# TRIALS OF EMBERS AND TRUST

## FLAMEBORN SERIES II

# K.J. ALTAIR

Editor: Jenny Sims (Editing4Indies)
Book Cover: Lennox Tocororo (@tocororoart)
Map and Graphics: KJ Altair

ISBN(ebook): 978-1-967591-02-2
ISBN(paperback): 978-1-967591-03-9

First Edition: September 2025

*To everyone whose path has been anything but smooth:
Falling is fine—as long as you keep rising. You've got this.
Now take my hand, another world is waiting!*

*And to my husband: you are my real-life hero.*

*Trials of Embers and Trust is the second book in the Fireborn series and is set in an unforgiving, fantastical world with magic, vicious creatures, gods, and high stakes. It includes elements of battle, violence, perilous situations, injuries, blood, death, grief, PTSD, and sexual activities that are shown on the page. Readers who may be sensitive to these elements, please take note and prepare before diving into these trials.*

# CONTENTS

N
BELARRA
BARRIER MOUNTAINS
BLACKSTONE
ARGONA
AVINA
MIST
THIAR
RYTUS
ALDEA
EKIAL MOUNTAINS
LAR
GORA
PLATORIA
MALVADA MOUNTAINS
OBALA
MOUNT ALBIÓN
MIST
THE DISCORDIAN SEA
TELOS

HAREA
RERE
RAY
ILYN
MIST
MUNTOS
MENDIA
SORTU
THE 5 KINGDOMS

XEO
THE ICE COAST
RÚN
AVINA
ALDEA
MIST
KYSTIS
BELARRA
LAR
TELOS
THE DISCORDIAN SEA
N
NE
E
SE
S
SW
W
NW

# ONE

## ARA

"The maid will be with you in a second," the butler tells me, and never have words sounded so threatening. The door closes, and I'm alone in an opulent room with golden walls, pristine and dainty furniture I'm afraid to touch, and a white marble floor I'm sure has my boot prints on it now, but I suppress the urge to check.

*What am I doing here?*

I rush to the door, but I'm not sure if it's to call my brother back or make a dash for it. Before I can push down the handle, the door opens, and I find myself face-to-face with a young dark-haired woman. Her simple dress in the dark blue and cream of the Belardi family lets me assume it's the maid. The same colors are present throughout the palace.

The woman's startled look morphs into a timid smile as she curtsies.

"I'm Ana, my lady, and I'll be at your service," she says in a bubbly voice, seemingly excited at the thought of being at my beck and call.

"I'm Ara," I tell her, and her eyes widen.

"I can't call you that, Lady Blackstone," she says, and despite her kind tone, I feel chastised. I sigh. Going up against three opponents in a hand-to-hand combat sounds lovely right now. What am I saying? I would fight ten rather than suffer through the next hours.

"So let's get you dressed, shall we?" Ana plows on, and I nod. I probably wouldn't have made it far anyway. The palace is too big, and too many people are around to get away unnoticed.

*"I could pick you up at your window,"* Solaris suggests, and I seriously consider it while Ana goes through my bags. They were miraculously waiting when I was shown into my room. She turns to me with a puzzled look.

"Is the rest arriving soon?" she asks, and I only blink. *Rest?* I had already scoffed at the twelve dresses my mother insisted I bring.

"Oh, never mind. You have some wonderful choices here, and I can get everything else from the royal seamstress." She gives me a careful once-over and hurries out the door.

An hour later, I regard myself in the mirror and have no idea who the person is that's staring back at me. I looked more like myself when I was posing as a boy.

The corset and dress push my breasts so high that I could probably rest my chin on them if I get tired, while the stiff fabric makes any relaxed posture simply impossible. I have no sleeves to hide my blades and can't strap them to my legs either, due to the heavy skirts. The result is that I feel naked and caged at the same time.

In a small act of defiance, I strap the dagger to the delicate belt circling my waist. I'm not going out there unarmed.

*"Are you alright?"* Solaris inquires. His amusement is loud and clear, so I wonder why I don't believe him when he tells me I look beautiful.

My hair is the only part of me left unbound, and I watch Ana wearily while she arranges the last curls to her satisfaction.

There is a knock on my door, and I meet my brother's eyes in the mirror when Ana answers it. His gaze wanders over my painted face —my red lips and my black-rimmed eyes—before taking in my hair and dark green dress.

"Don't say a thing," I warn him while I turn, pick up the gloves Ana insists I wear, and brush past him into the corridor. My dress is ridiculously long, trailing behind me on the floor. At least that explains why the floors are so spotless. Those dresses do half the work.

"You look beautiful, little sparrow, and very grown up." Dar falls into step next to me, and I snort.

"I look like a damn show pony," I reply, making him chuckle.

We turn corner upon corner, our steps loud on the marble floor. It's a good thing I didn't make a run for it because I'm already lost.

All the corridors appear identical, featuring royal colors and paintings and statues lining the walls. The view out of floor-length windows framed in curtains of dark blue is the only indication that we don't move in circles.

"*I probably would have starved before finding the exit,*" I grumble.

"*I would have picked you up before that happened,*" Solaris assures me, his voice full of laughter.

"*I don't belong here.*" I sigh, drawing my brother's attention.

"*Yeah, I wonder how that feels.*" My bird's sarcastic remark is accompanied by images of a crowd staring at him, and I giggle.

"*Okay, you win.*"

"Behave," Dar warns, before stepping through a massive door into what sounds like a verifiable party.

I follow, and a presence brushes over my skin like a swarm of fireflies, setting it aglow. Tate. I swear my insides change places.

*What is he doing here?*

Puzzlement and hope war in my chest while I get on my tiptoes, trying to spot him in the sea of strangers. Dar strides forward, oblivious to my turmoil, but stops when he notices I'm no longer by his side.

"What are you doing?" he spits, grabbing my arm.

There he is. It's only been a week, but my eyes drink him in like my body thirsts for his sight. Damn, he's so handsome. He stands alone, wearing one of his usual scowls, and everyone gives him a wide berth.

His skyrider uniform accents his powerful build, the dark gray highlighting him amid the colorful, fancy clothes everyone else prefers. His hair is tousled, his cheeks sport at least two days' worth of stubble, and his dark and commanding aura stands out even in this room full of influential people. I'm not the only one noticing, and who can blame them? He is beautiful, powerful, breathtaking.

I want to run to him, but that is out of the question, and not just because my brother is dragging me in the other direction.

Only now do I register the other people milling around in the giant room with the high ceiling. Again, it's decorated in the royal colors, and I wonder if you can hate a color just from its dominance around you.

The wooden floor and giant fireplace create a warm ambiance in the room, while two large chandeliers dominate the ceiling. There is shuffling and whispering all around us, and when my eyes sweep the crowd, I find many gazes trained on me.

Darren stirs me toward a blond man sprawled in a chair, holding court. There is no other way to describe the way everyone gathers around him, desperate for his attention. He is as light as Tate is dark—not just his hair and eyes, but his whole demeanor as well. He wears a carefree smile, his eyes crinkling at the corners and already resting on me. But there is also something calculating in his gaze.

"Your Highness. May I introduce my sister, Tamara Blackstone?" Dar says next to me, and I remember my manners and curtsy.

"Tamara, this is Crown Prince Frederick," he completes the introduction. Frederick kisses my hand.

I have no idea how it is even possible in a sea of people, but I feel Tate's eyes on me, and I can't help but meet them.

"Tamara, it's a pleasure to meet you." Frederick follows my gaze, and his mouth twitches. He beckons Tate over, who follows slowly, lazily, like he couldn't care less what the future king thinks of him, his eyes never leaving mine.

"May I introduce my brother, Prince Alexander? I assure you, his presence is as much a surprise to me as it is to you. He just arrived," Frederick says, his eyes on Tate.

*Brother? Prince?* Something niggles at the back of my mind.

*It seems the prince has a weakness for you.* The sentence pops into my head, accompanied by emotions and images. Smoke, pain, blood, my heart races, a metallic taste coats my tongue, a man's face, the desperate need to get away, trees. The impressions are there and gone in an instant. I try to hold on to them, but that only makes me nauseous. I sway.

*But that means ...* my eyes fly from Tate to Frederick and back. My fingers tingle, and the blood rushes in my ears. I try to draw a deep breath, but the corset makes that attempt futile. Why is it so damn warm in here?

"Are you alright?" Frederick asks, and I fight for composure.

"Yeah, I'm great," I press out, but don't dare to look at my brother or, even worse, Tate. If I don't do something, I'll faint right here in front of everyone.

"Actually, I think ... I need ... if you'll excuse me," I say and rush to a door that is to my right. I don't care where it leads, but I'll be damned if I faint in the middle of a crowd. My fingers tremble on the handle, my heart races, and no matter how much I struggle, there is not enough air.

I stumble into a hallway. My vision dims at the edges, and I focus on the bright light of the balcony doors at the end of it. If I can make it there...

I haven't come far when arms come around me, steadying me, holding me up when my legs give out. For a second, I hope it's Tate. That he has come after me, but when I blink up, I meet blue eyes instead of golden ones.

I blink again when I recognize the man from the library.

"Well, angel, so we meet again, and you end up in my arms once more." He winks at me. "And aren't you a vision?" His eyes flicker over my head, and his grin widens. "And in high demand, I see. Do you need someone to protect you from those brutes?"

"Get your hands off her." If the situation hadn't been so messed up, I would have laughed at Tate and my brother's twin demands.

"My, my, our rogue prince and the general are laying claim on you. Now I do have to know who you are, and if there is any chance, I can throw my hat in there as well." Mischief winks in his eyes. He obviously enjoys teasing them.

"Uh, air," I gasp and push against his chest to disentangle myself, but he doesn't budge.

He looks down at where his hands circle my waist and lifts an eyebrow. "No wonder you can't breathe. You wear an underdress, yes?"

I nod faintly.

"Well, then. Rest assured, I know my way around a corset," he says, and pulls out a dagger.

"One wrong move and we'll need a new admiral," Tate growls before I'm ripped out of the man's arms. Before I have the chance to topple, I'm swept up into arms I would recognize anywhere, and my already racing heart stumbles. The terrace doors behind me burst open, and Tate steps out with me into the cool air.

"Tate, what...?"

He sets me down gently and pulls me into him so my back rests against his chest.

"Just breathe, sunshine," he murmurs, and the use of his pet name sends shivers skating down my spine. "Just relax and breathe."

Yeah, right, as if relaxing is so easy with his breath caressing my skin and so much left unsaid.

I close my eyes, and for just a moment, I let myself pretend we're back in Tate's room, and everything is fine between us. I relax into him, and his arms tighten around my waist, his body solid and reassuring.

# CHAPTER
# TWO

TATE

THE MOMENT I SPOT ARA, I NEARLY SWALLOW MY TONGUE. SHE looks beautiful. I may prefer her in leather, but she looks stunning in the green dress. Her hair tumbles down her back in soft curls, one of them trailing over her collarbone in a way that makes me want to sample her skin right there.

She curtsies before my brother, and I have the urge to shove him aside when his lips meet her skin. I fucking hate it.

Her eyes find me, like she knew I was here from the start, and when they jump back to my brother, I crave her attention like it's a physical thing.

Frederick beckons me over, and I don't like the look on his face. It's like he knows something I don't.

He introduces me, but my attention is on Ara. Her eyes widen, her mouth opens as if she wants to say something, and the color drains from her face. Her breath comes too fast, too shallow. I step closer.

"Are you alright?" Frederick asks.

*What a stupid question.*

"Yeah, I'm great," Ara whispers, and all of us take a step closer. "Actually, I think ... I need ... if you'll excuse me..." Her voice sounds strangled, and she turns and flees.

I try to rush after her, gossip be damned, but just like Blackstone, the crowd my brother is always surrounded by delays me.

"Well, angel, so we meet again, and you end up in my arms once more." I recognize that voice, Lir Morgan. The biggest womanizer Avina has to offer, and the new admiral of our navy since he took over his father's position a year ago. Morgan holds Ara like he has a right to, smiling down at her. When he notices us, he pulls her even closer while his smile turns into a smirk. "And in high demand, I see. Do you need someone to protect you from those brutes?" He offers all flirt and charm while Ara blinks up at him.

"Get your hands off her," I growl, and I'm not surprised to hear the same sentiment echoed by Blackstone.

*Wait a minute, meet again?*

"My, my, our rogue prince and the general are laying claim on you. Now, I do have to know who you are, and if there is a chance, I can throw my hat in there as well." He only has eyes for Ara, and it's starting to seriously piss me off.

Ara says something too low for me to catch and makes a half-assed attempt to get away from him. His eyes wander over her before he lifts an eyebrow, still ignoring Blackstone's and my request.

"No wonder you can't breathe," he murmurs, and I miss the rest of what he says because I'm hung up on that.

*She can't breathe?* He unsheathes a dagger, and my thoughts turn murderous.

"One wrong move and we'll need a new admiral," I threaten before ripping Ara out of his arms and throwing open the balcony doors with my gift.

Then we are out on the balcony.

"Tate, what...?" Ara gasps.

"Just breathe, sunshine," I tell her, setting her down and pulling her into me. "Just relax and breathe." She relaxes into me, and I pull her closer.

Something inside me settles at her closeness, like I exhale for the first time in a week, and when she rests her head against my shoulder, I fight the urge to kiss her neck.

My back is against the wall right next to the doors, and we are out of sight, but that is not what's holding me back. There is a very real possibility she'll push me away, and I don't want to risk it.

Voices echo in the hallway, reminding me we are not alone.

"How do you know my sister?" Blackstone asks the question I burn to know the answer to.

"Your sister?" Morgan muses, "Fancy that! Of all the girls tumbling into my arms during our visit ... a small world indeed."

"You'd better explain that, or I swear, Morgan, you'll find my fist in your face in a moment," Blackstone threatens, but Morgan only laughs.

"I do enjoy seeing you go all barbarian, Blackstone." He chuckles. "Who would have thought there is such fire under that ice?"

"Morgan, would you think it funny if it were your sister we were talking about?" Blackstone asks, which shuts him up.

"Sorry, old man. No, I wouldn't think it funny at all if someone mentioned Marina in that way."

*Huh, I didn't know Morgan even had a sister.*

"Old man?" Blackstone scoffs. "You are ... what? Two years younger than me? Three?"

"It still counts." I can hear the smile in Morgan's voice, and it sounds like they have had that argument before. "But to get back to your sister... I was bored during our visit to the academy and went to the library, where your sister literally tumbled off a ladder and into my arms. She cursed like one of my sailors, laughed at me when I tried to sweet-talk her, and rushed off in a hurry, claiming to be late. So while it's safe to say she bewitched me instantly, we exchanged probably less than five sentences, and I had no idea she was your sister."

"What was Tamara doing at the Aerie?" my brother asks, alerting me to his presence, and I realize Ara and her brother must have just arrived, if he hasn't heard about her Phoenix yet.

"Where is Solaris?" I ask Ara, startling her.

"Oh, he's around. He said something about a rose garden last time we talked."

"My brother doesn't know you're bonded?" I ask.

"Yeah, about that. Your brother? Really? You didn't think mentioning that would have been kind of the obvious thing to do when I came clean about who I am?" she whisper-hisses and pushes away from me, and I regret saying anything.

She turns on me, color blooming on her previously pale cheeks, and her chest heaves distractingly.

"Who the fuck put you in a corset?" I ask, only now realizing why her waist looks so ridiculously tiny.

"My maid," she snaps, "but that is not the issue here." Her voice gets louder.

"It is if you have trouble breathing," I counter.

"No, I want to know why you never told me who you were, when —" She's interrupted by her brother calling her name. When I look up, all three men—Blackstone, Morgan, and my brother—stand in the doorway, watching us.

*Shit, I forgot about them.*

By the way Ara looks at them, I think she did, too. Her eyes glaze over. She is talking to Solaris. Only seconds later, shouts of alarm and wonder announce him before Solaris's brilliant form dives toward us.

"If you'll excuse me, I need a few minutes to cool down." Ara curtsies and jumps on Solaris's back, who is perched on the stone railing. We watch silently as Solaris takes to the skies, Ara's skirt hiked up inappropriately and her golden hair trailing behind.

"Holy hell, I might have to marry her," Morgan declares, only to start chuckling when all three of us stare at him with less-than-friendly expressions. "Sorry, I didn't think that through before it came out." He shrugs. "But hot damn, she's bonded to a Phoenix?" He shakes his head in wonder. "So let me get this straight, she is a skyrider, bonded to a Phoenix, sister of our commanding general, and promised to our crown prince ... what gift does she have?" He turns toward Blackstone.

"Fire," Blackstone answers, and it stings that I didn't know that until now.

"At least they'll think twice before trying to abduct her." He slaps Blackstone's shoulder.

*Trying to abduct her?* My eyes fly to my brother. What does Morgan mean by that?

"And the ball tonight is in her honor, right?" Morgan asks, and when Fred nods, he grins. "Then I'll make sure to attend. I can't wait to see the reaction to our future queen if they took weeks to accept the thought of Darren or me in the positions we're in." He chuckles. "This is going to be good," he predicts, walking away whistling after waving a cheery goodbye to all of us.

"Well, I'll get some rest, then," I say and hurry off before Blackstone or my brother can corner me. My brain is foggy with exhaustion. Flying through the night might have gotten me here, but it sure wasn't pleasant.

My feet carry me to my old rooms without even thinking about it. I hesitate, but then use my gift to unlock the door, nearly expecting the space to be empty or transformed into someone else's quarters. But to my surprise, everything looks exactly how I left it, apart from the chaos I caused while packing in a hurry.

Despite the sitting room being spacious, it's suffocating to be back. As if I've stepped into my past, and the missing years are pressing in on me. I continue into my bedroom, but everything looks the same here, too. The dark blue of my family and a big four-poster in dark wood dominate the room, which now seems unnecessarily big after years at the academy.

Curious, I open my desk and find everything where I left it, the paper still adorned by my name. A name that doesn't feel like mine anymore. Even the signet ring I left is still lying next to it, and not a speck of dust is in sight. As if the past four years never happened. Eerie.

I close the desk and wander over to my wardrobe, only to find everything still in order there, too. Even the red healer's garment is still there.

*"Are you alright?"* Daeva asks.

*"Yeah, I'm... I don't know, actually."* I look around the room again. *"I'll be fine. Get some sleep, and I'll do the same."*

When I wake in my old bed, in my old room, it feels strange, like the past few years have been a dream. Only I can't decide if it's a good or a bad one. A brisk knock on the door explains what woke me.

I never closed the curtains, and the sun is already low, the slanted rays nearly reaching me. It has to be well after the fourth strike. The knock sounds again, and while I'm tempted to ignore it, I know it's a servant sent to fetch me. He won't stop unless I answer, not daring to fail his king's request.

I groan and sit up, unlocking and throwing open the door with my magic. The man standing in front of it wears a servant uniform, wringing his hands and looking uncomfortable.

"What is it?" I ask.

"The queen wishes to see you, Your Highness." So my father didn't send for me himself. Interesting.

"Centurion will do. I no longer hold my old title."

"But..."

"I'll be out in a minute," I say, closing the door in his face. For a second, I contemplate donning some of my old clothes, but that comes too close to falling in line, like defeat. I slip into a fresh uniform instead. I'm not here for them. If not for Ara, I wouldn't be here at all.

The servant hurries ahead, and my curiosity is piqued when he leads me to my parents' quarters instead of the throne room. It's not like my father to pass up a chance to intimidate in the right setting.

Despite that change, I'm not prepared for the sight when I lay eyes on my parents. My mother hasn't changed much, but she looks worried and a little drawn. But my father... he has aged vastly in the past years. He's lost weight, his hair is gray now, and his once proud and strong frame looks frail and bent by age. Only his voice is as clipped and cold as ever.

"Where have you been?" he snaps. His eyes wander over my uniform. "A skyrider ... well, I guess it's better than a healer. Is that why you threw your legacy in my face and vanished without a word? You were looking for glory?"

"You told me to never come back," I answer evenly.

"And still you are here, standing right in front of me."

"I can find lodging elsewhere if that offends you."

"Don't be ridiculous." My mother intervenes, breaking our staring contest. "Your rooms are still yours, and we are happy to see you, aren't we, Reginald?" she asks my father, but he doesn't react, just continues staring at me.

Everything else would have surprised me. He is not a forgiving man, and I don't think he will ever forgive me for walking away. Not even if he ever learns my reasons.

"How have you been?" my mother asks, coming closer but stopping short of touching me. Her hands twitch, and without my father present, I think she would have hugged me.

"I'm good."

"That is all you have to say? After running off to the gods know where, the only thing you have to say to your mother is I'm good?" my father snaps.

"What did you hope for? That I come back begging for forgiveness, Father? That I'll tell you how miserable my life is and beg you to take me in? You can wait eternally for that."

"Please, could we not just talk civilly for at least a few minutes?" my mother asks, and I bite back the rest of my words for her sake. "How are Jared and Nan?"

"Jared and I joined the skyriders. Nan lives comfortably and doesn't miss a thing despite you cutting her off." The last words are directed at my father.

"You did not." My mother whips around to look at him now, too, and this time, he appears slightly uncomfortable.

"She chose her future when she decided to leave us."

"I will fix that," my mother tells me. "Please tell her I didn't know. She should have written me. After everything she did for us..." She shakes her head, disappointed at my father.

"Frederick is holding court now?" I ask, since he greeted Ara and Blackstone alone despite my parents probably knowing they were coming.

"He started taking over a year ago," my mother answers and looks at my father again, but doesn't say the obvious: His health is declining.

But the gods forbid someone would say that to his face.

# THREE

## ARA

"I HAD THE FEELING YOU NEEDED TO GET OUT FOR A BIT." DAR smiles at me while we walk down a bustling street.

"And you weren't wrong." I return his smile. For the first time since we arrived this morning, I can breathe freely.

We are in the old part of Avina. The streets are narrow but clean, and the sheer number of shops lining them makes me gawk. Dar laughs about my reaction.

A heavenly smell of something sweet and fruity tickles my nose, and when I find the source and stop in front of the bakery, my brother shakes his head.

"Why am I not surprised? I take you shopping in the capital, and the first thing you want is to buy food."

"Walking raised an appetite, and had we come by the smithy first, it could have been weapons." I wink at him.

He groans. "Mom told me to take you to get accessories, whatever that means."

I shrug. "A few new daggers seem to fit that description, and I have more use for them than for a fan, silk gloves, or ribbons."

"Fine by me. As long as you don't tell on me." We grin at each other.

Ten minutes later, I munch happily on an apple tart, the sweet and acidic flavor exploding on my tongue, ending in a warm note of cinnamon. I hum with contentment, and my brother grins.

"Good thing no one knows how easily it is to buy your loyalty," he teases, and I swat his arm.

"Bribery is not needed. I would do anything for you, anyway."

"The same goes for me, little sparrow." He pulls me into his side, ruffling my hair like he used to when I was little.

"Hey." I jump out of his grasp. "I'm not a child anymore, Dar."

"Oooh, is there someone concerned about her looks? Maybe because of a certain prince?"

"I have no idea what you're talking about." I feign ignorance. A commotion up ahead draws my attention.

There is shouting. A little girl clings to a woman while two guards try to separate them. Mother and child, by the looks of it.

"You can't have her," the woman screams. "She didn't do anything."

"Mom," the wailed word goes over into a high-pitched screech once the guard succeeds in pulling the girl away.

Dar tries to steer me away, but I slip past his arm. "What is going on?"

"Little sparrow, we need to go."

"We have to help," I disagree. "They can't just take her. Why are they taking her?"

"Ow, she bit me." The guard drops the girl. "Cursed spawn of the devil."

And realization dawns. "Are they taking her because she is cursed?" I hiss.

"Stay quiet," Dar warns.

"I don't think so." And I move in the girl's direction, who's now playing a life-threatening version of catch with the guard. But for now, she's winning. And I'll make sure it stays that way.

"Ara," Dar warns, grabbing for me, but he is too late, and I'm already crossing the street. The guard never sees me coming, or doesn't take me for a threat. Either way, my punch catches him off guard, and he falls like a tree.

The girl blinks at me before a smile takes over her face. The second guard is on me within seconds. But Dar steps in front of me.

"She attacked a royal guard."

"Now surely you don't want to tell me a delicate woman knocked out a royal guard," he placates the man, who instantly bristles. I scoff. *Delicate woman*, what a joke.

"I know who you are, General Blackstone. I will file a complaint about this," the man threatens and then helps his companion up, who slowly comes around.

Mother and daughter use the commotion to disappear, and I just hope they're smart enough to go into hiding.

They exchange a few more words before Darren marches off, seething, pulling me with him. He doesn't say a word until we're back in his rooms in the palace and the door is locked.

His rooms are large, representative of his status at court, and so tidy that they appear almost uninhabited. Our family's dark green color is prominent in the fabrics, and various maps decorate the walls, dotted with markings. Pictures of our family and the fortress Blackstone are the only personal touches to be found.

"That was incredibly stupid," he whisper-shouts. "Openly siding with a cursed, attacking a guard—are you out of your mind?" He paces the room, his steps muffled by the thick carpet.

"They would have killed her," I go toe-to-toe with him now, forcing him to stop pacing. "Would you have let them take me without a fight, too?"

"No, of course not." He drags a hand through his hair. "But my priority is you and the rest of my family. Your actions today could have gotten us all killed."

My eyes jump to the images of Elena and Tyre on his desk. Guilt settles in my gut. I haven't thought that far.

"What did you expect me to do? Just stand by and watch?"

He sighs. "We can't rescue everyone, and sometimes we have to accept that. You have a big heart, little sparrow, but one day it's going to get you killed."

"Maybe you're right, but I wouldn't be able to live with myself otherwise, anyway. I know I can't rescue everyone, but at least I can try."

"There will come a day you'll have to prioritize, and then you'll realize it's not that simple."

I cross my arms.

He sighs. "I love you, little sparrow, but you have to start thinking about the consequences of your actions. Far too many people are now interested in you, and it will only get worse once the betrothal becomes public."

"I will not marry Frederick."

"I thought you wanted to save everyone?" He raises his eyebrow mockingly. "And what better position to do that than as their queen?"

I open my mouth, then close it without saying anything.

"It's not that easy, is it?" he asks. "Just make sure you get your priorities in order before you enter this floor." He makes a sweeping gesture encompassing the palace. "Because there will come moments of uncomfortable choices." He rests his hands on my shoulders. "And I won't risk all of you for a girl I don't even know." He shrugs. "I'm sorry, but that is my truth. Now get some rest, before they start fussing over you, because they will."

THE ROYAL SEAMSTRESS WEARS A SUBTLE SNEER WHILE SHE looks at me in the dress. We are in my room, and this is the third dress she put me in. I don't have to be a mind reader to know what she's thinking. It's obvious in the way she eyes me.

I'm not soft enough, not fragile enough. Too many muscles, too many scars, too many calluses on my hands. I bet her list is longer, but those are the things that come to mind.

Remembering the way Tate had looked at me about a week ago makes me want to stick out my tongue and tell her at least one of the princes deems me adequate. Only memories of his reaction once he knew who I was dampen my mood.

What had I expected? My family's connections and influence come before me, always. I should know that by now.

A memory hits me.

*I'm eighteen and moping since Joel isn't home for Equinox like I hoped. He hasn't come home at all since he left a year ago.*

*I'm watching dancers twirl over the grass between tall pyres surrounding the meadow, keeping the mist at bay. I'm always just watching.*

*Everyone knows my family and my brothers. And they are too important to cross them over something as insignificant as a girl.*

*A hand enters my view, waiting, like... My eyes snap to the boy in front of me. I have never seen him before. Giddy excitement flashes through me when he doesn't take back his invitation.*

*A dance becomes many, spring flows into a summer filled with laughter, kisses, and secret meetings. He is sweet, he is charming, and I lap up his attention and think myself in love. I trust him and give myself to him.*

*He says the sweetest things, promises me the moon and the stars ... only to pretend we never even met when I accompany my brother to the smithy on the following day. My excitement had drained quickly, leaving me subdued and quiet. Bubbling energy turned to heaviness.*

That same night, I confronted him. *"You are sweet, you are fun, but you are not worth alienating your family over.”* Then he suggested that we should continue to meet in secret, and I kicked his ass.

I smirk, thinking about how surprised he looked. It was as if he'd suddenly forgotten who raised me.

*Tate walked away, too,* a little voice whispers. And still ... the way he acted earlier ... my stomach buzzes with a flock of birds at the memory.

“No, that doesn't work,” the seamstress says, drawing me out of my thoughts. “All those scars are too noticeable. We'll have to go with something else.” Her eyes are still on me, assessing and judging.

I was surprised when Frederick knocked at my door with the woman in tow, who now scrutinizes me. She came armed with a myriad of dresses and fabrics to get me presentable for tonight's ball, whatever she meant by that, when I had still been in the monster of a dress I wore before.

Okay, granted, it had suffered a bit due to Solaris's flames and sported new creases since I had been anything but gentle with it during the flight.

She rustles through the dresses on the hanger next to her before pulling out a dark blue gown. Pushing it into my arms, she ushers me back behind the changing screen before stripping me out of the current dress with efficient and quick moves.

“Wait,” she barks, then bustles off.

As if I would have fled the room dressed in the thin undergown I'm currently wearing. Yes, I admit the thought is appealing, but I'm still not closer to knowing my way around the palace.

She whispers with Ana, and then some drawers open and close before she comes back, another corset clutched in her hand, and I groan. She sends me a sharp look.

“We have to accentuate your figure in some way if we hide away all your skin. Your waist will look positively tiny,” she declares. I try to tell myself she only wants me to look stunning tonight.

Not for my sake, I'm not that delusional, but it was obvious she adores Frederick when he brought her here. So I am sure she will do everything to make him look good, and he informed me that I would be on his arm tonight.

Okay, she hates me. I'm sure of it, as soon as she fastens the instrument of torture at my back, it's even tighter than the last one. How is anyone supposed to breathe in that thing, let alone dance? But at least I don't have to worry about my posture.

Two hours later, I descend the staircase to the ballroom, and Tate's expression, when our eyes meet, makes all the torture worth it.

I hold his gaze while walking down the steps, and everything else melts into the background. I wish we were just two skyriders, with no pasts, no ties, no expectations. Maybe then—

"You look stunning, Ara." My thoughts come to an abrupt halt at Frederick's words. I look at him and only now notice the offered hand. Dammit.

I slip my hand in his while I descend the last few steps and can't help but notice how much smoother his hand is compared to Tate's. *Alec*, I berate myself, *his name is Alec.* But I'm not sure I will ever get used to it.

While Frederick guides me over to a group of people, everything in me pulls in the other direction toward Tate. I want to know what he's doing here. Why did he come? His threatening Morgan, the way he held me... It has to mean something, right?

Frederick's hand settles on my arm, and I look up, startled. His questioning look tells me I zoned out.

"Uh, could you repeat that, please?"

"I asked if your stay is pleasant so far."

*I'm completely out of my comfort zone. I knocked out one of your guards to protect a cursed girl. I'm gauged and judged like a brood-mare, I want nothing more than to throw myself into your brother's arms while technically still promised to you...*

"Yes, I'm splendid," I say with the fakest smile in history, but he seems content. Tate would have seen through my bullshit. Speaking of which, he is slowly coming closer, and all the hairs on my body stand on end.

I smile and nod distractedly to the phony pleasantries strangers whisper while their fake smiles are even worse than mine. There is no doubt that none of them are pleased I'm here, even if they pretend otherwise.

I take in the splendor of the ballroom around me. It's majestic. The soaring ceiling is hung with dozens of crystal-encrusted chandeliers, their light multiplied by the night-darkened windows and sparkling mirrors. The floor is polished wood, the walls covered in shimmering creamy silk, while the hundreds of people milling around are works of art themselves. Precious fabrics gleam and shine, while stones encased in glinting metals compete with the glimmering light from above.

"You shuffled the cards, and they can't place you yet." Tate's whispered words send a shiver down my back, and I suppress the urge to lean into him. His body's heat seeps into my back despite us not touching.

"Do you care to dance?" Tate asks, and my eyes widen. I look at him over my shoulder.

"You want to dance with me?" I whisper.

"A dance is the least I can offer after everything," Tate says loud enough for everyone to hear, holding out his hand. To them, it sounds like he is talking about our broken betrothal, but to me... My heart flutters, and a nervous buzz starts in my belly and works its way up while he leads me to the dance floor.

We fall into the rhythm of the music with ease, both of us moving seamlessly in the crowd of dancers around us. Content in each other's silence.

"You look stunning," Tate whispers while he guides me effortlessly over the dance floor. "I still prefer you in fighting leather, but you look beautiful in a dress, too." His eyes run over my arms. "Why the long sleeves? You must be melting in here."

"The seamstress was appalled at the thought of showing my scars."

"Why doesn't that surprise me?" He shakes his head.

The thought that he knows exactly how many scars are on my skin makes me evade his gaze. He lets go of my hand and tips my chin up so I look at him again, his feet not faltering even for a second.

"Your scars are nothing to be ashamed of. When we were kids, you told me they were your badges of honor, and you were right. They are signs of your strength, your resilience. And I love every one of them."

"Don't say things like that," I say, and swallow when my voice comes out hoarse.

"You are the most beautiful woman in this room, inside and out," he tells me. "I'm sorry about how I left things. I just..."

"Sweet-talking my future bride now, brother? You always were a competitive bastard." Frederick is suddenly next to us. "May I have the next dance?" he asks, smoothly intercepting. Tate's hand flexes on my waist before he steps back. I want to object, but humiliating the prince in public probably isn't the smartest move. So I grit my teeth and nod, even if it is the last thing I want.

I want to hear what Tate was about to say. I want to hear him grovel, and then I want him to whisk me off to his rooms, not dance with his brother.

But we dance, and if my thoughts hadn't been otherwise occupied, I may even have appreciated his efforts to draw me into a conversation. He is charming, and not as guarded as his brother. But that is the problem. I constantly compare him to Tate, and what can I say? I know who I'd choose.

I finally manage to excuse myself and make my way toward Tate, but I hardly take a few steps before someone intercepts me. I'm probed with questions under the guise of superficial chitchat, and I barely escaped the first before I'm stopped by the next. I nearly growl when I realize it will take me forever to reach him.

"You look like you need saving again." Morgan smoothly intercepts the next courtier and blocks me by turning his broad shoulders to the room. I exhale through my nose, and he chuckles.

"Not one for being swooned over all night?" he asks with a twinkle in his eye.

I laugh. "Whatever gave you that impression?"

"You ran from the library as if it were on fire when I started talking to you," he deadpans.

"You should have asked me to spar instead if you wanted me to stick around," I tease, but then sober and shake my head. "No, I was already late and hiding from Dar that I joined the academy."

His eyebrows jump up. "How did he take the news?"

I shrug sheepishly. "Not so well."

"By the waves, my sister would adore you." At my raised eyebrow, he continues. "She is a half siren and sure to bring me into an early, wet grave."

"I'd love to meet her." I grin at him.

"Ura be us hold, if that ever happens." He groans mockingly, making me laugh again. And I pester him for information on his half-siren sister. Marina sounds like fun, and he promises to introduce us when she's in Avina.

Unfortunately, he's called away by a group of men on the other side of the room.

Five encounters later, I've affronted at least three of the people I talked to. They don't seem to appreciate my kind of humor around here, and I'm close to screaming or threatening people at this point anyway. When I notice a balcony door, I slip outside.

On the balcony, I draw in what feels like the first full breath in hours. Or at least as much as I can breathe in this dress.

Despite the summer being close, the night air is still chilly up here in the north. Rustling lets me whirl around, my hand reaching for a dagger that isn't there, grasping layers upon layers of fabric instead. Then I remember I secured it once again at my waist.

Wide brown eyes meet mine, followed by a nervous laugh when she follows my movements, landing on my father's dagger.

The girl in front of me is delicate and beautiful. Dark curls tumble onto a stunning black dress that drapes perfectly over her petite figure. Her plush lips form a delicate O. She radiates class and elegance, and I'm a lump next to her.

"That is a pretty ... knife," she says nervously and swipes at her cheeks.

"Thank you." I trail my finger lovingly over the distinctive hilt, which depicts a bird taking flight. I look up again and only now realize she has been crying.

"Sorry, I'll find someplace else," I say, stepping back.

"No, it's fine. There is enough room for both of us." She is only being polite, but I need a minute, so I stay.

She fidgets with a pendant around her neck that depicts three grouped mountains, one in front of the others. When she notices my look, she slides it into her dress and stills her fingers.

"Are you in mourning?" I gesture to her black dress, so different from all the bright colors competing with each other inside. She looks down at her dress, running her hand over the rich fabric.

"In a way." One corner of her mouth lifts. When she looks up again, there is no judgment in her gaze, and she doesn't launch into probing questions either. I like her.

"You are the first friendly person I've met tonight." I give her a small smile. "And that's despite intruding on your privacy."

"They feel threatened by you."

I laugh before realizing she's being serious.

"By me?" I ask. "Why would anybody feel threatened by me?" I look at her incredulously.

She chuckles.

"Do I have to spell it out for you?"

"Please do."

"Alright, you are going to marry Fred. Your brother is the commanding general of our army. You flew here on a Phoenix." She ticks off the things she says on her fingers. "You are a skyrider. You walked through flames and emerged unharmed, bonded to a Phoenix. You challenged a dragon and lived to tell the tale. You are beautiful, and you manage to befriend not only Alec but also the head of guards and the admiral of our navy while only being here for less than a day. How should anyone not feel threatened by that?"

"But that's not—" I disagree. She waves me off.

"It doesn't even matter if you've never met a dragon..."

"Well, I did, but it was Tate—I mean Alec—who fought him."

"He fought a dragon for you?" Her eyes grow big as saucers. "That is exactly what I mean. How is a girl supposed to compete with something like that?" she cries out, throwing up her hands.

I laugh. "You have it all wrong, but thanks for making me feel better about the snooty looks and cold shoulders I got in there. Now I feel less like the country bumpkin."

"Oh, believe me, that is not what anyone is thinking."

"So how long have you been at the palace?" I ask.

"Nearly all my life," she tells me. "I came here with my father as a little girl. He is an adviser to the king."

"So you are used to all..." I gesture toward the ballroom with the light and noise behind us. "This?"

"Oh, you mean the splendor, the beauty, the backstabbing? Yeah, I'm used to it. Doesn't make it easier, but I have no illusions about it anymore." Her voice sounds sad. "Sometimes I just need a break."

"I like you," I tell her. "Would it be terribly rude of me if I ask for your help with navigating the waters around here?"

She laughs at that, shaking her head.

"What?" I ask.

"Nothing, it's just..." She shakes her head again. "I would feel honored. How about we meet for lunch the day after tomorrow?" she proposes, and I gladly take it.

The door behind us opens, and when I turn, Frederick steps out.

"There you are," he says when his eyes find me, then he notices the girl next to me. "Deliah," he inclines his head stiffly, while she sinks into an elegant curtsy.

"Your Highness," she whispers.

"Come, Tamara," he tells me, offering me his arm. I take a deep breath before taking it, stepping back into the warm air of the over-crowded room and giving Deliah an apologetic smile and a wave.

Even among all the gifted people in attendance, Tate's magic stands out. My eyes snap to him, only to find his already on me. I try to read his face, but his mask is back up, giving me nothing, and I'm too far away to read his eyes.

"How do you know my brother?" Frederick leans into me, his breath tickling my ear. How to answer that? I have no idea how much Tate told him or if they even spoke, but since he arrived in his skyrider uniform...

"He is in the same division as me at the Aerie," I start. "But I didn't know—"

"So I don't have to worry about him stealing you away?" And I decide this moment is as good as any.

"Look," I sigh. "We don't know each other, and I'm not going to marry a stranger. I bet you are nice and all, but—"

"So get to know me." His voice is somewhere between disinterest and command.

"What?"

"Since you *are* going to marry me, you should get to know me," he states.

"Hey, that's not—"

"I'll be king soon, and you don't tell a king no." His words, so casually spoken, sound like a threat. The hell I won't. I'll even make sure he remembers it bright and clear.

"There you are." My brother steps up to me, his gaze searching my face. "May I steal my sister for a dance?" he asks Frederick, and I raise an eyebrow while Fredrick nods and hands me over.

"You look beautiful, little sparrow, and like you were about to kill the crown prince," my brother tells me while smoothly maneuvering me onto the dance floor.

"I was close, and you look pretty handsome yourself," I tell him, and he does. His uniform jacket brings out the blue in his eyes, making them pop in his tanned face. His hair is styled back and not one lock is out of place.

"But I do have the urge to mess up your hair a little," I tell him, the tension slowly seeping out of me.

"Don't you dare." He gives me a mocking glare, and I chuckle.

"Thanks for the rescue," I tell him.

"Yeah, you looked ready to spill some truths there."

"He implied that I don't have a choice but to marry him," I say, and my brother's eyebrows jump.

"Well, what did you say?"

"I was about to show him how wrong he is."

He groans. "Ara, what did you do?"

"Relax, you interrupted us," I tell him. "There is truth to what you said earlier. But I don't want to marry him, especially..." I catch myself.

"Look, I'm not a moron. I know there is something between you and *him*." His eyes wander to Tate. "Or you wouldn't have kissed him the way you did while I was standing right next to you." He gives me a stern look. "But please don't do anything rash. Whatever you decide will have a rippling effect much bigger than you might think. Marrying Frederick would guarantee not only your safety but also everyone else's in our family who might be born cursed." My eyes fly to his.

"Elena is pregnant?" I ask, and he nods, a smile spreading over his face. I draw him into a tight hug, not caring that we stop in the middle of the dance floor. "I'm so happy for you," I whisper. "I promise I won't do anything impulsive. Even if his implication that I don't have a choice and that he kept interrupting me made me want to punch him." My brother laughs softly at my exasperation.

"Thank you," he tells me, kissing my brow while we continue dancing.

"You're a pretty good dancer," I tell him a while later while he accompanies me over to the bar.

"Don't sound so shocked." He laughs. "You are not the only one who was forced to take dance lessons. You had them with Ben after all, and don't think it wasn't the same for the rest of us. And for your information, it's not fun to dance with Ian or Luc." I burst out laughing at the image of my big brothers dancing together.

"I would pay to see that." I giggle.

"No amount is high enough."

Unfortunately, my brother is pulled away soon after, and my urge to scream in frustration grows with each passing hour. Only my promise to Dar keeps me from doing anything hasty, like drawing my dagger and threatening anyone who comes too close.

While many keep their distance from Tate, I'm always surrounded by people with no regard for my personal space, and the annoyance in his eyes matches mine whenever our gaze meets.

What does a girl have to do around here for some space and alone time?

# FOUR

TATE

The sheer mass of people around me has me on edge. There is too much noise, too much movement. It's too easy to miss something.

Thankfully, not many are brave enough to approach me, but the ones who are ask questions they have no business knowing the answer to and keep distracting me, which makes me even more anxious.

Yes, we aren't in Telos, but what if whoever attacked Ara tries again? It would be easy to get close in a crowd like this. Especially since too many are getting too close to her.

I get it, they are curious about her and why she is here, but if it wouldn't make it worse, I'd be glued to her side, making sure they step the fuck back and give her room to breathe.

My eyes return to the spot where Ara stood moments ago, but she isn't there. A chill runs through my body.

My eyes sweep the crowd again and again, but she's gone. My throat constricts. Panic rises.

"We were so concerned when you vanished into thin air. And that tragedy." The elderly woman in front of me sighs. "Of course, we never believed the rumors—" She seems to wear everything her jewelry box has to offer and now presses her hand on the tangle of necklaces while she pauses, hoping for me to fill in the silence. My brain catalogs away all the details, but I don't even acknowledge her prying, my eyes still scanning the room. She huffs and turns away.

I dive into the crowd, and it parts to let me through. Cold sweat dampens my skin, and when a man bumps into me, I'm just short of kicking him out of my way.

She has to be here somewhere. I scan my surroundings. She would have never reached one of the doors at the other end of the ballroom without me noticing. I search the floor, afraid to find a crumpled form. The noise seems to swell around me, and I do my best to calm my breath.

All of it, it's ... just too damn much.

And then there she is, stepping back through the balcony door on my brother's arm. Her eyes find me, grounding me. She's safe. My heartbeat slows, and breathing becomes easier again.

No one is attacking, at least not physically.

Another court member steps toward me and declares his outrage on my behalf. He assures me he never believed a word he heard, and with the number of people who assured me of that tonight, I guess there can't possibly be any rumors.

They seem to forget that I grew up here.

I take another deep breath, and I'm back in control.

Ara's and my gaze meet again. She's dancing with her brother now. She smiles, and warmth spreads through me, replacing the cold dread.

What do I care what people think as long as she still looks at me like that?

My hope to talk to her, and the need for people to remember

seeing me here has kept me longer than I intended. The sea of people between us is still endless, and when another person heads my way, I've had enough. I turn and leave, minutes later stepping out into the night and making my way through the gardens. There's a rustle of wings before Daeva lands next to me.

*"A wonder you didn't kill all of them,"* she tells me. *"I wouldn't have had the restraint."* I laugh softly and stroke her beak.

*"I guess it's good it was me in there and not you, then. But I guess you can put it down to years of training."*

*"How dare they speak to you like that?"*

*"Oh, I bet word has gone around that I'm stripped of my title,"* I say dryly. *"And I'm sure my father's displeasure about my leaving and Frederick's distaste at me showing up again play a role as well."*

*"We should leave,"* she tells me.

*"We'll leave soon enough,"* I promise her. *"But there are things I need to do first, remember? And tonight is perfect for that."*

I make my way to one of the less frequented entrances of the palace, and I'm on my way to my father's study when the rustle of skirts alerts me before another person turns the corner. Deliah stops short when she sees me.

"Alec." She curtsies. "I mean, it's nice to see you, Your Highness."

"Centurion," I correct her. "What are you doing here?"

"I wasn't in the mood for partying," she tells me. I raise my eyebrow because that doesn't explain why she's in this part of the palace instead of the guest wing.

"I'm just taking a night stroll and didn't feel like going out into the dark," she says. "Walking calms me."

"Then I don't want to keep you," I tell her. And she curtseys again before walking away. I wait for a moment, turning the once familiar ring on my finger. It feels heavy and foreign now. When everything stays quiet, I continue.

Wearing the ring is a precaution. I'm sure the news that I'm back has traveled through the palace like wildfire, but I have been gone for well over three years now, and I'm not sure that all the guards would recognize me on sight. The royal crest, on the other hand, they'll recognize for sure.

My stride is confident and purposeful as I pass the guards, and just as I hoped, no one stops me on the way to my father's study. Unlocking the door with my gift, I slip in and close it softly behind me, before taking in the room.

Nothing has changed.

Not that I expected it to. My father is not privy to quick changes, a frequent source of argument in the past.

The dark room is filled with memories awakened by the mixed scent of parchment, paper, and my father's aftershave. The bulky desk dominating the room is illuminated by the lamps lighting the perimeter of the palace, their warm glow entering through the window behind the desk. A big map adorns the wall next to the door, and shelves full of books fill the space in between.

I step up to the desk and my eyes flit over the papers lying on it and stop on a half-opened scroll, when the words "flight games" catch my attention. I step closer, unrolling it and using my dagger to hold one side down while I scan the information. It's organizational stuff about housing, food, and celebrations.

*"That is not what you came here for,"* Daeva chides me.

*"I worked so long toward those trials. Excuse me if I'm curious."*

*"Then be curious a bit faster or after you did the actual work,"* she grumbles, and I smile.

*"No one is going to come here tonight. My brother is busy dancing, drinking, and charming people, and my father is probably sleeping by now."*

*"It's your head you're risking,"* she tells me, but her worry belies her dismissive tone. I follow her advice and start looking for the information I came here for.

It takes me a while to locate what I'm looking for. Either my father changed his system or it's my brother's doing.

I pause when footsteps pass the door, accompanied by a hushed conversation. The words are too low to understand, but the voices and steps fade, so I continue.

After scanning rows of names, I find the one I'm looking for right next to the prison he's held in and the date of his execution. My father is nothing if not structured and thorough.

I copy the information onto a paper with his letterhead, then fold it and tuck it into my pocket. If that doesn't prove the information is real, nothing will.

I've just placed the records back where they belong when footsteps approach again. This time, they stop.

I duck behind the desk and curse wordlessly when the door opens. My dagger is still lying on the desk.

"Empty." My brother's voice sounds disappointed. "And I can't smell a thing over your perfume," he complains. The other voice is a woman, but the reply is too quiet to make out. My brother groans and closes the door. Despite the hurried steps fading quickly, I pick up my dagger and wait a while before making my way to the door. When everything is silent on the other side, I slip out and head to the guest wing.

Through Daeva, I know that I missed my chance to talk to Ara after the ball and that she is already back in her room. Daeva also told me Solaris is resting on the balcony, keeping an eye on Ara. Smart bird.

*"Daeva, can you tell Solaris that I'll only leave a letter? I don't want him to wake her."*

*"Done,"* she tells me, and I'm relieved to find Ara's door locked. Smart girl. But with my gift, it's as easy as turning the key on the other side to get in. I step into the room and come to a stop.

She sleeps peacefully, curled up on one side of the bed, the cover clutched to her chest. Mists, I want nothing more than to hold her, to feel her snuggle into me all sleepy and warm. A strand of hair moves gently with her breath, and my fingers twitch with the need to push it aside.

I stay where I am, though, and place the letter next to her with my gift. If I get too close, I'll climb in behind her, and someone seeing me coming out of her room in the morning is the last thing she needs. The news would spread within minutes.

I slip out the door silently, too awake to go to bed. I walk the corridors instead.

As if they have a mind of their own, my feet carry me to the room where I'd spent so many hours, bored out of my mind, observing my father handle meetings and audiences.

The years spent away turn the throne room familiar and foreign at the same time. It seems smaller somehow, and I notice details I never did before, like the intricate decorations rimming the arched ceiling or how my steps echo in this room that I have so rarely seen empty.

The carving on the armrests of the two silver-plated thrones is smoother, worn down by age and the touch of my family. Cold white marble dominates the room, fitting my father's personality perfectly.

A dark blue carpet displaying a pattern of my family's crest stretches from the main entrance to the steps leading up to the thrones. The crowned phoenix spitting flames is also depicted on the banner behind the thrones and countless other surfaces throughout the room.

How different my life would have turned out if I had never accompanied the trading party to the Ice Coast, or Kystis, as they call their realm.

*"How can I ask her to give up a crown for me?"* I ask Daeva.

*"What nonsense question is that? You could ask her to give her life for you, and she would probably do it,"* Daeva answers.

The thought is terrifying and—knowing Ara—unfortunately, not completely out of the blue either. And people close to me tend to get hurt.

*"Maybe staying away would be the best for her."*

*"That is rukhshit, and we both know it,"* Daeva grumbles. *"Tell her how you feel and let all four of us fly back together. The trials start soon, and Solaris doesn't like it here any more than I do."* Her unease

trickles through our bond. *"And don't lie to both of us by pretending you could do it ... walk away, I mean."*

She's right. I have two goals at the moment, and neither of them involves letting her go.

Win the trials and eliminate the threat. Keep her safe. Maybe not easy, but doable.

Tomorrow morning, I will catch her after breakfast and take her somewhere we can talk. I have quite a bit of groveling to do, but at least our interaction so far gives me hope that she will listen.

I turn around, ready to leave the room and my past behind me, when my brother steps through the door. Maybe sleeplessness runs in the family.

CHAPTER

# FIVE

TATE

"Congratulations, it seems you can't help but climb the ranks." My brother claps mockingly.

"Oh shut up, Frederick. Sarcasm doesn't suit you, and what are you complaining about anyway? You got everything you wanted, didn't you?"

"What *I* wanted? You want to tell me you did what *I* wanted?"

"I bet you felt so bad about being first in line," I scoff.

"I thought you were dead," he roars. "I woke up from the mark searing my skin, and I thought you died. Either because someone killed you or because you gave up. When I hurried to Father, he confirmed you were gone." He breathes heavily. "It was only when I started asking around for Jared and Nan that I learned you left ... all of you, without even saying goodbye."

"I never—"

"No, I see it now. You are a coldhearted bastard, like him. You are just better at hiding it, aren't you? So, Tamara—"

"Don't you dare pull her into this," I snap, but he continues raising his voice to speak over me.

"Don't pretend you care, I know you too well for that." He sneers at me. "She is not your type. The women you used to be with were prettier, more polished, more obedient, softer..." I shake my head at him, wondering where he is going with this shit. Of course, no one from my past can compete with Ara. That's why they are in the past, and she's my present and, if I have my way, my future too.

"But then what made her irresistible is her brother's position, isn't it? It's rather brilliant. Fuck his sister, gain his loyalty, and then use my own army to take back your throne." He lowers his voice. "Tell me, brother, how far did you get? Did you fuck her?" He only grins at the fury in my eyes. "Of course, you did..." He strides toward me. "Does she like it, or will I have to force—"

His head snaps back when my fist connects. He grunts and runs his tongue over his lip, smearing his teeth with blood in the process.

"So she is good between the sheets. That's a relief." He chuckles, barely avoiding my right fist, but not expecting the left. He stumbles back, grinning like a madman now.

"You know you gave me a gift. I resigned to marrying a faceless girl because our father demanded it, for the sake of her bloodline, her family. But this is so much better, knowing what she means to you—"

"She means nothing to me," I bluff, my blood running cold at his threat. Suddenly, I desperately want him to believe the scheme he accused me of.

"You were right. I used her for her connections." The lie rolls off my tongue without hesitation. "But I got tired of her ... so there's really nothing in it for you here."

My brother looks at me, then at my swollen knuckles, his tongue darting over his split lip.

"What can I say? I'm not good at sharing." I shrug. "Even if she is nothing but a willing body in my bed." Mists, I nearly choke on that last sentence, disgusted by my own words. She means so much more to me.

Frederick shakes his head, grinning. "You should have joined the theater. That was one hell of a performance. I almost believed you." He taps his nose. "Almost."

If he hurts her because of me... My hands clench into fists while I fight for control.

"You will not lay a finger on her," I threaten, dangerously quiet.

"First you lie, now you threaten me for her?" He sighs and shakes his head.

"You have no idea what I would do for her."

"Well, then, it's better if I take her off your hands. I'm going to marry her and enjoy every minute ... of your suffering." I lunge for him and get in two more hits before I'm pulled off him.

*He planned this.*

The realization hits as soon as he gets up, grinning despite his busted face. He planned to provoke me into attacking him, and I fell into his trap.

"Take him away," he orders coldly. "Twenty for raising his hand against me and ... another ten for daring to touch my future bride while I will ... fill her in."

"Frederick, if you touch her..."

"That is Your Highness to you, *brother*. And please go on ... threatening your future king in front of witnesses would be a new low, even for you."

"Don't you dare..."

"Oh, I already did." His cold grin freezes me from the inside out. "Let's see how you like it when everything is taken from you, and you have to deal with it ... all alone."

"What did you do?" I demand to know.

"You would love to know, wouldn't you?" He sneers at me.

Wind whips through the room, billowing the curtains, crashing the windows open, and throwing back the two guards who previously held me.

*I'd rather kill him than let him harm her.*

"Stop," Daeva snaps. *"You can't."*

"Oh, *watch me.*" There's buzzing in my ears, pressure builds in my chest, my gift unfurls and snaps like an angry beast.

*"She is fine. Think about it, you just saw her. She is probably still sleeping in her bed."* Her words penetrate the mix of terror and wrath controlling my mind. *"If you kill him, the throne will go to you—and they will win."* That sobers me. Daeva is right.

The wind dies down, and only seconds later, the icy cold of suppressants closes around my wrists.

"Impressive. Air magic, who would have guessed?" Fred turns to someone standing behind me. "Leave the suppressants on until tomorrow. I want the message to sink in."

The pressure in my chest collapses, taking all the air with it. I'm led away while I concentrate on drawing my next breath. Icy panic claws up my throat, constricts it. The distinctive cold of the shackles suppresses my magic, leeches my strength, and it's sickeningly familiar.

*"Daeva, contact Solaris,"* I order, but get no reply. *"I need to know she's alright. Protect her!"* Still nothing. The suppressants seem to cut my connection to Daeva, too. The icy numbness fills my veins, spreading.

I struggle against my captors, smashing one of them against the wall of the hallway. The grunt of pain is satisfying, but more hands reach for me, restraining me until I'm not able to shake them anymore.

Anger, helplessness, and terror swirl in my chest, restricting my lungs. I'm failing her ... failing them. I fight it, fight the lurking darkness, but it swallows me, pulls me under, and with it come the memories.

*Forest surrounds me. The ground is spongy and muddy under my knees, the cold seeping into my bones. Screams permeate the air, and the piney scent of wood has a coppery tang to it.*

*Blood soaks the earth, infusing it with the terror of the dying. My own breathing and pounding heart are so loud I can't make out anything but the screams.*

*The skin-crawling terror of what happened here will forever stain this place. I already feel it—the darkness, the evil. I'd bet the place is crawling with nightmares by evening.*

*Bodies litter the ground, and I can't help but look in the direction Louis lies. Only his right leg up to his knee is visible from over here, but my eyes get stuck on it. I will it to twitch, to move, anything that tells me he's not dead—but there is nothing.*

*The gash was bad. The way he jumped in front of me and took what was meant for me will haunt me in all the lives to come. Even if he isn't dead yet, he's bleeding out while I kneel over here, useless, the icy pull of suppressants cutting off my magic.*

*Not that I would have been of help ... healing and truth-telling are no use in battle. I only learned to heal myself. Everything else is beneath me—according to my father. I hate him for it right now.*

My arms are stretched above me. Pain explodes in my gut, my cheek, my abdomen. I dimly realize we are beneath the palace now and that I'm chained to a wall before the memory pulls me back under.

*Leo and his father are the only ones still alive apart from me. It's only them and me ... and our captors. Leo is my cousin, but also my brother's best friend. They share the same coloring from my father's side, with their blue eyes and blond hair.*

*He is shaking, his whole body quivering like a leaf in a storm. I feel cold too, but it's a different kind of coldness, one no fire will ever be able to chase away. They died because of me. My eyes run over the bodies again and stop on my cousin. His pants are darker around his crotch. His eyes show too much white. His terror has something animalistic.*

*It all seems like a bad dream, the kind where terror paralyzes you and dread drips down your back. It's the bone-deep knowledge that something bad is happening, and there is nothing you can do to stop it, no matter how hard you try.*

*The awareness that evil brushed you, stays with you, will never leave you again ... the kind of horror you need convincing and time to shake after waking ... only it isn't a dream.*

*One of our attackers runs his blade down my front, hacking off my shirt, leaving a burning path on my skin.*

The coppery taste of blood coats my tongue. It's my blood, and when I spit it out, it splatters on stone instead of wet earth.

*The man's eyes are fixed on the mark declaring me as the crown prince of Belarra, and a wide grin spreads over his face. He shouts something. His language is harsh and full of hissing sounds.*

*Men gather around me, laughing and poking at me, nicking my skin. They stop when someone else arrives, smaller than the others and not as heavily armed. He looks nearly harmless in comparison.*

*"We'll make a deal with you, and then we'll let you go," he says, and I spit at his feet. They killed Louis. I'm not giving them anything.*

Pain blooms in my chest with every breath I take.

*Nonchalantly, like it is no more than brushing lint off his sleeve, he runs his blade over my uncle's throat. Blood soaks me and my cousin, its warmth startling against my ice-cold skin. My stomach heaves.*

*I killed him. I killed him as surely as if I had wielded the blade myself.*

*Leo's eyes burn into me, and I make myself hold his stare. It's filled with pain, tears, fear ... and disgust. And I deserve it.*

The brilliant pain of my nose breaking nearly shatters the image, but not quite. The bloody forest is for a second replaced by a musty stone room, the flicker of torches replacing the soft light of dawn, and stained stone the bloody earth. Another blink and I'm back in the forest.

*"Let's try this once more, shall we?" The killer walks over to me and runs his dagger over the right side of my neck. It's not the burn that makes me jerk, but my uncle's blood running down my skin. Still warm but rapidly cooling. Marking me worse than the blade ever could. He chuckles and cleans the steel on the remains of my shirt.*

*"What do you want?"* I croak out.

*"That sounds much better."* He grins. *"You will promise to be a good prince and tell no one about what happened here, our little conversation, or our deal. The words will make you choke otherwise. Once you take over the throne, you will be our obedient slave and do whatever we command without exception, and in exchange, I promise to never harm you or the boy."* He nods in Leo's direction.

*"I..."* I start. He can't be serious.

The breath is driven out of me, and I sag. The shackles are now the only thing holding me up. Pain radiates through my wrists.

*"Uh, uh, uh ... not so hasty."* He walks back to Leo and sets his blade against his neck, and I instantly shut up. Agreeing to their plan is madness, but I can't let Leo die.

*They'll torture me until I agree anyway. Hopelessness washes through me. Too many have died already—for me.*

*I nod. I'll find a way out of this once we are safe.*

*"Well, you know deals don't work that way."* The man strides over to me, gripping my arm. *"Do you agree to the deal previously stated?"*

*"I agree."* A burn crawls over my skin, molding itself to the pattern of my gift. If I hadn't seen it form, I wouldn't know it's there. My gaze jumps up.

*"At least she's good for something."* I follow his gaze to a wispy girl with red hair, standing half hidden behind one of the warriors.

*Did she do that? What kind of gift does she have to accomplish hiding a promise so perfectly? Then my eyes go back to Leo. There is hope mixed in with the tears now, but the accusation didn't lessen. Had I agreed earlier, his father would still be alive. Hell, if they had handed me over instead of protecting me, maybe everyone would still be alive. And we both know it.*

Whatever held me up snaps, and there is rough, cool stone beneath me, my fingers sliding over it while I try to find my way out of the memory.

*The man who had been talking to me grunts something, and the girl gasps. Pain explodes over Leo's face only a heartbeat before the bloody tip of a blade pierces his chest.*

"No!" *The scream reverberates in my head, but I'm not sure if it ever leaves my mouth. The big warrior, the girl still by his side, pulls his sword back, and Leo slumps to the floor, his eyes unseeing.*

"What did you do to him?" a stern, familiar voice demands to know.

"The crown prince's orders," another replies.

"You are damn fools. Do you have any idea who that is?" He curses. "Get out of my sight, before I teach you a lesson you'll never forget," the voice orders. Someone leaves, the steps fading. "Let's get you up, Your Highness."

"Not my title anymore," I reply, or at least I try to, but what comes out is barely recognizable. My old mentor understands me anyway.

"How about we argue about that once we have you cleaned up and back in working order?" he asks while pulling me to my feet. "Get those things off him," Corin snaps to someone behind me.

"But His Highness ordered—" the voice replies.

"And I will take the blame if it comes to it, but get them off him. Now."

One of my eyes is already swollen shut, and my whole body hurts, but even worse is the throbbing in my chest, like someone poked around in a festering wound.

Corin, my father's head of guards and the one who trained me since I was a little boy, pulls my arm over his shoulders to steady me. A relieved sigh leaves my lips once the suppressants are off.

*"Is Ara alright?"* I ask Daeva.

*"Good to have you back. Forget what I said earlier. If your brother ever comes close to me, I will eat him, one piece at a time. How long do you think we can keep him alive if you heal him in between?"* she asks, but doesn't press for an answer when she feels my turmoil. *"Solaris is a pain in my ass, but he promises she is upset but unharmed."* Hearing

Daeva's voice and knowing that Ara is fine soothes me more than anything else could.

Corin accompanies me into the healing quarters. We are quiet while the healer on duty patches me back up.

I'm exhausted—physically, mentally, and emotionally. There is nothing left to give. I'm not even sure if I would have been able to heal myself.

The healer leaves the room, and the guard master's intense stare is on me.

"Frederick is a moron—I never said that, of course—but what did you do to provoke him like this?" he asks.

"He wanted to have something, and I told him no," I say. "Well, not just verbally."

"Hmm, that's what I thought."

"Did you now?" I rub my face, grateful that it's only the memory of pain lingering there.

"Oh, I have eyes, and I was at the ball last night, even if I was watching from the sidelines." He shakes his head at me. "Only make sure she is worth all of this."

"What is that supposed to mean?"

"You wouldn't be the first to be discarded for the shinier object or the better offer."

"She's not like that..." I shake my head and sigh. "But I messed up."

"Don't we all from time to time?" He grins at me. "When I sleep in the barracks on my missus's orders, crawling and groveling always helps. Not that I ever imagined seeing you on your knees."

"What should I say?" I shrug and give him a lopsided grin. "She cut me down before I had a chance to counter."

"No surprise, considering who raised her." He pats my shoulder. "Sounds like you've found your match, son."

CHAPTER

# SIX

ARA

MY EYES FLY OPEN, AND I SCAN THE ROOM, UNSURE OF WHAT woke me. I strain my ears, my eyes searching for anything, anyone moving in the dark, but there is nothing. All the shapes are accounted for by the furniture in my room. My heartbeat slows, and my breath comes easier. I sit up.

Maybe it's the unfamiliar surroundings, but something about the palace has me on constant alert. And Deliah's talk about backstabbing didn't help either. I wait for another minute, but when nothing seems amiss, I lie back down.

I roll over, trying to get comfortable, when something crinkles under my hand. It's a stiff, rectangular piece of paper with a blob of wax—a letter. I jerk up again, my hand reaching for the dagger on my nightstand. My eyes fly through the room, checking for movement, but again, there is no one.

"*Solaris?*" I ask and find him wide awake, his signature so close he has to be on the balcony. "*What are you doing on the balcony?*"

"*Keeping watch,*" he answers. "*I don't like it here.*"

That would make two of us.

"*Was someone in my room?*" I ask him even though I already know the answer. How else would the letter have gotten here?

"*He promised not to disturb you.*" An image of Tate accompanies his words.

"*Tate was here, and you didn't wake me?*" I chastise. "*You knew I wanted to talk to him.*"

"*Daeva told me not to wake you.*"

"*Oh, when Daeva said that...*" I huff out a breath.

"*How about you read the letter instead of swooning over it?*" Solaris suggests, and I stop my thumb, which had been tracing the seal.

I light the candle next to my bed with my gift and melt half—okay, nearly all of it—before a small flame flickers to life. IIan had started practicing my gift with me after I almost set the dining table on fire by accident. The wick sits now in a big puddle of wax, sooting unsightly, but it's burning, so who cares how it looks?

The paper is thick and heavy, a single word gracing its front. *Sunshine.* The wax bears the royal seal.

My hands shake slightly while I open and unfold the letter. His handwriting is sure and slightly slanted, and it makes me realize how little I know about him. I don't even know if he always writes like this or if it means he was in a hurry. My finger strokes over the paper.

"*Could you stop petting that damn letter and start reading it?*" Solaris grumbles, pulling me out of my thoughts, and I do.

*Sunshine,*

*I'm not sure if I'll be able to catch you alone before*

*I have to leave, and around here, you never know who is listening, so a letter seemed safer.*

*On patrol, a man approached me to warn you. He said his name was Tynan.*

*He didn't say much, only that you need to be careful. He claimed to belong to the mist court and have your best interest at heart. I don't know about that, but we both know something happened at Picking. I pray you remember soon, but since I don't know if you'll return...*

What? What does he think I'll do instead? Marry his brother?

The knock on my door startles me, but since my thoughts are still on Tate, I rise without hesitation. Only there is no one there.

I peer down the hall, and someone slips around the next corner. I hesitate, but when I reach out with my senses and find Tate moving in the same direction as the person who knocked, my curiosity is piqued.

I grab the dagger from my nightstand and rush out the door, with the letter still in my hand.

My bare feet are soundless on the cold marble floor. My nightgown is too thin for the chilly night and definitely not proper, but that is not enough to make me turn around.

I move swiftly. Twice more I spot movement ahead of me, and we are still moving toward Tate. Another set of footsteps has me slowing down. I creep around the next corner, but the corridor is empty apart from the curtains on a window and a few statues evenly spaced along the wall.

I pause. This is stupid. What am I even doing here? I'm just about to turn around when someone steps out of a corridor to the side, not ten steps in front of me. I freeze.

It's Frederick. He pauses, and I squeeze my eyes shut, already searching for a reasonable explanation, but the questions never come. His footsteps move away, and my eyes fly open just in time to see him step through a door into the same room Tate has to be in. He leaves the door ajar. I creep closer, and the murmur of voices reaches my ear.

At first, I can only make out a few words. "Coldhearted bastard ... father ... hiding."

I debate whether to turn around or go in, then Frederick mentions my name, and I move closer.

"Don't you..." Tate starts, but Frederick talks over him.

"Don't pretend you care, I know you too well for that. She is not your type. The women you used to be with were prettier, more polished, more obedient, softer..." The sneer of the seamstress pops back in my mind, the gazes of a hundred strangers taking my measure at the ball last night.

I shake my head. This is stupid, Tate told me I was beautiful. "But what made her irresistible is her brother's position, isn't it?" Frederick's voice is scathing. "It's rather brilliant. Fuck his sister, gain his loyalty, and then use my own army to take back your throne."

I jerk back like someone kicked me. No, that can't be true. He didn't even know who I was before... *But he met your brother before he took you to bed*, a tiny voice disagrees.

I shake my head in denial, but my stomach is heavy. I bite my lip, straining my ears, willing him to disagree to make this better, but it gets worse.

"So she is good between the sheets? That's a relief." Frederick's words make me sick. I press a hand to my stomach as bile rises in my throat.

"She means nothing to me." Tate's voice is cold, controlled, and foreign. There is a pause. "You were right. I used her for her connections. But I got tired of her..." His words strike my heart with brutal decision, slicing it into bloody ribbons. Blood pounds in my ears.

But how could I have been so wrong? Why then, acting the way he did with Morgan?

"What can I say? I'm not good at sharing." Tate answers that question as if he heard me. "Even if she is nothing but a willing body in my bed."

*No.*

I stagger.

He can't, how can... I shake my head, trying desperately to explain away what I just heard. How could I have been so wrong about him? But no matter how I twist and turn the words, I can't change their meaning.

A whimper claws its way up my throat, and I press a hand over my mouth to hold it in. Then I back away, nearly stumbling in my haste.

How could I have been so blind? A spiky little ball grows in my throat, making it hard to swallow, to breathe. My hands shake as I watch flames devour the letter that had still been clutched in my hand. It shrinks and blackens until it is no more than ash, marring my skin.

I turn and run. The icy cold of the floor seeps into my bones.

*He used me.*

The sentence hammers in my brain like his betrayal pulses through my body. How could I have been so stupid? How could I believe someone would overlook my curse and my secrets to put me first?

I should have known better. Power and family ties, that's what it always comes down to—priorities.

I wrench open the door to my room, and when I push it closed behind me, my hand leaves a perfect imprint on the wood.

My nightgown smolders, and I stare at it numbly while brown flowers bloom on the light fabric, black follows, before glowing lines eat away at it. It looks pretty.

I snap out of it when flames dance over my skin, realizing I will set the room on fire if I don't do something. I rush to the bathing chamber, turn the shower to cold, and drop to the floor beneath it. The water hisses as it hits my skin, filling the room with steam. Smothering me, hiding me.

*He used me.*

I watch the water disappear down the drain while I fight to control the flames swirling around me. My nightdress is mostly black now and plastered to my skin. Inky trails run down my body and over the floor to the drain. I watch them curl and writhe and vanish.

I don't even realize the flames are gone until Solaris's screech pierces the icy numbness.

*"Turn off the water right now, or I will burn down this damn palace."*

*"Go ahead. I don't care,"* I tell him, but turn off the water anyway. I'm shivering, my body too cold to move. Maybe I'll just stay here.

*"No, you won't. You'll come out here this instant, or I will make good on my threat,"* he snaps. I try to rise, but I'm so damn weak that my legs buckle.

*"Now, Ara."* His command rips through me, so menacing that I don't question it and start crawling.

*"I'm coming, you bossy bastard of a Phoenix,"* I grumble. *"Why didn't I see it?"*

*"You can cry, rant, scream all you want ... once you are out here."*

I pull myself up on the frame of the glass door, stumbling out as soon as I unlock it, right into Solaris. I sigh when his heat hits me. He is in full flame and gently envelops me with his wings.

*"Don't do that again,"* he spits. *"You nearly drowned your flame."*

*"My what?"*

*"Your inner flame. Dragons and Phoenixes have them, and it seems you do too. If your body temperature becomes too low, it will extinguish and you'll die."*

*"I'm sorry."* I bury my face in his side.

*"You are fine, and had I known, I would have warned you. You can cry now,"* he croons, his wing pulling me closer. I wish I could, but

the tears are a frozen lump in my throat, pulsing painfully and making it hard to breathe and swallow.

Soothing, gentle memories wash over me. Images of a forest, Solaris growing up, other Phoenixes—probably his parents. All of it is light and calming, and I slip into his mind, leaving the pain behind, until it can't touch me anymore.

Dawn breaks and brightens, the castle starts to buzz with activity, and I feel strangely removed from everything.

Ana enters and gasps when she catches sight of me, but I only shrug, not offering an explanation.

I let her fuss over me, sitting like a puppet on the chair she pushed me on. I refuse the dress she wants to put me in and grab a thin tunic and pants instead. Ignoring her protest.

When my brother comes to get me for breakfast, I go through all the motions, but everything flows past me, not connecting to the hollowness inside me. My smile feels brittle, my movements mechanical.

I'm a puppet playing a role in a game I no longer care for.

Tate isn't at breakfast, which is a relief. I'm not ready to face him. I pick at my food, not eating much and not tasting anything.

I absently rub at the ache behind my sternum, but stop when I catch my brother's worried look.

"I'm going to train," I tell him as soon as I can excuse myself and rush out into the courtyard. I silently step behind a group of guards and join their training.

They don't seem to notice me, and I'm grateful for that. I focus on the movements of the man in front of me and shut out everything else. I keep a steady distance while we run laps around the palace wall. The impact of my feet and the warming of my muscles are soothingly familiar.

Exercises for conditioning follow. The men give me curious looks at first, but I don't meet their gaze, and I'm relieved when they ignore me after a while. A thin sheen of sweat coats my skin, my breath comes heavier and faster, and I'm determined to push through.

Perhaps exhausting my body will stop the swirling thoughts in my head that I can't seem to escape.

"Pair up for sparring," an older man commands, then looks at me, sizing me up. "I'm up for a round or two if you want, Lady Blackstone," he offers, and everyone falls silent. I know they all want to know my answer.

"There is no need, Corin. I'll spar with her." I close my eyes and do my best to suppress a groan at the voice coming from behind me.

# CHAPTER
# SEVEN
## TATE

Exhausted from the night's events, I'm late for breakfast, and Ara is nowhere in sight. But my brother is far too happy to inform me that he helped Ara see me for who I am. I have no idea what he means by that, but it can't be good.

My appetite is gone, so I search for Ara instead.

I find her out in the courtyard, training with my father's guards. The sunlight teases out the gold in her hair, the short strands around her face lighting up like a halo whenever they catch the light.

She follows along without difficulty or hesitation, reminding me that their routine is probably close to the training she grew up with. There is so much I want to ask her, so much I still don't know about her, and the thought that I might not get the chance to starts up an ache in my chest.

The central courtyard bustles with activity while nobles and servants cross the white gravel and go about their tasks for the day. I earn curious looks as I lean against the palace wall, my eyes glued to Ara's movements, but I ignore them.

*"If she condemns you that easily, she is not who I thought she was,"* Daeva says. I try to let that thought soothe me, but I don't like the emptiness in Ara's eyes or the tenseness lingering in her body.

I never spoke about the attack. How could I? But I know that coming back alone, covered in blood that wasn't mine and refusing to talk had caused a lot of rumors and opinions. They never were brave enough to say anything to my face, their fear of what I might do keeping their tongues in check, but I'm not deaf.

What if she believes them?

Corin orders his men to pair up for sparring, and I straighten. I amble closer when the old man offers to spar with her.

"There is no need, Corin. I'll spar with her."

Corin shoots me a knowing look over Ara's shoulder, but Ara's eyes stay on the floor while we head over to a rack of weapons, not once meeting my eyes until we face each other, swords at the ready. My chest constricts. This is bad.

Her face is empty, emotionless, and somehow that is so much worse than anger, pain, or even disgust ever could be. It's like she's shut down completely.

"Sunshine..." I start, not caring that others can hear me, and she charges. Reflex takes over, and I parry and evade while she comes at me again and again.

Her slashes are fast and hard, betraying her empty eyes. When I soften my blows, she grits her teeth and her eyebrows draw together.

"Dammit. Fight me already!" Ara seethes, and finally, there is fire in her eyes. If sparring helps her get it all out there, I'm happy to assist.

We go round for round, focused on each other, the clashing of our swords a fast-paced rhythm. But since I'm not sure she would let me heal her, and the thought of someone else healing her sets my teeth on edge, I'm careful with my blade. Ara doesn't show the same restraint, though. She is clearly out for blood. I twist, barely avoiding a slash that would have gotten her there, and shake my head when she comes at me again.

"Talk to me, Ara," I murmur when our swords lock again and I push her back. She shakes her head stubbornly.

"*I don't think she wants to talk,*" Daeva comments.

"*I'm working on it,*" I tell her.

"*You're not doing a good job so far,*" she says, and I huff out a breath, refraining from telling her to shut up. I think she gets the message anyway and falls silent.

We go back and forth, and I'm so focused on Ara that I have honestly no idea how long we've been sparring for. While I try to get her to open up, she does her best to make a conversation impossible. And I want to smash my brother's face in.

Ara's arms start shaking. Her movements become slower and sloppier, her breath labored, but she doesn't let up.

"That's enough," I tell her, but she only shakes her head and keeps coming. Her creeping exhaustion, combined with her recklessness and determination, will get her hurt if she keeps that up.

Our swords tangle again, both our breaths labored huffs in the silence between us. Ara grits her teeth, not relenting even though my sword inches toward her.

"How could you do something like that?" she pants out, and my stomach drops. She believes whatever she heard.

"I would have told you—"

"And you think I would have ever let you lay a finger on me?" Her last words are nearly a whisper. I ease up on the pressure when my blade gets closer to her, only for her to press in. Fucking hell.

"Enough, Ara. Let me explain."

She shakes her head.

I grind my teeth in frustration, and with a flick of my wrist, I send her sword flying out of her hands. She growls at me, only to dart over and pick her blade back up to come at me again.

"I said that is enough," I snarl. This time, when I snatch her blade, I let it float back to the rack along with my own.

"It will never be enough," she growls, her chest heaving, impaling me with her glare. A few whistles and chuckles come from the guards who stop their sparring to watch us.

"Did I say you can laze around?" Corin snaps, and we're left alone. Or as alone as you can be in the middle of a courtyard filled with soldiers, servants, and nobles who are all too interested in your business.

We stand in front of each other, both our chests rising and falling. But her darting eyes tell me she is about to run. *Oh no, you won't, baby.*

I step closer.

"What are you doing?" she snarls.

"Fighting you." I flip her onto her back, trapping her beneath me. Which turns out to be a fucking horrible idea since it reminds me of the last time I had her pinned beneath me. Naked, in my bed.

Her chest heaves against mine, and her lips part on a gasp, drawing my attention. We both freeze. She is so fucking beautiful that it makes my chest ache.

Our gazes lock, and my lips tingle when her breath skates over them. Her pull on me is so strong that I lean in without even thinking about it.

"Don't you dare," she whispers, her voice rough. But it's the tremble on the last word that causes me to push up. I'm hovering over her, our bodies no longer touching.

"Please talk to me," I murmur, my body aching from her proximity.

Another whistle catches my attention and reminds me of where we are. As much as I want to, I can't keep her trapped beneath me until she listens. Not in the middle of the courtyard.

I get to my feet and reach down, but Ara ignores the hand I offer, getting up by herself.

She balls her fists, and for a second, I think she'll come at me again, but instead, she turns and hurries to a door and back inside. I follow.

# EIGHT

## ARA

I HURRY DOWN THE CORRIDOR, BUT HE KEEPS UP EASILY.

"Talk to me." Tate catches my arm, and his touch burns through the rest of the icy wall I erected around my heart. My chest heaves, but whether from sparring, running, or his proximity, I don't know. Probably all three of them.

I don't get the chance to object before he drags me into an empty room. It's open and light, with big windows and a set of doors leading to a little balcony overlooking the sprawling gardens. Still, the moment he shuts the door behind us, it's too small. He's too close. We are too alone.

A bitter laugh claws up my throat. How quickly things can change. Yesterday, I would have given everything to be alone with him, and now...

I turn away, my eyes wandering over the plush set of seats arranged on one side of the room, the silky blue of the fabric glistening in the sunlight streaming in. It matches the curtains framing the windows, and the color is found again in the light-colored rug on the wooden floor. I concentrate on all of this, trying to drown out my awareness of the man behind me.

"Could you please look at me, sunshine?" Tate asks behind me, and I want to slap him for using that name. How dare he pretend so convincingly?

"Quite a collection of paintings you have here," I say, fighting to keep my voice even, ignoring his request by going over to a big frame, depicting a festival in a parklike setting.

"Ara," Tate growls behind me, "I have to leave soon."

"Well then, leave."

"Ara, please could you at least look at me?"

"Maybe I don't want to look at you after everything I know now. Ever thought of that?" I round on him just in time to see the color drain from his face. His hair is tousled, and there is a slight sheen of sweat on his brow.

I avoid his eyes, looking at his chest instead. The damp fabric of his shirt clings to his body. Movement draws my eyes to his rolled-up sleeves and his muscular forearms, rippling with the clenching of his fists. His markings seem alive with it. Lines I traced while lying next to him in bed... There is a dull throb low in my abdomen, and I shake my head, angry with myself.

*He's a lying, deceiving bastard.* Sadly, that doesn't lessen his pull on me.

And because my traitorous body aches for him, I take a step back.

*She means nothing to me. I used her for her connections. She is nothing but a willing body in my bed.*

His words are burned into my heart as if he branded me, and now that he's pulled me out of my numbness, they hurt.

And I want to hurt him back. Gods, do I want to hurt him. Anything to lessen the pain in my chest.

"How could you do something like that?" I snarl, and he flinches.

"I trusted you." My breath is uneven and much too fast. "I let you... Gods, how could I not see it?" I bite my cheek hard to hold in the sob that wants to follow. "What kind of monster... And I let you... I let you touch me." I hurl the words like knives, satisfied to see his body jerk with every hit. "I hate you." My voice catches, and I make the mistake of meeting his gaze.

There is pain in his eyes, and my anger burns hot and bright, devouring everything else.

How dare he act hurt now?

I flush with fury, shake with it. The burn crawls over my skin. A wisp of smoke rising from my chest catches my attention.

It's not just anger heating me.

*Not again.*

"*I need you,*" I shout at Solaris.

"*Already on my way. Hold on just a minute longer.*"

"Ara." Tate's voice sounds scratchy, pleading. He swallows. "Listen to me, please, baby."

"Don't," I hiss, but he still reaches for me, and the worst thing is that some tiny part of me still wants him to. I back away and shake my head. "If you touch me, I'll burn you to ashes," I warn.

"You already did," he says, taking another step in my direction. I hold out my hand to keep him away, but he steps up to it and presses into it. I snatch my hand back, but the shape of it is already burned into the fabric right over his heart. He takes another step closer.

Emotions zip through me like lightning, and controlling my gift becomes impossible.

I turn and rush to the balcony doors. The hem of my right sleeve smolders, then catches fire. I fumble with the latch, the cool metal instantly heating under my touch. I step onto the balcony, the spring air icy against my too hot skin.

And as soon as Solaris is close enough, I jump on the railing and hurl myself at him. Flames erupt around me when I land on his back.

Tate shouts my name, but I don't look back. I can't. He's too good at this, and I'm too weak, too ready to fall for his lies again.

Everything blurs in front of my eyes while my arms come around

Solaris's neck. I bury my face in his feathers and let the heat kiss the tears off my face. My flames become one with his while he swiftly gains altitude.

I have no idea how long we are in the air, the time burned away in a swirl of orange and gold, accompanied by Solaris's comforting voice in my head.

I lose myself in our bond until the pain in my chest is no more than a dull, annoying pulse in a fiery ocean of emotions, memories, and impressions.

It's late by the time Solaris sets me down on the balcony of my room, and I'm quite literally burned out. My clothes did not fare well with the heat, and the thin cotton shirt and pants I donned this morning left nothing but black smears on my skin.

Ana throws the doors open, her eyes so wide they seem to swallow her face when she sees the state I'm in.

I'm sure between this morning and now, she thinks I've lost my mind. But I'm beyond caring.

"We have to hurry, or you'll be late for dinner," Ana tells me, wringing her hands.

"Is Prince Alec attending?" I ask.

"I don't think so," she says, and I nearly sag in relief. No reason to pretend then.

"I will skip dinner tonight," I tell Ana, intent on falling onto my bed right away. But Ana won't have it. She makes me take a bath while softly washing the soot out of my hair. Her gentle massage on my scalp nearly makes me fall asleep right then and there.

I don't even have it in me to protest when she towels me off like a little girl and pulls a nightgown over my head.

The bath doused all the fire that was left. Exhaustion crashes over me, and I'm out like a snuffed candle the second I fall onto my bed.

I dream of Tate, of him stroking my cheek, pressing kisses to my lips, and holding me. I sigh with contentment. But thinking of him starts a burning ache in my chest. And the images change. There is heat and fire all around me, and there is pleading and screaming. A face melting like a candle's wax, and it's changing.

Mariel, Calix, my brothers. Face after face consumed by my flames until Tate pleads with me to stop and not burn him to ash. There is so much pain in his voice, and I try and try, but I can't. Terror freezes me, and sadness rips me apart. I can't breathe, and then I start awake with a gasp.

I wake with gritty eyes and wet cheeks, bone weary and defeated, to a dark and empty room. I groan, rolling over, hiding under my blanket.

But reality crashes over me, making it impossible to fall asleep again.

*He used me.*

*I'm nothing to him.*

The dull pain in my chest flares up, and I turn again. Was it really only last night that I found Tate's letter and stroked it like a lovesick fool?

*The letter.*

I sit up. The mist court ... it always seemed no more than a tale, but... There are people in the mists, the titans. And if one of them tried to warn me...

*"Do you think that's a good idea?"* Solaris cautions.

*"They have to know something,"* I tell him. I jump out of bed and quickly get dressed, stubbornly ignoring all the reasons Solaris lists why this might be a mistake.

*"It'll keep me busy,"* I counter. *"It gives me something to take my mind off..."* I will not think of him. I will not fall apart.

My black worn leather armor, which I packed despite my mother's protest, is a comforting hug. Every blade I slide into its designated spot is another brick in my armor.

I braid my hair without needing to look in the mirror, as it is the same braid I've worn every day for months. I'm more concerned with keeping my hair out of the way than appearance, anyway.

Many people vanish in the mist every year, and it would be foolish to disregard that.

*"It could be a trap,"* Solaris cautions me, but the thought strangely doesn't bother me. Trust seems a strange concept right now anyway.

Let them come. Let them think they can take advantage of me, and I'll show them how wrong they are.

*"Ready?"* I ask Solaris while I stride over to the balcony doors.

*"Ready when you are,"* he croons, pushing off into the crisp air as soon as I'm seated.

# NINE

My chest feels raw, like someone used me for target practice, and there is nothing I can do about it.

She is hurting too. I saw it in her eyes while she landed blow after blow. And still, she didn't pull any of them, didn't even hear me out.

She took his word for the truth and stabbed me when I thought she had my back. And that hurts more than anything.

How can an event from four years ago cost me everything ... again?

Despite her words, I keep hoping she'll come back and give me the chance to explain. But she doesn't, and I finally have to leave.

Every breath is fucking torture, but I don't allow my mask to crack. When predators surround you, every drop of blood can be your demise.

I try to talk to my brother, seek him out in my father's office, but his bitterness sits deep, and he is hell-bent on getting back at me.

"I grew up with four brothers," he sneers at me. "And thanks to you, I have not one left. You got two of them killed, and you and Jared abandoned me."

"I was in no state to—"

"You simply left," he roars, jumping up from his seat behind the desk. "If you had at least told me, maybe I would have understood."

"You didn't talk to me," I snap. "Ever since I came back without them, you refused to talk to me."

"Because you refused to tell me what happened. All I wanted was to know what happened to them. I even begged you, and still, you stayed silent. No explanation. Nothing." He slams his hand down.

I shake my head at him.

"Really? Even now?" He laughs bitterly. "My life went downhill after you left, but you can't even give me the truth?"

I scoff. My brother was always envious of my position. I don't believe him for one second that he's sorry about that change.

"Our father took it in his hands to bring me up to speed in all the things I was lacking." He walks over to the window. "And in his eyes, that was everything since I wasn't you." His voice is harsh, accusing.

"He was never happy with me either," I offer, but my words don't seem to sink in. He turns to me and points an accusing finger at me.

"You cost me my best friend, my brothers, even the woman who was more of a mother to me than our own. Because you left, they broke my betrothal with Deliah since the girl you left behind had the better connections."

"You don't have to marry Ara. You can say no. That's—"

"Nice try. You shattered the life I knew and let me deal with the shards on my own, and now you think you can waltz in here and decide you want your bride back?" He laughs coldly. "I don't think so."

"Leaving like that was a shit thing to do..."

"Oh, you think?"

"I had no choice—"

"You cracked, brother, you crumbled under the pressure of a few rumors and suspicious glances, and instead of manning up, you walked away like a coward." He shakes his head. "You didn't care about me, so why would you think I care about you?"

"What about Ara?" Speaking her name nearly slays me, but I keep my voice even. "None of this is her fault. You want to punish her, too?"

"She's just a chess piece, Alec. Sometimes you have to sacrifice a figure to win the game. And she comes with connections and a bloodline I can't ignore." He smirks at me. "She will give me magically strong heirs."

The only reason I don't kill him for that comment is that Ara more or less promised she won't go through with the betrothal. No matter what my brother told her, she wouldn't take such a step without at least hearing me out, right?

I turn and walk away.

*"I'm still for taking him apart, slowly,"* Daeva caws.

*"Not. Helping,"* I tell her.

*"Oh, I think it would help just fine with all that rage bubbling inside you."*

*"Daeva,"* I warn. *"Focus on the greater goal."*

*"Yeah, okay, we'll take out the others first and then him."*

Since I haven't brought much with me, packing is done within minutes. On a whim, I slip the signet ring into my pocket. Who knows if it will come in handy? If my plans work out, I will be back in Avina soon, and the royal crest always held more power here than anywhere else in the kingdom.

I pace my room and delay departure again and again, hoping for an opportunity to talk to Ara. Only when I can't wait any longer, I leave.

We cut it close, but since my stubborn bird refuses to rest even when I try to order her, we make it back with time to spare. I lie down for a few hours, but sleep evades me.

"You want to talk about it?" Jared eyes me from the side on our way to the weight room.

I just look at him, our steps echoing in the empty hallway.

"Sorry, I forgot for a second who I was talking to." Jared shakes his head at me. "You prefer to let it eat you up instead."

"Have they made any announcements concerning the flight games yet?" I try to shift the conversation to a different topic, but I should have known better.

"No. How was it to be back?"

"Weird, unchanged."

"How is Fred?" I nearly groan at Jared's question.

"A bitter and hostile asshole, who feels like we abandoned him."

Jared winces. "I guess he isn't so wrong about that. Was he giving you shit about it?"

I laugh humorlessly. "He wants Ara."

"What?"

"You heard me. He wants to marry her to punish me and for her ... connections." I spit out the last word and can't bring myself to say anything else.

"She's smarter than that," Jared assures me.

"She hates me and regrets ever letting me close." My voice is rough on that confession.

"Surely, she didn't mean it."

"Oh, she meant it." Just thinking about the truth in her voice feels like a knife twisting in my chest.

"We all say things in the heat of the moment..."

"She meant it, Jared," I snap, desperate to stop this conversation. Thankfully, he takes the hint. I throw myself into training and work hard to keep my thoughts off her, but it's impossible.

I'm back for only a few hours when I get a message summoning me to the merchant quarter. I stop in front of the house I visited once before, and just like last time, I'm surprised the spider didn't choose the seedier area around the arena for his operations.

The bang of the heavy brass knocker hangs still in the air when the door opens silently. Even if I didn't know that the man in front of me—one of the spider's most trusted—there would be no way to mistake him for a servant. His clothes are too fine, his posture too arrogant, his striking green eyes too keen and calculating for that.

Just like last time, the silence around him is heavy, nearly solid. He steps back, and there is amused respect in his eyes when I don't speak either. He leads me down the corridor, his movements so soundless I would have questioned his existence if I hadn't been able to see him.

We enter a library, where the spider, a cruel-looking man with graying hair, thrones behind a massive desk. The spider marked on the back of his right hand lets everyone know who they're dealing with.

I'm not comfortable with owing him a favor, but he was my best chance for finding out what happened on Mount Albión that day, and who hurt Ara. Rumors claim he knows everything happening in and around Telos, and the fact that he learned so quickly about my return seems to confirm that.

Now I only hope he has what I need.

"You have the information I was looking for," he greets me.

I nod and retrieve the sheet of paper from my pocket with the information about one of his assassins. Silence, the soundless man with the green eyes, steps up to take it from me.

He opens it, and the corner of his mouth twitches when he notices my father's letterhead. He then passes it on to the spider. The spider nods and gives Silence a signal to go ahead.

"The attack on Mount Albión was orchestrated by a group origi-nating from Kystis." Silence sounds slightly rough, like he doesn't speak much. Until he took my promise, sealing this deal, I even thought he wasn't able to.

"They arrived weeks ago and asked around for two skyriders whose description matches you and your Phoenix rider. What piqued our interest is that they started by asking for a girl even though, if I'm correct, the Phoenix rider's gender was only revealed after bonding?" I nod my confirmation. "But they also asked for a Grayson Summer, which is the name the Phoenix rider used previously, right?"

I nod again, my head spinning. How had men from the Ice Coast been alerted to Ara's presence, especially if they had been looking for her under her false name? That doesn't fit my theory that they went after her because of her family. And why had they been looking for me?

I think back to the man who told me they were supposed to bring me back alive, and trepidation settles in my gut. Could it be that they had been after me? But how had they known about Ara?

"One of them mentioned a fight with a dragon."

I freeze. Shit. If that is what alerted them, then it is truly my fault.

"Does the name Foley ring a bell?" My jaw clenches, and he nods. "Yeah, I thought so. We have it on good account that they met. We don't know why or what they were talking about, but they have been seen together more than once. So my guess would be they work together." He pulls something out of his pocket.

"You're lucky. Our man providing the information is an illusionist. He was able to give me a face." He hands me a sketch. And I bite my tongue to hold in the curses that want to slip free. I know that face. I see it nearly every night. If this man is behind the attack, all of this is about me. Ara got sucked into this because of her connection to me.

"I take it the man means something to you," the spider observes.

I shrug. "He looks like someone I met a long time ago. Doesn't have to mean anything."

"Half of the little finger on the right hand is missing. Does that trigger anything?" he asks. And I'm thankful for all the practice I've had with hiding my feelings. I'm the reason he's missing it.

Bile rises in my throat. Once again, someone I care for was attacked because of me.

"Is there more?" I ask, surprised by my even tone.

"They're still around," Silence says. "Never staying long in one location, frequenting different taverns, different inns. Slippery as fuck."

I nod. The information doesn't surprise me. They haven't got what they came for, so it's only a matter of time until they try again. Suddenly, I'm glad Ara is in Avina.

Silence accompanies me to the door.

"Nice detail with the letterhead." He smirks.

"I thought it was good for authentication," I say, before I leave the house and walk back toward the Aerie.

My thoughts are racing. The man I have been dying to get my fingers on for nearly four years is here in Telos, the same year the flight games come up. That can't be a coincidence.

Ara. My chest aches just thinking of her. Maybe things do happen for a reason. Perhaps hating me is the best thing she can do for now. Her betrayal hurts, but shit, I'd rather rip my own heart out than be the reason for her death.

Maybe now she'll stay away from me, stay away from Telos. Perhaps it will keep her safe. And since Janus announced this morning that Foley will be in charge of the qualifying competitions for the flight games, I hope she stays away for at least another week.

CHAPTER

# TEN

ARA

Despite dawn lining the horizon, it's still dark. The palace and its grounds lie silent around us. Solaris tempers his flames so that his feathers resemble a bed of coals, with embers like glowing eyes nestled into the darkness.

Shouts of alarm echo out into the night while we pass one of the watch towers, but we gain height, and the noise falls back behind us.

Since we're close and I know the area, we head home. Giving the fortress a wide berth, we land half an hour later in the valley below, close to the mist. It's the same area where we leave the food and other offerings every equinox.

The swirling, wavering white mass in front of me is so thick that I can't see anything past three steps in.

*"If I ask you to wait here—"* I start, but Solaris's snort interrupts me.

*"You could try to snuff out my inner flame instead. It would be easier."*

*"Yeah, I didn't think you would go for it."* I give him a crooked smile. *"Well, then let's do this,"* I whisper and step into the mist.

The noises are instantly muted, the chirping of birds, rustling of small animals, and even the sound of my steps fall away until it's eerily quiet. My perception narrows to only me, Solaris, and the spongy ground we walk on. Other than that, there is only ... mist. The air is musty, damp with it, the moisture reaching for my face like cold fingers and never letting go.

The dark shapes of trees and bushes only become visible once you almost run into them, and the silence is starting to freak me out.

*"What do I do now?"* I ask Solaris.

*"This was your brilliant plan,"* he tells me. *"Maybe we should..."*

"Hello? I'm here to meet Tynan of the mist court," I call.

*"...stay as silent as possible."* Solaris finishes his sentence.

*"How else are we supposed to find anything in this white mess?"* I ask him.

*"I'm more concerned about what could find us,"* he replies dryly.

I cast out my perception, searching for magic, and ... it's everywhere. The mist around us is pure magic, its glow so bright it's blinding and so distracting that I nearly miss the dark spots of missing magic moving toward us.

*"We might have a problem,"* I say, and Solaris curses as soon as he plucks the images out of my mind.

I try to pierce the wall of white around us with my eyes, but it's utterly useless, so I stick to my other senses.

*"Can you fly in this?"* I ask Solaris.

*"I can, but we would probably end up in the next tree. I think we have a better chance if we go back to where we came from."*

We retreat but haven't gone far when a long, dark, spindly leg swipes at me, sending me crashing into Solaris. A big, ugly head rushes me, fangs ready to strike, and I scramble for my dagger. Solaris's beak strikes true, hitting one of the too many eyes of the monster, and it vanishes back into the white with a screech that makes me want to cover my ears.

*"Thank you,"* I sigh.

Unease settles over me, the leaking drip of fear, like something is watching us. That I can't see anything fuels the dread that starts to take over my body. My muscles tense with the knowledge that something is waiting for us.

Solaris cries out in pain and bursts into flames only a few steps later, and I nearly jump out of my skin.

The stench of burned ... something permeates the air and makes me gag.

I face Solaris.

"How bad is it?" I demand to know, but run out in a hiss when something slashes at my legs, drawing blood. I whirl around, but there is nothing.

*"Concentrate on staying alive, and don't worry about me. I'm hard to kill, remember?"* Solaris says, ending in an angry screech. *"Unfortunately, that isn't true for you."* He finishes a few beats later. The pain in his voice makes my temper flare. No one is hurting him and getting away with it.

Flames billow around me, and in my frustration, I push against the magic surrounding me, wishing we would see just a little more. To my utter shock, a circle free of mist forms around us. I look at Solaris, my flames burning bright and high next to his.

*"That is a handy trick you could have used earlier,"* he deadpans.

I move forward, trying to push in the direction we came from, but nothing happens.

*"It would be even better if I knew how I did it."*

"Who do we have here?" a deep voice asks, and I whip around. But I can't see anyone.

"I'm..."

"Oh, I know who you are," the voice replies.

"Why the fuck are you asking, then?" I snap. I hear two male chuckles before the mist parts, and a man steps out. His dark cloak swirls like the mist behind him, blending with it.

"If I hadn't known your gift's signature, I would never have answered your rude announcement, and Arachne's maidens would have taken care of you."

"Well, I feel honored," I reply dryly while he inclines his head.

"We have to work on your tact before you are of any use to us."

"Maybe I don't want to be of any use," I say, crossing my arms.

"But you want something, don't you?"

"Answers," I state.

"And why should I provide them?" He looks me up and down. "Why should I trust someone who is not just tactless but also has no control?"

"Oh, she has some control." Lorcan steps out of the mist. "We also already have an agreement." His eyes sparkle while he surveys the flames around me. "And I'm not worried about her burning me."

"You," I say dryly and stand my ground while he approaches.

"Are you not going to run today? I'm disappointed." He does his weird head tilt, betraying his non-human nature. "But I guess you're not afraid of fire anymore," he muses.

"No, I'm not."

"Pity. I could have done with a chase. Ready to start where we left off, then?"

I nod, but the dark stranger interrupts us.

"Let's get back to the keep first. And cease the fire show. You draw too much attention. Stay next to me, and you are safe." The warning is clear: if we leave his side, we are fair game.

Solaris is back to black long before I manage to wrestle down the flames. I scan him for injuries, relieved when I can't see any.

*"Are you alright?"* I ask Solaris.

*"Nothing a good night of sleep won't fix,"* he tells me. *"How about you?"*

I shrug. I've had worse, and we both know it.

We follow the stranger and Lorcan into the mist. Maybe I should be worried, but I'm rather excited at the prospect of finally getting answers.

*"I'm worried enough for both of us,"* Solaris lets me know, staying close by my side.

*"Hey, maybe I'm now hard to kill, if I have an inner flame like you,"* I muse.

He snorts. *"Yeah, let's not test that theory."*

*"Can't you ask other Phoenixes? Like your parents?"*

Solaris goes suspiciously quiet.

*"Solaris?"*

*"Hmm."*

*"What is it?"*

*"I'm not really on speaking terms with them right now..."* He trudges on next to me, without elaborating.

*"Why is that?"* I look up at him, but he is even harder to read than usual with his head fading into the mist above.

*"Eh... a disagreement, nothing to worry about."*

We walk in silence for a moment.

*"It's because of me, isn't it?"* I ask hesitantly.

He sighs. *"No, it's because of my decision."*

*"Your decision to bond with me?"*

His silence is answer enough. Great. Why do people have opinions or plans for my future without even talking to me first?

And how the fuck dare they punish Solaris for choosing me? I'm so sick of falling in line and being pushed around.

THE MIST THINS OUT, AND SOLARIS IMMEDIATELY TAKES FLIGHT. His relief at being airborne again floods my body, relaxing me. Walls appear next to us, and it's so unexpected that I'm startled. There is a city in the middle of the mists?

I crane my neck. The dark silhouettes of heavily armed men and women appear in the thinning white on top of the wall. We pass through a massive archway with a raised grate easily fitting six men marching side by side. Catapults and archers complete the lines atop the wall. They are well-prepared for an attack. For a moment, I'm worried about Solaris, but there are no shouts of alarm.

*"How often do I have to remind you I'm not that easy to kill?"*

*"I can still worry about you,"* I reply, and my lips twitch at his reluctant agreement.

As soon as we venture into the city, vigilance is replaced by what appears to be everyday bustle. Children are even playing in the street.

A wolf-pup and a cub tumble into my way, playing, but it seems I'm the only one startled. My two companions step around them without breaking their stride, as if it's normal to have wild animals running around in their city. It's only when a little boy runs towards them and turns into a fox mid-stride, shredding his clothes, that I realize they have to be shifters too.

I have never met a shifter before—apart from Lorcan—and even less so their children. What is this place?

We are greeted with respect and smiling faces, devotion even, and it's all directed at the stranger walking next to me, which seems at odds with his dark and menacing aura. I watch him out of the corner of my eye. He has the fluid movements of a trained warrior, reminding me of Tate. I shut that thought down immediately.

We close in on a tall building, a fortress, and pass through another heavily armed archway into a courtyard, the mist dancing around us, glowing in the rising sun.

The men head for the building, but I stop short. Solaris won't be able to follow.

*"I don't like it either,"* he tells me, circling above.

*"Will you be alright?"* I ask, and he snorts.

*"I'm worried about you. I'll be watching. Stay close to a window, so I'll be able to get you."*

*"Will do,"* I tell him before walking over to the two men who stopped next to a fortified doorway.

*"Don't do anything stupid,"* Solaris replies.

*"Like what? Erupting in flames?"*

*"No, there is nothing wrong with that. But don't take an ice bath."*

I roll my eyes at him and follow the men inside.

A dark-haired woman launches herself at the stranger right in front of me as soon as we clear the doorway. But I seem to be the only one surprised by the sudden movement. He catches her, and there is such devotion and love in their eyes that my throat closes up.

I turn away. Colorful rugs, curtains, and pillows give the large entryway the cozy feel of a home, rather than the military structure it appears to be from the outside.

"Do you like it?" The woman walks up to me. "You should have seen it when I got here..." She shakes her head in playful exasperation. The man steps behind her, wrapping his arms around her like he can't stand to be separated even for a moment.

She tilts her head back and smiles up at him. "I think men confuse cold with intimidating." Her grin widens, and it takes a moment before her gaze comes back to me.

"By the gods, where are my manners?" she says, pushing away from her partner. "Living with those grumbly men sanded them down, it seems." She beams at me. "I'm Lyla. Have you had breakfast yet?"

I shake my head.

"Well then, into the kitchen, all of you." She makes shooing motions like we are a flock of chickens and not three armed warriors, one even a dragon.

The warm kitchen is alive with chatter that stops as soon as I step through the door. A big wooden table occupies most of the space, and the scent of something delicious baking in the oven permeates the air. Fresh herbs in pots line the windowsills, and the countertop and cabinets are well-used, but clean, and were built for someone taller than Lyla's petite form.

"Don't let them intimidate you. They are harmless and sweet beneath all that bluster," Lyla whispers while passing me, shrugging at the disapproving look of her partner.

I grin. I like her.

Three men sit around the table, their eyes carefully taking my measure, and at least one of them finds me lacking, if his cold expression is anything to go by. I grin at the vase of wildflowers on a delicate tablecloth, which seems so at odds with the gruff warriors sitting around it.

If their icy silence is meant to intimidate, I'm happy to disappoint. I nod at them and take the seat Lyla directs me to without hesitation.

She grins at me and then at her partner, who shakes his head at her.

The silence stretches on.

Lyla places her hands on her hips and glares at the men.

"Really? You're not going to introduce yourselves to our guest?" she chastises. "Haven't I taught you better than that?" The men look apologetic, which is funny since she looks tiny next to their massive forms and probably doesn't reach past their shoulders once they stand.

"I'm Tynan. Welcome to my humble home," the man I met in the mist says, while mockingly arching an eyebrow at Lyla.

"Really? You, too?" She shakes her head and then looks at Lorcan.

"We already know each other," he tells her, winking at me. The rest of the men introduce themselves one after another, but apart from Ice—the one with the cold expression—and that one of them is Tynan's brother, I promptly forget their names.

And who cares? I'm only here for my answers.

I poke around in the food on my plate and eat a few bites for Lyla's sake, but I'm not hungry. I'm anxious to get to the real reason I'm here.

Finally, everyone finishes eating.

"Can we come to the answers part of my visit?" I ask.

"Hmm... I like that idea." Lorcan grins at me. "I'll just need your blood, then."

Apart from Tynan, there are questioning glances all around.

I snatch Lorcan's glass, dumping the last bit of water into the vase on the table, and draw my dagger. There is an instant tension in the air, but I ignore it. I nick a vein at my wrist and let my blood trickle into his glass. Then I hand it back to him.

"Here you go." I bring the wound to my mouth, the coppery taste flooding my mouth. The bleeding quickly subsides with pressure.

He looks disapprovingly at the glass.

"Takes away all the fun," he grumbles, but empties it without batting an eye and licks my blood off his lips afterward. He hums.

"Magic wielder, lots of power, a surprising amount of fire, definitely Margret's granddaughter, a very vicious undertone I wouldn't have guessed but like, and such a promising future." He grins at me.

"You can see my future, too?" I ask, and he throws his head back and laughs. "No, that is my conclusion after all I know about you, your family, and your family's ties, Tamara Summer Blackstone." The dragon purrs. "And the fact that you are here, of course."

Lyla claps her hands in joy. "Can we keep her now?" She turns to Tynan.

"Um, I'm not here to stay," I answer before he has the chance to.

"But where else would you go?" Tynan's brother asks, his name is something with a K... I'm sure of it.

"Back." I shrug.

"But—"

"Kian." Tynan shakes his head at his brother, solving the name mystery.

I turn back to Lorcan.

"I still want more information," I tell him, and he nods.

"What they now call cursed was once the most coveted gift of them all, an elemental power unlike the others—magic. Your element is magic." He grins when my mouth drops open. "You can form it, wield it, or snuff it out. Like every other gifted element, it can't harm you directly unless you are depleted or permit it. It might feel uncomfortable at times if you aren't shielding properly, but it won't cause lasting harm."

"So, essentially, gifted can't harm me with their magic?"

"No, that is not what I said. It's more nuanced than that. Psychic gifts like healing or emotion-bending, for instance, influence you directly. They won't work on you unless you have depleted your gift or permit it. With time, you will even be able to let someone heal you as long—"

"I already can," I interrupt him, and everyone gapes at me.

"What?" Tynan asks.

"I already managed that. I can be healed as long as I keep my curse ... my gift in check."

"I told you she has control." Lorcan smirks at Tynan. "Well, you can probably guess where I'm going with this. Elemental magic doesn't necessarily influence you directly. So if a water wielder floods a room, you will still drown, if an air wielder solidifies air, he can still trap you ... unless you take control over their magic ... but that is rather advanced. At first, you should learn to shield, which addresses most elemental magic thrown at you."

"You mean like a lightning wielder trying to grill me," I say dryly.

"Exactly," he beams. "I bet your gift is quite strong since it runs in your family for generations." I gape at him.

"It does?"

"She said she would write it all down for you," he grumbles.

"Who would write what down for me?" Now I'm confused.

"Your grandmother. She was a magic wielder as well, a very skilled one, and a very strong and capable woman on top. She pretended to be giftless all her life and covered up her markings to go unnoticed. Only her husband knew about it. Well, and us." He looks at Tynan.

Suddenly, my grandmother's quirks make a lot more sense.

"And you are sure she left me something?"

Tynan and Lorcan nod.

"She came to me when you were a child. Only months before her death," Tynan says. "And I promised to help you hone your gift once it started showing." He smiles up at Lyla, who hands out steaming apple cake, revealing the source of the heavenly smell.

"She made plans to keep you safe and change the future for the better. That is why I tried contacting you, but you ran."

"Wait, what?" I smile my thanks at Lyla, but my head spins trying to make sense of all of it. "When did you...? That was you in the library?"

"Yes, that was me. I did not anticipate that you would recognize gift signatures already or that you would feel threatened by me."

"You crept up on me in the dark." I quirk my brow at him. "While I sat alone in a drafty library with no one around."

Lyla slaps his arm. "You did not."

"Well, I knew you were there regularly." He shrugs, then winces, looking at Lyla even though she hadn't said a word.

"Could you use your voices, so all of us know what is going on?" one of the men asks.

"Oh, she is probably ripping him a new one for stalking women in dark libraries." Kian snickers.

"Tynan, you creep." The still nameless man shakes his head in mock disappointment.

"You see, the mist makes everyone a little woo-woo. I think you are better off staying close to me." Lorcan gives me a wide grin.

"So you want me to believe you are normal?" I ask.

"Oh, Lorcan is alright," Tynan says, his staring contest obviously over. "For a dragon."

The whole table erupts in laughter while the dragon flips him off. They remind me of my brothers and me, and I can't help but like them.

"Why did you think I would stay?" I finally ask Kian.

"Because they all do."

I look around the table for clarification.

"Magic gifted come here to be safe," Lyla says.

"All here are cursed... I mean, magic gifted?"

"No." She smiles at me. "But most of the people living here are not ... tolerated in the realm. We do our best to find and help them escape the king's persecution. And if they come with their families, they are welcome, too."

I swallow. A society where cursed ones live openly and are safe sounds like a dream, and I contemplate for a moment if staying isn't an option.

But leaving my family behind? Without telling them where I'm going?

Somehow, I don't think Tynan would be okay with me informing the commanding general of Belarra about their whereabouts. Would Dar even let me go and live with his enemies?

But the thought of meeting others like me ... of cursed children—magic gifted—growing up without fear. I love the idea, and something deep within me yearns for it.

"That sounds wonderful," I whisper, and the realization that I'll never have that settles like lead in my chest.

"We hoped you would say that." Tynan smiles at me like he can sense my turmoil. "With your future position, you could change everything."

I look around the table and swallow at the hope in their eyes.

"What ... what do you mean? I'm just one woman, just a single skyrider."

"You are not just a skyrider." Lorcan scoffs. "You are a Phoenix rider, you are the general's sister, and our future queen."

"How do you know about that?" The heaviness spreads to my gut.

"We told you there were plans in place, a path laid out for you," the dragon says.

"By whom?"

"Your grandmother, among others," Tynan throws in.

I swallow, my mouth suddenly dry. How can I be a part of something so big without knowing? How is this supposed to play out? Do they expect me to simply go along with everything they planned?

My first impulse is to tell them a resounding fuck you. How dare anyone plan my life for me? But on the other hand, here are six strangers who know my darkest secret, and they accept me without question, with nothing but hope and curiosity in their eyes.

I could learn from them, be myself without secrets. I'd make a difference, but...

*"I don't want to marry Frederick. I don't want to be a queen..."* My turmoiled thoughts wash around Solaris's calm ones. I cling to his steady, calming presence, drawing strength from him. *"But how can I say no?"*

*"You don't have to make a decision right now,"* Solaris soothes me. *"We can get out of here if you want?"*

"I ... would you give me a minute?" I jump up.

"Of course," Lyla says, her eyes narrowing at Tynan when he opens his mouth. "I can show you the way to the garden or a quiet room, if you prefer that."

"Actually ... the quickest way to the roof would be more like it," I tell her. She nods and leads the way like nothing about my request is odd.

# ELEVEN

## ARA

THE VIEW OF THE TOWN FROM THE ROOF HAS A DREAMLIKE quality. The mist swirls around us, fading everything in the distance to a white haze. The slate shingles beneath me are damp with the tiny drops of the mist and catch the light like precious jewels.

But as pretty as it looks, it also makes maneuvering them treacherous. A concept that seems to fit everything around here, beauty and death hand in hand.

Solaris is next to me, and I'm more thankful than ever for his presence. I dangle my legs and watch the people moving about in the courtyard below.

*"Without you, I would go insane,"* I tell Solaris, and it's true. All this scheming is doing my head in. Everyone has ulterior motives and plans. How am I supposed to trust anyone?

*"If you considered yourself normal before today, maybe we should talk..."* Solaris says, and surprises a choked laugh out of me. I scoot

closer and lean into him, and he rubs his head affectionately against my hair.

*"Do you think we could simply hide up here or leave and live in the woods somewhere?"* I ask.

*"Running away won't solve your problems."*

*"You sure? I'm ready to give it a try."*

Solaris snorts. *"No, you're not. You're too stubborn to give up, and your conscience would steal the rest of your sanity."*

*"Hey, I could become this crazy bird lady everyone just speaks about in whispers."*

*"Whispers and you don't go together."* He chuckles.

*"So what is your suggestion, if you don't like mine?"*

*"Hear them out, collect information, don't commit to anything if you can help it, and we'll take it from there."*

*"Alright."* I get to my feet with a sigh. *"I'll do it your way, oh wise one."*

*"We can keep that name. I like it."* Solaris fluffs his feathers, and I run my hand over his beak.

*"Of course you do."* I rest my brow on my hands. *"But if everything goes sideways, we'll go with my plan,"* I tell him. But he is right. Running away is not my style.

Back in the keep, I find Lyla in the kitchen, and before she even says a word, footsteps come down the hall.

"Are you keeping tabs on me again?" She playfully scolds Tynan, who steps through the door.

"What can I say? I like to check in from time to time." He grins at her.

"From time to time ... right." She snorts, then turns to me. "That was a lot, huh?"

"Yeah." I give her a weary smile.

"I can only imagine what you went through to keep your secret growing up, but you are always welcome here, and we won't pressure you into anything ... isn't that right, Tynan?"

He holds her stare for a moment before he agrees. "Of course not."

"Let us show you around and tell you about all the ways you could help us, if you decide to do so. But there are a lot of lives depending on us not being found, so we have to swear you to secrecy." She looks at me apologetically.

I nod. It's not like I didn't expect something like that.

Tynan holds out his hand, and I clasp it.

"Just a reminder, breaking a promise is deadly. You are aware of that, right?"

I nod.

"And you also realize that once the promise is made, causing my death will also end your life? And vice versa?"

I nod again.

"Okay, then. You swear to keep any information concerning us or our location a secret. You won't be able to speak or convey it in any other form to a person who doesn't already know. Whenever you try to formulate the words with the intention to report us, you won't be able to. Do you understand?"

"I do."

A promise sears into my skin, keeping the one to Lorcan company, its twin blooming on Tynan's skin, where it's nearly hidden between all the lines already there.

Tynan and Lyla accompany me into the city, where people greet me, a stranger, with open arms. Their intention is clear, but it's still working. When we get back to the keep, the people living in the mists, the titans, aren't faceless strangers anymore.

"Why titans?" I ask, and Tynan laughs.

"It was Tynan's originally, but since it sounds close enough, and titans were something people had heard before ... it evolved." He shrugs. "And we never tried to correct them. After all, people turning us into strong, mystical beings is in our favor." I look at the armed men and women guarding the fortress. With the tendrils of mist softening the edges and smudging the details, they do seem like something belonging in myths.

"What do you want from me?" I finally ask, watching the man and woman in front of me closely.

"Supply us with information," Tynan says. "Help us get access to records of families with cursed ones, and once you are on the throne—"

"Let's not get ahead of ourselves." Lyla interrupts.

"Why do you attack the borders?" It still doesn't add up for me. The people I met today and the atmosphere here are friendly, peaceful even. Yes, the walls and every person old enough to carry weapons are heavily armed, but they don't seem hostile.

"The mist protects us," Tynan says. "But at the same time, it limits the sunlight. Many crops have problems with that."

"I thought you control it?"

"It's a precarious balance." Tynan shrugs. "Tipping to one side means being discovered, while tipping to the other means going hungry. We seldom have enough provisions to last the winter, and whenever our numbers grow too fast, they dwindle even faster."

That's the reason for the raids. They're fighting to stay alive.

"Are there more places like this?"

"Yes, there are three cities in the mists, Rún being the biggest, since we are close to the river and your family always provides us with offerings."

"But..." I gape at him. "Do my brothers know about this ... you?"

"No, it's a ritual established over centuries, one that pays off since we never attack those who provide for us."

"What about the mist creatures?"

"They are the reason this city is as fortified as it is. They fear me because of my connection to the mist, but they will attack everyone else who walks in it. They navigate mostly blind. Sound, heat, and vibration are what draw them in."

"Are you ... a magic gifted?" I ask.

"No." I wait for him to elaborate, but he doesn't.

"What do you think?" Lyla asks and looks at me with hopeful eyes.

I want to help them, but supplying them with information means spying on my family, my friends, and my flight.

How can something feel so right and so wrong at the same time? And how can I not help them? I'm reminded of the little girl and her mother a few days ago. I have to at least try, right? I swallow.

*"Solaris?"*

*"I agree with you."* Having his support makes me feel better. I hesitate, but then nod, and I'm greeted with a relieved smile.

"So how is this going to work?" I ask.

THE COMMENT ABOUT MY GRANDMOTHER LEAVING information for me keeps circling in my mind, so instead of going straight back, I stop at home. I know my mother's routine. She's usually in her garden at this time of day, and I spot her right away.

She's bent over in her herb garden, plucking out weeds between her precious plants. A big straw hat casts shadows over her face, and she straightens when I walk up to her. The air is heavy with a scent that reminds me of the tea she always made me drink when I had a cold.

"What did you do?" she says as a way of greeting, with a frown on her face.

"Nothing." The response is so natural, I don't even think about it. "Can't I just visit you?"

"Sure." She still sounds suspicious, and we are both quiet for a moment.

"Why are you so adamant that I marry Frederick?" I finally ask, curious what she'll answer.

"You rejected him?" My mother watches me wide-eyed.

"No ... but—"

"Ara, listen to me. You have to marry him."

"But why? Is it too much to at least want to know why?"

My mother sighs, then beckons me over to the little bench next to her rose bushes, the giant elderbush casting shade on part of it.

"When we discovered your curse, your grandmother went to an oracle to seek guidance. The oracle told her that marrying the crown prince would keep you safe. So we worked toward an agreement." But is that the truth? Or was it just my grandmother's way of persuading them?

"An agreement about me and ... Alec," I say. The name feels as foreign as the man I thought I knew.

"When he left, we agreed on you marrying Frederick instead. The oracle only spoke of the crown prince after all," she says, and I narrow my eyes. Is that really all it is, or is something else at play? Why have I never heard about this before?

*Gods, I'm turning paranoid.*

"Frederick was always such a sunny child, and everyone likes him. I'm sure you'll get along," she continues, and I swallow the bitter laugh before it can spill from my lips, then switch the topic.

"Did Grandma Blackstone leave anything for me?"

"We weren't close." My mother's words remind me of my grandmother's favorite piece of advice. *Never trust a healer, Ara.* Damn, how I wish I'd followed it. Unaware of my turmoil, my mother continues. "She would have handed whatever she left to your father. Why?"

"Just ... a hunch."

"You could check the study. I haven't changed anything in there since Darren only uses the drawing room when he is home."

"Thank you." I give my mother a quick hug and turn to leave when her hand stops me.

"Please don't do anything hasty," she pleads, and I give her a small smile, not promising anything.

The moment I step into my father's study, something tightens around my ribs, and my throat constricts. It still smells like him in here.

I lock the door behind me and just stand there for a minute, my eyes closed, pretending he's sitting behind his desk and will look up with a smile once I open them. But of course he won't.

He would have known what to do. He even knew the princes better than any of us. He would have known if his mother had left me something. He would have had answers to at least some of the questions burning in my chest.

A sob catches in my throat, and I sink into the armchair I used to sit in while he worked. I always hid in his room when I was in trouble, and he never ratted me out.

His booming voice, so easily commanding a battlefield, was never raised in anger at home. He spoiled me, but he also made me see reason and my mistakes without being harsh about it.

A knock on the door rips me out of my head, and I quickly dry my cheeks, a habit that is hard to shake, even if my brothers are far past the age of teasing me for crying.

"I know you're in there, Ara."

I get up at Ben's voice and unlock the door, but instead of opening it, I curl back into the armchair. He steps into the room, closing the door behind him, then comes over to me.

"Scooch over."

"We don't fit in here together," I protest.

"Then we aren't trying hard enough." He picks me up and places me next to him after he sits down. I'm now sitting mostly on the armrest, partly wedged next to him. His shoulders take up too much space for this to be comfortable, but it makes me grin. When he shifts, I nearly tumble off, and he catches my arm to prevent it.

"Now tell your favorite brother what's going on and who I have to beat up," he says while smiling down and coaxing another weak smile from me.

"Adult life sucks," I say, making him chuckle.

"Is this because of you marrying that prince? Then say no."

"Yes, no ... part of it." I exhale through my nose.

"Then it's not worth it."

"But what if it is?"

"Then I would say start talking because I don't like the look in your eyes."

I hesitate, but this is Ben, my twin, and he has neither the same weight on his shoulders as Dar nor the strict moral compass Ian does.

"You have to promise to never breathe a word to anyone, not even the others."

"Now I'm so in." He grins and clasps my arm. "I promise to never betray a secret you tell me to another person and to stand behind you no matter what." He looks at me expectantly. "You have to agree." With his unconditional trust, warmth seeps back into my chest. "Ara, you have to say it," he repeats.

"I agree," I say, my throat thick, and I hiss at the by now familiar burn. Ben's grin widens.

"Spill it!"

And I do. Telling him about Tynan's people is tricky since my own promise binds me, but we know each other well enough that I can give him an idea without breaking it. And I tell him about Grandma and her plan.

I leave out Tate, though, maybe because I'm still ashamed he fooled me, or perhaps because I'm not ready to talk about him at all. For sure, sex is the last topic I ever want to discuss with one of my brothers, even my twin.

"I'm going to join the Aerie next winter," Ben says as soon as I finish my story. I blink at him.

"What?"

"Did you think I would let you do all this alone? And hey, I get a second gift out of the deal, not to mention a badass magical bird." He grins. "You couldn't stop me if you tried."

"Ian is not going to be pleased," I predict, but Ben's grin only widens.

"What are you doing here anyway?" Ben asks, reminding me why

I came. I tell him about the notes our grandmother supposedly left for me, but even though we search the entire room, we can't find anything.

"I'll keep looking," my brother offers. "And I'll have to train more on the obstacle course." His grimace makes me laugh.

"Well, what are we waiting for?" I ask. "This may be the only chance I get to teach you something about climbing."

And this is how we spend the next hours on the obstacle course. My arms feel like my bones have dissolved, and my legs are as heavy as stone, but spending time with Ben, talking things through, helped a lot.

It's late afternoon when I get back to the palace. To say Darren is not amused is about as accurate as calling a thunderstorm a drizzle. I'm glad I can offer Mom and Ben as an excuse for where I've been. Otherwise, I think he would have chained me to him.

"I'm sorry, okay? I just really needed a break."

Dar scrubs a hand over his face.

"I thought you did something stupid ... thoughtless. That Prince Alexander left around the same time didn't help."

"Oh..." I scoff. "No need to worry about him."

My brother's eyebrows jump up in surprise.

"So you are going to...?"

"I don't want to talk about it, okay? And no, I haven't decided yet. I need more time."

Dar squeezes my shoulder. "I'm proud of you for thinking things through this time," he says, and I squeeze my eyes shut. He wouldn't say that if he knew what I did. Guilt tries to swallow me whole.

But I did the right thing, didn't I?

For the following two days, I train with the guards, wander

through the gardens, and have tea with Deliah. I only see Frederick while others are around, and I'm glad about it.

In public, he is polite, funny, and pleasant enough, but that doesn't erase his words. Maybe I would have liked him if I hadn't seen his other side.

Every night, I retire as early as I can get away with and leave for the mists as soon as darkness falls.

Now that I know what to look for, it's easy to navigate the mist via the signatures of all the gifted living in the city. When I ask Tynan about it, he assures me that only magic gifted, the fae, and some shifters can sense it, which makes the mists the perfect hiding spot.

My nightly visits, full of planning, and my sleepless nights make it hard to concentrate during the day. More than once, I find myself zoning out during a conversation, covering it up with smiles and nods. No one notices.

I miss the academy and my friends, and I can't wait to leave the palace behind, but first, I have to make a decision. A decision I push away, ignoring that my time is running out. But the signs are there. Frederick tried to initiate a conversation yesterday, and my brother has also become impatient.

I'm standing in the garden outside the breakfast room with my eyes closed, enjoying the sun on my face. It's a warm day for spring, the air already whispering with the promise of the coming summer. The scent of roses permeates the air, and I can hear the honey flies and other insects buzzing from one flower to the next. Off in the distance is the synchronized step of guards moving as one, the tinkle of a laugh, and the peal of metal on metal. I miss Telos. And something about the quiet around me makes the ache in my chest worse.

Footsteps approach from behind, nearly muffled by the lawn, but I don't open my eyes to acknowledge him until he clears his throat.

*Time is up.*

Frederick stands next to me. His eyes rest on the scars on my arm, prominent in the glaring sunlight. When he sees me noticing, his face morphs into a reassuring smile.

"We have healers who can easily deal with those."

I never felt protective of my scars, but his comment irks me. I remember Tate kissing them, declaring them a sign of my strength... But that was all a lie.

"Do you mean to imply my family wouldn't have the means for a healer skilled enough or that my mother and brother aren't skilled healers?" I ask sweetly.

I watch Frederick squirm, clearly unsure how to deal with my enormous blunder of tact. But I don't even feel anger or satisfaction. Instead, a treacherous silence fills my chest.

Frederick ignores my comment and changes the subject.

"My father's health is declining. He plans to hand the crown over to me soon. So I think we should plan the wedding for..."

"No," I snap, startling him and drawing an affronted gasp from the servant hovering a few steps away.

"No?" He looks as if he doesn't know what to make of that word. "Have you forgotten what I told you at the ball?"

I laugh and cross my arms. "And I'm still telling you no."

Perhaps I'm starting to understand what Dar meant. It's what is expected, and it would be best for everyone else ... but I can't do it. The thought of letting him touch me makes my skin crawl. Frederick waves the servant away, and suddenly, we are alone. I swallow.

"Are you sure of your answer?" he asks, his gaze watchful. "Even though I could make this go away?" He waves the scroll I only now notice him holding. "I had the impression you and your brother were close..." He turns and I should let him walk away, but ... dammit.

"What is it?"

His smile is too smug, too sure. Something heavy settles in my gut, but I hold out my hand for the scroll, and my stomach plummets as soon as I read it. It's a complaint about my brother interfering with the arrest of a cursed girl. *Shit.*

"So he stepped accidentally into someone's way. Big deal," I say, fighting hard to keep my voice unimpressed. *It's my fault.*

"I think you don't understand." He gives me a condescending smile. "A guard was hurt, and a cursed person escaped. He aided the enemy. That is treason and punishable by death."

My stomach rebels, and I empty it into the rose bushes a second later.

*"You have to think about the consequences of your actions."* My brother's words run through my head. *"There will come moments of uncomfortable choices."* It seems the moment is here, and it's my own damn fault.

The emptiness inside me spreads until it's hard to draw a proper breath. Everyone wants to use me for their goals.

I can't let my brother be blamed for my mistakes. I exhale and concentrate on Dar's words about the position of a queen. My grand-mother's plans. The cursed hiding in the mist.

"I'll marry you." The words sound strangled and hollow, but a satisfied smile curves Frederick's lips.

"Well, that is splendid, then—"

"But I have conditions," I quickly add.

His eyebrows jump up.

"Come on, you clearly have something to gain out of this, or you wouldn't blackmail me into it."

"I don't like your forwardness, but ... go on." He nods. "Name your conditions."

"I want to finish my training at the Aerie. I don't want our arrangement to start before I'm done, and above all, we keep it a secret."

"And why should I go along with that?"

"We barely know each other, and I'm pretty sure you have your pick of willing suitors, so like I said, you have other reasons to marry me than love or pleasure." I remember his words about Tate using me to get back his throne and add, "Like my brother's loyalty. Like your army's loyalty to my family because of my father's sacrifice."

Frederick doesn't have his brother's stoic face. His eyebrows rise, and he looks at me like he has never seen me before.

"Okay," he agrees, but keeps looking at me.

"What do you want now? A kiss?" I ask sarcastically.

"A promise." He holds out his hand. After a few beats of hesitation, I clasp it and trade my life, my future, for my brother's and for Frederick's promise to make the problem go away as long as I hold up my part of the agreement.

Numbly, I watch as the pattern forms on my skin, binding me to him. But even though I feel frozen to the bone, I would do it again.

I guess I learned something about my priorities today.

# CHAPTER
# TWELVE
## TATE

Since I'm back, I throw all my energy and focus into preparing for the flight games. Except my best friend currently challenges that concentration by pacing my room like a caged animal. If I had to guess, his restlessness is likely due to Zaza. The way they dance around each other and sneak glances when the other isn't looking is getting ridiculous.

I'm sitting at the desk in my room, reviewing and sorting the notes piled in front of me. It's the work of years of careful research and compiling everything I could find about the flight games. Since they happen every ten years and started about 300 years ago, it's a lot to go through.

"Do you really think you can plan like that?" Jared's voice has me looking up.

My brow furrows. "Of course I can plan it."

"But we won't even know what we'll be up against until the trials start."

"There are still patterns, repetitions. And the qualification phase is close to the same every time." I point at my notes, and Jared steps closer, looking over my shoulder. "There's always a race of some sort, often an obstacle course, as well as one-on-one challenges." I point at the next list. "The elements are always involved, and gods seem to love mind games." I look up at him. "So let's say a flight has gifted from various elements, and is good at shielding against mental attacks. They have a far better chance." I pull out another list. "I studied the winning teams from the past century. Their gifts were always well balanced, and their skills too."

"Where the mists did you get lists of their gifts?" Jared's eyes scan my notes, and I understand his confusion. Gifts are personal and often closely guarded since knowing them gives your opponent an advantage.

So if anyone compiled an official list of a flight's gifts, they would probably be shot without a question asked. But by observing, you can guess many gifts easily, especially elementals.

"I read through all the records and eyewitness reports I could find."

"Did you sleep at all over the last years?"

I ignore his question because I never sleep well, and he knows that. The only quiet nights I've had lately were those I spent with Ara in my arms. Another reason why she's better off without me. I don't want that darkness to ever touch her.

Since the incident with the suppressors, my nightmares are even worse—more vivid and more frequent. Only the empty eyes too often belong to Ara now.

Knowing that my enemies tried to use her to get to me and are still waiting in the shadows for me to mess up... I exhale. I can't let that happen.

"We got fire, we have ice and air... Zaza is great with arrows and knives. We have you for shielding, healing, and truth. Confusing people is my pleasure..." Jared's finger is halfway down the list of the members of our flight by the time I jolt out of my thoughts. "You could add Ara for the obstacle course and her Phoenix—"

"No, absolutely not." I shake my head, my eyes still on the list. "I won't bring her into this." I know Jared, so it's obvious her skills are not the only reason he suggests her. "And she might not even be back before I hand in our final lineup for the games."

"But she is exactly what you... What we need." He keeps poking.

"What if she doesn't get back at all?" I raise my eyebrow at him. "And the last time I saw her, she was more likely to spit in my face than follow my orders," I counter.

Jared raises his hands in mock surrender. "I just thought spending time together would do you good."

"Well, think again," I snap.

"Damn, your mood is even worse since you two broke up," he grumbles. "Do you already have some riders in mind?"

Instead of answering, I tap the bottom of the page he just read.

"No first years?" he comments. "Hmm, you think Cassius will go for it? Give up his chance to rise in rank in the coming years?" Jared looks up from my notes.

I shrug.

"If we had a certain someone, he would be sure to jump at the chance."

I only glare at him.

"Just saying. It's not my fault he likes her," Jared adds innocently.

So it's not just my...

"*Jealousy,*" Daeva supplies helpfully.

"*Perception,*" I correct her. But I'm reminded of Blackstone and Cassius's conversation back when I didn't realize they were talking about Ara.

*I always thought you would have ended up together if she hadn't been promised to the crown...*

How can it be that she had been mine for half my life without me knowing it? And fuck, yes, it bothers me that he wants her, even if she seems oblivious. The way Jared's mouth twitches tells me he knows it too.

"Stop trying to mess with my head. And if you have nothing helpful to say, just shut up or leave."

Jared sighs. "Okay, let me see your list again." After some consideration and back and forth, we have a list of four people to add to our crew and a flight that I'm confident can win the games.

"She would be good for the obstacle course," Jared comments.

"Still not going to happen," I press out.

"So who did you plan for the obstacle course?" Jared asks and groans when I only smile at him. "And who else?"

"I thought you and Zaza would make a good team."

"Of course you would," he grumbles, and now it's my turn to smirk.

"How about taking some of your own advice? Or I could talk to her?" I offer, my grin widening at Jared's horrified look.

"You clearly haven't been around when she told Ara that she isn't into younger men or that she advises any woman to stay away from the guys in our flight," he snaps.

"I don't think Ara's age was the problem, more that she looked like a kid," I point out.

"Solve your problems, not mine," he gripes.

"So you want to annoy the hell out of me, but I can't tease you back?" I ask. "That's not going to work."

We look at each other for a moment and then change the subject back to the flight games. That's what I'll focus on. To win the trials, earn a favor from Iza, the goddess of hunt and secrets, and make the bastards pay who cost me everything.

# CHAPTER
# THIRTEEN
## TATE

Two days later, I'm jogging up the stairs on my way back to my room when Daeva's announcement nearly has me missing the next step.

*"Solaris just landed,"* she informs me.

*"What?"* I curse. She has the worst fucking timing in history. Two more days, just two more days, and the flights would have been finalized. Then there wouldn't have been a thing Foley could have done to throw her in there. I groan. But now that she's here... Hope mixes with panic while I drink her in through Daeva's eyes and change direction.

She looks different, harder somehow, much more the skyrider than her usual cheerful self.

She removes the harness from Solaris's back when I reach the atrium. She spots me the moment I step through the door, and her expression falls—she is not here for me.

My approach doesn't falter. I'm her centurion. She is my responsibility, even if she doesn't want to be. I stop in front of her, both of us silent for a moment.

"How is everything?" I finally ask.

"Unchanged."

She might as well have plunged a dagger into my chest. The pain is crippling. Despite her assurance, she is going to marry my brother.

"Good to know I can't trust your word," I say slowly.

"I'm no longer the naive girl I was," she replies. Seems like Corin was right after all.

"How easily he changed your mind." I shake my head. "Get back to Avina, Ara, go back to my brother. You don't belong here."

She shrugs and turns away, meticulously arranging Solaris's harness on one of the benches along the wall. Her bags already rest next to it.

Her movements are efficient and unhurried. The tension in her shoulders is the only indication that we aren't talking about something trivial like the weather.

Do I know her at all? Or did I just see what I wanted to?

"I'm still staying," she says after a long pause. "If you'll excuse me, I have to get the stuff to my room and report back."

"I'll handle that." Despite everything, having her walk into Foley's office on her own makes my skin crawl, and Janus is in a meeting.

"I don't need your help," she says, but her actual message is loud and clear. *I don't want your help.* I rake my fingers through my hair, take a deep breath, and count to ten.

"Ara—" I'm not even sure what I'm going to say, but she raises her hand.

"Not now, Tate, or better, not ever." She exhales. "Let's just pretend nothing ever happened between us, and I'm just another first year in your division." She turns back to her things. "I sure as hell wish I had never met you."

I flinch. "You're not even going to let me explain?"

She turns back to me, fire in her eyes now.

"No, I don't want to hear your excuses. It's too late. I've already made my decision. There is no way back."

Numbness spreads through me while her words lodge like splinters in my chest. Letting my guard down was a fucking mistake.

Her eyes wander up to the window of Janus's office.

"I said I'll handle that," I repeat, my voice clipped, emotionless. "Get your stuff sorted, then go to class. You've missed enough already." When she hesitates, I add, "Just do it."

She huffs out a breath. "I'm supposed to hand over a letter—"

"I'll take it."

She rummages around, then pulls two letters out of her bag. I reach for them.

"Not that one." She snatches one back, but I don't miss the royal signet it bears.

I keep my mouth shut, not sure what I'll say if I open it now. Instead, I watch her walk away in silence. There is no hesitation, not a hitch in her step, while my chest feels like someone removed every organ with a dull knife.

I'm a fucking idiot.

I try to shake it off and rise above it, convince myself that it's for the best, but it's about as easy to ignore as a fatal wound. I knock on the wooden door that bears Foley's name.

"Come on in," his muffled voice orders through the door.

Deputy Commander Foley continues writing when I enter. The quill hovers next to him, scribbling away while his gaze is fixed on the paper in question.

Aside from the permission to enter, he ignores me. I wait, not betraying my impatience, not buying into his power game, something I have far too much experience with.

The feather sweeps over the paper, the soft scratching the only sound in the room, a very efficient use for Foley's telekinesis.

Despite my efforts not to think about Ara, she occupies my mind like it's her home. Her cinnamon scent, the feeling of her curled up against me. The tickle of her hair on my skin when she'd lean over me for a kiss. And then there is her wicked humor, her tendency to throw herself at life without hesitation, her smile.

*"This is a load of rukhshit,"* Daeva complains. *"Why did you let her walk away?"*

"She made her choice," I snap.

*"And you just give up?"*

*"What do you want? Do you expect me to crawl and beg when she can't even be bothered to listen? Don't—"*

*"Then make her listen. Trap her in a room, bind her in chains..."* Daeva's suggestions go downhill from there.

*"I don't envy whoever chooses you as a mate one day,"* I reply dryly. *"The connection to me nearly got her killed, my brother is after her because of me, and now you want me to chain her up?"* The clearing of a throat pulls me out of our conversation.

"Thank you for your patience."

I blink at Foley. I forgot for a moment that I stood in his office. He steeples his hands, watching me with a haughty expression. "What brings you here?"

"Ara Summer is back from Avina," I say. "She brings a letter from the general, and I told her I would pass it on." Foley looks at me, contemplating.

"Has our Phoenix rider already the power to let centurions do her bidding?" He sneers. "Seems like the general whisking her away to meet the king went to her head. That was to be expected."

"I sent her to class. She's missed enough already," I state calmly, not rising to his bait.

"Since we are on topic, I was informed about some interesting ... rumors. Riders were telling me that Summer was severely burned when she came out of the flames, that she collapsed, and that her Phoenix wouldn't let anyone near her but you." He tilts his head, his gaze unblinking.

I try to recall who saw Ara up close, but I honestly can't remember since she had been my sole focus.

*I should have shielded her better.*

Daeva helps me out by sending mental images down our bond, and it takes everything in me not to flinch. Her memories contain far more details than any human's would even though Daeva was circling above us most of the time.

"Don't you have anything to say to that?" Deputy Commander Foley inquires.

"I didn't realize there had been a question," I say coolly. "What would you like to know?"

"Is it true?"

"She did collapse off her Phoenix, but that was more exhaustion than injury, and she had some superficial burns, but nothing serious." I gloss over the situation that nearly cost me my sanity back then.

"Why are there no records of her being healed for those burns?"

"I could easily deal with it, and she needed rest." I shrug. "The healers were quite busy that day."

He ponders my answer.

"How come we don't have any records of Summer ever being treated in the healing quarters?"

"I'm only her division leader." I never wished more for words to be lies than at that moment, the truth scraping over my skin. "She is one of many first years in my line of command. I don't have all their medical history memorized." *Only hers.* "Maybe she didn't need treatment?" I offer.

He narrows his eyes.

"How is it her Phoenix let you close and no one else?" There is suspicion in his voice.

"I had convincing arguments," I answer.

"Which were?"

"That he needed to let one of us check if she was fine and that I could help her because of my healing gift."

He looks at me, waiting. Maybe hoping I'll divulge more if he keeps quiet long enough, but that's not going to happen.

Finally, he nods. "I'll keep an eye on things. Please remind

Summer to use the healing quarters like all other students." He gives me a small smile. "We can't have her thinking she gets preferential treatment." Then he adds as an afterthought, "And scars look so ugly on a girl's skin, don't they?"

He dismisses me, but his gaze follows until I close the door.

I take a deep breath, releasing it slowly, and open my fists, flexing my fingers.

My arms are numb and my knuckles raw when Jared finds me in the weight room.

"Do I have to get used to this?" he asks.

"Would you prefer to help me dispose of a few bodies?"

"Maybe." He grins at me. "If it solves this permanently."

"She's back."

"Yes, Zephyr told me. I hazard a guess and say your conversation didn't go well?"

I huff out a humorless laugh.

"She told me to forget anything ever happened between us. That she regrets ever meeting me."

Jared winces. "I could talk to her," he offers.

I shake my head. "She clearly isn't the person I thought she was, when she doesn't even let me explain." And doesn't bother to keep her word. I remember the man who hurt her because of me. "It's better this way."

"But..."

"No. This is over and done with."

"I don't think..."

"Jared," I warn, and he falls silent. I head over to the weights, intent on exhausting myself until I'm too tired to think. Thankfully, we have patrols lined up, so we'll be leaving in a few days. And maybe just maybe, Foley will let it go and not drag Ara into the flight games?

"I still think," Jared starts again, and I round on him.

"I should have kept my distance from the start. So do me a favor and keep your talk about 'letting people in' to yourself from now on.

It isn't for me." The laugh that escapes me is sharp and without warmth. "After everything we went through, she took my brother's word over mine without even letting me explain, so just drop it." I turn back to the weights in front of me. "Don't you think that if she'd given me a chance, I would have tried everything?"

"Would you?" he asks, but I stay silent.

"You know it's okay to be happy, right?" He tries again, but instead of answering, I shut him out and work my body until I'm ready to drop. Maybe I'll at least get some sleep tonight.

THE FOLLOWING MORNING IS TOO BRIGHT AND SUNNY FOR MY liking. My whole body aches from last night's training, and still, it's nothing against the stubborn pain in my chest. If I didn't know it to be incompatible with life, I'd consider asking someone gifted with petrification to turn my heart to stone. I bet Cassius would be happy to do it.

I'm on my way to the coop when all my hopes of keeping Ara out of the games are dashed.

"Kyronos." Vega jogs up to me. I stop, waiting for him.

"I was ordered to pick her for my flight," he says as soon as he reaches me. And I have a sense of foreboding.

"Who?" I ask, still hoping I'm wrong.

"When we fill up our flights for the flight games, I'm ordered to pick Summer for my flight." Fuck. There goes my plan to keep her out of it. It took her one fucking night to throw all my plans out the window. It's not her fault, but couldn't she have stayed in Avina?

"But she isn't in your division."

"Because of her, they will open it up so we can choose from other divisions as well."

I stare at Vega. I shouldn't care. She doesn't want my help, but...

"Why are you telling me this?"

"I don't agree with Foley, but I won't go against his orders for her either. So how about you ensure I don't have to?"

I knew it. I knew Foley would try something.

I give him a stiff nod. "Consider it done."

"That's what I thought. The way you jumped in to save her ass last time..."

I narrow my eyes at him. "What are you implying?" I ask, not even trying to hide the warning in my words.

"Nothing." He shrugs. "Just saying, I can't blame you either." His grin carries too much meaning for my liking, but sadly, any reaction would only support his suspicions.

So I don't say anything else while he walks away.

Maybe we haven't been as cautious as we thought, and that means there are potentially more people who could try to get to me through her. I curse.

*"Just warn her,"* Daeva suggests, and I snort.

*"We both know how good Ara is at heeding warnings..."* I sigh. *"No, the only way to keep her safe is to keep her close."*

Picking her for my flight means she'll be around all the fucking time, but how else can I keep an eye on her? And what alternative is there? To let her die?

I curse again.

I can keep her close and keep my distance at the same time.

*"Yeah, because you were so great at that last time,"* Daeva comments, but I ignore her. Making Ara leave would be another option, but I don't hold my breath. Talking to her will probably only make her dig in her heels even more. Stubborn woman.

# FOURTEEN

## ARA

Being back is harder than I anticipated. Not the part about seeing my friends again. That is great. But everything at the Aerie reminds me of him. The spot in the library where we shared our first kiss. The place in the refectory where I teased him about cake. And don't even get me started with the storage room I pass every damn day.

And as if all of that isn't enough, there's also the fact that my awareness of magic encompasses the whole academy by now. So if Tate is here, I'm aware of him. And even staying out of his way is easier said than done since he is still my centurion and about as easy to ignore as a damn lighthouse.

"Is it just my imagination, or does he push us harder than usual?" Mariel pants. I lie next to her in the sand of the atrium, both of our chests heaving, our bodies covered in a mix of sweat and dirt.

"Summer, Tethys, this is not a tea party," Tate interrupts before I have the chance to answer.

"Oh wow, I would have never guessed," I mutter while I will my trembling arms to hold me long enough to get up again.

"What was that?" Tate stops next to me.

"We're trying," I spit.

"Then try harder," he snaps before stalking off.

"He is definitely in a bad mood," Mariel observes.

"When isn't he?" I ask, but images of him grinning and joking pop into my mind. The teasing spark in his eyes back then is a world away from the cold and guarded expression he wears now.

After Picking, we started training with the other riders. And what's even worse, whenever Joel's flight is on patrol, Tate takes over to whip our asses into shape. And he is a damn bastard about it.

"Please tell me that whoever takes over as our decurion will oversee training." I gasp half an hour later while Mariel pulls me up after she threw me down for what feels like the millionth time. I won't ever reach her level when it comes to weaponless combat.

"Nope, Joel will have the honor until we're split up." So by default, Tate will torture us whenever Joel isn't present. Great. Thank the gods, Joel is scheduled to be back by this afternoon. I glare over at Tate, who is explaining something to another rider.

"Are you alright?" Mariel asks.

"Why wouldn't I be?"

"You look like you want to murder someone and haven't heard a word I said."

"I didn't sleep well." The excuse comes easily since it's the truth.

"Yeah, I noticed. You were turning and sighing all night."

"Shit, I'm sorry if I kept you awake," I apologize.

One of the benefits of being a rider is that I share a room with Mariel now instead of my whole flight.

She waves me off good-naturedly. "As long as it doesn't become a habit, we're fine." And I vow that from now on, I will head to the common room instead of keeping her awake.

"Hey, girl." Zaza comes up next to me, pulling me into her side. "I miss having you around, especially now that I know I had female reinforcement without even knowing it."

I grin. "I miss you, too. But I can do without Tate's version of hell every morning."

She laughs. "Yeah, he can be rough, and I have no idea what crawled up his ass today. But you'll thank him whenever you are seeing action, believe me."

That thought sobers me since the men I'll fight are probably going to be Tynan's. How can I do that while knowing they only do their best to save people like me? People the king deems too dangerous to live.

Zaza notices my face.

"Don't worry, you still have time until then." She gives me an encouraging smile.

"She seems nice," Calix comments when Zaza leaves us to join her own flight for breakfast.

"Sorry, but I'm pretty sure she goes for blondes." I look over at their flight, just when Jared throws his arm over Zaza's shoulder, and I grin.

"That is not what I meant," Calix protests, making Mariel and me snort with laughter.

"Sure you didn't," Mariel deadpans.

"Can't I comment on someone's behavior without you assuming I want to sleep with that person?"

"On a gorgeous woman's behavior, who has legs for days, curves in all the right places, and hair so amazing that even I want to bury my hands in it, not to mention the fact that with her skin she'll never look like a boiled lobster?" Mariel asks. We look at each other and say simultaneously, "No." Only to start laughing.

"I have no idea why I'm friends with you. I'm not that shallow," Calix grumbles.

"We know you aren't." I gasp, catching my breath, and throw an arm around him when he looks genuinely hurt. "You are the best friend a girl could wish for. Look at you suffering through our teasing to brighten our mood." I wink at him.

"That's what I always was, the funny, chubby guy everyone wanted to be friends with," he grumbles.

"And now you are the funny, ripped skyrider every woman—but us—wants to jump, and we won't judge you for enjoying it ... only tease you a little now and then," I tell him while we start loading our plates.

Calix sighs, and Mariel changes the topic, but I tune her out, my thoughts still on how I can get my fingers on a patrol plan to make sure Tynan's people can avoid them. Hopefully, that would prevent casualties on both sides.

I keep making plans in my mind, pushing thoughts around while I do the same with the food on my plate. But I avoid thinking about one person at all costs.

Unfortunately, he doesn't avoid me.

"Summer, a word, please." Tate stops me as soon as we step into the corridor.

"I have class." I don't look at him, but Mariel's and Calix's eyes widen at my tone. Shit.

"And it'll take even longer if you argue," Tate says and steps to the side, clearly expecting me to follow.

I gesture for my friends to go on without me.

"You're part of Beak Flight First Squadron from now on," he says and turns like he wants to stride off. I grab his arm, but drop it when his body goes rigid at my touch.

"I don't want to be part of your flight," I mutter.

"And when did I ask for your opinion, rider?" He looks at me over his shoulder and arches one eyebrow.

"There has to be another way." I'm close to begging because being around him all the time might actually kill me, or him.

"You could quit and leave Telos," he suggests.

"I will not quit." I grind my teeth. Considering how that leads to a premature marriage with Frederick, I would rather fail the first year a few times.

"Then we are out of options, it seems." His voice is emotionless. "Tomorrow, fifth strike, weight room," he says, turning as if the conversation is over.

"I want to have Mariel and Calix on our flight."

That grabs his attention, and he scoffs while turning back to me.

"Sure, why don't you pick all your friends, and I'll fill my whole flight with them?" he says sarcastically, raising his eyebrow again. My stomach flutters with annoyance.

"You have to take them. They—"

"I have to? It seems someone is embracing their future role? Well, *I hate to* disappoint you." He stalks closer. "I don't take commands from you ... never have and never will." He leans in, his breath fanning my ear. "And no, harder, deeper, faster doesn't count." He smirks when I jerk back, my cheeks glowing.

"You're such an ass," I hiss.

"Only fulfilling expectations," he replies.

He wants a fight? Fine. I smile at him sweetly, fluttering my lashes, and his eyes narrow in suspicion. He'll get a war.

"My mistake. Let me rephrase. You'd better make sure Calix and Mariel are in your flight too, or I'll have you removed from this Aerie."

He scoffs. "You don't have this kind of influence."

"Hmm, let me see..." I tap my finger against my lip. "Who will I write first? Your brother or mine?" The thought of going through with it turns my stomach, but I won't back down.

"To tell them what?" he challenges.

"Whatever the fuck I need to." I turn and smile at him over my shoulder. His jaw and his shoulders are tense, and his eyes ... a thunderstorm.

"Weight room at fifth strike," he snaps.

"We'll be there," I tell him, and don't look back while I stride off to class, already late by now.

I should be happy that I won. But my chest is heavy, and my lip is nearly raw by the time I get there since I can't stop biting it.

*He started it*, I remind myself. Only it doesn't make me feel better.

The next weeks are going to be hell, I just know it. Tate is not one to take a threat like that lying down. But I can't join his flight without someone having my back.

I scurry into the classroom, smiling apologetically at Professor Myrsky before I slide into the row with my friends.

"You're going to be in the flight games. I hope you aren't angry with me," I say as soon as I drop into the empty chair between Calix and Mariel.

"What?" Mariel's eyes go wide.

"How in the mists did you manage that?" Calix asks.

I fidget. "I might have threatened Kyronos with my brother," I whisper.

"Do we want to know who your brother is?" Calix asks.

"Hmm ... no?" I slide deeper into my seat when Myrsky's gaze lands on us.

"Spill it, Ara," Mariel demands.

"Darren Blackstone." I sigh, and both heads whip toward me.

"As in General Darren Blackstone?" Mariel squeaks.

I hide my face in my hands but nod.

"Sorry I didn't tell you before."

"Now I know why you vanished while he was visiting," Calix says. "Any other surprises we need to know of?"

I stay silent because how do I answer that without lying?

"There are, aren't there?" Calix looks at me and groans. "Fuck, Gray, you might be the person with the most deceiving first impression I've ever met."

"Guess she can't hide behind her Phoenix now," someone whispers behind me. And I don't have to look back to know it's Livia. I haven't even been back three days, but she tries to provoke me all the time, and I've heard similar comments from other riders as well. It wouldn't surprise me if she's behind that, too.

"I don't hide behind anyone," I say loud enough for the whole class to hear. A few heads turn, but I don't care. I meant what I said. I don't hide.

*"See it as a compliment. Envy only means you have something others want,"* Solaris says.

*"Was that a backhanded compliment to yourself?"* I ask, and his amusement washes over me. *"I'm glad I didn't hand over Frederick's letter. If being your rider draws that kind of attention, I don't want to know what being under the crown prince's protection would add."*

*"Don't mind them. You're doing great."*

*"That's a lie, and we both know it."*

Missing two weeks of class is coming back to bite me in the ass. Just now, I wasn't able to answer even one of Prof. Etario's questions about the big fallout between the guardians, and this morning, I didn't do much better during Prof. Myrsky's class, where we're currently learning all about the mist creatures and their strengths and weaknesses.

"Are you alright?" Mariel asks, looking at me sideways while I gather my things. She has asked me that repeatedly over the past few days.

"Why wouldn't I be?"

"I don't know. Something is off about you since you've been back. Is your family alright? Did something happen?"

I do my best to appease her worries, but the looks she keeps sending me tell me I haven't done a better job than the past few times.

Practical Magic brings down my mood even more. While I think my progress is decent, Professor Galdur has a different opinion entirely.

"Sloppy and weak. That hit wouldn't have stopped a lame cat, not to speak of anything more substantial." She steps up next to me. "I expect more."

We're standing on the sandy ground of Telos's arena, probably to keep the damage to the Aerie to a minimum.

The stone structure around us rises tall and proud, and the magic barrier in front of the now empty rows of stone benches is invisible but easy to detect. Keeping everyone outside of it safe from our gifts.

While I glimpsed some movement in one of the arched entryways earlier, it is only us on the sandy ground. Perhaps it was one of the gladiators, curious to know who was occupying their space.

"Concentrate," Galdur snaps next to me, and I do my best, but after an hour in the midday sun wrangling with my gift, my brain is fried. If it's because of the magic or the heat, I don't know, but I'm uncomfortable, itchy, and tired all the same. It's unfairly hot for this early in the year, and the fact that there isn't the slightest breeze doesn't help either.

"Do you need a break?" Galdur asks sweetly, jolting me out of my thoughts.

"Maybe," I answer.

"Then you should have chosen a different unit," she barks. "Since you'll fight from your bird's back, your gift will be your main weapon. I want to see five precise and measured hits on the target. Now."

It's a disaster. At first, there is nothing, not even a spark. Then a flame not bigger than that of a candle flickers to life in my palm, but never reaches the target. Galdur scoffs, and my temper stirs.

"Maybe you shouldn't have taken so much time off." She shakes her head. "You're clearly struggling to keep up, and we see again, a strong bird doesn't equal a strong gift."

Her dismissive tone pisses me off even more, and a familiar heating of my skin draws my attention. Dammit. I concentrate and try to temper it, but it only gets worse when she gives me a pitying smile. Fuck this.

I take everything I have left, channel all my anger into it, and ...

the fireball is bright and so hot it raises the temperature of the air around us and annihilates the target made of straw within seconds. There are a few gasps, and wary glances fly my way.

"By the mists, Ara," the rider next to me mutters, staring at the black dust that is all that remains.

"Sloppy. We have a long way to go," Galdur comments dryly, clearly not impressed. "Extra practice. I will coordinate it with your centurion," she says before walking on to the next rider of my squadron.

I ball my fists. This was my first class with her, but I already know we won't get along.

And that she is going to tell Tate—Centurion Kyronos, I correct myself—I suck at magic, is not earning her any bonus points either. On the other hand, maybe he will kick me off his flight? A girl can hope, right?

THE FOLLOWING MORNING ERASES THAT HOPE. WE STAND IN formation, and the air is electric. Since no one talks about anything else lately, it's no surprise when Janus announces the upcoming flight games as well as the lineup of the competing flights. The list had been hanging in the common room the previous night, but since we had already started training with them anyway, I didn't need to consult it. My best friends, along with Joel and me, are part of Tate's flight now.

I don't share the whispered excitement around me. It's just a silly tournament, and I have no intention of wasting my time on it. The only plus is that I have a patrol plan now.

"For the last century, the flight games honored Otero," Janus starts, and everyone hushes. "This year, and the nine games to come, will be dedicated to Iza, our goddess of the hunt and secrets. Now doesn't that sound promising?" There are a few excited whoops, and I roll my eyes. Considering the fickle nature of the gods, every participant is just as likely to be prey instead of a hunter.

"But this year, we not only honor our gods and the peace with neighboring realms..." Janus pauses for dramatic effect. "The king also announced the coronation of his heir for the end of the trials." Another round of cheers goes up into the morning air, covering my groan.

Dammit, now I really wish I were not part of this.

"So expect this year's festivities to be more lavish than they ever have been, and the royal family will be more involved." He looks pleased, but I stifle another groan. "You'll have a few weeks until we start with qualifications. Deputy Commander Foley took over planning." I look up and find Foley's gaze on me, with a cruel smile on his lips. That can't mean anything good.

"In Avina, you'll then face competitors from all over the continent to earn the favor of Iza herself." I blink, and the formation hums like a nest of honey flies.

"A favor of the gods?" I whisper to Mariel next to me. "What is that supposed to mean?"

"An audience, maybe?" she whispers back while looking straight ahead.

"Quiet!" The buzzing stops immediately, and Janus has our full attention again. "Apart from the honor of competing in this challenge and the favor, it also holds the chance to win as a flight and bring back the trophy to our Aerie." Another cheer. "You'll face a combination of single and group challenges, just like you do in your service. You'll need a full flight to compete and throughout the competition. Losing a member means disqualification of the whole unit." There are gasps.

"You heard it. No dying, everyone," Jared mutters in front of me, and I snicker while Zaza jabs him in the side.

"Ouch," he complains, overly dramatic.

"Seems like we are already one down," Zaza counters, blinking at him innocently.

"If you want to take me down, you only have to say it, and I come willingly." Jared grins down at her, and Zaza rolls her eyes.

Nothing changed between those two. I grin. Maybe all of this is not going to be so bad. I'll just have to ignore Tate, who happens to be standing in my line of sight, facing us.

"Centurions, you'll have the next weeks to bring our young riders up to speed. I hope you chose them wisely." A prickle of awareness skates over me, but I avoid meeting Tate's gaze and keep my eyes locked on his chest. Okay, maybe ignoring him will be harder than I anticipated.

# FIFTEEN

## TATE

I KNEW ARA HAD A STUBBORN STREAK AS WIDE AS THE CENTRAL plains of Belarra, but it seems she also has a ruthless side I missed so far. Needless to say, my careful planning didn't work out as I had wanted it to. I now have three inexperienced riders in my flight, and not all the gifts I planned on.

Ilario's emotion-bending could come in handy, but having two fire gifted instead of another element and Tethys's necromancy ... not so much.

Sure, I could have hoped Ara was just bluffing, but the truth in her voice and her expression told me she would have gone through with it. And my brother would have been too eager to assist her to risk it. I'm not going to let pride get in the way of avenging my friends.

Her actions prove I don't know her, can't trust her ... and yet my eyes and thoughts keep coming back to her. Combined with the need to keep her close, it's a disaster waiting to happen.

We get back from our run and head to the atrium for training just when the sun rises over the horizon.

"While we are on patrol, I want you to stay and attend classes," I address our first years. "At least until you master your gifts. The last thing I need is one of you dying out there and disqualifying our flight before the trials even start." My eyes land on Ara. But against my expectations, she doesn't argue. Instead, she looks ... relieved?

"The first trial will be a group operation, the second will be more about single competitions. The results will be summed up and make up our final score. The flight with the highest score represents our Aerie."

Everyone nods.

While Ara's threat fucked with my plan, I have to grudgingly admit that she was right about her friends. They not only hold their own in training and sparring but also fit in with my flight. Another plus is that Ilario, Tethys, and Cassius stick to Ara's side, so I don't have to.

Cassius bumps Ara's shoulder and they both laugh over something he said, as we head for the obstacle course. I tell myself again that it's good that he stays close. Maybe one day it will override my irritation.

Everything goes well until it's Ara's turn. She shoots through the course like a squirrel, with no regard to caution or safety. Didn't she hear a word I said earlier? I grind my teeth.

If I didn't know better, I would say she did it solely to piss me off. I wait until I no longer have the urge to yell at her, and then motion her over from where she stands talking and laughing with Cassius again. Her face falls, but she comes over, her movements screaming her reluctance.

"Cut the risky bullshit," I tell her. "If you want my attention, talk to me."

"You are delusional if you think my world revolves around you," she snarls. "I was simply having fun, but I should have known you wouldn't recognize that basic emotion even if it bit you."

"Huh, did my brother forget the part of his tale where I bartered away my heart and replaced it with a stone?" I ask dryly. "I gave you a way out, you chose to stay, so I expect you to pull your weight in this flight and not risk the whole competition because you're having fun." I take a step closer, looming over her menacingly. "And don't even think about pulling something like last time again. You don't want me as an enemy, Ara. And you are not the only one with connections."

She tilts her head back and looks at me with pure defiance. Holy mists, that should not turn me on like it does. And the fact that she isn't the least bit intimidated? That shouldn't make me want to kiss her.

"What are you going to do?" She smirks. "Write my brother?"

"Fuck no. I deal with my problems and don't run for help." And mists, if she isn't the most irritating and tempting problem I've ever met.

Her mouth drops open, and I turn and walk away, the corner of my mouth creeping up at the angry huff behind me.

If she thinks she can push without me pushing back, she is sorely mistaken.

CHAPTER

# SIXTEEN

ARA

I'm furious and limping when I arrive at breakfast. It's been a little over a week since we switched flights, and Tate seems determined to make my life hell.

Calix is already seated, and I slump down into the chair opposite him. My body aches all over, since Tate singles me out every damn time during training and lets me repeat movements over and over until they please his perfectionistic expectations.

If I make a mistake, I can be sure he'll point it out, and if I'm ready to quit, he'll provoke me until I go over every one of my limits to prove him wrong. Only I always regret it the following morning, when I can barely roll out of bed. So it's safe to say, my mood is not up to my ordinarily cheery self.

I let my head fall into my hand, poking listlessly at my bowl of fruit, seeds, and oats.

"The first competition is going to be in a week's time." Calix destroys the pile of food he heaps on his plate every morning.

"I have no idea how you do that." I look at him, shaking my head.

"What? Eating?" He raises his eyebrows, stuffing his mouth as soon as the question is out.

"That too. You are eating enough to sate a dragon, and in half the time I need for a fraction of it." I grin at him, rolling my eyes. "No, I mean getting the info before anyone else does."

"First of all, you should eat more..." He eyes my untouched food. "And second, I have my sources." He waggles his eyebrows. "Miss Carter was very helpful."

"You did not." My mouth falls open. "She is like ... ten years older than us?"

"And beautiful." He smiles like the cat who caught a bird, or Janus's personal secretary, for that matter.

"Gods, you're impossible." I laugh.

Mariel sits down next to me. "What's going on?" She looks from Calix to me and back. "Or do I not want to know?"

I snort. "Probably not."

"I'd rather live while I can." Calix sounds defensive all of a sudden.

"You are right." Mariel attacks the food on her plate like it offended her. "Better to keep the heart out of it anyway. You'll only get hurt otherwise. If they aren't emotionally unavailable, they die," she grumbles.

"I don't think—" Calix starts.

"Nah, don't listen to me." She waves him off. "I dreamed of Scott."

Calix looks confused. So I whisper, "Her dead fiancé." And sling an arm around Mariel in comfort. Calix's eyes widen.

"If you want to talk—" I offer, but Mariel interrupts me.

"No. Let's talk about something else, please."

"Umm, since you mentioned dragons," Calix obeys her request, addressing me. "Have you heard there is one in town at the moment?"

I perk up. Could it be that Lorcan is here to meet me?

The conversation stays light and helps pull Mariel out of her dark thoughts. By the time we head to class, her sorrow is nothing but a shadow in her blue eyes.

The announcement of a dragon in town has me on alert for the rest of the day. So when his unmistakable presence pops up at the border of the academy, it's a relief.

I leave my friends in the common room under the pretense of checking on Solaris, and he takes me to a place outside the city walls, our agreed-upon meeting point.

"Your bird is too obvious," Lorcan greets me.

"Well, then we have to meet somewhere else, because walking out here will take me forever," I tell him. He stares at me, like he waits for something, but when I only stare back, he chuckles.

"Okay, let's meet in the city next time. You know the fountain at the start of the merchant quarter?"

"The one with the siren?" I ask and he nods.

"It's in the old part of Telos, plenty of small alleys to go unnoticed or lose a tail." I agree on the new meeting point, and pull our patrol plan from my pocket.

"That's all I have so far, since this is my flight from now on, I would appreciate them not running into Tynan's men."

"Beak flight, first squadron, southern division." He grins. "Seems like someone is keeping an eye on you for his brother, huh?" When I glare at him, his grin widens. "I think I'll stick around a while. You promise to be the most entertaining human I've met in years. Actually, one of your distant ancestors holds that title so far." His voice becomes a little wistful at that. "Seems to run in the family."

"Glad to be of use," I deadpan, and he laughs. A vicious sound that should frighten me, but doesn't.

"Okay, little warrior, until next month, then," he purrs and starts walking away.

"Little warrior, really? I'm not that much smaller than you."

He laughs. "Your life is a blink of an eye in the span of mine, and you are tiny." With those words and in a ripple of light, he turns into a beast of a dragon. Proving that I'm indeed small compared to him.

He snorts at me when I refuse to step back, and my feet get coated in snot; a rasping sound follows, laughter.

"You are disgusting," I tell him. Every one of his bronze-golden scales is bigger than my face, but I refuse to be afraid of him. He takes off, and the wind of his wings nearly throws me to the ground and shrouds me in clouds of dust that make me cough.

"Show-off," I mutter, after I cough up a desert's worth of dirt and dust myself off. Another benefit of meeting in the city next time is that there won't be enough room to repeat that little stunt.

"Your extra training starts today," Galdur tells me when she stops me on my way out of the classroom. "Be at the gate at the third strike." That means it will cut into my time with Solaris. I open my mouth to protest, but another rider asks her a question, and she turns away before I have the chance to object. Fucking perfect.

*"You should work on getting better, then,"* Solaris tells me.

*"I'll give my best."*

I make my way to the gate five minutes late and stop short when I see who is waiting for me.

"You've got to be kidding me," I mutter and make my way over to Tate.

"You are late," he snaps.

"Sorry, I was busy polishing my attitude, but I shouldn't have bothered you brought enough for both of us."

"When I'm training you, I expect you to be on time."

"Well then, it's your lucky day. Find someone else. I'm not training with you." I reply.

"Yes, you are," he tells me.

"Why you? Why can't someone else teach me?"

"Because anyone else would go too easy on you, and we don't have time for that."

I roll my eyes at him.

"Get moving, we're wasting time." He signs us out at the gate and starts down the street. I follow reluctantly. The prospect of spending even more time with him, alone, makes my body buzz with nerves and my stomach flutter with trepidation. I'm physically aware of the missing buffer our flight normally provides.

"I want rules," I mutter after walking alongside him in silence for some time.

"Really? And here I thought you abhor rules, since you were ready to throw the towel after I requested nothing but punctuality."

I ignore his barb. "No touching, no speaking, unless it's about training."

"That's all?" He raises his eyebrows at me, an infuriating smile on his lips.

"Yes."

"And by touching, you mean we keep our hands to ourselves?" he clarifies.

"That is what touching refers to, isn't it?"

"Well, good to know you are not opposed to being kissed, licked, fucked, or bitten by me as long as I keep my hands off you," he drawls, and heat zings through my body.

I hit his arm ... hard. "You infuriating, smug bastard. You know quite well that is not what I meant."

"Look at you already breaking all of your rules only seconds after you made them." He mocks, shaking his head at me, and keeps walking while I seethe quietly, telling Solaris about all the ways I intend to make Tate Kyronos's life hell.

We reach the arena in silence and enter through the main

entrance only to veer from it just before reaching the ranks. Descending downward into the belly of the round building, we follow a tunnel that ultimately leads into the sand-covered heart of it.

Everything about the man next to me annoys me. How well he moves, the heat of his skin, when he gets too close, and especially his beautiful face. He is the perfect trap, too alluring, too dazzling to see the darkness beneath.

No, that's not true. There is a vicious darkness to him, a coldness, only I had ignored it, because it was never visible when he was with me.

"You're staring," Tate says with an annoying smirk on his face.

"Only trying to figure you out," I snap.

"I thought you had me already all figured out, down to my black soul. Scared yet?" he drawls.

I scoff. "I'm not scared of you."

"Maybe you should be." He sets up a target. "Let's see what you've got."

I don't have a problem calling on my fire this time. It jumps into my hand the minute I think about it. But that is about all that works. My fire is all over the place, and the more agitated I get, the more erratic it is. That Tate stands right behind me, witnessing my defeat, doesn't help either.

I growl in frustration.

"Stop," he orders.

"I can do it." I try again.

"I said stop," he snaps. "Your fire is linked to your emotions. It's easy for you to call it when you are angry. What is holding you back when you aren't?"

"Who said I have trouble calling it?" I retort.

"Galdur. Get your emotions in check, and let's try again. We have to find the root problem so we can address it."

"You are the problem."

"So you're thinking about me constantly?" He quirks one eyebrow.

"That is not what I said," I seethe, and I swear his mouth twitches. "You enjoy this."

"Irritating you?" He hums. "It's my pleasure."

I narrow my eyes.

"Take a deep breath," Tate orders. "Hold it, release it. Let it take all your anger and tension."

"I have better ideas on how to get rid of my anger and tension," I grumble. His eyes jump to mine, and heat ripples through my gut. A slow throbbing joins when they trail over my body lazily.

The way my body reacts to his gaze is ridiculous. His mouth stretches into a knowing smirk, and I want to kill him.

"That is not what I meant. But removing your head permanently would work," I say sweetly, and his smile widens.

"Breathe, Ara," he taunts, and I swallow because his words remind me of how concerned he was the last time he said that and how he held me.

I stare at him, my throat suddenly too tight.

"Is that too hard for you?" he asks, and for a second, something flickers in his eyes, then they harden again.

I glare at him. I bet using him as a target would improve my strikes considerably.

Then I huff out an irritated breath. This training is not about him, and I want to improve, so I do as he asks.

"Again."

I comply, and he has me simply breathing with my eyes closed for what feels like eternity. It doesn't help against the anger burning my skin from within, but I do manage to wrangle down the urge to attack him.

"Now try again," Tate states calmly, and at first, my magic flows up easily. My hand heats, and a small flame dances over my palm.

But then memories come up, my handprint on the door, the one on Tate's chest. My breathing picks up, and the images of my nightmare are back. Faces engulfed in flames, twisted in agony. Tate is begging me to stop. My breath becomes ragged. I shake the images off and try to catch my breath.

Tate watches me with an unreadable look. My hand is curled into a tight fist, my nails digging into my skin. The flame is gone.

"What happened there?" Tate asks, his voice softer now, but I evade his gaze and shake my head.

"Don't act like you care," I hiss.

"I can't help you if you don't let me in."

"You are the last person I'd let in," I tell him. He tenses, but otherwise shows no reaction. None. Anger floods me like a tidal wave. Why am I still so affected by him when he is not?

"Try again," he instructs.

I call the fire, and a darting flame shoots up into the sky. It's even more erratic than before, and just before I'm about to release it, there's a surge of power, like my gift is spilling over. I grasp for it, trying to hold it back, and the coolness of my magic gift tangles in it. The result is an explosion unlike anything before. It knocks me on my ass. Tate swears behind me and quickly smothers the flames that are billowing up into the sky.

"What the fuck was that?" he asks, his eyes running over me. My skin is hot. Whether it's due to my embarrassment or my gift, I don't know. I swat at a small flame dancing along a hair band wrapped around my wrist.

"Somehow, my curse became tangled up in it," I grumble. Tate checks our surroundings, but it's still just us. I get back up.

"Let's not do that again," he finally says, running his eyes over me again. "That's enough for today. Until we are back from patrol, I want you to do the breathing exercises at least twice a day and practice getting your emotions under control." It's an order, but his voice isn't as cold as before. He's sounding more like the old Tate again. I swallow.

*There is no old Tate*, I remind myself. He was just a lie.

When I realize he is waiting for an answer, I nod, my cheeks burning.

We walk across the sand and then step into the shadow of the cool passage leading out of the arena, our steps echoing on the smooth stone. There is the clatter of metal against metal somewhere in the distance, but we don't see anyone apart from the guards at the entrance.

The silence is too heavy between us, vibrating with everything unsaid, and when my eyes fall on the guards at the door, I blurt out the first thing on my mind.

"Who would try to attack a building filled with warriors?"

Tate gives me a strange look. "They are for keeping people in, Ara, not out," he says, and I feel foolish. I have never been to a gladiator fight and never thought about where they originated or why they fought. But there are some big names even I have heard of, and now he implies...

"The gladiators?"

"Them, the slaves serving them." He shrugs. "One of the many things my father and I fought over many times."

"But how can the king...?"

Tate shakes his head at me. "Don't say it ... not while others can hear you."

We pass the guard, and he barely spares us a glance.

"How do they know who to keep in and who to let go?"

"They have marks, Ara. The gate might be enchanted, too, and the guards probably know everyone living here."

I'm disgusted by this whole new side of the kingdom. Tate's eyes soften a bit when he sees my face.

"I take it you didn't have any slaves at Fortress Blackstone then?"

I shake my head.

"You grew up even more sheltered than I thought possible," Tate murmurs, and I'm afraid he's right.

The way back is silent, and I don't even want to know what is running through Tate's head. He's probably laughing about my naivety. Only next to the revelation that there are people forced to fight for the entertainment of others and the debacle with Tynan's people do my own problems seem insignificant.

"How did it go?" Calix asks when I'm back in the common room. I slump down onto the couch next to him. Joel sits on the opposite couch, with Mariel curled up next to him. They stop talking, their attention on me.

"Don't ask." I push a strand of hair out of my face, and his gaze snags on the charred band around my wrist.

"That good, eh?"

"Worse." I pause. "Did you know that gladiators are slaves?" I ask, but I already know by the look they give me that they did.

"They are enemies captured during battles or criminals. Everyone knows that," Mariel says.

"Well, I didn't," I snap and get back up. "I need a shower." But what I need even more is time to myself. It's time to come to terms with the fact that if Mariel's claims are true, my family may have played a part in putting those people there.

It suddenly makes me question the image I had of my father and my brother. I remember that Dar was ready to sacrifice a girl to keep me safe. What else did they do over the years to protect me?

And what about Tate? He said he is against it, but is he telling the truth? And even worse, once I end up on the throne next to Frederick, and he doesn't intend to change it... Would I even have the chance to disagree openly?

More sheltered indeed. I'm a blind woman trying to play a game I don't even know the rules of.

My guilt about helping Tynan lessens. At least I'm doing something.

# SEVENTEEN

## ARA

"Something is up with you, Gray," Calix voices. We sit in the library where I do my best to make up for everything I missed in Professor Myrsky's class.

I roll my eyes at him. "Really? You too? Isn't it enough that Mariel badgers me all the time?"

"Hey, I'm concerned for you," Mariel speaks up. She and Calix pore over a big map, while she does her best to drill the most important landmarks into Calix's head. Judging by his sighs, I'm not sure it's working.

Okay, maybe I'm a little on edge. Our flight is on the first patrol since Tynan's men know their route and schedule ... because I handed it to them. What if I misjudged? What if they ambush them? What if one of them gets killed because of me? What if Tate... I shove the doubts back into their dark box and bury it in the depths of my mind, only it refuses to stay put.

The flames in the two lamps sitting on the table flicker in reaction to my nerves, creating dancing shadows around the books, notes, and maps spread over the table. The eyes of my friends land on me again.

"What?" I ask.

"The tension radiating from you is bad enough to give me a headache," Calix mutters. "I'm tempted, you know."

"If you tamper with my emotions, I'll smother you in your sleep," I warn, but there is no heat behind my words.

"Same goes for me," Mariel chimes in, and Calix grins wickedly.

"You mean all I need is my gift to get both of you in my bed?" he says in mock wonder and gasps when Mariel nearly sends him to the floor by throwing her shoulder into his side and tipping his chair at the same time.

I dissolve into giggles, and the smug grin on Calix's face tells me he succeeded in his mission. I shake my head at him.

"Let's go out tonight," he suggests, and Mariel nods enthusiastically. "Since you bailed on us right after Picking, we didn't even celebrate that we're riders now. And if I'm not allowed to improve your mood, maybe alcohol will." He grins at me.

I don't feel like celebrating. I look at my friends, ready to decline, but at their pleading looks, I catch myself nodding instead.

Since our flight left this morning, we only have classes and training with the other first years for the next few days, so basically, we are on a break compared to what Tate is putting us through. Maybe celebrating is in order.

It's already late by the time we leave the library, and even though I copied Calix's and Mariel's notes, I don't feel like I know more than before. It's frustrating.

That same evening, we put Calix's suggestion into action. Heading to a tavern flanked by Calix and Mariel and accompanied by the rest of our old flight is a strange feeling. When we step up to the gate, I nearly expect someone to stop us, but of course, no one does.

We sign out and head into the center of Telos. Mariel and Calix grew up here and know exactly where they want to go.

"Do you mind if my cousin joins us?" I ask when we pass into the merchant quarter, reminding me of the last time I was out for a drink.

I haven't seen Sloan since the encounter with my brother, and I'm sure she would enjoy the company despite her aversion to fighting.

The others don't mind, so we make a small detour to her house. The butler's face when our full flight shows up at the door is priceless.

"Holy mist, your family is loaded," Mariel says, eyeing the atrium of my uncle's house, and I'm reminded that not all of us have a wealthy background. I eye the open room with its intricate pillars and variety of plants. The leaves of the trees rustle in a gentle breeze, accompanying the burble of the fountain, which dominates the center of the room. Just like in the garden, the fountain depicts Ura, who is emptying her amphora into the basin.

"I grew up at an outpost," I remind her. "But yes, my family is well off, I guess."

"You can say that again," Calix murmurs, his eyes trailing the mosaics decorating the floor and the abundance of magical lights illuminating the space now that the sun is setting.

A squeal announces Sloan, who flies down the stairs to the side and hugs me.

"You did not have to compensate for showing up alone the last times." Sloan chuckles, her eyes wandering over the other riders. I make introductions, and then we are on our way again.

Sloan's gaze sweeps over the guys around us repeatedly while walking between Mariel and me.

"Like what you see?" I tease.

"Maybe I do understand now why you joined that academy after all," she says, winking at me. "Even though you had a nice view from your window at home, too."

At Mariel's questioning look, I explain. "Sloan enjoyed watching the men train while visiting during the summer—shirtless." Sloan's cheeks pinken, and I laugh.

"Oh, if you like that, maybe you should come over some time." Calix leans between Mariel and Sloan from behind, treating her to his dazzling smile. "We are the real deal." He winks at her, and Sloan's color deepens. Mariel swats at him.

"Listening in on conversations is rude," she chastises.

"I'm sorry, Blue, but how else am I supposed to stay up to date on what my favorite flight members are up to?" Since Calix still calls me Gray, he dubbed Mariel Blue. It seems red had been too obvious for his taste.

"You only say that because the rest are mostly men," Mariel accuses jokingly, and Calix laughs, pulling her into his side.

"Now you wound me."

I smile at my two best friends joking around.

"Are you happy?" Sloan asks. I look at her, startled.

"Of course I'm happy. Why would you ask that?"

She eyes me for a moment. "There is something different about you, darker." She shrugs. "Are Jared and Tate coming, too?"

I look away, pretending to watch Mariel and Calix. Her question reminds me of the night she met them, and that they are out there, possibly with a target on their backs. *Shit.*

"No, they're on patrol." My voice sounds off, and I'm grateful when she doesn't prod.

We end up at the same place Sloan and I were last time, and Calix's reasoning that they have the best beer in Telos explains a lot.

My mind goes back to the night I ran into Tate, to the tantalizing, delicious temptation of hiding in his arms. A shiver runs through my body, followed by sadness. Gods, what would I give to go back to that moment?

More memories follow. How he accused me of spying, while holding me captive against a wall (the irony is not lost on me), him attacking Lorcan, and how he kept me close and above water after flinging us off a cliff. His anger, then concern in front of the fire, and our kiss in the dark library. The moments in his bedroom, when Foley nearly caught us. He hadn't known who I was for any of it. The all-too-convenient knock on my door, allowing me to eavesdrop on him and Frederick, comes to mind.

Doubt worms its way into my chest. What if...

No. I stop my spiraling thoughts.

I heard him. *She means nothing to me. I used her for her connections. She is nothing but a willing body in my bed.* He'd said that, and ever since then, I can't get those damn words out of my head. So what if the physical attraction was real? What if someone arranged for me to overhear them? He still said that. And if I've learned anything from growing up among men, it's that just because they want you doesn't mean they love you.

Arriving in a group with eight trained and armed men has the benefit that we are left alone.

Despite Sloan's objection to violence, she blends in seamlessly and seems to have a good time. I tell her as much when we make our way to the toilets.

"Your friends are great," she agrees, looking at me, and I grab her shoulder to keep her from running into a man coming the other way.

"I'm sorry," she stammers, looking up at him, but he only grins.

"There are worse things than a beautiful woman running into you," he counters smoothly. "May I ask your name, darling?" His voice is gravelly, rough.

"Sloan," she breathes, holding his gaze.

"Sloan." He savors the name while repeating it. My eyes narrow. He's good-looking with thick brown hair and startling green eyes and impeccably dressed—a man used to Sloan's circles. But something about him whispers of danger.

I squeeze Sloan's hand.

"Oh, and this is my cousin Ara." She introduces me, like she only now remembers I'm still next to her. The stranger's eyes land on me and run over my skyrider uniform before smiling.

"The Phoenix rider," he states, and the hairs on my neck stand on end. How does he know that? "Everyone in Telos talks about you," he continues, like he read my mind. "A very interesting family." He smiles at my cousin, who promptly blushes. "May we run into each other again." He winks at Sloan, then tips his head at me and passes us.

"He was strange."

"He was charming and so well-mannered." Sloan nearly sighs. I shake my head at her.

"That was a predator in disguise if I ever saw one," I tell her.

"You are overly dramatic." She dismisses my words, and I leave it at that. We won't see him ever again, so why burst her bubble if she enjoyed the encounter?

THE FOLLOWING MORNING IS SUNNY, AND I DO MY BEST TO keep my mood bright as well. Today, we will practice flight maneuvers, and I'm excited for that. I walk down the path toward the coop that houses our birds, with Calix and Mariel next to me. A tree we pass is in full bloom, humming with insects as they move from flower to flower, the air sweet with their scent. A light breeze tickles my face.

"Your cousin is nice," Calix comments, making Mariel roll her eyes.

"She's not into men fighting for their living," I tell him.

"What?" Both look at me now.

"Weapons, fighting, war, and all that are not her thing. So save your breath. She will never go for someone who is into 'killing and be killed' like she words it."

"But men who can handle a sword are hot," Mariel utters incredulously.

"Aw, thanks, I think you're hot too." Calix grins at her and chuckles when Mariel shoves him.

"Get over yourself, I didn't mean you specifically."

"Oh, come on, I know you love me."

"Of course we love you," I tell him to stop the ensuing argument. "And we know better than to land in your bed, so you're stuck with us." I pat his cheek, and Mariel cackles at his expression. "And I assure you that is a compliment, because my taste in men is seriously flawed," I add.

"I knew it!" Mariel cries. "Something happened while you were gone, didn't it? Details," she demands. "I still owe you a life, and I'm happy to claim one instead."

"Seriously, you'd better give us a name," Calix warns, and warmth fills my chest. Who needs men if you have friends like mine?

Even though they continue badgering me, I don't give them a name or details, of course. That would make the situation only worse.

Half an hour later, we have our birds harnessed and ready in front of the coop. Solaris tempered his flames and is once more mostly black.

I ordered a custom harness from the metal gifted who crafts all the weapons for my family, but for now, I have to make do with enchanted leather, and I'm not going to test how long it will withstand him in full flame. Especially not while practicing flight maneuvers.

"Okay, we set up targets over there." Sanders points at a row of targets out in the open field, removed from the buildings. "I want you to lead a coordinated attack. That means swooping in, loosening your arrows on command, keep going, turn, and again. Who wants to lead the first round?"

Some hands raise.

"You should spend some time observing the riders in charge over the next days. Every flight will pick a decurion next week. Some of you have joined active flights already. But the rest of you will also start operating like it." He pauses. "So putting effort into mastering your gift and becoming one with your bird, as well as getting used to forming an entity with your flight, is advisable.”

His words create a buzz.

“Concentrate,” Sanders snaps. “I didn’t tell you that to distract, but to motivate you.” We all fall silent. “Ilario will take charge first, and remember, arrows only. I don’t want anyone using their gift here until all of you are solid in controlling it, understood?”

We nod, but his words still run through my mind once we are up in the air. I’m far from controlling my gift, even on the ground, and the flight games are creeping closer.

Our first sweep is chaotic, and arrows striking a target are more chance than anything else. On the third go, at least the release is synchronized. Hitting a target mid-flight is something else entirely.

*I think we have to practice that,”* I tell Solaris, and he agrees. After three attacks, Sanders has us land and goes over our mistakes and strengths, and then we go again and again, with someone else taking the lead on every round.

We empty more than two quivers each, and I feel my arms and every other muscle in my body by the time we walk along the targets and pick up the stray arrows.

“It definitely looks easier than it is,” I grumble, and Mariel agrees.

“Are you excited for the flight games?” she asks.

“The way I’m handling this”—I indicate the target next to us—“and my gift, more trepidation than excitement.”

She scoffs. “You’ll do great. You are the Phoenix rider.”

“At the moment, it’s more likely I’ll set our whole flight aflame.”

She waves me off. “You’ll get the hang of it. When is your next training with Kyronos?”

“Once they’re back, I guess.”

“How’s it going?” she asks, and I just shrug, trying very hard not to think of all the hours I’ll be spending alone with him.

# EIGHTEEN

## ARA

"Summer and Vaccari." Arkwright goes on reading from his list of pairings for sparring, but my gaze locks on Livia, and I groan internally. Dammit.

"Just what I need, someone trying to poke holes in my body," I mutter, which earns me concerned glances from Calix and Mariel.

I smile at them reassuringly before I head over to Livia, who is already waiting, glaring and tapping her foot.

"I'll end you, Summer," she says as a greeting.

"Then let's see what you've got," I taunt her. I eye the fresh markings running down her arm, and I'm glad that using our gifts is prohibited. I have no idea what hers is, and I'm still far from controlling mine.

She comes at me hard the second Arkwright gives the go. The impact of her strike vibrates down my arm when I meet her blade with mine, stopping her from cutting me open.

She's out for blood, and I don't go easy on her either.

We exchange blows while circling each other like crows ready to feast, always looking for the one weakness that would give us the upper hand. The room around us falls away.

This is more than just sparring. Her expression and movements tell me that if I give her the slightest chance, she will make good on her promise. I'm not going to.

The longer our fight lasts, the more desperate Livia seems, like ending me is vital to her. She grows angrier with every feint I call and every attack I stop. Soon, she starts spouting insults under her breath.

Not loud enough for others to hear over the commotion, but I have the eerie feeling I've heard those words before.

A headache starts brewing, and frankly, I've had enough of her insults. So the next time she comes at me, instead of meeting her attack like before, I duck and slip past her, making her stumble.

She curses me, audibly this time, before lunging at me with a scream of rage. Suddenly, her image blends with another, one set against a background of trees swaying in the wind. Distracted, I react just a smidge too late, and I know I won't parry in time.

I drop instead, rolling to avoid her blade, bringing myself into a vulnerable position. I twist and scramble back when her sword comes down again. There is a slight sting down my side where she grazes me. But she mostly missed.

I jump up and jerk my blade up, stopping her next slash, only to stumble back when her fist lashes out and hits my cheek with enough force to stun me. I blink, trying to get rid of the black spots obscuring my view. There is the whisper of steel on leather, and something grazes my side. I brace for the pain that's sure to come, but instead, I'm pushed aside by a big body, steel clanging against steel, before gentle hands pull me aside.

"Jealousy doesn't look good on you, Vaccari." Calix chuckles. "And I hate to disappoint you. As enticing as your suggestions sound, I neither had her alone nor shared her with Kyronos and Cassius. But do tell me more of your fantasies."

"Are you alright?" Mariel inquires, still gripping my arms. I shake my head to clear it, only to follow up with a nod when her brow furrows.

"Yeah, I'm fine," I reassure her, gingerly moving my jaw from side to side and prodding at my face. No blood, so at least that is something. I shift, and the sting at my side reminds me of the blade that caught me there. *Not too much blood*, I amend my previous statement, when I inspect the shallow cut. It's more of a scratch.

"You should go see the healers," Mariel suggests, but I wave her off.

"I've had worse."

"We don't get caught up in a fight emotionally," Arkwright's stern voice comes down at Livia. "Neither during training nor combat." He shakes his head at her. "I don't want to see..." He goes on in his lecture, but I tune him out.

My face hurts. My whole damn head hurts. When he's done, he comes over to me, looking me over.

"Head to the healing quarters, Summer," he instructs and dismisses me. My head is killing me by now, so the last thing I want is to wrangle my gift down so a healer can do his work. I head to Mariel's and my room instead.

I kick the door closed behind me and only remove my boots before lying down on my bed. The images of Livia dance through my mind, as well as her insults. Did I run into Livia during Picking? And had it been before or after I met up with Calix and Mariel? Was it her I fought, or is my imagination filling her in since she is the most likely candidate?

*"What do you think?"* I ask Solaris, replaying the image again. *"Do you think I just made it up, or did it happen?"*

*"It doesn't matter. The way she came at you today, I'd say, let's just dispose of her and be done with it."*

I laugh softly at his suggestion, but he isn't wrong. If her actions today are anything to go by, it may come down to that.

"Shit, that looks like it hurts." Those are Mariel's first words the following morning. A look in the mirror shows me what she's talking about. My right cheek has taken on different shades of purple and looks worse than it feels. I shrug.

"It's not too bad." I lift my pillow and peek under my bed. "Have you seen my dagger? The one my father gave me," I elaborate when she frowns at me.

Realization brightens her face, and she helps with the search, but despite looking everywhere, the dagger remains missing. We have to leave, or we'll be late.

"We'll find it," she assures me while we walk down the corridor, and her gaze catches on my face again. "If you hurry, you can make it to the healers between our run and breakfast," Mariel suggests, but I shake my head. I have no desire to have a healer's hands on me this morning either, and it doesn't inconvenience me. Who cares how it looks?

It seems the answer to that is more than I thought. Calix promises retribution when he sees me, Joel looks ready to explode, and Tate...

I'm startled by the anger washing over Tate's features when our eyes meet on my way to class. They just got back from patrol. He is still in his dusty armor and his hair windswept.

He stalks toward me, his mood radiating out like a pulsing storm. What have I done now to draw his anger?

Since I'm not in the mood to deal with him, I turn around and make my way down the corridor. Not running, but accelerating my steps when he comes closer. A hand clamps down on my arm, and my momentum swings me around.

"What?" I hiss.

He doesn't say anything, only clamps my chin in his hand and tilts my head, his eyes zeroing in on my cheek. And I remember the bruise.

"Let me go," I demand. "I don't need your help."

"Do I need to hold you down this time?" he replies.

My eyebrows jump up. "What?"

"I think I made my view on risking others because you are too proud to ask for help very clear, haven't I?" he growls.

"It's just a bruise. That's not—"

"Shut up and hold still for a second, would you?"

"No, I will not. You—"

That's as far as I get before invisible hands hold me in place, gentle but firm, and when I try to speak, I can't.

*Oh, he did not.*

But no matter how much I try, I can't move. His hands frame my face lightly along my jaw. And the gesture, combined with his magic flowing into me, feels too intimate, too damn familiar ... too good. Heat rushes through me. And maybe it's a good thing I can't move since my body gravitates toward him.

How dare he make me feel this way?

I want to push him away, lash out at him, anything to cut this connection. Only I can't move a damn finger.

I narrow my eyes at him, but he doesn't even blink. Asshole.

When he's done, he takes a step back before releasing me.

"The next time you force your magic on me like this, I'll stab you," I hiss as soon as I'm free.

"A funny way of saying thank you," he remarks dryly.

"Why would I thank you if you gave me no choice, Tate?"

"I wouldn't have to if you would take care of yourself. A unit is only as strong as its weakest..."

"Are you calling me weak?" I hiss, but he goes on like I didn't say a thing.

"Member. And it was more than a bruise. The slash was already infected." He glares at me.

"And why the fuck would you care?"

"I—" Tate starts, then shakes his head. "I need all of you alive and healthy for the trials. You know that." He pauses. "Looks like Fred thoroughly changed your image of me," he adds quietly before he turns and walks away without a backward glance.

My heart constricts painfully, and I breathe past the lump in my throat. Damn him.

I start walking, only to realize I'm headed in the wrong direction. I squeeze my eyes shut and take a deep breath. I can't let him affect me like this.

"Oh, you went to the healing quarter," Mariel comments once I fall into my seat between her and Calix. I don't correct her since I wouldn't even know where to start.

I do my best to pay attention while Sanders goes through different flight formations and their use in combat, but my thoughts drift off again and again, replaying the earlier situation... Had there been concern in his eyes? Was that sadness in his voice when he said Frederick changed my image of him?

Argh. All this second-guessing shit is driving me insane. When did my life become so muddled? Action and reaction, that is my way of living, not turning in dizzying circles.

I force my attention back to Sanders because, dammit, I really should pay attention.

*"Relax, I'm listening,"* Solaris assures me, then snorts. *"If we do that, our partner would not appreciate it."*

I look up. Sanders explains a maneuver that would put us in very close proximity to another bird and its rider—not for long, but I see the problem.

*"I don't think that was drawn up with Phoenixes in mind,"* I tell him.

*"Shortsighted planning,"* he comments. *"Don't you think it strange that a human teaches flight maneuvers when he doesn't even have wings?"*

*"Oh, would you like to teach this class then?"* I ask dryly.

*"Yes, let's ask him ... you could do the talking, and we could incorporate demonstrations, and—"*

*"I don't think so,"* I tell him.

*"You spoil all my fun,"* he complains, and I shake my head, drawing Calix's attention.

"Solaris would like to teach us flight maneuvers," I answer his unspoken question.

"Aella had a few comments, too." He chuckles, his eyes on Sanders again. "But I guess we would throw in our opinions too if our birds were suddenly teaching us fencing or something." I nod in agreement and then make an effort to stay present when Sanders starts asking questions.

"How would you have to adjust your maneuvers fighting titans compared to mist creatures?" That question turns my stomach, reminding me that it will come down to that one day if I don't find a solution.

A rider from the northern division raises his hand and goes on explaining the benefit of quick attacks and splitting up the flight into smaller units, to be less predictable.

"Is there an instance when this approach would be wise with mist creatures, too?"

"Yes, if there are otrov around or snakes," a woman from the fifth squadron pipes up.

"They can't reach us up there," a dark-haired rider scoffs.

"Not true," she disagrees. "My brother is stationed at an outpost in the Malvada mountains, and a rider of his flight was plucked right out of the sky."

"Then they were not keeping the proper height."

"No, I have to agree with Miss Florentius," Sanders cuts in. "If you see a otrov around, act as if you had enemies pointing an arrow at you, if they spit their venom, the reach is nearly the same. And never underestimate the height a snake can reach if it propels itself upward. Since the mist hides them from view, it is even more important."

"Why then use any other tactic at all?" the same rider from before grumbles.

"It saves your strength, and if you have mainly Arachne's maidens or piatta you're dealing with, you don't have to worry about them coming up."

I'M EVEN MORE IRRITATED ABOUT TATE'S BEHAVIOR THE following morning. My awareness of him is a constant thorn in my side and gets more annoying the harder I try to ignore him. On top of that, it's like he is obsessed with those stupid trials and perfecting every one of our movements.

This morning, we are at the obstacle course again, and I just completed the round in record time. That should shut him up, but no, he calls me over immediately.

My breath is still labored, and I dust my hands off while stalking over to him.

"What?" It comes out more like a snarl than a question.

"Seems like someone is in a bad mood," Jared comments, only to lift his hands in surrender when I glare at him. "Already shutting up."

Tate, on the other hand, seems cool like a glacier. He raises an eyebrow at me, and I'm ready to tackle him. I don't do it, but I want to.

"What?" I bite out again, sounding only marginally more civil this time around. And Tate doesn't even blink. Of course.

Somehow, that pisses me off even more.

"Next time, cut that stunt at the beam. You could have easily missed, and being quick doesn't help you if you fall off."

"Well, I didn't, and this is how I like it," I say.

"Change it."

I only look at him, crossing my arms, and Tate steps closer. My heart skips a beat.

"Your request was to treat you like every other first year, wasn't it?" he asks under his breath. "So how about you act like it, too? And not like an entitled queen? You aren't ... yet."

"I'm not acting like an entitled queen," I hiss back.

"My bad. A spoiled toddler throwing a tantrum, then. I think I gave very precise instructions the last time. Was there anything to misunderstand?"

"Why would I go slower? It doesn't even make sense," I complain.

"Because I said so," he replies.

I roll my eyes.

"Is that not a good enough reason for you?" he asks, his voice still calm. But there is irritation in his eyes now, anger steering. Good. I fight a grin, but his gaze drops to my mouth, and his irritation multiplies.

"You wanted to be treated like the others. Didn't you?" There is a warning in his tone.

I nod, but let's face it, right now, I want to get under his skin. I want to see a reaction, a real one, anything to prove that I'm not the only one affected by this crackling friction between us.

"So next time, are you going to follow orders?" he asks, and I tilt my head like I'm thinking about it, then give him a slow grin.

"Maybe."

"Then *maybe* you want to help out in the coop," he states.

"If that's all it takes. How about I move my bed there and don't follow any orders?" I ask, and my grin widens when Jared turns away, his shoulders shaking with silent laughter.

"Why didn't you leave if orders are so abhorrent to you?" Tate takes another menacing step toward me, and I start picking imaginary dirt from under my nails. "Ara," he growls, and I bite my cheek to keep from laughing at his irritation. He stands so close now that his shadow falls over me. I look up at him and shrug like I don't have a care in the world.

"Eh, you know me. I'm here for the fun and giggles."

Mariel gives me an incredulous look while mouthing, "What are you doing?" behind Tate's back.

"You will follow my orders." Tate's voice is dangerously quiet now.

"Or what?" I hold his stare, and my heart skips a beat. There is not just anger in his eyes. There is heat too.

"Or you won't like the consequences." His warning is a low rumble that should not cause heat to zing through my body.

"Maybe I would," I whisper under my breath, but by the way his body freezes, I know he heard me. "I think I prefer sleeping with the Strix," I add quickly. "At least with them I know what beast I get."

"Say that again," Tate takes another step forward, so we are nearly nose to nose now. I open my mouth to push him over the edge, when...

"Kids, kids"—Jared interrupts—"as entertaining as this is, you have an audience. You do realize that, right?"

"Three days," Tate snaps, then turns and stalks over to the other side of the atrium.

Mariel comes over to me. "Did I miss something?"

I scoff. "Of course not."

Her eyebrows rise. "Well, you could have fooled me."

# NINETEEN

## TATE

It's not hard to find out what happened to Ara's face, and when I corner Vaccari in an empty corridor, her smile slips. Grim satisfaction floods me.

"Maybe I wasn't clear enough the last time around. Unfortunate accidents happen if people try to play fate. Do I have to remind you how very easy it is to cover up something like that around here?" I address her quietly.

"You're threatening me?" She lifts her chin.

"If there was any room for doubt, let me rephrase. If you go after Ara again, we'll have a problem."

"Do you know who my father is?" She lifts her eyebrows, and I laugh. She takes a step back. I shake my head, still chuckling.

"You sound like I'd care." I shrug. "I don't."

"But..." she splutters.

"All snakes die the same," I muse. "Who cares about their

origin?" That message finally seems to get through to her, and she pales.

"So to make sure there is no misunderstanding. Ara is part of my flight. If you threaten her, you threaten me, and you don't want that, believe me." She swallows and gives me a hasty nod. And on a hunch, I add, "Oh, and maybe you want to tell Foley I said that, too." She pales even more before hurrying off. *Interesting*.

I leave the nearly empty academy behind and make my way to the training field. Today, it would have been easy to find it with my eyes closed, the commotion audible long before it comes in sight.

Do I hope that threat solves the problem with Livia? Yes, but I won't hold my breath. She seems to be the kind of person who doesn't know when to give up, and if she is in it with Foley... Perhaps we should address that problem more permanently.

"Where were you?" Jared greets me as soon as I set foot onto the field, which is bustling with activity. Sixteen flights are competing, and every rider who isn't part of it or on patrol is present to see us off.

"I had to take care of something," I tell him while my gaze wanders over the birds and people crowding the field. Thanks to Daeva and the now black Solaris, our flight is easy to spot between the mainly white and brown birds.

"Quite the spectacle, isn't it?" Jared comments, and I have to agree.

Our flight and the other three flights of my division have gathered on the south side of the field, so we make our way over to them.

## ARA

Our first trial is what I would describe as a messed-up scavenger hunt. Every flight has to find three eggs hidden in the mountains. We have maps, provisions, our birds, and three days to find them. The messed-up part about it is that we are allowed to open fire and steal them from each other, too.

A flight is allowed to return as soon as it has three eggs. The order of return will be the placement.

"We will build three teams. Smaller groups will make us faster and less noticeable." Tate eyes the groups we have already built and stops on me and my friend. "Absolutely not." He shakes his head. "One first year per group, not a group of first years." I huff out a breath and cross my arms, but Mariel and Calix nod. Traitors.

Mariel heads over to Joel and Tanner, and I make a beeline toward Miller, Boko, and Zaza. There is no way I'll pair up with Tate. So Calix ends up with Tate and Jared.

Tate narrows his eyes at me like he wants to object, but then just shakes his head and turns away.

"Well, let's go then. Every group has a map?" he asks. Zaza and Tanner nod. "No unnecessary risks—"

"And no dying," Jared says, making everyone chuckle. "We know, we know."

"Is everyone aware of the meeting point?" Tate goes on as if Jared hadn't said anything. "If you get separated from your team, go there and keep your head down until the rest of us are in. If someone needs help—"

"Our bird will let the others know," Jared throws in again. "Tate, you mother hen, this is not our first mission," he complains.

"Not yours, maybe, but there are some who haven't been out with us yet." Our centurion raises his eyebrows at his friend, then looks at Mariel, Calix, and me. "Do you have any questions?"

We shake our heads. His briefing yesterday was pretty extensive, so I doubt there'll be anything we haven't heard about yet.

"Fine." He nods. "Then let's head to our birds and wait for the signal."

I clamber on Solaris's back, and the added height gives me a good overview of the field around us. It's the one we used for target practice with Sanders, but with 160 huge birds occupying the space, and countless riders running around, it seems smaller than usual.

White, black, and brown feathers rustle. Cawing, excited murmurs, and shouts hover over the field, the atmosphere a mix of excitement and nerves.

I strap myself in, cursing when the stiff, snug leather of the breastplate limits my movements in ways I'm not used to yet. It's the first time I'm in full armor, and while the armor makes it hard to bend over, the helmet limits my perception.

It's still early morning, but I do not doubt that I will cuss at the extra layers of protection later when the sun is up and I hike through the mountains. I twist and check my bags, secured to the harness behind me, then my bow, spear, and sword. Once I'm sure everything is in place and won't go anywhere, there is nothing left to do.

The commotion slowly dies down as more and more riders mount their birds, bringing on a silence loaded with tension.

I pat Solaris's neck, who shifts restlessly from one leg to the other.

*"Is the excitement getting to you, too, handsome?"* I ask him.

*"I don't know about you, but the thought that someone will shoot at you soon makes this somehow less fun,"* he answers.

*"I'll be fine,"* I tell him, patting my armor, more thankful than apprehensive now.

A fanfare gives us the go. Tate's hand mirrors the command only a heartbeat later.

We rise as one, the sight breathtaking. A sea of birds surrounds us, the collective beating of their wings drowning out even the cheer of the crowd that came to see us off. Then the feathered cloud breaks apart into sixteen units, Tate and Daeva taking over the lead of our flight. Huge V-formations fill the sky, drifting apart, heading for the mountains.

Flying on Solaris's back is effortless. Our thoughts being one, I don't have to rely on the cues they taught us during flight classes. I only have to think about the direction and often not even that, since he knows our destination as well as I do.

We head for the location that Tate chose as the starting point. We approach low, using the surrounding mountains and then the trees as cover.

Just like Tate instructed, our birds rise as soon as we dismounted, heading farther north to conceal our exact location. They still wear their harnesses and our packs as well as the spears. Bow and quiver are strapped to our backs now, as well as the swords and daggers.

I follow Zaza uphill. Tate's plan of separating into groups helps us cover more ground quickly. And we have two more areas to cover after this one.

"No climbing," Tate shouts after me, but I ignore him. I'm not going to promise that while we are surrounded by mountains.

*"Daeva says you'll be a sitting duck on the face of the cliff. If they spot you, they can easily shoot you down, and you have no chance to counter. Also, if you disobey this time, Tate will chain you to him."* Solaris's voice sounds distant.

I scoff, dismissing it.

*"What he doesn't know won't rile him up,"* I answer.

*"Is that what you want me to answer?"* Solaris teases, before turning serious. *"Please be careful. Daeva showed me how they found you after you slipped."*

His words spark memories of the day Tate learned my biggest secret. A secret he's still keeping. Unconsciously, I seek out his signature and fight the urge to check if I can still spot him.

"This is stupid," I utter under my breath, continuing instead of looking behind me. I recognize the three gifts of the riders in my team, and there is a faint pulsing above us.

I peer up at the cliff next to us.

"It's right above us," I whisper, but Zaza, who walks right in front of me, still hears and turns around.

"What?"

"I think what we are looking for is right above us." I point up. It's stronger now that I concentrate on it.

"How would you—?" she asks, then checks her map. "That is not where it is supposed to be." She shakes her head.

"I saw something up there," I insist.

"Well then, let's continue up and we'll double back to check it out," she says, still not convinced. I look up at the cliff and then the winding path in front of us.

"How about I climb up there and save us the time?" I say.

"Ara, you heard Kyronos. He said no climbing, and I don't think he was talking to us."

No, he wasn't. But this is stupid. I'm not going to stop climbing just because I fell one time.

"Tate isn't even here," I tell her.

"Ara," Zaza warns, "he will be furious."

"Then we're not going to tell him." I grin at her. "Just think about how happy he'll be when we have the first egg before noon."

Ahead, the two men realize we stayed back and turn around.

"What's going on?" Boko asks, and Zaza explains the situation. I use the chance and get started.

"I still don't think—" She turns back to me, but stops when she finds me already on my way up. My helmet dangles on my belt, which I moved so my sword is at my back and not in the way. She sighs.

"I'll be right back," I call down and continue up.

My body starts to heat despite the cool morning air, and I enjoy the feeling of freedom. There's nearly no wind, but the wall is still in the shade, and the stone is cool beneath my fingers.

I carefully choose every hold, but the rock is more stable than the last time, and I feel myself relax. My racing heart calms with my progress, and as far as Tate's threat goes... He won't even know it, and even if he finds out, he won't chain me to him. That's ridiculous.

The cliff is rough, giving me enough purchase for steady progress, and I grin when my fingers reach the edge. I look back down and give Zaza a thumbs-up to let her know I'm fine before pushing fully up.

Only for my eyes to land on a pair of boots. *Shit.*

# TATE

THE MOMENT DAEVA TOLD ME SOLARIS'S ANSWER, I KNEW IT was bullshit. Never ever would Ara simply agree to my demand to keep her two feet on the ground, and sure enough, here she is scrambling up a cliff again. What I didn't expect to find is the small golden egg I currently hold in my hand. How did she know it was up here?

I've checked my map twice since arriving, but this is not where it was supposed to be. *One problem at a time.* I slip it into my pocket and wait with my arms crossed for Ara to clear the ledge.

If I weren't so mad at her, her reaction would have been quite funny. Her eyes land on my boots first, and she drops her head. I approach her while she is busy cursing.

Her eyes come up to me, and I'm not prepared for what that little tilt of her head does to me.

Her kneeling in front of me, her big, beautiful eyes fixed on me and full of defiance. Holy mists. I'm instantly hard. She bites her lip, and I know it's a nervous habit, but my cock doesn't care. I swallow down a groan.

"I thought we talked about this," I say, and somewhere on the way up my throat, my voice dropped an octave. I swear that woman was created to tempt me.

"You talked about it," she tells me, "but I never agreed. What are you doing here anyway? Your group went in a different direction."

"And you thought Solaris happily agreeing to my demands wouldn't make me suspicious?" I ask, glad that came out as a coherent sentence. "I know you, Ara. I see you. That we weren't so far off helped too."

I point behind her, and when she turns, I use the chance to adjust myself. She harrumphs upon seeing Calix and Jared in the distance, then turns back with a glare.

"Were you spying on me?"

My eyebrows rise. "Keeping my flight in line is my job," I say dryly. "It's not my fault that to keep you in line, I have to get a little more creative." I step closer and notice her body going rigid, when I lean past her to let Zaza know we'll head to the next location. "Oh, and Ara is with us now," I shout down before turning back to her.

"I warned you," I tell her, and her eyes narrow. Oh, she is going to hate it.

Daeva approaches and lands behind us.

"Get on," I order, and just as I thought, she declines.

"Thank you, but I have my own bird."

"That would be difficult," I tell her, and nearly laugh at her expression when she realizes the solidified air circling her wrist.

"You've got to be kidding me," she hisses, her eyes snapping to mine.

"I keep my promises," I tell her and nod toward Daeva. "Now, get on, or I'll make you."

"I will not sleep next to you," she hisses. Huh, I haven't thought of that, but then when has Ara ever slept next to me? She always seems to prefer to sleep on top of me. I tell her as much, and her reaction makes me grin.

"That's not what I meant," she snaps. And maybe I get why she loves to drive me up the wall. This is the most fun I've had in days.

"So you want me to sleep on top of you?" I pretend to ponder her imaginative offer and hum.

"As if I would want—" She stops and shakes her head, huffing out in exasperation. "Just get this off me."

"That I can't do." I grin down at her. "Consequences are earned after all."

When she makes no move to climb on Daeva's back, I get up first and hoist her up in front of me.

It's only when she ends up with her back snugly against my front that I realize I haven't thought that through properly. She leans forward, probably to create distance, but with Daeva's slanted back, that only presses her perfect ass more firmly against my crotch. Holy mists talk about sweet torture.

She quickly leans back, but now her head rests against my chest and neck. Her scent floods my senses, and the temperature increases rapidly. I'm hyper aware that I only have to slightly turn my head to press my lips against her temple. Her left arm is crossed over her stomach and still connected to my right arm, which is resting on my thigh near her hip. I swallow.

Daeva launches, and the movement causes Ara to slide back against me. Even if she didn't notice it before, there is no way in hell she can miss what her proximity does to me.

Thankfully, it's a short flight.

Jared greets us with a smirk, while Calix looks confused, when Ara slides from Daeva's back and waits for me to get down, her tapping foot expressing her annoyance. I stay next to Daeva and talk to her to give myself time to cool down before facing the others.

"What was that about only one first year in each group?" Ara asks behind me.

"I'd say I don't have to worry about you straying from my side now. Do I?" I look at her over my shoulder.

"As if I have a choice," She grumbles. "Yes, he chained me to him," she says, seemingly answering Jared's or Calix's unvoiced question.

"You didn't give me a choice," I reply evenly, while Jared snickers.

We hike to the next location, and as soon as we reach it, I look at Ara expectantly.

"What?" she asks.

"Where is it?"

"I have no idea what you're talking about," she says, but she is lying. I step closer.

"We both know that's bullshit," I whisper into her ear, and goose bumps spread over her skin. I try to ignore it. "You want me to believe that you climbing up there was a coincidence? Come on, Ara."

"You can believe anything you want."

"You can feel or see magic or sense it in another way, can't you?"

She stays silent.

"That is how you always know where I am. You recognize my gift, don't you?"

"Those are some interesting theories." She looks off into the distance.

"Haven't I proven again and again that you can trust me?" I ask, slowly getting frustrated. She lifts her eyebrows at me.

"Have you?" She looks down at her wrist. "Funny, I must have missed it."

# CHAPTER
# TWENTY
## TATE

Binding her to me was a mistake. Every time the wind blows her sweet and spicy scent right in my face, every time her arm brushes mine by accident, every time she bumps into me, because one of us forgot she was chained to me, her proximity drives me fucking crazy.

After a full day of that, I'm ready to come out of my skin. And the thought of sleeping next to her tonight? I exhale.

But what other choice do I have after uttering that damn threat? There is no way to take it back now. And how can I expect her to respect my orders if I don't go through with the consequences?

I run a hand through my hair only to make her stumble into me again. Gods be damned, having her this close and still so far out of my reach is the worst kind of torture.

She steps away from me and displays her frustration by kicking against a stone, sending it flying. I suppress a grin. At least I'm not the only one who is aggravated by the situation. Discovering her ability to sense magic could have made all the difference, but she refuses to acknowledge my observation.

Could she have climbed up there to get a better overview, like she claims she did? Sure. But I know she's lying, and it doesn't explain all the other things I noticed over the months. Like how she was able to find me in a crowd of people at the palace, or how she had noticed my shield when she shouldn't have been able to.

That she's refusing to use it to help us win is starting to piss me off, though.

While Jared seems to think our bickering is entertaining, Calix still looks confused, which only means Ara didn't tell even her closest friends about me. And I don't know why that thought pisses me off even more.

By the time night breaks, Tanner's team has found the second egg, not due to Ara's help, I might add, and again, it was far from the spot it was supposed to be. By now, I'm pretty sure who is responsible for that.

When we settle down for the night, I'm on high alert, and that's not just because of Ara's proximity. No, another flight descended close by not long ago. And with us already having two eggs, that also means we already have things worth taking.

"Change of plans for tomorrow," I declare once we have the whole flight gathered, "Since we already have two eggs, other flights only have to ambush us to take the win. So it's important to protect what we have."

"Cassius, Tethys, and Tanner, you'll be the core group and will protect the eggs. Everyone but Ara and I will accompany you, ready to throw up a diversion or draw others away, if they come too close. Ara and I will go find the third."

"Why just you two?" Cassius asks.

"I would've gone alone," I tell him. "But since Ara proved I can't trust her to follow orders when I'm not around, she will stay with me for now."

Cassius's brow furrows, but Ara only rolls her eyes. We make camp before the last light fades and retire early to take advantage of the next day. Our birds will take turns and alternate the watch, as they require less sleep.

"I'm still not the magical bloodhound you seem to think I am," Ara whispers, while she rolls out her bedroll next to mine.

"We'll see about that," I tell her.

"You're really going to make me sleep next to you?" She challenges.

"What do you think?"

"I'm not going to run away," she grumbles. "Or you could attach that to someone else for the night." She gestures at her arm and looks up when Jared walks past us. "Like Jared."

"Oh, hell no," Jared quickly answers. It seems he overheard her question. "I want to wake up tomorrow morning."

Ara furrows her brows. "You think I'd stab you in your sleep or something?" She asks. "Maybe we do need some bonding time."

Jared laughs. "No, Ara. I don't think you'll stab me. But he might." He motions his head toward me and grins when I glare at him.

Ara shakes her head. "Whatever. How about you chain me to Calix or Joel, then?" She points out the two who settled down close to us.

"No, and hell no," I tell her. Having her snuggle up to Cassius is the last thing I need after today. Her sleeping draped all over him might actually turn me violent.

"I think they want to wake up tomorrow morning, too," Jared says, patting Ara's shoulder. "Sorry, you're stuck with him. Even if he snores."

"No, he doesn't." Ara disagrees and instantly has Calix's and Cassius's attention. "I mean, I'm sure he doesn't."

Jared throws his head back and laughs. I smirk.

Calix's gaze jumps from me to Ara and back. Mariel comes over with her bedroll and drops it between Calix's and Joel's. She takes in Ara, who is pointedly ignoring all of us.

"What did I miss?"

Jared grins. "We were just discussing sleeping arrangements."

"For a discussion, other opinions would have to be at least considered," Ara grumbles.

"No, it's definitely not a discussion," I agree and bite my lip to keep from laughing at Ara's annoyed sigh.

We retire early, and Ara is out cold as soon as her head hits the cushion. I stare at her for a long moment before I quietly turn, trying to get more comfortable without waking her. Despite my exhaustion, sleep seems impossible, so I lie in the dark, listening to her quiet breathing. I turn again, but freeze when she shifts next to me.

She mumbles something unintelligible, and her hand lands on mine.

All the hairs on my body rise, my pulse jumps, and I hold my breath.

*Is she awake?*

When she doesn't move again, I put that down as a no. The place where our hands touch seems to pulse and tingle, and while I love the connection, the thought that she wouldn't reach for me while awake stings.

Slowly, I extract my hand from under hers, but she shifts again and rolls over only to end up snuggled into me. Her head rests on my chest right over my racing heart, her hand sits on my stomach, her pinky grazes bare skin where my shirt rode up, and her leg is hooked over mine. I'm a marble statue, not even daring to breathe.

"Ara," I whisper, but only low breathing answers me. I try to nudge her over softly, but she only tightens her hold on me, her fingers find their way under my shirt, trailing over my abdomen and sliding up to my chest.

My abdominals clench, and her fingers leave a burning path. Bubbles fizz through my blood.

Holy mists.

Every one of my tries to push her over to her bedroll has her clinging to me even tighter, so I give up and wrap my arm around her. And I allow myself to enjoy having her in my arms, even if it is only for a night.

I wake from someone tugging at my arm and trying to wriggle free, remembering who slept next to me has me tightening my hold on her.

"Tate, if you don't let me go now, you won't like the consequences. I really have to pee."

I crack open one eye, and I'm greeted by Ara's sleepy face against a barely lit sky. The camp is still quiet around us. "Good morning to you, too. And I was right."

"About what?" She huffs out an irritated breath.

"That you prefer to sleep on top of me."

"You cuddled me like a cushion, so it's hardly my fault," she whisper-hisses.

"I just got comfortable since you clung to me like a burr, no matter what I did." Not that it bothered me.

She scoffs. "And why would I do that? You aren't even soft, but all hard and muscly..." She trails off. "Whatever, I really need to go, so..." I release her and my hold on her to give her some privacy. But keep tabs on her whereabouts through the air around her. It would be just like her to run solely to piss me off.

## ARA

"When I tell you to run, you fucking run," Tate whispers.

I raise my eyebrows. It's the second day of the competition, and Tate and I are on our way to find the last egg.

"Just to prove you right?" I lower my voice, trying to imitate him, "It's just like you to run when it gets hard." I switch back. "I don't think so."

There are other riders close by, and Tate is suddenly acting all tense and worried.

"You could just leave me here." I offer. "If you get this off me, I'll climb one of the trees and stay quiet until they are gone."

"I'm not leaving you behind," he rumbles, gripping my hand as if I could disappear any moment, even though I'm still chained to him.

"Why does this feel familiar? You, tucking me on, while we run from someone?" I ask.

"Not my fault that you always draw that kind of attention."

"Now you have it all wrong." I disagree. "Last time it was all you. Lorcan and I were just talking." He is right about this time, though. It was me they spotted and started to chase, that is why we are currently trudging through this forest trying to lose them.

Tate scoffs. "Just talking. Well, let's just talk then."

He pulls me behind the next tree, his body caging mine in.

"What are you doing?" I hiss. But he stops me with a finger to my lips. His gaze is not on me, but in the distance, intently listening.

"Could you stop touching me?" I try again.

"Could you stop talking?" He whispers back. I nip his finger just enough to sting.

He sucks in a breath, and his gaze snaps to me.

"Ara."

"Keep away from my teeth if you don't want to get bitten."

A twig snaps not far off, and Tate curses under his breath. He grabs my hand, and we start running again.

"We have to get out of this damn forest so Daeva can get us."

"And here I was thinking you were hoping for a cliff to throw me off."

He doesn't reply, but I swear there's a grin on his face.

We are running from other riders. I'm accusing him of wanting to throw me off a cliff, and that is what makes him smile? I shake my head.

Over the sound of us hurtling through the woods, I start to make out something else—the sound of water. *You've got to be kidding me.* I curse when I realize Tate is heading right for it.

"That was a joke," I tell him. "I swear Tate, if you throw me off a cliff again, there is nothing that can save you from my retribution."

"Oh, I would love to see that, but unfortunately, there are no cliffs around," He tells me. "Or rather, there is no ocean around. But there should be... Yes." He breaks off when we reach a riverbank. "I can lift you over it, if you're afraid to get your feet wet," he offers.

"I'm not afraid," I snap back, but any discussion is cut short when there are shouts behind us. Tate's grip on my hand tightens, and he pulls me after him and into the floods. I gasp. The water is freezing.

"Keep breathing," he tells me.

"Can't," I wheeze. The water reaches up to my chest now, and I swear my ribs are frozen. After a short moment of prickling pain, numbness creeps into my limbs.

*"What are you doing?"* Solaris screeches in my head.

*"Taking a damn ice bath."* And I swear even my mental teeth are chattering.

*"Get out of there now,"* my bird commands.

*"I'm on it, I swear,"* I croak back. Finally, the water level sinks, and we stumble to shore just seconds later.

"I can't feel my legs," I complain. Then the pins and prickles set in. "Never mind, I wish I couldn't feel my legs," I mutter.

An arrow whizzes past us, our pursuers already scrambling down the riverbank.

"We have to keep moving," Tate tells me. And I know that, but there is no chance I'll outrun them in this condition.

"Or we have to stop them," I say when an idea strikes. I concentrate on the stream. And just like I practiced with fluid in a tea mug, I channel my gift into the water, heating it. Steam billows over the surface. And one of the men, who was just about to step in, yelps and jumps backward.

"What are you doing?" Tate barks, pulling me behind a boulder, and throws up a shield just in time to stop another arrow midair.

"Discourage them from following," I say.

"Are you crazy? Do you know the amount of energy that takes?"

Well, yeah, I feel it. My gift is depleting rapidly.

"I only have to keep it up long enough so they turn away." I grit my teeth. By now, the water is boiling. Steam rises, hiding us from sight. Tate scans our surroundings and pulls me with him, while I observe with growing unease as my gift weakens. I won't be able to hold it much longer.

*"Don't use all of it,"* Solaris warns just seconds before my gift sizzles out. I've run empty.

*"Too late,"* I answer.

*"Get somewhere where I can get you,"* Solaris demands.

*"I'll try."*

"Come. I've found something." Tate pulls me to some brushes, and I want to protest, but he slips behind them and tugs me into what seems to be a small cave.

I hunker down, shivering, leaving room between us.

"How much did you use?" Tate asks calmly, and I bite my lip.

"Ara," he warns.

"All of it," I whisper.

He curses. "You're cold."

"Very observant of you," I snap back.

"Get out of the armor. It will take too long to dry," he instructs while stripping out of his, leaving him in a wet tunic plastered to his skin. I tug on mine, but the soaked leather is stiff, and my shaking fingers don't help either.

He sighs. "Would you stop being stubborn and come here already?" I inch closer. "You slept glued to my body last night. Do you think now is the moment to keep your distance?" He helps me with the last straps and pulls me into him. The moment my body hits his, I sigh.

"So warm," I hum and wrap my arms around him.

He chuckles and pulls me closer, then slides down the wall so I end up in his lap, straddling him, his magic settling around us.

Slowly, I stop shivering, and with the returning warmth, I realize just how intimate our position is.

Awareness hums between us and prickles over my skin. There is an unnatural stillness to Tate's body, like he is afraid to even breathe. My head rests against his shoulder, facing away from him, and I don't dare to move either.

It's like both of us feel that one move could change everything. And it would, because if I look at him now...

An aching need unfurls in my core, and he's not unaffected either. I can feel him harden beneath me. Our breaths pick up speed, but still neither of us moves. This is absolutely the wrong place, the wrong time. But damn, I've never felt for anyone what I feel for him, with him.

"I'm sorry—"

"No need to be sorry." I cut him off. "It's me who's plastered against you like ivy." I pull back, but that's a mistake. Now I can see his eyes. And they are filled with such longing, such ... pain that I lean in without thinking. I know there are like 100 reasons I shouldn't do this, but at the moment, I can't even think of one.

"Whatever you need, sunshine," Tate rasps, and I crash my mouth to his. Despite his words, he's not passive. He doesn't surrender but takes as much as he gives.

"You're going to be the death of me," he whispers between kisses. I hum. This feels so damn right. My body is on fire, the cold forgotten. I move my hip against him and moan when the length of his cock hits my throbbing need.

His hands tangle in my hair and tug to expose my throat, where he places nipping, hungry kisses before his mouth comes back to mine. I know we should stop, but at the moment, I don't care. All I want is to taste him, feel him close, against me, inside me, his magic around me, filling me.

"Shh," he whispers against my lips. "You have to be quiet, baby."

I wasn't even aware I made a sound.

He grabs my hips, grinding up against me, helping me to get the friction I seek.

"I need you inside me," I moan, and he crashes his lips back on mine, swallowing the sound.

"As much as I would love that," he rasps, "here is not the place nor the time." How can he be so reasonable? How can he even think?

A sound of pure disagreement leaves my lips, and his lips curl into a grin against mine.

"Whatever I need, was it?"

"You are such a demon." He bites my neck and sends sparks shooting through my body, but then pulls back. "But we still have a competition to win. So as much as it pains me, not now."

His words sober me quicker than anything else could. The competition. The egg. The reason he took me with him. How badly he wants to win.

I scramble off his lap so fast I nearly fall, since I forgot for a moment I'm still chained to him.

"Get that off me," I snarl, gesturing at my hand.

"Whoa, what happened just now?" Tate's eyes search mine.

I step back, but of course, he follows.

"I forgot for a moment whose lap I was riding," I spit.

"Nice try, but you were cold, not drunk, when you cuddled into me, so I'm not buying this shit. Try again."

"Was that your way of softening me up, so I would play your bloodhound for this damn competition?"

"What the fuck are you talking about? You kissed me, remember?" His gaze jumps between my eyes, trying to read me.

"And you played me ... again," I mutter.

"I ... what?" He grabs my chin, bringing my eyes back to his. "Now listen closely, I have no idea where all of this is coming from, but I have no time for this shit. I have exactly two goals at the moment: keep you alive and win the flight games, and you are doing your damned best to sabotage both." He runs a hand through his hair. "And still I'm here, still I can't stay away from you, still I—" He shakes his head, releasing my chin as he steps back.

"If the thought of helping me win this competition is so abhorrent to you, then don't. It's not like I worked years for this." He laughs humorlessly. "Stay here and don't move." He grabs his armor and leaves, and because I want to follow him, I do for once as he asks, and stay where I am. It's only when he is gone that I realize he cut me free. And somehow, that hurts.

# TWENTY-ONE

## ARA

WE COME IN THIRD AFTER A FLIGHT OF THE EASTERN AND THE Northern division, but all I can think about are Tate's words.

*And still I'm here, still I can't stay away from you.*

My heart aches with a mix of hope and fear. If he truly cares about me... I bury the thought before it can fully unfurl. Getting out of my promise is impossible, and the thought that Tate's feelings might be real ... it shreds me.

Despite her threats of making my life miserable, Livia has ignored me so far. Fine with me since my life is bad enough as it is. Tate is back to treating me with cool indifference, and who can blame him if... I push the thought away. No, spewing pretty words doesn't make them true.

My gift remains unpredictable and is still all over the place, especially when he stands next to me. At least my grasp on my magic gift has improved, and my hold on it is even tighter since the incident with the fire.

I don't sleep well, and my nightmares come more and more often. Next to the one about me burning everyone and everything around me, there is also a strange man threatening me, torturing me. And like the incident with Livia, something is strangely familiar about it.

I do my best to exhaust myself during training to keep them at bay, but it doesn't always work. And worrying about everything else has cost me my appetite.

"The stronger your magic becomes, the more regularly you have to release it," Galdur says as she steps through the door and walks over to her lectern. She's always like that, starting right away, not bothering with greeting or niceties, as if she had already been lecturing on the way here.

"Yes, you can go days, some of you even weeks, before you feel the effect of the accumulating magic, but I wouldn't advise it. First of all, your magic will become harder and harder to control the longer you bottle it up. Second of all, your strength will grow with daily use, and third, unless your gift is premonition, you'll never know what the next day brings, so it's better not to wait too long before releasing it.

"In short, you have to find ways to use it in your everyday life and not just for full-blown attacks." She starts pacing the front of the room, her steps on the stone echoing off the bare walls.

"Fire gifted can use their gift to warm their bath, their tea, or themselves, for instance. And most of you already handle that quite well. Ice can do the opposite. Ice baths are supposed to be healthy," she says, drawing a few laughs from the class.

I'm grateful I have fire. I hated cold showers and baths, even before what happened at the palace. But since Solaris explained to me that it is dangerous if my core temperature drops too low, and the bath in the river, my motto is the hotter, the better. Cold water seems to be especially dangerous since it leeches warmth so effectively.

"No, roasting your fellow riders is not an acceptable way to use your gift," Galdur says and earns a few more laughs. "But seriously, I know some of you have it harder. Decorating your room with illusions, playing with shadow or light, or letting something hover in the air for fun is easy to accomplish without involving others. But those with healing, necromancy, influencing, or emotional manipulation, for instance, have little chance to use their gift without involving others. That doesn't mean there aren't ways to release it without breaking the rules." She looks over the rows. "Everyone with elemental gifts, you should be able to figure something out. If you need pointers, ask other riders with the same magic or come to me after class. Psychics who need training partners, please get up."

She looks over the group of about twenty riders, assessing.

"Healers, I already talked to Professor Medella at the healing quarters. She expects you every day for an hour after lunch. Those of you gifted at understanding animals are always welcome in the coop to chat with the birds, or you could seek out other animals. Your fellow riders won't be much help even though some might behave like animals," she says dryly. And the slight smile at the responding chuckles lets me suspect she enjoys her role.

"Simeon, don't get too comfortable. The king will likely graduate you early and appoint you as an ambassador. A gift for understanding all languages is on his list, and reported as soon as a rider shows it. Petrification." She shakes her head at two riders, one from the northern and the other from the western division. "I won't let you practice by turning your fellow riders into stone. Sorry, you'll have to start with plants. Our head gardener marked an area where you can practice without risking anyone. Necromancers, we already talked." She nods at Mariel and another girl from the northern division.

"That leaves the rest." Her eyes wander over the group of about ten people still standing. "I will assign you a new rider every week, and you will train with them daily. Since they have to learn how to shield their thoughts and emotions, the training will benefit both of you."

"Great, someone poking around in my head or my emotions sounds fun," I grumble, and Mariel grimaces.

"Ask me how much I look forward to spending time with the dead," she shudders. "I swear, the first time one of them starts talking to me, I'll run away screaming." She sighs. "And it's not like I would get out of the other fun. I'm not even sure what is worse, someone knowing my feelings or my memories. No offense..."

"None taken," Calix says good-naturedly.

"But if you poke around in my emotions, I'll castrate you," Mariel finishes.

"Now I do feel offended," he complains, and we laugh.

"I'm glad I don't have many secrets," Calix says while we file out of the room. When I stay silent, he sighs. "We know you have too many of them." He bumps my shoulder.

"I'm sorry," I whisper.

"No, don't be. After that announcement"—he nods at the room behind us—"I'm glad I don't know."

"Me, too," Mariel agrees.

My eyes prickle. I have the best friends in the world. And things could be worse. I was paired with an emotion-bender, not an influencer or mind reader.

My appetite hasn't come back, and if possible, the added worry on how I will partly shut out the emotion-bender next week without losing control of my fire in the process has made my sleeplessness worse.

The result is occasional dizziness and feeling like shit, which, turns out, is not ideal while dealing with sharp weapons.

I curse, looking at the blood running down my arm.

"Sorry, Ara." Simeon looks apologetic, but I wave him off.

"My fault," I assure him.

"Here, let me," he says, snatching the shirt he discarded and wrapping it around my arm. "Unless you want to leave a bloody trail for effect?"

I snort. "No, thanks." I sway a little.

"Let's get you to the healers," he says, and after letting Arkwright know we are on our way, Simeon accompanies me down the corridor. And I try very hard not to think about the fact that this is the first time I visit the healing quarters and that someone else besides Tate will heal me. It freaks me out.

There is no reason for it, of course. I have such a tight handle on my gift that it doesn't react at all when I come in contact with magic anymore... I could ask Tate instead. No, the thought of having him this close, of his hands on me, is too tempting.

"Ara, what happened?" Jared asks from behind us. I turn and nearly sigh in relief when Tate isn't anywhere in sight.

"I'm heading to the healing quarters. I'll take her," he dismisses Simeon, who only nods and drudges back to class.

"What are you doing at the healing quarters?" I ask.

"I asked first," he says and looks at me expectantly.

"Accident during training. I stumbled." I shrug. It's not like I haven't had it before, and my body has the scars to prove it. But the dizziness does worry me.

"Are you alright?" Jared asks.

"Nothing I didn't have before." I smile at him.

"No. I mean, are you alright?"

"Why wouldn't I be?" I bristle. I really have had enough of everyone asking me that lately.

"I don't know. Maybe because you and my best friend used to look at each other all moony-eyed, and now you both act like a cat I'm trying to give a bath to as soon as I mention the other's name?" He looks at me while I focus straight ahead.

*And still I can't stay away from you.*

"Leave it," I say.

"Funny, that is the same thing he says," Jared replies dryly. For once, his humor seems to be missing.

"Maybe you should listen. Wait," I stop short. "That is not the way to the healing quarters."

"No, it's the way to your personal healer."

"No." I shake my head. "I can't. I don't want his hands on me."

Jared's look changes from empathetic to disappointed.

"Fine, have it your way." He sighs, and even though he doesn't say anything, judgment flows off him in waves.

"You don't need to accompany me." I quicken my step, but he easily stays next to me.

"Right and risk him ripping my head off if something happens to you? No thanks."

I scoff. "You could tell him you never saw me."

"Lie to him?" He shakes his head at me. "You really don't know him at all, do you?"

"What do you mean?" I look at him, waiting for an explanation, but it never comes.

The rest of the way is cloaked in a heavy silence. I mumble a goodbye and rush into the healing quarters as soon as we arrive, too eager to get away from Jared and his silent judgment.

A young healer takes me into a room and cleans the wound. His smooth hands feel strange when I'm used to the slight rasp and tickle of Tate's callused ones, but I quickly shut down that thought.

*"Maybe you should hear him out after all,"* Solaris suggests.

*"And what good would that do?"* I ask him. *"Even if he means it, if he has an explanation for everything, even if I trust him again, there is still Frederick..."* And the promise he blackmailed me into.

The healer places his hands on my skin, and his magic flows into me. I flinch. It feels strange to have someone else's gift invading my body. The coolness tries to rise at my agitation, but I double down, not giving it the chance.

I thank the healer and hurry out of the room as soon as possible, promising myself to be more careful from now on.

As I leave the healing quarters, I run straight into Tate. His cool gaze wanders over me, taking in the blood-covered remains of my tunic and Simeon's blood-stained one in my hand.

"So Jared ran right back to report on me?" I snap, and Tate's brows rise at my tone.

"I'm on my way to a meeting," he says evenly. "Was there something to report?"

I instantly feel foolish. What did I expect? That he would rush to my side, concerned and demanding answers?

*And still I can't stay away from you.*

Yes, dammit, that is exactly what I had hoped for.

"No, of course not." I raise my chin, trying to keep my face as stoic as his. For a second, I think he's going to say something, but he doesn't.

I walk past him and don't allow myself to look back while I stride down the hall, determined to put as much distance between us as possible until I see him again tomorrow morning.

# CHAPTER
# TWENTY-TWO
### TATE

I look over at where Ara is joking with Joel as they leave the sparring hall. And the way he looks down at her ... sees her as a sister, my ass.

I can't see her face, so I don't know if she's oblivious or lapping up the attention.

I shouldn't care. It's better to stay away, safer. Her accusation that I am trying to use her ... mists if that isn't a sign we are far past saving, I don't know what is. And still, only a few days later, I couldn't help but rush to the healing quarters as soon as Jared told me she was hurt.

Mists, I would cut my own heart out and lay it down in front of her, if I thought that would buy me the chance of getting her back. I shake my head at that thought. No, I wouldn't, because staying away is the goal here.

*I need to stay away.*

They walk past me, Ara's eyes meeting mine for a heartbeat before she looks away.

"Does your betrothed know you throw yourself at other men?" I ask before I can stop myself.

"Wait a minute..." Joel says, his eyes widening. His gaze flickers from me to Ara and back. "Do you mean..."

"Yes, she is still going to marry him."

"First of all, that's none of your business." Ara's voice is icy when she addresses me. "And second..." She turns to Joel, her voice much softer now. "Don't look so shocked. You knew this since we were kids."

"But you said you didn't want to marry him," Joel says aghast.

"Well, I changed my mind," she snaps. There is fire in her eyes now, but also something that looks close to desperation.

"Why didn't you tell me?" he asks her, and isn't that an interesting question.

"I don't have to tell anyone anything." Her gaze flies from me to him and back. "And I sure as hell don't have to let you two judge me for it." She turns away, and I see her eyes filling with tears before she stomps down the corridor ahead of us. I instantly want to rush after her. My hands curl into fists, and I stay where I am.

"What happened?" Joel asks quietly.

I give him a cold look. "I have no idea what you're talking about."

For a second, he looks like he wants to add something, but snaps his mouth shut and sighs.

"I guess it's for the better," he finally says, and just like that, I want to smash him into the next wall. So I turn and walk away. Nothing about this situation is even remotely good, and I will have another practice session with Ara this afternoon. Just her, me, and an empty arena. Fucking great.

I should have anticipated it, considering how our conversation ended, but I'm still surprised at how tangible silence can be. It's like a third person in the sandy round of the arena.

Ara hasn't said a word to me since she met me at the gate. No comment, no sass, nothing. Whenever I give her instructions, she follows them without complaint, and it grates on my nerves in a way I never thought obedience could. So it's a damn relief when she finally opens her mouth, even if it is to snap at me.

"It's not your place to talk about my business with other people."

"Other people?" I say. "Last time we talked about him, you tried to convince me that Joel is *like a brother* to you. So he's hardly other people."

"It's not your business."

"So you're telling me it's not my business even though you know how I feel about you, even though you will be part of my family? You'll be my sister-in-law, for fuck's sake." I pause. "Do tell, when is the big day?"

"First of all, I'm not your anything." She takes a step toward me, her eyes shooting fire. "Second, we haven't set a date because I'll finish my training first."

*"You still have time to win her over then,"* Daeva comments.

Hope wiggles in my chest, but I smother it.

*"No, I won't,"* I tell her.

*"And you call me stubborn,"* she says.

"Well, then I'll be sure to mark down the date next year." I take another step closer and sneer down at her. "Sister," I add mockingly, and she explodes. It's the only way to describe it.

She reaches for me, grasping my arm a heartbeat before we are engulfed in flames so bright they blot out everything else. I expect heat and pain, but instead, there is silky coolness. I stare stunned at the flames surrounding us, yet they don't burn me.

"I'm not your sister," she hisses. "I'm not your family. I'm not your fucking anything." She lands one verbal blow after another. "I don't even know why I put up with you and those stupid trials."

"Oh, so you want to quit now and leave us hanging? Abandon us?" I snap right back, not even caring about the flames around us anymore. "I don't know why that even surprises me."

"Are you kidding me?" she seethes. "You are the one who walked away, who betrayed me."

"What?" I search her eyes, but she closes them, shutting me out.

"It doesn't matter." She takes one deep breath after another until the flames sputter out, and she is back in control.

"The fuck it doesn't matter. What are you talking about?" I ask, but she shakes her head. "Talk to me," I insist, but I see it on her face. She is not going to give me anything. Irritation crawls over my skin. How many more dismissals is it going to take until I can finally let her go?

A glint catches my eye right where Ara stood, and I squat down, getting a closer look. A small, rounded piece of glass glints in the sun, and I reach for it, but pick it up with my gift when I notice the heat radiating off it.

Seems like her flames burn hotter than any fire wielder's I've met before. So why am I still standing here? Why didn't her flames burn me? I've never heard of a fire wielder shielding someone else from their flames.

Is Ara's gift different because of Solaris? Or does it have something to do with her other ability? Something I know far too little about.

I look up, only to see Ara heading toward one of the arches leading out of the arena's round center. She is simply walking away ... again.

## ARA

"So you are giving up?" Tate calls after me, and my skin heats again.

"I'm not giving up. I'm ... taking a break," I shout back. Anger joins the terror squeezing my chest.

"Running away won't solve anything. And we need to work on your control."

I huff out a breath. I'm so far from controlled, it isn't even funny. The image of a few minutes ago dances through my mind, eerily matching my nightmare—Tate engulfed in my flames. And I have no idea how I managed to shield him from it. I ball my fingers into fists to keep them from shaking.

"Excuse me if we aren't all made of ice and stone," I walk faster. If I don't get some space between us, I'm not sure what will happen ... and that would sadly enough only prove his point.

"We aren't done yet," Tate shouts after me, but gods, I'm so done right now.

"Five minutes," I yell back. "Unless you want me to set everything on fire," I add under my breath. I storm around a corner to be out of his sight and run smack into another person. She gives a surprised gasp before she lands on her ass.

"I'm sorry I wasn't looking..." I huff out a breath and reach down to help her up. Only now taking her in.

Her eyes are red-rimmed, her cheeks wet, and when I pull her up, I notice fresh bruises on her wrists and neck. She ducks her head and hides her arms behind her back as soon as she sees me noticing.

My anger flares up brighter, drowning out the terror. Forget Tate, I have a new, much more satisfying target in mind.

"I'm happy to set someone on fire for you if you point me in the right direction," I tell the girl. Her eyes widen, but then a small smile tugs on her lips.

"I would like that," she whispers, "but it would get you in trouble, so thanks, but no thanks."

"I hope you kneed him in the balls at least."

A surprised giggle bubbles out of her mouth before she claps her hand over it to hold it in. She shakes her head.

"I'm not a fighter." She eyes my tunic and pants in their telltale gray, and her eyes land on the skyrider insignia on my shoulder. "Not like you."

"So you are not one of the gladiators then?" I ask. My eyes land on the mark on her wrist, the emblem of the arena. "You take care of them." I realize, remembering Tate's words.

The girl blushes at my words, but nods.

"I could teach you a few moves, if you want," I offer. "To defend yourself." The girl's eyes widen again. I guess she hasn't had it easy in life if such an easy offer stuns her, and I'm even more determined. "I'm here daily in the afternoon."

Her eyes dart behind me, but since I feel him approach, I don't have to look.

"If you are done playing with your new friend," Tate snaps, "we can get back to practice." The girl instinctively cowers at his harsh tone, and I glare at him over my shoulder. His whole demeanor shifts from menacing to something softer the moment he takes in the scene. I blink.

He steps up behind me so close our bodies nearly touch. And while I want to ease back from his warmth, I make myself stay when I notice the girl's weary gaze. He is not a threat. Whatever else is wrong between us, he would never harm me or her. She relaxes visibly.

"That has to be painful," Tate says softly and gestures to her throat. Damn, I love this softer, warmer version of him. The girl glances at me but nods when I smile encouragingly.

"I'm a healer. If you give me your hands, I can make it go away," Tate offers, and I soften even more. Could it be that I have it all wrong?

Tate holds out his hands, palms up, and waits patiently. The girl looks at me and places her hands in Tate's when I nod, the only contact coming from whatever she is offering. Her bruises fade quickly, and her hand flies to her throat as soon as Tate is done.

"Thank you," she whispers. Then her eyes widen. "But I have nothing to pay you with unless..." She bites her lips, her eyes flying from me to Tate and back, seemingly unsure if she should go on with whatever she was about to say or not, but Tate beats her to it.

"I don't expect payment. I see it as my part to balance out the lives I claim." He nods at her, then turns. "I'll wait in the arena for you. Don't dawdle," he adds to me before striding off.

Damn that man. I look after him.

"You are a lucky woman," the girl comments.

"Oh, I'm not ... we're not..." I stammer.

"It wasn't my place to comment on, my apologies."

A bell tolls in the distance, and the girl flinches. "I have to go. Thank you so much, both of you." She smiles and then hurries off into the dark corridor. Only then do I realize she never agreed to let me teach her how to defend herself.

"That was nice of you." I approach our encounter with the girl on our way back. "To heal her, I mean."

"I'm not a monster," Tate snaps.

"I never said you were," I counter.

"Oh, didn't you?" he remarks dryly while quickening his steps until I have to nearly run after him. I wince when I remember he is right, I did say something like that at the palace.

I keep my eyes open for the girl over the next few days, but I don't see her. I even try to excuse myself to go looking for her at the end of our session, but Tate won't have it.

"You stay where I can see you at all times," he snaps. "No wandering off, do you hear me?"

"Yes, master," I salute him mockingly, but that doesn't go over well.

"Oh, you think what happened to your little friend was funny?"

"No, of course not," I splutter. "Something like that won't ever happen to me."

"You're damn right it won't." When he sees my stubborn look, he sighs. "Who do you think has to sign off on their pardons once they have fought and killed their way to freedom? Just because I don't agree with my father's ways doesn't mean every man in here is harmless. And they have very little to lose."

"You're only worried I'll burn down the building," I retort because that sounded awfully close to caring. And he can't care for me, he can't.

He huffs out a laugh that misses every trace of humor. "Sure, that's it. Get to work. We aren't here for talking."

Tate is never easy on me, but today, he pushes me until the ground beneath me starts to shift, only to growl at me for stumbling into him, like it is my damn fault.

Later at lunch, a cup of tea and a plate with all my favorite foods land next to my hand. I look up from the food I have been pushing around for the last ten minutes and meet familiar golden eyes. My heart skips a beat.

I don't know who I expected, but not him, not after the way he snapped at me earlier. My eyes wander back to the plate.

"I can get my own food."

"Eat it," he growls.

"Why?"

"If you faint during training, you'll waste my time."

"You don't think I can keep up?"

"Eat and drink ... all of it. That's an order."

"I'm ordered to eat fruit, cake, and ... cookies?" My eyebrows rise.

"Yes." His face is deadly serious before he turns and stalks away. I meet Mariel's and Calix's puzzled looks and shrug.

"The good thing is I know he's not trying to poison me since he needs a full flight for the trials," I joke while I pop a grape into my mouth.

I take a sip of the tea, and my eyes fly down the table to where Tate and Jared sit. The tea is just how I always drink it and contains the perfect amount of honey.

I make an effort and finish the tea and half of the things on my plate. The rest goes to Calix.

Again, doubt creeps in. What if he does care? What if it's not just an act? What if I'm wrong?

But that would mean I messed up even worse and lost more than I thought.

I don't hear a word of what Professor Riku says during geography.

CHAPTER

# TWENTY-THREE

ARA

Even though I'm allowed to leave the grounds now, I'm tempted to sneak out just for the fun of it and as a tribute to old times, but my brother closed the gap, and flying is a lot more comfortable anyway.

I'm invited to dinner at my uncle's, and I jumped at the opportunity. I'm looking forward to seeing Sloan, and avoiding Tate is a plus. It's a warm night, and in contrast to the night I got locked out, not only are there enough windows open but the others also know where I'm going. Even Tate.

Okay, I let Jared know. But I'm sure he told him by now.

The sun is just setting on the horizon when I climb onto Solaris's back, and we swoop down from the roof of the sleeping quarters. We win in height with every powerful stroke of his wings. The city spreads out beneath us, the higher structures of the arena, temple hill, and the academy tinted red by the sun's glow.

Despite Solaris not being in full flame, I still spot some faces turned skyward, watching us while we close in on the merchant quarter and descend over my uncle's house.

We land right next to the big fountain I hid behind when secretly visiting Sloan, and the big glass doors to the parlor are thrown open as soon as my feet hit the ground.

"Took you long enough." Sloan envelops me in a hug. "Are they not feeding you at this Aerie of yours?" Her eyes scan over me.

"Lots of workout and learning magic. I burn through everything I ever could eat." I grin.

"Maybe I should try it sometime, too," Sloan jokes, patting her hip. "Our cook created a new dessert. She's making it tonight, and I tell you, it's to die for." She ushers me into the house while a sweet older woman spreads a big variety of food in front of Solaris.

I look back at him.

*"I'm good,"* he tells me, and I chuckle while the woman oohs and aahs about Solaris's beauty.

*"Do I have to borrow a cart to get you home later?"* I tease.

*"Quite possibly,"* he replies.

"That I will have to get used to," Sloan declares while watching me. We stopped just past the doors.

"Sorry, I just checked in with Solaris." I grin at her. "What were you saying?"

Sloan launches into stories about the people invited tonight, but my thoughts drift off.

Somehow, people affronting each other and petty rivalry seem so … inconsequential. Why do they even bother with it? And for the first time, there is a wall separating Sloan and me, a wall made of ignorance, and I'm not sure if I should pity or envy her for it.

The dinner just started when I'm already bored out of my mind. And the thought that this could be my future... I repress a shudder, feigning interest in the story of a merchant's son, who claims to have made the deal of his lifetime with... I can't even remember what it was, wool of blind sheep from Kystis or something like that?

"Those goats are amazing..." Oh, right, it was goats. I tune him out again, giving him an empty smile and a nod now and again.

*"Do you think he will stop talking if I scream?"* I ask Solaris, and his amusement floods me.

*"Worth a shot,"* he agrees, and I contemplate it. Since we were introduced, he talked about nothing but how great he is.

*"You could also stab him with your fork,"* Solaris suggests.

*"And say what ... oops, I missed my plate?"* I bite my lip to hold in my laughter while twirling the fork between my fingers. My aunt intervenes, either because she pities me or dreads the drama.

"I'm sorry to interrupt, but may I have a word with my niece? I see her so rarely." There is blissful silence next to me at her words, before the man turns to Sloan on his other side and continues his story like she's been attentively listening all along.

I sigh in relief.

"It's so nice that you make time to visit Sloan regularly. She is so much happier lately." My aunt beams at me. "But take the front door next time, yes?"

*Visit? Front door?*

I plaster a smile on my face to hide my confusion. I have no idea what Sloan told her, but I'm not going to land her in trouble by contradicting it.

"Yeah, now that I'm here in Telos, I have to make use of the time we have." I nod.

"It's great that you girls get along so well. Maybe we'll send her with you to Avina." She winks at me and turns to the guest next to her. Her statement makes me want to throw up.

Why did she have to speak of me going to Avina when I so successfully banned Frederick from my mind?

The food is good, and Sloan didn't lie about the dessert, but I don't get much down. My aunt's comment has ruined my appetite.

The night is warm, and after hours of sitting, I decide a walk is just what I need.

Since Solaris wouldn't be comfortable circling in the dark, I send him back.

# TWENTY-FOUR

## TATE

I HAVE HAD ENOUGH OF WAITING FOR SOMEONE TO MAKE A move, enough of setting my hope solely on winning the trials while the men I'm searching for are still roaming the streets of Telos. So I find myself once more at the door in the merchant quarters.

Again, Silence answers the door, but instead of letting me in like all the other times, he steps out and closes it behind him.

"Let's walk to the market," he says in his raspy voice, and I follow. What else am I supposed to do?

"Someone else showed interest in your Phoenix rider." He stops at a stand of an older woman selling fruit. He lifts a fruit from the piles occupying the straw baskets and continues talking, not looking at me, but at the older woman.

"I suspect they made a deal with my boss."

"Why are you telling me this?" I use my gift to transport the sound to his ear, startling him.

"Well, that makes things easier," he comments. "So we can talk across a distance? Even in a noisy tavern?"

I nod.

"Play along, then head to the tavern on Rope Maker Lane," he says before spinning around to face me. "The spider isn't available right now and neither am I," he says, before pushing past me and walking away. I huff out a breath and glare after him, before leaving.

In the tavern, I eat a spoonful of the watery stew in front of me, hoping I made the right call in trusting Silence. I still have no idea why he would help me, but I'll take my chance. After what he said, I also need to hear the rest before even thinking about walking away.

When he comes through the door, I nearly don't recognize him. Silence changed his usually impeccable clothes for the ragged ones of a sailor. Grime covers his hands and parts of his face, and one of his green eyes is covered by an eye patch. He even carries one of the bowed sabers many sailors prefer. He settles on the other side of the room, and as soon as his lips move, I let the air next to my ear mirror the vibrations of his voice.

"Is this good for you?" he asks, and I nod. As long as I can see him, it works for me.

"He gave me orders that have me believe he sold you out, or rather, your friend," he says, and my blood runs cold.

"Why are you helping us?"

"Everyone protects his interests, and helping you protects mine," he states matter-of-factly, which makes him more believable than any declaration of his good intentions ever could have. And he speaks the truth.

"He didn't give me any orders, and I don't think he will, so keep her close, keep your eyes and ears open, and if you can, get her out of Telos."

I nod, already planning how I can make that happen. Silence finishes his wine and leaves shortly after. I take my time and then head back to the Aerie, glad that I already told everyone to stay in groups of two or more whenever possible.

I sit in the common room with the others in my flight. Tanner is dealing out the next round of cards while Boko makes a show of checking Jared's sleeves for hidden cards.

"You have to be cheating," he complains. "No one has that much luck."

"Maybe I made a deal with Sreca to grant me good luck." Jared grins while Boko huffs and leans back in his seat, examining my best friend with narrowed eyes. I shake my head at Jared and wait for the moment Boko realizes that with his gift, Jared doesn't need extra cards.

Nearly our whole flight is here. Actually—I scan the room again—everyone but one person is here. Calix and Cassius lounge on one of the couches, talking. Mariel is curled up between them, but Ara's golden locks are missing. That is odd.

"Where is Ara?" My gaze wanders over the room again, but she isn't here.

"Visiting her cousin," Jared says next to me.

"What did I say about no one going out alone?" I ask, my irritation leaking into my voice.

"Hey, don't shoot the messenger. Or did you expect me to invite myself to a family dinner?" He tilts his head, contemplating. "Maybe I should have..."

"How did she get there?"

"She took Solaris."

"Well, that is at least something, I guess." No one would be stupid enough to attack her with a Phoenix around, right?

I try to concentrate on the game and the conversations around me, but catch myself looking at the door every time it opens. It's getting later and later, and Ara still isn't back. Maybe she went straight to bed?

"*Is Solaris back?*" I ask Daeva.

"*Just came in,*" she answers after a few minutes. The tension in my muscles lessens because that means she is safely back on the academy ground, then. "*Ara should be here soon, too. Solaris says she is walking.*"

"*What?*"

I'm out of my chair before she has the chance to respond. The chair crashes to the floor, and I ignore the confused inquiries of my flight as I rush to the door. This woman is going to drive me up the wall. What is it going to take for her to stay safe for once? Do I have to chain her to me again?

"*Now that is a good idea,*" Daeva comments, but I ignore it.

"*Meet me in the atrium,*" I tell her, while I grab my swords and hurry down the stairs. She'd better be breathing when I find her, or I will tear this city down, stone by stone, if I have to, until I find the men responsible.

Daeva is already waiting for me. I don't bother with a harness this time, and she takes off as soon as I'm on her back. I grab on to the base of the wings, careful not to impair her movements, while she shoots up into the sky.

The city is a sea of shadows and pinpricks of light beneath us. Only a few of the shadows are moving. Trees sway in the evening breeze blowing toward the sea, while a few animals skitter in the darkness, and people roam the streets, their movements often revealing their intent.

Using Daeva's sight, everything is as clear as in broad daylight, and I keep my eyes open for Ara's familiar form, while we head for the merchant quarter.

A few days ago, the thought of Ara being close to whoever caused those bruises on the slave had turned my thoughts murderous. Now cold terror squeezes my heart, and it has nothing to do with the fact that we would lose the trials, if... I don't finish the thought.

*You're only worried I'll burn down the building.*

I snort. She could burn down the whole damn city, and I

wouldn't blink an eye as long as she walks out unscathed, and that is … insane in its own right.

However much I try not to, I still love her. Even though she hates me and even though she proved that she is ready to blackmail me to get her way.

Fuck, I love her tendency to drive her head through a wall rather than give up, and the fire in her eyes when she goes toe-to-toe with me. I love every reckless, stubborn fiber of her, which makes her exactly what my enemies have been looking for, and she doesn't even see it.

# TWENTY-FIVE

## ARA

"WHAT DID I SAY ABOUT WANDERING ABOUT ALONE?" TATE drops down in front of me like an avenging angel or Otero himself. The night, the shadows around him fit his dangerous tone as he stalks toward me. Every delicious part of him radiates anger.

Since Daeva blends with the darkness around us, it seems like she isn't even here, making it seem like the sky spat him out right in front of me.

"Should have expected it," I mutter and start walking again, determined to brush past him, but Tate has other plans. I find myself caged between him and the house next to me. My heart skips a beat, but I only arch an eyebrow.

"This seems awfully familiar," I tell him dryly.

"Stop fucking disobeying my orders," he seethes, and a thrill runs down my spine. He is well and truly pissed, and I probably shouldn't enjoy it so much, or provoke him—but I can't help it.

"Or what?" I lean back against the wall behind me, grinning up at him. I love that, for once, he doesn't look all calm and collected.

Tate slams his palm against the wall right next to my head. I don't even blink. How can he feel so safe and dangerous at the same time?

I watch him. He looks skyward like he is praying for something, his chest heaving with the anger rolling off him in waves, charging the air between us. He takes a deep breath, releases it, before facing me, leaning even closer.

I swallow, and tingles shoot over my skin.

His eyes burn into me, setting me on fire, my body not getting the message that kissing him is not an option ... shouldn't be an option. It's like I'm fighting a wildfire with a bucket of water.

My eyes drop to his mouth, but I jerk them back up again.

"Or what?" I repeat, my voice husky.

*"What are you doing? Riling up your centurion is everything but smart,"* Solaris admonishes, and he is right. My centurion, that is all Tate is now to me. Centurion Kyronos.

"You are on coop duties for two weeks, report there right after formation tomorrow morning. And never disobey my orders again, are we clear?" He leans in, his stare piercing, and I involuntarily hold my breath. "I mean it, Ara. One day, it will get you killed."

"And that would screw up your plans," I say.

"Exactly," he replies, then pushes off the wall and gives me one last long look before starting down the sidewalk.

"Use your feet, rider," he snaps. My breath rushes out, and I gasp in a new one.

Why, oh why, does he still affect me like this? And why, oh why, do I want to do that again?

We start our way back to the academy in silence. It's easy to be quiet with him, and somehow, that is worse than any awkward silence could be. We snap more at each other than talk, and still, I crave his company. What does that say about me?

Tate starts cursing next to me, and I look up. We just entered a small alley, and two men are walking toward us, blocking our way. They are both dressed solely in black.

"Don't argue, and don't disagree. Go along with whatever I say or do. Got it?" Tate commands.

I huff out a breath at his clipped words. I probably would have argued or at least asked questions, but the men have already reached us.

"Get lost," Tate says, his voice low and threatening.

"And who might this be?" one of the men drawls, looking me up and down.

"Step back and take your eyes off her before we have a fucking problem," Tate barks, his stance menacing.

"Easy, man. I'm only admiring the view," the man replies and steps closer, reaching for a strand of my hair that has fallen in my face. I freeze, unsure how to react after Tate's warning. Who are they, and what do they want? No one has drawn weapons yet, but...

The man closest to me is slammed into the next wall. My eyes widen, but I don't make a peep.

"You don't get to touch her," Tate growls while stepping next to me. Did I think he was angry before?

I was wrong. The air is charged by his magic, pulsing with it. Power radiates off him in waves, prickling my skin.

He's the embodiment of the deadly quiet right before a storm. A storm you won't escape, no matter what you do.

"Walk away," the second stranger says, while his friend's face slowly turns purple. "We are only here for her."

"Then I'm here for you," Tate says, his voice a warning rumble, like thunder in the distance.

The storm has arrived.

Gale-force gusts lash around us, tangling my hair and caressing my hot cheeks. Tate's gift saturates the air until it throbs with it and pulls me in stronger than ever before. The need to reach for it to open myself to it becomes stronger and stronger until I can no longer resist.

Warmth floods me, so familiar and still different from his healing gift. A laugh escapes my lips while I bask in the raw power around me and become one with it, with him.

The second man lunges for me, but never reaches me. I knew he wouldn't. I felt the power shifting, reaching for him. He ends up next to the first, both now struggling against the invisible hold Tate has on them. But his attention is on me, his face unreadable.

The men start screaming, and he whips around, shutting them up. And my attention is drawn back to the magic around me. It feels accelerating, freeing, amazing. I feel amazing.

I spin in circles, the sky above me a glittering blanket of beauty, until I'm stopped by Tate's arms coming around me, and I melt into him.

"Dance with me," I hum, while I rest my head on his shoulder.

"We have to go," he says softly, guiding me out of the alley, but I spin away with another laugh, taking up my dance again.

"Look how beautiful everything is." I grin back at him, but the smile on his face is tinged with sadness. I spin back to him, gripping his face. "Don't you see it?"

"Oh, I see the beauty, sunshine." He picks me up. "But now we really have to go." He carries me down the street, and I snuggle into him.

"Hmm, you smell good," I tell him.

"And you are an adorable drunk."

"I didn't drink anything," I protest.

"You opened up to my magic, didn't you?"

"Hmm." I shudder in his arms. "It felt so good." I sigh.

"You seem drunk," he states. "I've only read about it, but... You're probably power drunk." He looks down at me. "Looks good on you, though." There's a smile on his face, and I like it.

"Sorry for tonight," I tell him. His smile widens.

"Are you always this agreeable when you're drunk?"

I scrunch up my face. "I was only drunk once. Ben stole a whole variety of bottles from the vine cellar and dared me to try every one of them. I was so sick that I've stuck to one glass only since then."

Tate chuckles and shakes his head. "Seems like your brother is a handful, too."

"He is my twin." I shrug.

"That explains it all," he teases, and I close my eyes, content and happy.

I wake up in my bed the following morning.

"You've got some explaining to do," Mariel greets me as soon as I open my eyes.

I blink at her.

Images of an angry Tate pinning me to a wall flash in front of my eyes, then the encounter with the strangers, Tate's power saturating the air. Then it gets a bit hazy. I scrub my hands over my face.

"What do you mean?"

She gives me a stern look.

"Our delicious and slightly scary centurion rushed from the common room like a demon last night, then he gets back and deposits your drunken ass in your bed and tells me we are excused from training and you should rest..." She raises her eyebrows. "And you want to know what I mean? What the fuck happened last night?"

"I was at dinner at my cousin's and drank a bit more than was good for me." I jump out of bed, and the world spins slowly and unsteadily. My stomach rebels.

I rush into the bathing chamber and fall to my knees in front of the toilet.

"Yeah, that part is obvious," Mariel comments dryly, pulling my hair out of my face before I spill the meager contents of my stomach into the bowl. "Better?"

I nod weakly.

"Nice try, but that doesn't get you out of answering me," she teases as I rinse my mouth and splash water on my face.

I roll my eyes, making her smile.

"I decided to walk home and ran into Kyronos on the way. That's all." I shrug and try to shake off the guilt about lying to her.

She doesn't look convinced, but leaves the room while I jump in the shower.

My thoughts drift back to last night as hot water cascades over my body.

Who were those men cornering us, and ... what the hell was that with Tate's gift? A shiver runs down my spine when I remember how good his magic felt as it seeped into me. How good it felt when he held me.

He called it power drunk. But how is that even possible? I got drunk on Tate's gift? Even in my head, that sounds ... dirty.

Wait, what happened to those men?

I get ready as quickly as possible, and we arrive just in time for the last part of training.

"Look who got done with their beauty sleep," Miller comments. "But it worked, ladies." He grins at us.

"You want to tell us we looked ugly yesterday?" I ask and chuckle when he blushes and backpedals. "I'm just fucking with you." I grin.

"I hope not," a calm voice says behind me, and I close my eyes. Shit.

His gift is like a physical caress on my skin, and a pleasant shiver runs up my spine. "Feeling better?" he asks, and I nod, not trusting my voice.

I clear my throat and make sure everyone is out of earshot. "What was that yesterday? Who were those men?"

"A power play, nothing more."

"If you think you will get rid of me with just that tidbit, think again." I cross my arms, stepping right in his way.

He huffs out a breath. "Alright." He grabs my shoulder, sending sparks through my body and steers me farther away from the others.

"We had a no-touching agreement," I grumble, hating how much I want to lean into him.

"You mean the one you broke last night, when you snuggled into me and asked me to dance?"

"I did not..." *Shit, I totally did.* "That doesn't count."

"Of course it doesn't." I'm unsure if he's agreeing or mocking me. My getting drunk on his power hangs between us, unspoken but tangible.

"What happened to the men?" I ask.

"I couldn't let them walk away," he states, watching my reaction.

"I'm sorry," I whisper, and his eyebrows jump up.

"There is nothing to be sorry for. They were there because of me. Trying to get to me through you." He shakes his head. "If anyone has to be sorry, it's me."

I swallow at the implication that someone can hurt him by hurting me.

"I... I still don't like that you had to kill them for—"

Tate interrupts me. "Oh no, I killed them very much for myself." He chuckles darkly. "Maybe that makes me the monster my brother tries to paint me as." He pauses, adding more softly, "Some things color a soul, I guess." There is something else in his eyes, another message, but I can't grasp what it is.

We are occupied with training and classes, and still, I can't stop thinking about what happened.

When we head to the library to study and I have to look up something for Herbs and Poisons, I add a book about *Rare Medical Conditions in Gifted* to my stack of books before making my way back to my friends.

Calix and Mariel are busy with their own studies, so I pull out the heavy tome and check the glossary. My breath catches when I see the phrase Tate used: Power Drunk. With sweaty fingers, I find the page indicated and start reading.

*The phenomenon described as power drunk happens if a gifted person, who is able to draw from the power of gifted or other sources, takes in too much power in a short amount of time. The symptoms are described as euphoric and slightly intoxicated.*

Well, that matches how I felt that night and my rather hazy memory of it.

*If the state is kept up over long periods through repetitive power intake, or the patient takes in more than he can handle, it can develop into a full-blown intoxication. For more information on symptoms, consult Magic Intoxication.*

No, thanks. I have no intention of giving myself nightmares by looking up how I could have ended up.

*There are varying reports on toxic levels, which lead to the belief that toxicity depends on the person's innate power.*

*The occurrence of the condition is overall rare, as the transfer of power requires a high level of trust from both parties. Historically, there have been a handful of instances where the person drawing power was able to overpower the other, taking their gift by force...*

What? I look around, sure that anyone watching me has to be able to see what I did. But the library is still empty apart from Calix, Mariel, and me. And they are not looking at me.

It didn't feel like I was taking from Tate by force. With the amount of power he displayed, I don't even think I would have been able to. So does that mean he let me?

*...other than that, there are only reports of power being shared between family members or lovers, since the process is an intimate one. Allowing the other's gift, a part of them if you will, to enter your body...* My eyebrows rise. Shit, that does sound intimate. The visual description sparks memories, making me squirm in my seat. I close the book.

Okay, no more getting drunk on Tate's power, but how did I do it? Through my magic gift? Through our past? Or both?

Since the night of the attack, something changed between us. We still have awkward moments and love to piss each other off, but it all has a more teasing note now. And as much as I try, I can't shake his comment that someone would be able to hurt him by hurting me.

I'm slipping, I'm truly slipping, and all my previous arguments sound hollow now.

"Tate has kindly volunteered for this demonstration." I grin at him, and the look he gives me in return has Alessia, the slave girl, chuckling nervously.

He stands next to me after our training ended to help me teach her. He is indulging me in his spare time, and that warms my chest in a way it shouldn't.

Alessia shifts her weight from one foot to the other, betraying how uncomfortable she feels out here in the arena. Her soft, slender figure and pale skin declare that all of this is out of her comfort zone. But she is here, and I admire her for it. She wants to learn, so I'm happy to teach.

The sun is as harsh as ever, and there is only a thin sliver of shade starting to spread over the scalding hot sand. Tate has lost his shirt, and I do my damn best not to stare at him. Or to notice the slight sheen of perspiration on his skin. Or to remember how his body would feel under my fingers. No, not thinking about it at all.

He raises his eyebrows at me, and there is a slight smile on his lips. I narrow my eyes at him, and he throws up a shield.

My grin widens. No reason to hold back then.

I attack. In quick succession, I slam my elbow in an upward motion against his nose, only to pivot, striking his Adam's apple with my other elbow. My fingers slam into the shield in front of his eyes, before I bring my arms out and slam my palms over his ears, and then knee him in the groin. He doesn't even flinch.

"Yes, don't hold back," he comments dryly. "I could get the impression you care otherwise."

"Just trying to make it realistic. Don't whine, I just hit your shield."

"Yeah, thank fuck. Only you didn't know that when you went for my nose. Or did you?"

"Maybe I wanted to give you a chance to practice healing," I comment sweetly.

"Too kind of you."

I chuckle. "Relax, I knew you had your shield up." That instantly catches his attention, but before he can ask questions, I turn back to my student.

"Memorize those targets, it's where you can do the most damage with the least effort." I go through the motions again, with explanations this time.

"The nose is sensitive no matter the species." My fist connects with Tate's shield. "Since you are not used to hitting, don't use your hands. You'll probably break something." I show her again, using the heel of my hand and then my elbow. "Your elbow and knee are the best bets. It's less likely you'll hurt yourself." I demonstrate how kneeing a man in the groin would make him double over, which in turn makes it easy to reach his nose with a knee next. Tate goes along with it.

"Don't hold back," I tell her. "You are going for maximal damage. Envision you want his nose to come out the other side."

Alessia nods.

"If he needs force to get a girl to notice him, it will probably improve his looks too," I add with a smirk, and she giggles.

We go through the simple but effective strikes again, and since she is too shy to train with Tate, I do, while he shields me. I show her a few moves to get out of a man's hold after that, and the half hour flies by quickly.

"You did very well," I tell her proudly, and the way Alessia beams at the praise transforms her whole face. "If you find someone to train with, do it daily. Until you don't have to think about it. And whenever I'm here, we can train too."

"Thank you so much!" She throws her arms around me, and I make plans to get her out of here. Maybe Tynan would help me with that?

However, I don't say anything. I don't want to get her hopes up until I know more. So I just squeeze her and give her an encouraging smile, before she vanishes back into the belly of the arena.

When I turn, Tate is watching me.

"What?"

"The way you care for others..." He shakes his head. "It's hard for you to shut someone out, isn't it?" And there is something like hope in his eyes when he says it.

"Yeah, I've heard it all before." I roll my eyes. "I should be harder, control my feelings, blah, blah, blah," I say.

"No, I think it's admirable."

That comment throws me. Is he joking? I narrow my eyes at him, trying to figure him out, but he gives me nothing.

"Let's get back. You need your flight practice."

I scoff. "Thanks."

"I didn't mean it like that."

I glare at him, but he is right. I have a really hard time shutting him out lately.

# TWENTY-SIX

## TATE

Today is the final part of the competition. This evening, we'll know the flight to represent our Aerie, and I pray to all the gods who are willing to listen that it will be ours. We came in third in the first round, a fact that irks me. I try especially hard to ignore the fact that Ara could have secured a win easily, but chose not to.

We still have a chance, but we also have strong competitors.

The atrium is already filled with everyone competing, while riders, who are not part of the trials, line the windows of the building around us. Some even climbed up on the roofs. There is chatter, laughter, and excitement.

Despite what is in it for us, most riders see this as a day full of entertainment, a friendly competition, nothing more.

Everyone hopes for a flight of their own division to win, and I have seen coins change hands more than once, but overall, the atmosphere is festive, and no matter who wins, they will celebrate it. But that is not enough for me, I need us to win.

"Okay, everyone, we went over this." I raise my voice to be heard over the ruckus around us. "You all know which competitions you are in?" My flight nods. "You planned it out as well?" I address the decurions of the other three flights, and they confirm. "Well then, riders, may the gods be in your favor and all your strikes hit true. And remember, no unnecessary risks," I let my eyes rest on Ara. At first, she gives me nothing, but then there is a nearly imperceptible nod, and that is more than I hoped for.

My sword fight is up first, so I don't have time to dwell on it. My first opponent is a middle-aged rider from the northern division. Like many riders, including myself, he fights with two short swords. And while he is very skilled, I'm faster, a detail that helps me win the first round.

All of the competitions today are elimination style. Two riders of every flight compete per discipline, so thirty-two riders start.

Three rounds will occur in the first half of the day, with a resting period following. The semi-finals and finals of every discipline will take place in the afternoon and evening. It will be a long day and hopefully a victorious one.

Everyone starts in two disciplines, and there isn't much time to observe others, but since our names keep showing up on the blackboard announcing the next rounds, we are doing great so far.

I planned for this since I started at the Aerie, choosing every member of my flight for their skills and gifts. Everyone but Ara and her friends, another way she manipulated my efforts, while accusing me to manipulate her.

*Was that your way of softening me up for this damn competition?*

The crowd cheers, and I turn toward the noise. Just in time to see Ara rise and dust herself off. Her victorious smile dims when she notices me, then Cassius hugs her, congratulating her on the win.

Irritation sweeps through me, and I turn away.

Keeping her alive and winning the trials is all that matters.

My opponent doesn't even know what hit him when I work off my anger on him. He doesn't get to do anything but parry, retreating again and again, and finally ends up in the dust, my crossed swords at his neck.

I take a deep breath and release it slowly, centering myself once again. It doesn't matter ... it can't matter what Ara is doing.

My other discipline is less action and more concentration, focus. Ara sparring, watching someone go at her, maybe even hurting her, would not help with that, so I leave the sword fights behind and watch Mariel Tethys destroy her opponent by locating areas on a map at lightning speed instead.

Observation is ingrained in my soul, it's survival. So spotting the illusions created to camouflage and trick us is easy, and I breeze through the competitions, effortlessly advancing to the third round.

"You look pleased," Tanner steps up next to me, studying the blackboard, and then grins. "And I see now why. Even our first years are still in. I'd say this round goes to us, eh?"

"Let's not count the chicks before they hatch, but yes, we are doing pretty well so far." My eyes run over the list. The names for the third round of competitions with spears, swords, crossbows, and daggers are already complete. The other rows are still missing a few names. "Have you had a chance to watch one of the newcomers compete?"

"Our redhead threw a guy nearly twice her size to the mat as if he weighed nothing, and Ara flew through the first round of the obstacle course. I didn't have the chance to watch their other rounds, though."

"What about Ilario?"

"He is the flirting champ, and wrapped Zaza around his fingers last time I saw him," he winks, and his white teeth sparkle against his sun-tanned face. "No, all jokes aside. Zaza said he did well in his first two rounds. And since she is a queen with daggers, I'll take that to mean he dominated them."

I nod, watching a rider write down the missing names in the rows of the map orientation and obstacle course. We are still in. All of us, and I dare to hope.

Zaza is laughing about something Calix said, while they walk up to us. Seems like Jared is getting competition.

*"And you don't?"* Daeva taunts, but I don't allow myself to get distracted by that thought. Today is only about the qualification. There is no space for anything else.

The first ones to drop out are Boko, whose opponent's aim with the spear was just a tad better, and Calix, who did great at tracking, but the seasoned rider he was up against was a bit quicker.

It's alright, I tell myself we can still make it, but the two flights competing with us for the top are not doing badly either.

## ARA

"And I thought for the final rounds, we'd change it up a little." Foley's eyes land on me. This can't mean anything good. "Since I don't want to spoil the surprise, the candidates will start right after each other. Please take your marks."

I exchange a glance with Jared. That we are both still in bodes well for our team, but after Foley's comment...

A loud gong gives us the go, and I start into the obstacle course that has been changed again. But how much so becomes clear once I'm balancing over the first beam. Suddenly, it shudders and starts to rotate. Right when I'm in the middle of it, how convenient.

I leap for the platform and grunt when my feet miss it by a finger's length. I throw my arms out, and the air is driven out of me when my upper body hits the edge, my fingers searching for purchase on the wooden boards. A splinter lodges under one of my fingernails, and I curse.

A short push against the still rotating beam helps me push myself fully up, and I scramble to my feet, trying to ignore the pain in my chest and fingers. I hiss as I pull out the splinter and curse when it breaks off.

This round will be different, alright.

My relief of having solid planks under my feet is short-lived when something whistles past my face and makes me stumble back a step. Huge alternating pendulums swing in front of me; they must have been released once I stepped on the platform. They swing in a pattern that requires me to get the timing right or risk being pushed off the beam that starts right in front of me. Great.

I focus on my next steps. And once the pendulum passes me, I slip past it. The next one swooshes past my face before I take another step and inch my way across.

I'm careful this time and prepared for something else to come at me as soon as I leave the last pendulum behind.

Whatever else Foley planned for me, it won't surprise me. Or so I hope. Because let's face it, he did plan this for me and not the other three contestants.

It's a good thing I'm alert, and I managed to duck in time for the blade to miss me. Ducking, weaving, jumping, and rolling, I make my way to the rope waiting for me at the end, pretending I'm in a sword fight instead of an obstacle course.

Misjudging the speed of a blade coming at my foot makes me stumble and fall, but thankfully, the leather holds. Doing the rest with a cut-up foot would not have been fun at all. My hands throb from the impact, my finger pulses, a shallow scratch mars one of my palms, but other than that, I'm fine.

I'm nearly through the slashy part of the course when a blade comes hurtling out of nowhere, thumping to a quivering stop where my hand was seconds ago.

I stay low, conscious of the metal rotating above my head, and try to figure out where it had come from. When I find Foley's hateful gaze on me, I have the answer. Another blade comes flying, and I charge forward. My only hope to get out of this alive is to be faster. To make myself into a difficult target.

I'm gaining on Jared, who is right in front of me, hangmanning over open space.

Dammit. I will be a sitting duck on there.

I look around searching for alternatives, when I spot a dangling rope on the stud right behind me. I don't take the time to consider, but grab it and take a running start, just when Jared reaches the other side. At my pounding steps, he whirls around, his eyes widening slightly, but I'm already airborne. I have one take at this. Swinging back will slam me against the wood it is attached to. So, when I reach the highest point, I let go and pray it is far enough. I drop down, the platform coming closer.

Shit, this is going to be close again. I brace for the impact and collide with a solid body. Jared's arms come around me, steadying me.

"I've got you. Thank the heavens I have you," he mumbles, pulling me away from the edge. "Why did you—"

But he doesn't get farther than that before an arrow sinks into the space I just occupied. "Fuck," he breathes. "Let's go. Go ahead so I can see you," he instructs, while we run for the net right in front of us.

My senses are sharp for any sounds or movements while I speed up even more, taking the course in a well past reckless manner, determined to get out of here alive.

A gift is reaching for me, and when I realize it's Jared's, I let it. There is a thump behind me when a star-shaped throwing blade comes to a quivering stop, a few steps behind me. Thank the gods the aim was off.

I glance at Foley, and I'm surprised to find his gaze focused on the space between Jared and me. Then I realize what's going on—illusions. Jared is keeping me safe from Foley's special treatment by making it seem like I'm a few steps farther back.

There is a gasp behind me, followed by the sucked in breath of the crowd below. When I whirl around I find Jared missing. Then I spot the fingers at the edge of the platform.

I hurry back and throw myself on my stomach at the edge of it, clasping Jared's arms.

"Go on, I've got this," he grunts. But one of his hands is bloody and slipping because of it.

"On three," I tell him. Ignoring the sting when something grazes my right leg.

"If you get shot because of me..." On my command, he hoists himself up, while I pull and then scoot back to give him room to scramble up the rest of the way.

"That I wasn't yet is thanks to you," I tell him. "So it would be especially shitty to let you fall, don't you think?" I help him up, and both our eyes widen when something hurtles through the space between us.

"Go," he yells, and we turn and run.

I concentrate on the course in front of me and try to speed up even more. Jared's magic that faltered during his fall is back, but it's only a matter of time until Foley realizes what's going on.

I don't even think of our competitors, while we rush through the rest of the course. When I jump to the ground, Jared drops his illusion. I land, roll, and come up. My hands instantly find my knees, taking in gulping breaths.

My throat is raw, a coppery taste on my tongue, and my heartbeat is so loud it drowns out everything else, but I'm still alive. I'm tempted to flop down on my back, but that would be a bad idea since someone might still be aiming at me. Jared is next to me within seconds.

"Let's get you out of here," he murmurs, stepping between me and Foley, shielding me with his body.

"Thank you," I whisper.

"Don't mention it. And I thank *you*," he says. "Not many would have come back."

"I'm glad I did," I tell him, and I'm rewarded by one of his brilliant smiles.

"Me too. Let's go see the healers."

# TWENTY-SEVEN

## ARA

While the solo competitions have gone well for us, my refusal to use my ability to find the objects has cost us. We are all gathered in the atrium while Janus announces the winner.

It's the flight from the Eastern Division. We only come in second.

My stomach drops, my whole body suddenly heavy with dread, while my eyes find Tate.

His posture is tense, his jaw clenched, and the look in his eyes is like a slash to my soul. It's like he lost much more than a competition.

The need to comfort is like a physical pull and if I could take away some of his pain, I would. I step up to him, but he only notices me when my hand lands on his arm.

"I'm sorry—"

"It's fine." He shrugs off my hand. The subtle movement is like a blow to my core, my breath suddenly stuck in my chest. "Who cares about those stupid trials anyway, right?" He throws my words back at me.

"No, that's not—" I shake my head.

"It's over," he snaps.

"If—" I try again, not daring to touch him this time.

"I'm fine, Ara. Just leave, okay?" He walks away while I draw in a stuttering breath and fight to keep the brittle smile on my face.

It shouldn't hurt like this. It's what I wanted, isn't it?

I press my lips together to hide the trembling, while the pit in my chest grows until I wonder why I don't fold in on myself.

"Hey, you okay?" Jared asks me.

I shrug. "Yeah, sure."

"That wasn't about you. You know that, right?"

I shrug again, because it felt damn personal.

Jared searches my face, and whatever he finds makes him take a deep breath. Oh, how much I wish I were able to keep up a mask like my brother or Tate.

"He worked toward this since we lost my brother in an attack years ago." He looks over at where Tate is packing up. "Our brother," he corrects himself. "Louis always was as much his as mine." He gives me a sad smile. We both watch Tate, while he moves around and talks to people, who seem oblivious to the pain radiating from him.

"Have you experienced one of his nightmares?" Jared asks softly.

I shake my head, not trusting my voice.

"They give me the chills just listening to him," he whispers.

"What are they about?"

He gives me a sad smile. "He never talks about any of it. Everything I know I pieced together from what he spilled while sleeping and his actions." He looks at Tate, who was stopped by another rider. "I might not know why he renounced his title, but I know him. So I stick around and go along for the ride, no matter how bad-tempered or grouchy he is, because I know it's worth it. He is worth it."

"He's lucky to have you," I murmur.

Jared shrugs. "That's what brothers are for."

I nod, thinking of my brothers, but then grimace when I think of Tate's.

"Or should be," Jared amends. "The next time I see Fred, I'll set his head straight. Entitled bastard."

That surprises a snort out of me. I would love to see that.

"What?" he asks. "Not my fault if he can't see past his bruised ego."

A giggle escapes me. "You are aware that you're talking about our future king?"

Jared just shrugs. "For me, he will always stay the little bugger who ran after us and tried to compete with Tate at every turn." He pauses, his face grim. "But he can hold a grudge, I tell you that. And now with a crown on his head." He grimaces. "Don't get me wrong, Fred is not a bad man, but I don't remember him as a farsighted, wise, or even-tempered person either, so I'm not sure what to expect of him as king."

I watch Tate walk away. His pain is not visible in his posture, which is still straight and unyielding, but it's in the angle of his head in his downcast eyes, and I ache to hug him, to hold him, but he would push me away. And that hurts more than I ever imagined.

"Please don't give up on him," Jared murmurs.

When I don't show any reaction, Jared sighs.

"He cares." His words jolt through my body, but he continues oblivious to the chaos inside me. "You should have seen him when you were out after Picking..." He shakes his head. "I've never seen him like that. He's lost so much already, but I'm not sure he would survive losing you." He squeezes my shoulder, and when I still don't react, he gives me another sad smile and walks away.

"All right, everyone. Let's get moving," he hollers at the rest of our flight.

I'm frozen, lost, unable to process Jared's words.

*He cares.*

*I'm not sure he would survive losing you.*

He has to be lying. My breaths are shallow pants, my eyes not focusing on anyone or anything.

*"Just keep breathing, you're doing great,"* Solaris coos, feeling my struggle for composure.

A single tear gets away from me and lands in the dust at my feet. Without a word to anyone, I head back to the sleeping quarters. I have to reach my room. I have to reach it before the ice melts off and bares the destruction beneath.

*"Don't you think talking to him would be a good idea?"* Solaris asks.

*"What would be the point? I promised to marry his brother. I'm not getting out of that. If what Jared said is true…"*

I hug myself, like it might help hold me together. As if my arms could keep the pieces contained so I can shatter in silence.

*"If I give him hope now and then, he has to watch me marry his brother…"*

A sob escapes me, echoing in the empty hallway, and I walk faster.

*"How about you just tell him that? Put it all out there."*

*"Now? On top of this defeat?"* I shake my head. The defeat I caused. The thought is like a claw digging into my chest. I'm responsible for his pain. All the past weeks … it's my fault.

*"So what now?"*

*"I don't know."* My heart breaks for him. I quite literally feel a crack, like something shatters inside me. *"It has to stop hurting at some point, right?"* I whisper.

*"We can still go for the crazy bird lady,"* Solaris tells me, and my chuckle ends in a sob.

Tears blur my view as I rush down the corridor, desperate to reach my room. Jared has to be lying, though. Right? Because if he isn't … my chest cramps.

I bend over, bracing my hands on my knees, desperate to draw in a full breath. But I can't fucking breathe.

If Jared was telling the truth… Tears cascade down my cheeks.

*What have I done?*

A whimper claws up my throat.

"Ara? What happened?" Hurried steps accompany the words, and then Joel pulls me into his arms. I hold on to him like I'm drowning, a shuddering sob ripping out of me. There is another voice I dimly recognize as Mariel's, but I just concentrate on my fingers digging into Joel's back.

"You're scaring me," he murmurs. And I don't blame him. I'm scared too. "Talk to me," he urges. But where do I begin?

How do I speak words I buried so deep I can't grasp anymore? How do I tell him what I fear and want to be true at the same time? How do I tell him that I destroyed the one thing that could have been the best part of my life?

When I stay silent, he shuffles me along, and I hold on to him. He is familiar, he is safe. There is a hushed conversation and a door closes, and then there is silence.

It's only when I quiet down and get myself back under control that I realize we are in Joel's room, and I soaked his shirt with my tears. But he waves off my mumbled apology.

"If Kyronos did something..."

"No, he didn't do anything." I shake my head. "It's just..." To my embarrassment, my eyes fill again. "Uh shit, not again." I hiccup, causing a tiny smile on Joel's face.

"You never liked crying in front of others," he remarks. "But if you need to talk, or a shoulder to cry..." he offers.

I lean into him, resting my head on his shoulder. "Then I know where to find you." I give him a watery smile. "Thank you, I guess I needed that."

"Anytime."

# TWENTY-EIGHT

## ARA

IT'S BEEN TWO DAYS SINCE MY BREAKDOWN, AND I AVOID TATE as much as I can. I don't meet his eyes. I make sure to leave the room before anyone else. Since we are no longer competing, there is less training. When Tate lets me know he'll pause my training for a few days too, I'm nothing but glad. Mostly.

I miss him, but I try to convince myself that he did me a favor. The fates didn't plan a happy ending for us, and that won't change.

I walk next to Joel, and we are on the way to the refectory. Ever since my breakdown, he hovers around me, looking at me like he expects me to crumple again. It's driving me nuts.

Someone laughs, and I look up.

Two female riders stand in the corridor ahead, next to Jared and Tate. I recognize one of them as the woman who went looking for Tate months ago at one of the outposts.

I shouldn't care. It's the confirmation I needed. It's abso-fucking-lutely great if he's moved on and there is nothing to Jared's words. If...

But there is pain. Pressure, like someone wrapped his hand around my heart and squeezed. A damning jolt like I missed a step.

The woman throws her head back and laughs again, only to flutter her lashes at Tate a moment later. She taps his chest playfully, and there is a twist in my chest that is anything but pretty. Joel touches my shoulder, and I only now realize I've stopped in the middle of the hallway, my eyes glued to Tate.

His demeanor is as stoic as always, but *she* can't keep her damn hands off him.

I glare at the disgusting appendage, currently attached to his arm. When my eyes come back up, I find Tate's gaze on me, a barely there smile curling the corners of his mouth. So he shakes my hand off, but her hands can be all over him?

My blood starts to boil.

Message received. So much for all the guilt and pain of the last days.

Bastard.

My skin heats. I walk away and ignore Joel calling my name.

I'll not give Tate the satisfaction of turning into a fireball in front of his eyes.

But he follows me. I feel his presence behind me, and quicken my steps. I barely set a foot into the deserted corridor to the sleeping quarters when I realize my mistake. I whirl around, but he is already there, stalking toward me like a wolf scenting blood in the snow.

His gaze is intense and fixed on me, and he still has that tiny smile on his face, as if all of this amuses him. I see red.

Instead of backing away, I move forward, my blood boiling. His smile widens when I push him.

Oh, he finds this entertaining? How dare he make me believe he cares only to dismiss me? How dare he let her touch him?

I keep pushing him, and he lets me, only to spin us around lightning-quick once we reach the wall. His body cages me in, his arms braced against the wall on either side of me. I swallow.

"You only have to say it," he growls.

"Fuck you."

"A damn shame, change one of those words, and we both get what we want," he purrs.

"If you touch me, I'll remove your hands—permanently."

"And here I thought we were making progress. Don't worry, I won't touch you until you beg me to."

He gives me a smirk that makes me want to bite him ... hard. His grin widens like he knows exactly what I'm thinking.

His presence, his scent, his magic, the heat of his body ... he is all around me, muddling my senses, drugging me. A small gasp leaves my lips, and he shifts closer.

"I'm sorry I snapped at you," he whispers. "I'm sorry I pushed you away," I shake my head in denial of what I see in his eyes.

"Just ... just go," I rasp.

"Are you sure?" He looks down at his chest, where my hands are fisted in his shirt. How did they get there? I let go and cross my arms to keep them from reaching out again. He smirks.

"Who is now not able to keep her hands off?" His voice is low and seductive, and I have to lock my muscles to keep from leaning in. He is so close. His breath caresses my neck, and I just know my knees will go weak if his lips make contact. I close my eyes.

His chuckle is dark and sultry, and my eyes pop open at the sound.

My breath is shallow, too fast. My head falls back against the stones, baring my throat, as if in surrender. His eyes flare.

"Say it," he whispers.

I roll my head from side to side, denying him. And myself. Because this will not end well. There is no future for us, and letting him close only to have to let him go will destroy me.

"You want me," he breathes onto my skin, and I shudder. "If I'd touch you, we both know what I would find, how fast you would come undone for me." His eyes trace over my skin, where it pebbles at his words, and his voice turns husky. "And you would let me, wouldn't you?"

I don't say anything, because let's face it, he is right.

"But unlike you, I keep my word!" He pushes off the wall, taking a few steps back. "You might want to take your time. You look flushed." He turns and strides off.

Asshole.

I stay where I am, my chest heaving like I just came back from our morning run, my whole body still humming from his closeness. My core pulses and throbs with the need ... for him.

I close my eyes and take a deep breath.

"I never thought you'd be cruel." My eyes fly open, and Mariel steps out of the shadow next to the staircase.

"What are you talking about?"

"You know that Joel loves you, right?"

I stare at her. "What?" I laugh. "He loves me like a brother, nothing else." I shake my head at her.

"No, Ara, he doesn't, and that is why your behavior is..." She shakes her head. "How can you get his hopes up one minute only to be with *him* in the next?" She tilts her head in the direction Tate just left.

"Mariel, you have it all wrong. I've known Joel all my life, and there is nothing between us." I cross my arms. "And I was not with Tate in any way."

"I have eyes, Ara. Both of you were that close"—she lets her fingers nearly touch—"to ripping each other's clothes off. And just a few days ago, you let Joel hold you while you cried and crashed in his arms."

"Joel knows there is nothing between us but friendship."

"So you don't love him?"

"I do love him ... like a brother. And he knows, Mariel. He knows about Tate, and he has always known that I won't end up with him."

"Why? Isn't he good enough for you?" She suddenly sounds accusing.

I shake my head at her. "No." I sigh. "I'm promised to someone. I have been since I was a little girl, and he knows."

She gapes at me before shaking her head. "Betrothals can be broken."

"No." I give her a sad smile. "Believe me, there is nothing but death freeing me from this one."

"Are you serious?"

"Deadly." A snort escapes at my choice of words, and I bite my lip to keep in the sob that wants to follow. "I screwed up so bad, Mariel." I give her a sad smile.

"So something is going on with our centurion." She watches me. "I figured as much, with all that tension between you two. Do you love him?"

I give her a long look. "I'm promised to his brother."

Mariel's eyes widen. "Fuck."

"You can say that again." My shoulders slump.

# TWENTY-NINE

## TATE

ARA IS QUIET AND MONOSYLLABIC FOR THE REST OF THE DAY, and if possible, she avoids me even more. Maybe I shouldn't have pushed, but when I saw her reaction to Jen touching me, I didn't stop to think.

I don't want to stay away anymore. I can't. Her reaction gave me hope, and I'm determined to explore it. But I have to eliminate the threat first. It might also be my only chance to get closure, now that we are out of the trials.

I don't know why Silence helped me, but I hope whatever his interests are, they'll sway him to help me again.

Instead of going to the spider's house myself, Daeva keeps an eye on it and trails Silence once he leaves. I catch up to him two streets down.

With the precautions he took last time, I don't make the mistake of approaching him again and use my gift to address him from afar instead. At my voice next to his ear, he whips around, looking more shaken than I have ever seen him before. He glares when he spots me, and I suppress a grin. So he's not as unflappable as he always seems.

My initial request for help is met with reluctance.

"Why would I help you with this?" he asks, while continuing down the street.

"You spoke of interests last time, and I thought maybe it would be in your interest if I eliminated the threat."

He sneaks a glance over his shoulder.

"What is your plan?"

I elaborate my plan, which essentially comprises of offering myself as bait to draw the men out. If Silence leaks information about a meeting with me in a dark and quiet corner of Telos, I hope they can't resist making a move.

I rely on their desperation after weeks of no progress to bring them out and make them careless.

"It's risky," he replies.

"It's my risk and not yours."

"You just want me to leak information, nothing else?" After some contemplation, he agrees, and I'm about to turn away when he adds something that lets my blood run cold.

"They found a dead rider not far from here this morning, a blond woman."

My thoughts instantly jump to Ara, but I saw her this morning.

"When?" I breathe

"Early, just after sunrise. It wasn't her."

The weight that falls from my shoulders has me nearly floating up. Of course, it's not her. She's heeded my warning so far and hasn't gone out alone again. But still, for a second, I wasn't able to breathe.

"I just thought I'd let you know."

"How do you know it wasn't her?" I ask, still puzzled why he's showing so much interest in all of this.

"I checked." That's his scarce answer before he turns onto another street and vanishes from sight.

I turn back to the academy, my thoughts already spinning like wheels on a chariot, planning the upcoming encounter.

What I'm doing is dangerous. I'm well aware of that. There are a lot of variables I can't control, but I'm also out of options. I need the threat gone, especially now when another sky rider—a blond woman —has turned up dead.

The coincidence is too big.

I have a date and a time. Now, I just need to make sure that no one else gets involved. I have to think of a good excuse for Jared's sake. Otherwise, he'll come, and there is no way I'll risk getting Nan's second son killed, too.

Once I'm back at the Aerie, I check my armor, sharpen my swords, and contemplate writing letters to Ara and Jared. There is a very real chance that I won't come back. But writing notes feels too much like planning for it, so I don't.

I do not doubt that my enemies will show tonight. For them, there is a kingdom to gain after all.

Finally, there is nothing left but to count the hours until it's evening.

*"I flew over the address you gave Silence,"* Daeva tells me. *"The alley is too small for me."*

*"I know, beautiful,"* I tell her. *"I won't risk you."*

*"That is such rukhshit,"* she explodes and continues to curse me for the next two hours before giving me the silent treatment for two more. We are barely back on speaking terms when I make my way back to Telos's center.

# THIRTY

## ARA

Guilt swamps me while I make my way to the fountain in the merchant quarter. It's evening, and while the sun is still low over the horizon, the shadows are stark and prominent in this old part of Telos. Houses huddle together, and often seem to lean in as if to whisper to one another, arching over the small streets below.

The lamps are not yet lighted, and the bigger streets pulse with life like the main vessels of an organ. But the bustle trickles off the deeper I venture into the small alleys. To blend in, I'm dressed in one of the few dresses I brought, but that is not what makes me uncomfortable.

Since the competition is over for us, I don't think I'm in danger. I'll meet up with a dragon, so why should I be worried? But I go against Tate's orders again. And after our last encounter, the thought of going toe-to-toe with him fills my stomach with swooping

Phoenixes. And the thought of him finding out why I'm here fills my chest with stone.

Nothing happened after I handed over the patrol plan last time, no attack, no engagement at all. And while I heard riders whisper about it, clearly alarmed, it helped to dispel my doubts. Reinforced my trust in Tynan and his men. Nevertheless, I don't even want to imagine how Tate would react if he found out what I did ... and will do again.

I'm early, since I seized the chance to leave without raising suspicion, even if it meant waiting, so when I cast out my perception, looking for Lorcan, I don't expect to find him yet.

But whom I expect to find even less is Tate. Alone.

My interest is piqued.

He moves in the same direction as me, but a little farther down, probably on the next street over. There is still no sign of Lorcan, so I turn onto the small street to my right, moving silently and staying in the shadows while closing in on Tate.

But I'm not the only one.

Three gifted close in on him from three different directions. My brow furrows. That doesn't feel right. Why would they circle him like that? Unless...

He is far from helpless, and he has Daeva. I try to calm myself, sneaking a glance at her dark silhouette against the darkening sky. There aren't many birds that would circle over the city at night, so it has to be her or another Night Raven.

As soon as I reach the alley Tate is in, my stomach drops. It's so narrow that there is hardly enough space for two people to walk shoulder to shoulder, and the roofs are close to touching. There is no way Daeva could come to his aid down here.

I accelerate my steps, and he comes into view ahead of me, his form and movements so familiar. He stops, then leans against a wall in a small square enclosed by houses. I strain my eyes for the others, but I don't see anyone. They can't be far away, though.

Their gift is less powerful than Tate's—whose isn't?—but they should be only a few steps away from him. Where are they?

There is a ripple in the air, and if I hadn't paid so much attention, I would have missed it.

"Tate, shield!" I shout. He whips around at my shout and … shields me. Idiot.

"Watch out!" I scream and witness, horrified, as two shapes jump out of nowhere, wielding daggers. I rush forward only to land on my ass when I run face-first into Tate's shield. Blood trickles down my face, pain radiating from my nose. He closed me in.

"Release me!" I yell, while my eyes are glued to the struggle in front of me. Four men now surround him. One body drops, and I release a relieved breath when I glimpse light hair instead of dark.

My hands trace the wall in front of me, searching for an exit.

*I need out. Out, out, out,* I chant in my head.

There is a sound of pain, and I know it's his. Fury burns through me. This can't be happening. I will not watch helplessly while they cut him down. This damn wall will release me now, or I swear I… I stumble forward, barely catching myself before going down on the uneven cobblestones.

Tate released me, or he is too distracted to keep up his shield. I hurry forward, drawing a dagger, and throw myself at the attacker in front of me. My blow aims for his back, and I growl in frustration when my blade stops with a metallic clang. I should have slit his throat.

The man whirls around, and I block his blade with mine. My body sings with the impact. I jump back, drawing him away, giving Tate more room. My opponent's slashes come fast and sure, at odds with his rugged, beggar-like looks.

He's a trained soldier.

I stumble back a few steps, watching him closely. He sneers at my dress and my long hair and comes at me with swaggering confidence. His mistake.

My dagger grazes his throat, but he is too fast, evading the otherwise deadly strike. He lashes out, his blade aiming at my face. I duck and kick at his legs, trying to destabilize him, but the skirt gets in my way, making me just a little slower than usual. It's enough for him to catch my foot.

Pain radiates up my spine and my arms when I hit the cobblestones. The impact echoes through my body, sharp at first, then dull and throbbing. I scramble backward, jump up ... and trip again. *Damn dress.*

A hand closes around my throat, cutting off my air and shoving me back against a wall.

"And we meet again," a voice whispers in my ear.

I know that voice. I freeze.

Hot pain. Icy terror. Helplessness. Anger. Heat. Emotions and impressions flood my mind, making me dizzy. Why do I know his voice? Whispers of pain and using me ... of plans and princes...

I shake my head. The man pinning me to the wall isn't speaking at all. He increases the pressure, watching me with a smile on his face.

I'm lightheaded and disoriented. This feels surreal, paralyzing like the seeping trickle of a nightmare. My heart beats too fast, and I'm desperate for air, but nothing comes.

Tate roars my name in the distance, cut off by a sound of pain. The sound cuts through my terror like a honed blade, and fury bleeds out of the cut, filling my body like liquid metal. It heats my skin, and my attacker releases me with a yelp.

I don't know who he is, but I know what he is—dead. He tried to hurt me, to hurt Tate, and the knowledge feeds my ire. I erupt in flames, and the man stumbles back.

My blood sings with the panic on his face. I advance slowly, feeding on this fear, on the power of seeing him scared. He hurt me in the past. Glimpses of hazy memories tell me that much, and I will make him pay. And for the first time, the thought of someone being consumed by my flames does not fill me with horror; no, I crave it, but first I want answers.

One look in Tate's direction assures me he is still standing, still fighting. I know he can hold his own, so I suppress the urge to rush to him and instead focus on the man in front of me.

He has answers, and I intend to hear them, preferably screamed.

My flames burn higher, hotter, wrapping me in a nearly white glow. I grin at my prey. His face is sheet white, perspiration on his brow. I've backed him into a corner, and he has nowhere to go.

The dagger in my hand glows red while I play with it, tapping its broad side against my palm.

"I seem to remember you were fascinated by my scars," I murmur, and his eyes widen even more. I keep tapping the glowing metal against my skin in contemplation, and the sight seems to unnerve him.

"What do you want from him?"

"I'm not telling you anything," the man spits.

I shake my head, clicking my tongue.

"That doesn't work for me. How about we give you something to admire, then? To remember me by." He closes his eyes and mumbles something under his breath, a prayer maybe. But a prayer won't help him now. I bring the glowing metal up to his face, and his skin reddens instantly.

I paint a sizzling line starting at his hairline, running along his left eye, past the edge of his mouth to his chin. The stench of burnt flesh sears my nose, but his screams make me smile. More and more memories surface. Of his cruel words and how he enjoyed hurting me.

"And now you're at my mercy. The fates have an interesting humor, don't you think? Let's try this again. What do you want?" He looks left and right, but there is nowhere for him to go.

His eyes come back to me, and he spits, but it never reaches me, consumed by my flames.

I feel his gift reaching for me. His voice turns hypnotic while he instructs me to plunge the dagger I'm holding into my heart. There is a crazed smile on his face when my face goes slack, and I lift the arm. I study the dagger pointing at my chest, before lowering it again.

"No, I don't think I'd like that." His face loses all the color he had left, and he presses against the stones behind him.

"Witch," he hisses.

I tilt my head. "I have no idea what that's supposed to mean, but I think your face needs a bit more symmetry." I grin.

"Ara." Tate's voice sounds desperate, and I whirl around. He's staggering in my direction, his movements sluggish and stiff. He's hurt.

A crackling, bluish light draws my attention to my right, emanating from a ball that illuminates a cruel smile. The man raises his hand, aiming at me.

I've survived it before. I can take it. I steel myself, but when his arm moves down, he pivots and throws the ball ... at Tate.

"No!" I scream, rushing forward even though I know I'm not fast enough. I throw my arm out, flinging my magic at Tate, willing it to keep him safe.

There is an animalistic roar and the wet sound of blood and flesh being scattered. Lorcan has arrived. I recognize his magic. But my eyes never leave Tate.

The lightning envelops him, dances over him, while he shudders and falls, crashing to the ground only seconds before I reach him.

I'm cold to the bone, my flames sputter and die.

No.

Please, no.

The lightning is gone, but he lies still. Too still.

I collapse to the ground next to him, pulling his head into my lap, searching for a heartbeat. But my whole body pulses with panic. How am I supposed to separate his? My fingers tremble while they feather over his face.

"Tate?" Tears mix with the blood of his busted lip and a cut on his cheek. "Gods, please. Please." I sob. "Elet, don't take him from me," I whisper. The thought of him being gone leaves me cold and empty.

My eyes trace his form, searching for movement. *Is he still breathing?* It's hard to tell since he's wearing armor. There is blood on the ground, soaking my skirt, soaking his tunic—it's too damn much blood. But I can't see where it's coming from, and the falling dusk doesn't help either.

My hands slide over the edges of his armor, and as soon as I find a spot that is sticky and warm with his blood, I apply pressure to stop the flow. His markings look harsh against his pale skin.

I exhale, rest my forehead on his, and do the only thing I can. Pray. Promising everything I can think of, if only Elet gives him back to me.

It's at that moment that I realize I might lose him, but I'll never get over him.

"I thought you hated me," Tate whispers. His breath warms my skin, and my eyes fly open, drowning in his. They are filled with a tenderness I thought I'd never see again.

"Yes. Gods, yes, I hate you so much." A laugh mixes with a sob, garbling the last word.

"Liar."

"Shut up and heal yourself, before I strangle you for scaring me like that."

He looks up at me, his gaze so intense my breath catches. "I heard you, you know."

I have no idea how to answer that, so I don't.

"How bad is it?" I break his stare to search his body for injuries.

"Nearly done," he groans. "I hate healing myself."

My eyes trace the alarmingly large patch of darkness at his side. And neither of us has to say it, but we both are aware that he is only breathing because of his gift.

"I promise, red is not your color," I joke, trying to hide my panic at the amount of blood he must have lost.

I wait patiently until he is done healing himself, then I help him up and pull his arm over my shoulder when he wobbles. My gaze wanders back to the spot where I cornered the stranger, but of course, it's empty.

The short way out of the alley is slow going.

The street is quiet again, and a few scared faces peer out at us from windows along the way. As soon as they register Tate's uniform, they nod at us, and no one calls for guards. A small mercy.

My eyes scan our surroundings constantly, ready for another attack. But everything stays quiet. Lorcan seems to have chased off whoever was left. I sense him trailing us.

Daeva is already waiting, and I use the time Tate needs to pull himself up onto her back to reassure Solaris that I'm fine. As soon as he is seated, Tate reaches for me, but I step back.

"Get some sleep and rest," I tell him.

"I'm not leaving you here," he protests, but his eyes are glassy and drooping, and I'd bet he is asleep before they even reach the Aerie. The fight, the wound, and the healing took a lot out of him.

"I'll be fine," I say, deliberately keeping my eyes on Tate's face and off the dragon waiting in the shadows.

Daeva launches into the air, carrying a still protesting Tate away. Once they are gone, I turn to Lorcan.

"Thank you for your help."

He waves me off. "You're not much use if you're dead. What have you got for us?"

"And here I thought we were on the way to becoming friends." I pull out the sheet of paper on which I noted the patrols for next month and hand it to him.

"I don't know about friends, but you're entertaining to have around," he concedes and grins when I roll my eyes.

He slips the paper into his pocket. "See you next month," he says and turns away.

"Wait, I won't be in Avina next month, so we'll have to meet here, and there is a message for Tynan on the back of the plan. If you could make sure he gets it, that would be great."

"Who do you think I'll hand this to? Of course, he'll get it."

"Thank you."

Without another word, he turns and walks off into the dark. I watch his back for a second before I make my way back to the Aerie.

# CHAPTER
# THIRTY-ONE
## TATE

The refectory is alive with chatter and the clinking of cutlery and tableware. Oregano, rosemary, and the scent of roasted meat hang in the air. Our flight is spread out around the table, and I'm content. And the news Janus gave me this morning has nothing to do with it.

Ever since the night of the assassination attempt, the warmth in my chest hasn't lessened. I smile.

"Livia Vaccari is dead," Jared says, setting down a close to overflowing plate before squeezing in next to me. I slide over to make room for him.

"I know," I answer. After Silence's statement, I looked into the supposed robbery. Not that I buy any of it. Who chooses an armed skyrider when there are so many easier targets out there? And why take all her weapons?

Jared's gaze jumps to me. "I would have helped hide the body, you know."

I snort and shake my head at him. "Your impression of me is truly flattering."

"Don't tell me you haven't thought about it," he retorts, and I shrug. What should I say? I have.

"I bet she had a lot of enemies," he adds after a brief pause. It's probably true, but I can't shake the suspicion that she wasn't the target.

"Or someone mistook her for someone else." I voice my worries.

Jared's eyes widen. "You think..."

"You don't? After the men in that alley, Foley's attempt at the obstacle course, and those bastards who tried to cut me down, you think it's a coincidence that a blond female skyrider turns up dead?"

"When you say it like that ... not really."

I give him a grim nod and look over at Ara and her friends. She's magnificent ... the way she jumped in to save my ass ... she can hold her own. But her words, her pleas, still haunt me.

She looks up, giving me a small smile tinged with sadness. Why is she so adamant about pushing me away?

The gods know I'm done fighting my feelings. Now, I only have to convince *her* to do the same.

Jared taps my chin, drawing my attention back to him.

"Just checking if you are drooling already." He smirks and bursts out laughing when I glare at him. "You should talk to her."

"I'm working on it," I grumble, then decide to share the news I just got from Foley.

"The competing flight came back one man short."

That catches his attention. "You mean..."

I nod.

"We are still in the flight games!" Jared shouts loud enough for the entire room to go quiet.

Smiles spread over the faces around me. Ilario is the first to whoop, and then there is whistling and cheering, but nothing compares to Ara's dazzling smile. Her eyes are on me, and the warmth filling my chest grows. Maybe, just maybe, we still have a chance.

It's only hours later that I get proof that something changed between us. Ara bursts into the common room, her eyes finding mine, and I'm up before she reaches me.

"I need your help, please." Her eyes are big and pleading, and no matter what she'll ask, I already know the answer. Her coming to me for help smooths something inside me, like a shard slipping back into place.

"Okay." I follow her out the door.

"It's Sloan," she whispers. "She's in trouble."

"What happened?"

"I don't know. A messenger boy came for me. Sloan needs a healer, and it has to be someone I trust." Her words fill me with warmth.

"Who sent him?"

"I don't know. It wasn't my aunt or uncle. They're away on business," she says. And I frown.

"It could be a trap."

"I know. But I won't stay here and wonder all night if she might be hurt. I need to see her."

She hurries over to the coop, her hands shaky while she drags down Solaris's harness.

"We'll take Daeva. She is less obvious and more comfortable in the dark." Ara bites her lip as she nods. I want to hold her, only I'm not sure she would let me.

I harness Daeva quickly and efficiently, and Ara mounts before I slide in behind her. Her back rests against my front, and I wrap my arms around her. The moment she settles into me, another shard finds its place.

"Where are you meeting her?"

"At Sloan's house."

We are silent during the flight, and only part of it is Ara's worry.

The rest is filled with memories, unspoken words, and a mix of caution and regret.

We have barely set down when the patio doors fly open and out strides... Silence.

"You." The word tumbles from Ara's and my lips, and my insides turn to ice.

How does Ara know him? She gives me a curious look, as if she's wondering the same. We'll definitely discuss this later.

"Hurry," Silence's voice sounds anguished, so we quicken our steps. I'm alert, my hand resting on the hilt of my sword when we enter the house. But I'm not prepared for the sight that greets us.

I've only seen Sloan once—and I was focused on Ara at the time —but when I say I wouldn't have recognized her, it's not due to lack of attention.

No, her face is a beaten, swollen mess, her usually light hair streaked with blood and matted, clumps missing.

Ara makes a sound of distress and hurries to her side, taking her in without daring to touch, her hands hovering over the girl who is like a sister to her. She whirls around, her eyes promising murder.

"If you did this, you're dead," Ara threatens Silence, and I tense. Either she is not aware of who he is, or she doesn't care. With her, it could be both.

"And if I did, I would let you," he bites out, surprising me. "I would never hurt her." He shakes his head, glaring at Ara's suggestion, but his entire demeanor changes as soon as his eyes land on Sloan. And I believe him. The soft brush of his trembling finger pushing Sloan's hair back speaks even louder than the torment in his eyes. "And still it's my fault."

"Who did this?" Ara asks, her stance proclaiming she is ready to take on whoever is responsible.

"I killed him," Silence answers coldly.

"Good." She nods. They share a look of grim satisfaction, forming an unspoken alliance, while they step aside, giving me room to work on Ara's cousin.

Sloan's eyes are closed, but pop open as soon as I touch her, too wide, too twitchy, flitting around until they land on Silence and Ara talking behind me, then they still. Slowly, the tension seeps from her body, like honey melting in the sun.

Nothing I say will make her trust me right now, but having people close who mean safety to her is enough for her to let me proceed.

"I'll have you back in working order in no time," I promise, then get to work. But I can only heal her body. Her mind must heal on its own, and that will take time.

The men who tried to intercept Ara on her way home pop into my mind, and the thought of seeing her like this has me clenching my teeth.

I'm as gentle as possible, and still I can't avoid causing Sloan pain while setting her bones.

"Be careful," Silence snarls. Every whimper draws his attention and has him fighting for control, but I don't hold it against him. The mists know I would be even worse if someone else were healing Ara.

"I wish I could resurrect him, only to kill him again, slower this time." Silence mutters behind me when I straighten Sloan's collarbone. "To see her like this..." His voice breaks, and in my periphery, Ara wraps a comforting arm around him.

She is amazing like that. No matter if admiral, slave girl, or assassin, she treats everyone around her with the same care and respect unless they are stupid enough to get on her bad side. Then she is ruthless. But I'm pretty sure a person's status doesn't make a difference then either.

"She is strong, and Tate is very good. She will be fine in a few minutes," she murmurs, and her trust gives me a peace I didn't know I had been missing.

I concentrate on the woman in front of me, who shares Ara's coloring, and let my healing gift flow into her. She sighs, and the tension trickles from her features, the fine lines next to her eyes and mouth smoothing out one by one.

Her chest rises more noticeably as breathing becomes easier, and her body sinks into the couch beneath her, her eyes drooping.

"Sleep," I tell her. "Your body needs to replenish."

She searches out Silence again, who is still talking to Ara.

"I don't think he's going anywhere," I tell her, and her eyes drift closed.

Ara and Silence are in a heated discussion when I reach them.

"You need to take her with you," Silence says, his eyes finding mine. "Healing and taking her with you—I'll take it as payment for your promise." His voice is a demand, but his eyes are pleading.

"What?" Ara asks, looking from him to me and back, but I nod. He is obsessed with his woman and desperate to keep her safe. I understand that.

"You're leaving for Avina, and I want you to take her with you. Maybe even bring her to the mist court," Silence elaborates, looking at Ara this time. The entire statement makes me frown.

"How do you know we'll go to Avina? And mist court?" I look at him for clarification.

"Of course I know. Interests, remember?" He shrugs. "Mist court is only an expression. I want her so safe no one can find her." He dismisses my question, but Ara's brow furrows while she studies him. "I have a lot of enemies," he continues. "And Telos won't be safe for a while, at least not for anyone close to me."

"What about the spider? Won't he mind about the promise?" I ask.

He waves me off. "Don't worry about him."

Sloan sleeps soundly while we plan.

"I still need to pick up Solaris's harness at Blackstone," Ara offers. "I could leave tomorrow if my centurion lets me go early." She looks up at me. "I would meet the rest of you as planned in Avina a few days later." She shrugs.

Silence nods, but I shake my head.

"You're not going alone."

"I could take Joel," she offers. "I'd bet he would love to see my family and his."

"Absolutely not." I shake my head again.

"How about Calix and Mariel, then?" She goes through every name on our flight until she huffs out a breath in exasperation. "You don't want me to go alone, but I'm not allowed to take someone either?" She throws up her hands.

I bite my lip to smother a grin. "You didn't ask me to accompany you."

Her eyes widen. "I'm supposed to take you home to meet my brothers? No! Absolutely not."

"And still it's going to happen."

"No, Tate, you don't understand…" she groans. "At least one of us will die—either me from humiliation or you because you got too close to me." She throws her hands up. "You don't know what you're asking." She continues explaining why going home with her would be a bad idea, not realizing that every word makes me more determined. She's certain her brothers will come between us, and I'll prove that's not true. They are important to her, so they have to get used to me being around.

CHAPTER

# THIRTY-TWO

TATE

Fortress Blackstone is a formidable keep situated on a summit in the Barrier Mountains. On three sides, its walls end right where the ground drops off into nothing, and since its color matches the dark stone of the rocky cliffs, it appears to be an extension of the mountain itself, granting a majestic view of the valley below.

Nestled at the foot of the mountain lies a small village, with the surrounding fields and pastures bleeding into the lurking mist. The air is colder, crisper, and has a bite that you'll never find in the south. The late afternoon sun casts long shadows, enveloping the valley in premature darkness. It's been three days since we left Telos. The journey had been slow, especially with Sloan coming along, since we made many more stops than we would have otherwise.

She had wanted to fly with Ara, but Ara could not shield her from Solaris's flames for such long periods, so she spent most of the time with me on Daeva.

A fact my bird did not appreciate. That she gave in, I suspect, had as much to do with her adoration of Ara as it did with my orders. Ever since Ara saved my ass in that alley, she can do no wrong in my bird's eyes.

The sound of a horn signals our arrival and draws quite a crowd. A man with the same coloring as Ara, who introduces himself as her brother Luc, helps Sloan off and offers her an arm until they disappear into the main house. Despite all the stops, she still sighs as soon as her feet hit the ground and hobbles along.

Ara, meanwhile, explains the situation to a man with dark hair and eyes and the rank of a commander, smoothing over quite a few of the events of the past weeks, from what I can hear.

I might have bristled at the man's protective stance or the way he pulled her into his arms, if there hadn't been the uncanny resemblance to her oldest brother, Darren.

In combination with his rank, I'm pretty sure this is Ian Blackstone. He confirms my assumption when he introduces himself with Ara by his side.

He whispers something that makes Ara groan and shake her head.

"Centurion Kyronos"—he steps closer—"if I catch you too close—"

"Ian," Ara warns, "don't finish that sentence."

The corner of my mouth twitches. If he thinks he can scare me away, he is sorely mistaken. His brows come down.

"The stable hands will take your harnesses," Ian says, his voice clipped, but Ara shakes her head.

"I have to make a quick trip to the smithy," she tells him, ignoring his disapproving look.

"Don't you want to show our guest his room first?" he asks.

"I'll accompany you," I cut in before Ara has the chance to answer.

"Well then, that's settled," she says. She looks around. "Where is

Tyre?" she asks Ian and then adds for my benefit. "My niece. I would have thought she would be the first out here to meet our birds."

"She and Elena are in Avina with Darren," Blackstone answers.

"Hmm. Then I'll have to introduce her to Daeva there," Ara answers and climbs on Solaris's back. She sounds as if Daeva is a pet that is suitable for a little girl to cuddle. I shake my head. But I shouldn't be surprised, after all, they're related. If she's like Ara, I can even imagine it.

Our birds launch, and after a few quick swoops of their wings, they catch a thermal, circling.

The valley stretches out below us. Despite the looming mist, the sight is peaceful. Tiny white and brown animals dot the luscious green, while horses and carts amble along the road, and tiny figures work the fields.

I turn back to the keep, noticing a half-crumpled tower. The drop next to it is especially steep, like someone cut off part of the mountain. The view from up there is probably quite similar to the one we have now. No wonder Ara is so comfortable flying. She grew up in a place that seems to hover over the world.

We descend in slow circles, details filling in the closer we get to the ground. Most houses are timber-framed, with straw roofing. The road leading to the fortress is the only one paved. It cuts through the middle of the village, coming from a wide stone bridge spanning the nearby river.

We land in front of one of the few stone buildings. The smoke curling out of the chimney, despite the mild temperature and the clanging of metal, would have made it evident where we are, even without the wide-open doors displaying the insides of the smithy.

We dismount and just pass the threshold when Ara groans. The room is hot despite the open doors, the forge radiating heat like the midday sun in Telos. But that doesn't seem to be the problem. Ara's eyes are narrowed at a young man, whose smile slips. He puts down his hammer.

"Ara, so nice to see you," he says, and I bristle at the way his eyes run over her.

"Unfortunately, I can't say the same," Ara snaps. "Is your father in? I'm here to pick up my order."

"Now don't be like that." He comes over, and I step closer. His eyes come to me, and I grin as he stops in his tracks.

He's a little smaller than me, his strong arms and shoulders betraying his profession. My eyes wander over his face, dark hair, dark eyes...

"Yes, you are prettier than him, happy now?" Ara grumbles under her breath, making my grin widen.

"I bet kissing me in front of him would get your point across," I whisper while the smith, after a last look at Ara, wanders off to the back, getting either his father or the harness.

She steps closer, looking up at me, and leans in, but her lips stop just short of touching.

"I'm not some tree you can piss on to mark your territory."

I chuckle. "Well aware. And if they are sniffing, they're already too close."

Ara rolls her eyes but doesn't pull back. Our breaths mingle, and every damn fiber of me yearns to close that gap.

"Who is he?" I ask.

"A mistake. I'm good at choosing the men who run as soon as they learn my name." Her words hold an edge.

Fuck. My stomach twists, and not only because of the implied history. It seems like I truly messed up and hit a sore spot with my behavior.

"Ara, that's not—"

"Ara Blackstone, good to see you again." A loud voice booms through the room, and Ara eases back slowly, deliberately, still holding my gaze. This conversation is far from over.

After a few minutes and some chitchat about countless people, whom I assume live in the village, Ara calls for Solaris to try on the harness.

Metal flows like water under the gray-haired Smith's administration. He makes changes until the harness sits perfectly, and Solaris bursts proudly into flames.

Ara laughs at her bird, the sound flowing over me like liquid sunlight. Flames reflect in the smooth metal, making it seem more gold than silver, and I'm not the only one admiring the sight. Ara stands in front of her bird, her head thrown back, looking up at him while he flares his wings, silhouetting her in flames.

"*Show off,*" Daeva huffs, who circles above, eyeing the spectacle.

We are back in time for dinner, and I receive more than my share of death stares from her brothers when I pull her in front of me to let someone pass on our way to the table, my hands resting on her waist for just a second. Ara grins up at me over her shoulder.

"Ignore them," she whispers. But the impression that they don't like me is only amplified by their pointed comments during dinner.

"You were not exaggerating about your brothers," I tell Ara later when she shows me to my room. She snickers as she leads me down the corridor.

"Every suffering is purely of your own hands," she tells me. "I told you this was a bad idea."

"And I don't mind." I give her a slow smile.

"Okay, well, here's your room." She tucks a strand of hair behind her ear and opens a door, but I'm too focused on the woman standing next to me.

"Why this one?" I ask since I overheard a hissed conversation between her and Ian, who insisted that I'd be in this specific room.

She sighs. "Because it's next to Ian's. And you'd have to pass his door to get to mine... And he's a light sleeper."

I chuckle. "So you didn't tell him I have air magic, then?"

One corner of her mouth curls up into a cheeky grin. "Of course not."

I hum. "And would you open your door when I come knocking?"

She shakes her head, with a tiny smile on her lips. "Good night, Tate."

And when she walks off, I'm left wondering whether she is softening toward me or if it's wishful thinking.

# THIRTY-THREE

## ARA

Being back home is strange, and even worse is knowing Tate sleeps only a few doors down from me. Originally, I planned to visit Tynan and Lyla right away, but with Tate around, I'm hard-pressed to find a convincing excuse to head out, and he can't come.

Sloan is quiet. She hardly spoke during the whole flight, and then shut herself in her room as soon as we arrived. She eats with us, but even then, she only pokes around in her food. Every time someone comes too close, she flinches, so I give her room.

As long as she doesn't talk to me, I can only imagine what she went through. I have a hundred questions, also concerning the man Tate called Silence, but I try to be patient.

I'm edgy. Nervous energy crawls through my veins, making it impossible to fall asleep. After turning and tossing for what has to be more than an hour, I get up and decide to bake.

It's been a long time since I had time for something as simple as that, and it calms me. I started it out of necessity. The only way to get sweet baked goods around here is to make them myself or walk down to the village. So I learned to bake.

We eat most of our meals with everyone else in the Big Hall and don't usually use the small kitchen in the main house. Rustling through the cupboards, I'm pleasantly surprised when I find all the ingredients for chocolate cake.

It seems fitting that I should indulge in the cake I compared Tate to all those weeks ago, when it's him I'm craving.

*Don't go there,* I tell myself.

I set up, and the rhythmic clatter, the easy process of mixing ingredients, is relaxing. Slowly, the muscles in my shoulders loosen, and I lean against the counter, cradling the bowl with one arm while I whisk the batter, keeping up a steady rhythm. My thoughts wander, and I nearly drop the bowl when someone clears his throat.

"Jumpy?" Tate asks from the doorway.

"I nearly dropped the bowl." I scowl at him.

"What are you making?" He steps through the door, and the room suddenly feels so much smaller. I look at the dark batter in the bowl and then up at him.

"Chocolate cake." It's like I threw a spark into a puddle of alcohol. The tension, the heat, it's just ... there. I avoid his eyes by looking back down at the bowl in my arms.

"You had a craving for chocolate cake in the middle of the night?" Tate asks, his voice lower, huskier now.

I swallow. Dammit, why didn't I make something else ... anything else?

"It relaxes me, okay?" I say defensively, and as soon as the word relax comes over my lips, I want to swallow it back down. My gaze flicks to his, and the expression on his face makes my mouth go dry.

Suddenly, I'm too aware of my nightdress, too aware of my bare legs and feet.

*Don't be ridiculous*, I chide myself. He has seen more skin than that before, even during training.

I put the mixing bowl down, turning my back on him, then reach up to get the form for the cake. The dress slides up, the whisper of fabric sliding along the back of my thighs torturously soft, when it's his fingers, his lips I crave. His gaze runs over me like a caress and sets my skin on fire.

Keeping my back to him, I mentally list all the reasons giving in would be a bad idea, but somehow, they are not enough. The air is thick with tension. It's like I'm trying to breathe water instead of air.

Transferring the batter into the form, scraping the bowl clean with a spoon—I have to concentrate on the simple tasks like never before. Then I help the rest of the batter slide off the spoon with my finger, and it's done. I exhale.

The finger comes to my mouth unconsciously, but a firm hand wraps around my wrist, stopping me. Sparks shoot out from where he touches me, heating my blood, and my eyes fly up to meet his.

He is so close. When has he come so close?

"May I?" Tate asks in a low rumble, and my mouth is too dry to speak, so I nod. I pick up the spoon to hand it to him and nearly drop it when his mouth circles my finger instead, sucking it clean.

I can't help the moan falling from my lips, and it vibrates between us, echoed by his groan. His tongue glides over my finger again, and I melt. That's the only way to describe it. My bones liquefy at his touch.

The spoon clatters to the counter, and my hand moves into his hair. The warning bells in my head play a whole concert, but my body gives a resounding fuck you.

I shouldn't.

I should.

I...

Gods be damned. I pull his head down and devour his lips like a starving woman. Our tongues wage a war, the kiss filled with hurt, frustration, and anger—both of us fighting for control.

I only dimly register Tate hoisting me up on the counter, or my legs wrapping around him, pulling him closer. What I do notice is him.

He still tastes of the batter he sucked off my finger. The way his body fits against mine, the heat of his skin through the thin fabric of his shirt. The arm that is wrapped around me possessively and the light rasp of his fingers on my jaw, in my hair. How his lips, his mouth are so achingly familiar. I tighten my hold on him.

This will end in disaster. It will make everything worse... There surely are a lot of reasons this is all wrong, but somehow, they slipped my mind.

"Why?" he whispers against my lips. I pull him closer, silencing him with another kiss. But he stays persistent. "Why are you pushing me away?"

I look pointedly down at the missing space between us. "I'm not."

His patience unravels right in front of my eyes, but that is not the only emotion on his face, and the hurt cuts deeper than anything else.

"Why don't you talk to me?"

"Because there is nothing left to say," I whisper and push against his chest.

"Why are you lying to me, Ara?"

And damn that sentence hits its mark. I'm lying to him on so many levels that hoping it will somehow work out is delusional.

"Let me go. I'm clearly too tired to think straight."

"Oh really? And what about the cave?"

"My brain was frozen."

"You know what?" he leans in, whispering in my ear. "That sounds like a lot of excuses to me."

I shrug. "They are still my excuses, and they are holding up so far."

"Don't be so sure of that," he tells me, and the promise in his voice sends a shudder up my spine. He steps back, both our chests heaving.

"I will finish this cake now." I hop down in the space he created and duck out from the delicious cage of his arms. "You are welcome to stay."

I expect him to leave, to be angry, to demand answers, but he doesn't do any of that. Instead, he sits down at the kitchen table and we talk. He tells me about growing up at the palace and the trouble he and Jared got into. And I tell him about my family and me. We even talk about my curse and my father.

I grin at his surprised face when he tries the still warm cake.

"What? Did you think I'd make you wait for it, and then it wouldn't be edible?"

"Maybe," he answers, and his soft laughter when I swat at him makes my stomach flip-flop.

"I'm great at baking cakes and cookies," I huff in mock indignation.

"Are you sure you didn't mean you're great at devouring them?" he teases, and I nearly swallow my tongue.

I missed him. I missed this light version of him so much that my chest aches with it. He is beautiful on any given day, but like this, with his lips curled into a smile and his eyes sparkling, he is breathtaking.

"A midnight party?" Ian's voice from the doorway breaks the spell I'm under.

"I was just in the mood for baking." Popping the last piece of my cake into my mouth, I rise, very aware of Tate's gaze, when I nibble a few stray crumbs off my fingers.

I want it to be his lips. I want to kiss him again.

"I'll head off to bed. Good night, Tate," I say, my brother's eyes jumping from me to Tate and back.

"Good night, Ara," Tate murmurs.

I press a kiss to my brother's cheek while brushing past him.

What am I doing? There's no way to undo my promise to Frederick. Letting Tate close again is madness. And still, I want to.

I head off to bed, but I don't get any sleep. The only advantage of that is I'm awake before the sun rises. I dress quietly and sneak out before anyone wakes.

Or so I thought.

# THIRTY-FOUR

## TATE

SHE SURPRISED ME AGAIN. SOMEHOW, I NEVER PICTURED ARA AS someone who enjoys baking, but it fits perfectly. The memory of tonight—and I don't mean just the kiss—of her opening up, telling me about her childhood, glimpsing traces of what made her who she is today, is something precious. If we hadn't been interrupted, I would have been content to talk the night away.

The interruption currently stands in the doorway, pinning me with his gaze, while I get up to leave the room.

"If this is your attempt at scaring me away, don't bother," I tell him, and Ian's eyebrows rise.

"She's promised to the crown," he warns, shifting, so he bars my way.

"She was mine long before she was my brother's."

His eyes widen slightly when realization hits.

"Still, she's promised to your brother now," he persists, and the mention of my brother makes my mood plummet. My voice drops to a threatening growl.

"What you and everyone else need to get in your head is I'm hers. And she's mine. And short of killing me, there's nothing you can do about it."

"Well, that can be arranged." He bristles.

"Why would you waste your time keeping away a man who is ready to kill or die for your sister when there's a real threat waiting for her?" My curious tone is conversational despite revealing the depth of my feelings. "I would never harm her. I'll always have her back and keep her safe." I shake my head. "I'm at her mercy. And you think you can change that? Why would you even want to?"

His brow creases at my mentioning of another threat.

"What do you mean?" he asks.

"I mean that someone attacked her during Picking, that I killed two men who tried to harm or take her in Telos two weeks ago. A blond skyrider turned up dead in Telos just a few days before we left." I pause, letting what I said sink in. "I mean that someone is targeting your sister. Until you have eliminated that threat, you would be stupid to keep me away from her."

Ian watches me, contemplating. "When was that? I need details." His eyes narrow. "I'll look into it." As if I made it all up.

"I already did," I tell him. "But while one attack came from men from Kystis, the others were from Belarra. Maybe someone targets her because of her role as our future queen." *Or because I'd do anything to keep her safe.*

Ian curses. "Does she know?" he asks.

"Of course, she knows. But I didn't make her see the connection to the dead skyrider. She doesn't need the guilt."

Ian nods, then steps aside to let me pass. We walk down the corridor to our rooms in silence.

"I do my damn best to keep her in sight, to keep her safe. That's why I'm here," I tell him, while I reach the door to my room. He pauses in front of his and turns to me.

"And who is keeping her safe from you?" he asks, and I chuckle.

"She's doing a pretty good job of that herself." With those words, I enter my room and close the door firmly behind me.

Sleep doesn't come easily that night, and when I hear silent footsteps creep down the stairs just when the sun rises, I dress in a rush.

Out the window, I spot a familiar shape hurrying around a corner.

*Where is she going now?*

Within minutes, I'm out in the courtyard, my eyes trailing the silence around me, when a hand lands on my arm.

"Sorry, I didn't recognize you," the guard says and takes a step back when he spots the skyrider insignia on my chest. The courtyard is quiet. Ara is already gone.

I curse. I'll have to trust she'll come back unharmed.

Since there is no way I'll be able to sleep, I make my way over to a space that seems to be used for training.

"And who might you be?" I turn at the voice behind me, and I don't have to guess who the man standing in front of me is. He can only be Benedict, Ara's twin. The resemblance is too obvious. He hadn't been in yesterday. His unit accompanied a merchant, from what I gathered at dinner.

Somehow, the same features that seem soft and feminine on her work for him, too, and there is nothing soft about him. A strong jaw and muscular build drive that point home. Hair of the same golden blond is shorn short on the sides and longer on top, and falls slightly into his face. Ara's brothers truly are a bunch of handsome bastards.

"I'm looking for Ara," I tell him.

"That doesn't answer my question, and where my sister is or isn't is none of your damn business."

I bristle at that because the fuck it isn't. But this man is important to Ara, so I will be nice, even if it kills me.

"I'm Tate Kyronos, her centurion," I tell Ben coolly. "So it's very much my business." Trying to dispel the tension, I add, "I've already heard much about you."

"I can't say the same," Ben states, smirking, while his eyes size me up. He reminds me very much of Ara at that moment, and I fight a grin. "If I see her, I'll tell her you're looking for her," he finally says.

"I'd appreciate it," I reply and turn away before I say anything Ara would hold over my head later.

I go through training and a shower afterward, but she still isn't back, so I go to her room.

Her scent hits me first, wraps around me like she did last night, making my pulse spike and my cock ache. Holy mists, this woman has me in a chokehold.

The room has two windows with breathtaking views. One overlooks the courtyard and the gate, the other looks out over a small garden, a healer's paradise with mostly herbs, some flowers, and fruit trees.

The room itself is light with whitewashed walls. The soft dark green curtains, pillows, and a duvet, along with the plush rug next to her bed, give the room a warm and cozy feel, while the assortment of weapons cluttering the surface of a desk, armoire, and nightstand makes me smile.

Her bed looks like she just crawled out of it. Her wardrobe is open, displaying various dresses next to training gear, armor, and two longbows. A stack of books lies next to her bed, with a dagger acting as a bookmark in the one on top.

While not exactly neat, her room is clean, and every weapon is well cared for. Displaying the same mix of chaos and dedication that is purely Ara.

It takes a long, long while until she opens the door, and she stops short when she sees me sitting on the edge of her bed, reading the book that she had marked.

"Tate." Her eyes trail over me. "I would have hurried if I had known you were waiting for me." She arches her brow, clearly asking what I'm doing in her room. Then she notices the book, and her eyebrows jump up even more, before she clears her throat. "Interesting choice."

"That's what I was going to say." I put the book down. "I saw you leave." *Where were you?* The question hangs unspoken between us.

"Last time I checked, I'm not your prisoner." She crosses her arms, tilting her head.

"You're doing your best to piss me off, aren't you?"

"No, I'm not even trying." Her face splits into a grin, and I can't help but reciprocate.

# THIRTY-FIVE

## ARA

Having Tate in my home works better than I thought. Toward the end of our two days there, Ian even shows something like grudging respect for him. And I successfully dodge Ben's questions by keeping Tate close, enjoying his company more than I should.

I enjoy everything about him more than I should. *Don't think about it*, I tell myself while we descend over Avina.

We are five days early for the official start of the flight games. The others arrive today, too, giving us time to get comfortable and rest.

Our housing is close to the arena, and I'm very relieved that we won't be staying at the palace. With Tate and me part of the flight, that's what I dreaded. But, well, we did replace Telos's previous team, or maybe this is an effort to treat everyone equally. Whatever it is, I'm glad about it.

The city is even more bustling than the last time I visited, and the crowd is a colorful mix of people from all five realms.

Pale-faced warriors from Kystis with their long, braided hair and beards look like they don't know what to do with the balmy temperatures. Their traditional layered clothing and fur-lined jackets are too warm for this kind of weather.

There are people from Harea, their hair wrapped in colorful cloth, their thin and bright garments, in comparison a little too flimsy for the sometimes still cool season.

We descend, crossing the river, and something moves in it. It looks suspiciously like one of the water creatures I read about in books, and I wonder if someone from Ilyn brought it. The ships stay close to shore, avoiding its long scaly body as best as they can.

I have never seen so many flying creatures circling above the city.

Dark gray gargoyles defy every natural law by whizzing through the air despite their weight. Beautiful winged horses, their coats gleaming in the sunlight, canter over the sky, and creatures looking like a mix of dragons and snakes wind through the air in arctic colors. They have membranous wings and two legs, their bodies scaly and sinuous.

Hippogriffs, a peculiar mix of the winged horses and our birds, make up the fifth group of flying beasts, their feathered front blending with the sleek coat of their back, their clawed feet easily finding purchase on the roofs.

Despite all those creatures, the crowd stares in awe when Solaris arrives, blowing his ego out of proportion.

*"I disagree,"* he grumbles, and I chuckle. *"It's not my fault if I'm prettier than those things."* He sends me his view of one of the gargoyles, and I have to agree. They look scary, hideous even.

We set down in front of the building we will stay in for the next three weeks, and Solaris flares his flames, causing people to give us more room.

The building doesn't look like a typical inn, more like the townhouse of some nobleman, built from light stone with big enchanted windows and a wrought-iron gate.

"Well then, let's see if the others are already here." Tate steps next to me, eyeing the building in front of us. After freeing our birds from bags and harnesses, they swoop up into the chaos above while we step into the building.

My earlier suspicion of this being a home is confirmed when I spot a family crest in the mosaic floor of the entrance hall. Contrary to atriums, which are open to the sky, this room sports a glass cupola spanning it, combining light and protection from the much harsher elements up here in the north. We hand over our things to the approaching servants before crossing the hall in search of the other members of our flight.

We find all of them gathered in a big dining room, occupying one of the three tables set up there. Mariel sits between Joel and Calix, and while laughing, leans into Joel in a way that has me grinning. Maybe I understand her questions about him and me now. I'll have to needle her for details later.

Our friends greet us enthusiastically as soon as they spot us, and while we talk, joke, and eat, two other flights of skyriders enter the room, claiming the other two tables.

It turns out we share the house with the flights from Lar and Aldea. But since we have different training schedules, and every flight occupies a different floor, we have little contact apart from the meals.

Two days later, the girls and I are gathered in my room. The official start of the flight games is approaching, and we spent the past two days training and getting comfortable in the new city.

Tonight, a ball at the palace will start the festivities. While the rest of my flight buzzes with excitement, trepidation coils in my gut, and my hands are clammy.

Frederick, Tate, and I in a room of watchful eyes ... with Ian and Dar.

*"That sounds like the recipe for disaster,"* Solaris agrees, and I grimace.

Sloan came with my brothers and is staying with us for a few days. I think my family hopes the festivities will distract her, but I'm not sure it's working.

She's quiet, and I'm not chatty either, but Mariel and Zaza make up for our silence.

Zaza looks stunning in a buttery yellow dress that glows against her skin, while Mariel went with a more subdued dark green, complementing her hair beautifully.

I close the door behind the maids Frederick sent and look down at the royal-blue gown I'm wearing, the one he picked. As if he wants to make sure I don't forget.

Mariel shakes her head at me when I turn back with a sigh. "Are you a princess and didn't tell us about it?"

"No," I say, rolling my eyes.

"But marrying the future king anyway," Sloan teases, then stills and slaps a hand over her mouth.

"Really?" I stare at her, too glad over her teasing to be angry.

"Wait a minute," Mariel butts in.

"You mean *our* future king? The handsome blond one?" Zaza asks.

"I thought you were promised to Tate's brother?" Mariel finishes her thought, and Zaza's eyes go wide while I hide behind my hands and groan.

"Yes," I hiss. "And I would be absolutely delighted if you wouldn't remind me." Three pairs of wide eyes are trained on me when I peek out from behind my hands. "Any chance you forget about all of it, and we can talk about something else?" I ask.

"So our future king and Tate's brother are the same, which..." Mariel starts and pauses.

"...makes Tate the prince who abdicated," I fill in her sentence. There is no use in denying it, anyway.

"The same prince she was betrothed to for half her life," Sloane supplies.

"And the one she's in love with." Mariel continues.

"And how the fuck did I not know any of this?" Zaza jumps in.

"Because my life is enough of a damn mess without telling everyone about it," I grumble.

"So tonight we're at a ball with two princes in attendance, who fight over your hand?" Zaza asks, glee in her voice.

I groan and bury my face in my hands again. "No. No one is fighting," I disagree.

Mariel laughs. "Yeah, you keep telling yourself that."

"And don't forget her overprotective brothers," Sloane offers.

"So basically, we have a room full of testosterone, just waiting for the spark." Mariel makes an explosion motion with her hands. "And that with Ara in the middle, who's *so* agreeable and doesn't enjoy riling people *at all*."

"Well, shit, when you put it like that," Zaza says. "Now I do understand why you didn't want to go."

"Oh, do you now?" I ask dryly. "How about one of you kills me now and spares me the drama?"

"No can do, girl," Zaza says. "We still need you for the flight games."

"Well, isn't that comforting?" I quip. "Gods, I'm royally fucked."

"Literally," Sloane throws in, making everyone laugh.

I roll my eyes. "Thanks."

But it's good to see a grin on Sloane's face. Her cheeks, for once, are back to their rosy color, matching her dress.

"If any of you breathe a word about this," I threaten, slashing my finger across my throat.

Mariel makes a motion as if she seals her lips, and Zaza nods.

"I'm not telling anyone ... else, I promise." Sloan looks contrite.

But somehow, them knowing what a shit show tonight might become helps a little.

Zaza raises her glass with pearling champagne. "To an unforgettable night, ladies, and three weeks of fun and glory."

Sloan snorts, but Zaza only arches a brow. "Would you have preferred me to say to slaughter and gore?"

"Nah, your words sounded a lot better," Mariel tells her. They both chuckle. I plaster a grin on my face as well, hoping the slaughtering part doesn't start tonight.

We head down to meet the rest of our flight in the entrance hall, and the guys whistle when we come down the stairs.

"Well, look at that, our girls can knock out a man without touching him," Jared comments, his eyes sweeping over us and stopping on Zaza's form. I giggle when he taps Tate's chin as if he has to close it.

I meet Tate's eyes for a brief second before looking away. I'm pretty sure he can guess who picked the dress. There's no way he didn't notice the color. And I dread his reaction.

Zaza laughs about something Tanner says while we walk to the two waiting carriages and then head to the palace together. I'm sharing a carriage with Sloan, Boko, Tate, Calix, and Mariel, while the others ride in the next.

Tate's eyes are on me the whole ride, but I avoid him by looking out at the nocturnal streets of Avina instead. The palace, lit by what has to be thousands of magical lights, slowly creeps closer, nerves ricocheting through my body like trapped fireflies, looking for an exit.

The cheering starts as soon as we set foot into the ballroom. It's illuminated by the warm glow of magical lighting, which fills the chandeliers and reflects in the mirrors and dark windows. The darkness of the night is erased by the reflections.

The people moving around nearly swallow the smooth wooden flooring. Giving me hope that I'll be able to hide among them.

But Belarra's nobles crowd us quickly, dashing that hope. Just what I need—even more attention. I sigh.

"Do you need saving again?" a smooth voice asks next to me, and I grin up at Admiral Morgan. "Huh, I wonder how you survive without me around."

I laugh, drawing Tate's attention, and when he sees who stands next to me, his scowl deepens. I roll my eyes at him and turn back to Morgan.

"So is Marina visiting during the trials?"

"She is actually." His eyes drift over to a woman, marching in our direction. "And I have to go. But I'll introduce you two soon," he promises. "It was nice seeing you again." He kisses my hand with a wink and leaves in the opposite direction from the approaching woman. I grin.

"Who was that delicious man?" Zaza whispers next to me.

"Admiral Morgan," I say, and my eyes bounce back to the woman, who now searches the crowd. "And he was fleeing from a past conquest if I had to guess." We laugh.

Observing the surrounding crowd is quite entertaining, and if there are new rumors circulating tomorrow, it might be our fault, as we pass the time by making up stories based on the behavior of the people around us.

"I didn't expect to find you here." The voice has me turning around, where I find Deliah's pale face.

"It's good to see you." I hug her, careful not to spill the drink she carries, and glad for another friendly face in this sea of strangers.

"Here, take this." She pushes the drink into my hand. "The gods know when you'll be able to get your own." I thank her, and she vanishes back into the crowd. But I don't get to take even a sip before Frederick steps up to us.

I fight hard to keep the smile on my face, but relax slightly when he greets us formally, congratulates us on our role as part of Belarra's champions, and wishes us the best of luck. Then he turns to me.

"May I have a dance with the most beautiful woman in the room?" he asks, offering me his hand. The way his gaze flicks to Tate, I know it's just to bait him. I grind my teeth.

My pause is slightly too long, but there isn't much I can do. So I graciously accept his offer and place my hand in his. He plucks the drink from my other hand, placing it onto the tray of a hovering server.

Everyone's gaze is on me while Frederick leads me to the dance floor. But I don't look at my flight, afraid to meet Tate's eyes.

"Was that necessary?" I ask as soon as we are far enough away.

"Can't I compliment my future bride? The dress looks stunning on you, darling."

"Don't darling me," I snap.

"What should I call you then?" he asks, and I swear there is humor in his voice.

"How about by my name?"

"Tamara, it is." We reach the dance floor, and he pulls me in. Closer than I want to be, but it's what the dance asks for, so it's hard to disagree.

"Why do I have the impression you knew exactly which dance was coming?" I ask him.

He grins down at me. "Of course I did. I made the list."

"We had an agreement to keep this a secret."

"And I complied with it. I didn't address you as my soon-to-be wife or my future queen. Did I?" I look down to hide my grimace at the titles.

We move to the music, everyone giving us too much space for my liking.

"Why do you hate your brother so much?" The question slips out before I can stop it, and Frederick stiffens slightly.

"I have no brother," he says, and my eyebrows rise.

"Funny, I could have sworn you introduced me to him the last time I was here," I mock.

He doesn't answer.

"Couldn't you just ... talk to him?" I'm well aware of how laughable the suggestion is, since I refuse to do the same, but then talking will resolve nothing in our case.

Frederick releases my hand and cups my face in what I'm sure looks like a tender gesture, but there is nothing soft in the way he makes me look into his eyes, his grip nearly bruising.

"If this is your attempt at getting out of this, don't bother. I planned this, and I'm very much looking forward to seeing him suffer while he has to watch you on my arm. Your body swelling with my heir."

"You're disgusting," I hiss.

"We have a deal," he reminds me. "You're mine as soon as you're done at the academy, and he won't change that. You'd better make him see reason before I have to take more lasting measures."

My eyes widen. "Are you for real? Are you threatening to kill your brother if I don't play along?"

"Those are your words, not mine," he says just when the song ends, and gives me a cool smile and a nod before releasing me. All previous charm forgotten.

My legs tremble with the rage flowing through me, and I stalk over to the next seating area, focusing on taking deep, measured breaths the way Tate taught me. Struggling to keep my temper and gift in check.

"What did he say to you?" While quiet, there's such a threat in those words that I simply close my eyes and concentrate even harder on breathing. The couch next to me dips. Tate's touch is soft as he guides my gaze toward him. I open my eyes, taking him in, making sure he is okay.

But I can't bring myself to repeat Frederick's words. It will only cause more drama, so I shake my head. His knuckles skim over the place where Fred gripped me.

"I could kill him for this," Tate murmurs.

"Don't," I tell him, not entirely sure if I mean don't kill him or don't touch me. Probably the latter.

# THIRTY-SIX

## ARA

"I... THIS IS A BAD IDEA." I GET UP AND MAKE MY WAY BACK TO our group. Joel takes one look at me and offers me his hand, along with the perfect excuse, by asking me to dance. And since I need to get away from Tate, I take it.

"You know I'm here for you, right?" Joel asks. The breath I release comes out shakier than I want it to.

"I don't like the tension you're under," Joel continues. "You look like you're about to shatter."

"That bad, huh?" I give him a humorless smile.

"No, you look beautiful. You always do."

My eyebrows jump up at that.

"It's the truth. Don't look so shocked. I have told you that you're beautiful before, right?"

"No, I don't think you have, Joel. I'm pretty sure your words to describe me were more like annoying, reckless, or even stupid. And let's not forget that you like to shout at me, too."

He looks shocked. "Ara, that's not ... that's not at all what I think of you."

I shrug. "It's fine. I'm your best friend's little sister who always tagged along even when you didn't want me to." His eyes widen even more, and I hurry to reassure him. "You were never mean about it. It's fine, Joel. I would even say we are friends now, right?"

"Ara, I care about you."

"I know that. You are as overprotective as my brothers, and the way you panic when I get hurt." I incline my head. "Oh well, now that I think about it, that could be because you fear the repercussions," I tease.

He shakes his head, looking stunned.

"No, I'm..." He swallows. "But that is not the point. What is going on?" Joel asks, and there are a thousand questions in his eyes. How am I supposed to answer that? Gods, I wish Ben were here. However much I hate talking with my brothers about men, I would do anything for one of them to hug me and promise that everything will be okay.

"I miss them, Joel," I say, going with the easiest truth. "I would give everything for one of Dar's hugs right now." My eyes wander over the crowd around us, but my brother is suspiciously absent. Now that I think of it, I haven't seen Elena or Tyre either. That's odd.

"I'm not Dar, but..." Joel says while cautiously pulling me against his chest. When I don't protest, he wraps his arms around me. "Better?"

I nod, finding comfort in his familiarity. We sway from side to side to the music, and Joel slowly steers us to the periphery of the dance floor.

"Thank you, Joel, for not rubbing it in," I finally mumble and look up at him.

He chuckles. "Oh, it took some restraint." He pauses. "What happened?"

"Short version, Tate is Frederick's brother."

Joel's eyes widen. "Wait, you mean ... holy fuck." He looks at me, eyes still wide, mouth open.

"Yeah." I shrug, and to my absolute horror, tears gather in my eyes.

"And now?"

I shrug again because I don't know anymore. I tried to push him away, to hate him, but I can't, and since the kiss in the cave, in our kitchen, my walls are not just cracking, they are tumbling one massive chunk at a time.

"Hey, you're not one to give up, so don't start now." He presses a kiss to my brow and gives me a sad smile. I nearly break and confess it all when I'm ripped out of Joel's arms.

"You've got to be kidding me." Tate's voice brims with anger.

"Hey," I protest, but he already starts walking, dragging me after him. "What are you doing?" I hiss and try to dig in my heels, a hopeless mission on the sleek floor.

"What *I'm* doing?" he growls, but keeps walking. "I swear, Ara, you either come with me right now or I'll throw you over my shoulder and carry you out, screaming and kicking if I must. I don't give a shit what anyone in here thinks, but we will talk now. My patience is fucking over."

This talk is long overdue, so I follow Tate without a fight.

It shows that Tate knows his way around the palace. We take only a few turns before we find ourselves alone.

He drags me into a room, a small office. A desk occupies most of the space. The walls are filled with shelves full of some sort of records. Tate closes the door behind him, and the lock clicks into place.

"What the fuck are you trying to accomplish, Ara? Are you trying to drive me mad with jealousy? Congratulations, mission accomplished."

"What?" I look at him. "No. In case you weren't there, they asked to dance with me, not to fuck me."

There is a humorless laugh as he drags a hand through his hair.

"My brother... I get it. I hate it, but I understand. You couldn't very well affront our future king in front of everyone. But Joel, to let him hold you like that in front of me, to let him kiss you while I'm very aware that he wants to fuck you..."

My mouth drops open. "What the hell, Tate? We're talking about Joel here. I told you he's like a brother to me."

"You also told me that you had a crush on him. So tell me, what sister has feelings like that for a brother?"

"He's not actually my brother, and—"

"Exactly."

"You're not making sense right now." I shake my head at him.

"Okay, whatever. But after being careful not to offend my brother, you think he is okay with you cozying up to another guy on the dance floor right in front of him?"

"He wouldn't care."

"He wouldn't care?" Tate repeats incredulously and takes a step forward, his eyes blazing. I step back, too aware of the pull between us.

He scoffs, obviously not believing me. "You want to tell me he's okay with you fucking other men?" He stalks closer, and my heart speeds up. I take another step back and bump into the desk behind me.

"Yes, I'm free to do as I want," I hiss.

"You really want to tell me..." He spins me around so my front faces the table with him right behind me. "If I bend you over this table." He grabs my neck and pushes me down so my chest and cheek rest against the smooth surface. "And fuck you until you're hoarse from screaming my name..." Heat pools in my belly and wetness between my legs. He steps even closer, his breath labored, his erection hard to miss where it rests against my ass.

His breath skates over the shell of my ear when he leans in. "You want to tell me my moron of a brother would be okay with that?"

I bite my lip to hold in a moan, but can't help arching my back, pressing into him. Tate groans.

"You want to tell me nothing is stopping me from having you right now?" His voice is rough, lower.

Gods, I want him.

Our situation is already miserable. Is there even a way to make it worse?

He bites my neck when I stay quiet. And I can't stop the moan this time.

"Do you want me to fuck you?" he whispers against my skin, and my whole body lights up. My breath is already ragged, and he hasn't even started touching me. Why is he still so much in control when my world is going up in flames? How can he stand there all cool and dominating and still leave the choice up to me?

"No?" I croak out.

"That doesn't sound like you're sure," he mocks, skimming his nose along my neck.

I shudder. Dammit, I want him.

"Are you wet for me, sunshine?" he asks. And the question alone heightens my arousal.

"No," I lie, and his eyes flare.

"Don't lie to me," he growls. "Let me ask you again. Do you want me to fuck you?"

My heart races. I bite my lip, trying to keep the word in. I should say no. I know I should. But damn, I need him, and I don't care about the consequences.

"Yes," I whisper, and Tate goes unnaturally still. I look at him through my lashes while he looms over me, my cheek still resting against the smooth wood of the table, his thumb caressing the base of my neck.

I lick my lips and watch him watch me. His eyes are dark with desire, his face tense with hunger. But that he is still so restrained won't do at all.

I meet his gaze, and remembering his words when he cornered me in the hallway, I deliver the final blow to his control.

"Please fuck me, Tate."

He snaps, explodes into motion, and all I can think is *hurry*.

Cool air caresses my wetness briefly before he slams home, replacing it with the heat of his body.

I whimper at the sudden intrusion, the fullness, the delicious stretch of him finally filling me. And at least for this moment, he is mine.

He pauses for a heartbeat as if he heard my mental claim or is as overwhelmed by the sensation as I am.

"Fuck, you're so wet for me." He squeezes his eyes shut as if he is fighting for control. But I don't want that. I push back against him, prompting him to move.

The pace he sets is fast, nearly punishing, anger, hurt, and frustration of weeks transformed into pleasure. I embrace it, crave it, and tilt my hip to let him slide even deeper.

Every one of his thrusts hits that delicious spot, causing sparks to flare and tension to coil. His hand still rests on my neck, the soft caressing motion of his thumb a stark contrast to the way he claims my body. Longing and sadness tinge the need in his eyes. And the knowledge that I caused it, that this beautiful, broken man is in pain because of me, makes my chest tight.

My emotions nearly choke me, while my physical pleasure builds until I'm teetering on the edge, only moments away from exploding. Tate stops. Then he changes pace and angle and pulls me back from the high.

I growl in frustration, and he chuckles darkly.

"You love having control, don't you?" he asks. "Driving me crazy with jealousy, shredding my control, pushing me until I'm on the edge of insanity..."

I shake my head, but he's right. A dark part of me does love it. The knowledge that I can bring this powerful man to his knees ... a shudder works its way through my body. But I would never use it to harm him.

Tate leans forward, seating himself so deeply inside me, my muscles flutter around him in anticipation, but he doesn't move. Instead, his mouth hovers over mine.

"I don't mind the control you have over me," he whispers against my lips before claiming my mouth in a kiss that is as demanding as his following words. "But I need to know that you are mine." I clench around him, satisfied when his breath catches.

"What do you want?" I croak.

"I want you to say it."

I glare at him.

"So damn stubborn." He chuckles wickedly. "But we have time."

He keeps up his pace, building me up only to change rhythm again, denying me the release I desperately crave.

I make a whiny sound that would have mortified me if I weren't so desperate.

Loosening the grip on the table, I reach for my clit, determined to take things into my own hands.

"Oh no." Tate's gift wraps around my wrists, bringing them back. "You only get what I give you. Just as you like to do with me." He starts his maddening slow pace again. "Admit it, and you get whatever you want."

"Bastard," I growl, only to moan loudly when the vibration of his laughter flows into me. I arch my back, let him slide deeper, squeeze him with every thrust, and feel dark satisfaction at every one of his curses, his praises. But despite all of it, he stays in control and pulls me back from the edge again.

And again.

Until I'm a shuddering, whimpering bundle of need.

"Holy mists, Ara. Simply admit it," Tate growls, his whole body tense with the effort of holding himself in check.

But I can't. I won't. We have no future.

"Please. Can't you see I'm drowning here?" he whispers, and

something in my chest cracks at that. He is the only one I'll ever want, but admitting that...

It won't change a thing, I realize. It doesn't make it less true if I deny him the words. It won't make it less painful.

"Only you, Tate," I choke out while my emotions go haywire. Tears start pouring down my cheeks, and my skin heats.

"Thank fuck," he growls. "I want only you, and it's driving me insane."

The wood beneath my fingers crackles and hisses.

*Oh shit.*

I throw my gift around him while I soar higher and higher, and just when I slip over the edge, I burst into flames.

# THIRTY-SEVEN

## TATE

Was pressuring her into a confession wrong? Probably. Do I regret it? Not at all. She is all I ever want, and knowing I'm not alone soothes something inside me I didn't know needed soothing.

However, her tears are killing me. I still don't understand her sadness or her reluctance to let me in. But I know what her body craves, and I can give it to her.

She tips over the edge, bursting into flames, but they don't burn me. I pull her up against my chest, regretting now that I didn't take the time to fully undress her.

I contain her gift so she doesn't set the room aflame and claim her lips in a desperate kiss. And while her body still quivers and shakes around me, I follow. I come so hard my vision blanks, and for a moment, my world comprises only her in my arms, our labored breaths, and my blissful release into her body.

The room is filled with panting silence and the smell of charred wood. It feels like the aftermath of an explosion. Surreal and different, with no chance of going back to how it was before. Not that I want to.

The moment Ara pulls away from me, sorting herself out, I can nearly see her stacking up the stones of the wall separating us, but I'm done with that.

I dress quickly, ready to stop her as soon as she moves for the door.

"Talk to me, sunshine."

She flinches.

"Yell if you must, curse me to the mists and back, but fucking talk to me, please."

"I heard you, Tate." She sounds tired, defeated. "I heard your conversation with your brother about what a good lay I am, your plan to use me, and that I mean nothing to you." A sob catches in her throat. "But then you act like you care, and I doubt what I heard, make excuses for you, feel guilty ... only for you to push me away again like I mean nothing to you..." She angrily brushes at the tears running down her cheeks, but steps back when I reach for her.

"What are you talking about? I didn't talk..." I start, but then remember the conversation we had weeks ago, the one where I tried to convince him she meant nothing to me. "Fuck."

"Yeah." She laughs humorlessly and tries to get past me to the door, but I block her. "Just let me go."

"Ara, I need you—"

"For your damn trials, I'm aware," she grumbles, and my irritation grows.

"...to fucking listen to me." When she crosses her arms and glares at me, I want to shake and kiss her at the same time.

"My brother must have known you were listening. Everything he said was meant to provoke me. I tried to protect you by denying my feelings, but... How could you ever believe that?" I search her eyes. How can she not see what she means to me?

"When people find out who I am, one of two things happens:

they run or they try to use me for their goals," she whispers. And in her eyes, I did both. Fuck.

I tell her what really happened that night. And the way she shifts, nearly reaching for me twice, gives me hope that I'm not too late.

"I would never do anything to threaten what I have with you," I say. All color leaves her face, and I push on, desperate to make her see. "You are it for me, Ara. You are everything I don't deserve but will keep anyway."

She shakes her head, looking frantic now.

"Do you want to see me beg? Crawl? Tell me what I need to do." My words are rough, raw, broken, but for once, I don't care. If she needs to see me bleed, I'll bleed. A shudder runs through her.

"Nothing," she whispers, breaking the silence and shredding my heart. "There is absolutely nothing you can do." That she believes it cuts even deeper than her words. I search her face, her eyes, hoping for once my gift is wrong, and she is lying. But all I find is pain. Pain that mirrors my own.

I shake my head. This is wrong. "I'm not giving up."

"What is there to give up?" she cries out. "What we had was built on lies." She looks away, and tendrils of smoke dance around her. "You are like completely different people, caring and cold, soft and hard. Sometimes I don't even know what to call you. Centurion, Prince, Alec, Tate." She shrugs, still not looking at me.

"You can call me whatever the fuck you want." I step into her line of sight. "As long as you call me yours."

Ara sucks in a breath. "Let it go. Let me go." Her eyes are pleading with me now. "Before it destroys us both."

"So you do have feelings for me." I latch on to her last words like a drowning man to a helping hand and step closer.

"Didn't you listen to a word I said?" She huffs out, stepping back, small flames licking over her skin now. "You need to give up, to let me go."

"And I told you I'm not going to. I love you, Ara." Her eyes widen, and her mouth drops open at my admission. "And that will not change. Loving you woke me up, changed me. It's part of who I am now. You exist, and I'm yours. It's as easy as that." Admitting my feelings doesn't leave me vulnerable, as I expected. It feels right. Loving her is not a weakness. It's the best damn thing I've ever done. But she doesn't look convinced.

"I'll prove that I'm worthy of your trust and love. Even if it takes me several lifetimes, I will never give up on you. I'd rather die trying." She pales even more.

"Oh gods, you're going to hate me." She bursts into tears, but they sizzle and evaporate instantly on her too hot skin.

"Believe me, I tried, and I can't." I move closer until the hand she holds up to stop me rests on my chest.

"Are you crazy?" she snaps, pulling her hand back.

"Maybe," I say. "But I'll get there for sure if you keep pushing me away." She still shakes her head, but when I pull her into my arms, there is no pain despite her flames.

"I don't know what to do." She buries her face in my chest, and I hold her even closer.

"Shhh, just give me a chance. Please?"

"It will destroy us both." Her voice breaks.

"We are stronger than that," I assure her.

"This is such a mess, Tate."

"Just let me love you ... pain, scars, secrets, and all." I bury my face in her hair and wish I could have a go at whoever caused her to doubt herself, doubt what she means to me.

"Okay." Her reply is hesitant and so quiet it's barely a whisper, and still, it's everything.

## ARA

I should push him away. It would be so much easier on both of us. But I'm tired of fighting him and my feelings. I'm simply tired. And so I agree, despite knowing I'll doom us both, because walking away would burn me to ash.

Another sob shakes my body, and Tate picks me up, settling against the wall with me in his lap, his lips resting against my temple.

"Shhh … the situation is not so different from before," Tate murmurs into my hair, but it is. It's so much different, only he doesn't know it yet. His brother will never let me go. I only pray that he is too content with seeing Tate suffer to go through with his earlier threat. And then there's the other secret I keep.

Spying for Tynan. His offer sounded like everything I wanted when I thought I had lost Tate. Acceptance, friendship, answers, and a goal to fill the void he left behind. But now?

Shit doesn't even begin to cover it.

We spend hours in that room, in that alternate reality we created for ourselves, and I cling to him like he is my shelter on a cold, stormy night. I try to ignore the cracks threatening my glass house, but even as he takes me back to my room, shielding me from prying eyes, I know it's borrowed time.

In the following days, my emotions are all over the place. Tate is so sweet. I'm walking on clouds while I can't help but wait for something to shatter the fantasy we hide in.

We agreed to keep the change in our relationship a secret for now, but I hate it. Even though I know it is necessary.

Tate's knuckles brush along my arm, and our fingers tangle for just a breath while he passes me in the arena's tunnel on our way to training.

Yesterday, Solaris's harness already sparkled when I picked it up to clean it after a messy training in the mountains, and at dinner, Tate saved me my favorite dessert when I was arriving late, sliding it over to me with a barely there smile, while he was talking to Jared.

His little gestures of attention help keep my doubts in check, but I still wait for him to push me away again.

Because nothing has changed. I'm still betrothed to his brother, my family is still the same ... and I still have secrets he can never know about.

# THIRTY-EIGHT

ARA

Avina's arena is massive. Telos's would fit inside it without a problem. Just like in the other arena, charms are embedded in the wall separating the first row of seats from the sand. The charms surround the open space, creating an invisible barrier that keeps anyone from leaving the deathly games, while also protecting the spectators. I can't see it, but I sense it.

Today will be the first time I set foot into the massive white stone building with its elaborate arches and statues outside of training. The figures gracing the walls and arches depict fight scenes, beasts, warriors, or the gods themselves—details I noticed during training.

The most impressive statues are the gods that line a ledge above the royal terrace. They are more than life-sized, if you compare them to humans, that is. Some stand, while others lounge on seats in an arrangement that resembles a casual gathering.

Approaching from the sky, I have little time to appreciate the details. One by one, the competing flights drop to the sand-covered ground, while the rest circle above waiting for their cue, turning the sky into a whirlpool of activity, blotting out the sun with swirling shadows.

There is a hum, an excitement blanketing the entire city and the stands of the arena. A crowd gathered outside the walls as if they wanted to be close to the event, even if they didn't have the luck to get a hold of seats.

The scent of garlic, bread, and roasted nuts permeates the air, originating from vendors roaming the rows of seats, selling a variety of items, including fruits, olives, and other food. Others sell beer and wine, and some offer trinkets and mementos of Iza, the flight games, or Frederick's upcoming coronation.

We are the third flight to be introduced, and there is a hush all around us when they spot Solaris. Everyone is in awe of my Phoenix.

*"And so they should,"* he comments. *"Most of them will never see another Phoenix in their lifetime."*

*"But they will see plenty of you over the next three weeks."*

*"Doesn't mean they can't appreciate me now."*

I slide off his back, walking over to our designated spot, while our birds take off, making space for the last of Belarra's flights. We stand next to each other around the perimeter and occupy about one-fifth of the area. The competing riders from different countries will fill the rest.

After Belarra, the gargoyles from Muntos follow with their riders. The ground trembles with the impact of each of the massive beasts.

Their gray skin is as smooth as marble, stretching into giant wings that look like a bat's. With their strong and muscled bodies, their arms and legs ending in massive claws, and their thin, pointed tails swishing the air restlessly, they look intimidating.

But their faces are truly terrifying—like demons or devils, sporting horns of different sizes and shapes. Their yellowish eyes, glowing in their dark faces, complete the horrifying combination.

"Yikes, I would not like to fight them one-on-one," I say, and Tate's head snaps to me.

"I'd hope not. If you ever do, concentrate on using your gift. Most weapons shatter on their stone-like skin."

I nod, watching the last of them take off.

Next are the riders from the Ilyn with their winged horses. Their beautiful white coats gleam in the midday sun.

"Now they are much nicer to look at and probably more fun to ride," Zaza comments.

"I hope you mean their animals and not the riders," Jared grumbles, and Zaza laughs.

"Now that you mention it... Girls, what do you think of that one?" She points at the dark-haired rider who led the flight that just landed.

*Do they even call their units flights?*

Zaza continues commenting on the incoming riders, and I'm not sure if she enjoys teasing Jared or if she is oblivious to his rigid posture behind her.

The hippogriffs of Harea land with a shriek that makes most people cover their ears. I heard they breed their animals by crossing the wild griffins living in the desert with their fastest mares. White clothes and headdresses adorn their riders. Typical of their sandy country, they keep their hair covered, but unlike others I have seen, only their eyes are free, making it hard to discern if there are women in their ranks or not.

The riders of Kystis are the last to join us, and Tate tenses next to me. I look at him in question, but he stares at the warriors in their layered armor and furs and their beasts, a mix of dragon and snake in varying shades of gray, blue, or even white. Unlike Muntos or Ilyn, they don't have any female riders. And instead of leaving like all other beasts, their creatures shrink in size and wind around their rider's throat like breathing necklaces.

"Well, that is handy," I comment under my breath.

"Or terrifying," Mariel throws in. "Think about it. They could hide anywhere, only to take on their original size and swallow you whole." She shudders. "I think now that I have seen them, lindwyrms even beat the gargoyles in the category of creatures I don't want to see in the wild."

I nod, grimacing at the appalling picture she painted.

Soon, the arena's sand is filled with contestants, and the crowd hushes at the blare of a horn. Everyone's eyes settle on the big stone balcony housing the royal family.

And there they are. The king and queen sit on huge thrones, hewn from the same white stone as the rest of the arena, their heads adorned by crowns that sparkle like shards of ice in the sun. Frederick stands by their side, his posture ramrod straight. Just like his parents, he wears a crown and the royal colors. Only his is smaller and less sparkly.

Even if they are far away, I could swear their eyes are on Tate and me.

The hushed mass of people surrounding us heightens the tension until I'm nearly ready to shout something, just to break it.

## TATE

"Bear witness as the flight games start anew." My father's voice booms, answered by a cheer from the crowd. His voice is strong and loud thanks to the sound gifted standing right behind him, but he looks even frailer than the last time I saw him.

And it must be even worse than he looks—my father handing off power is something I thought I'd never see.

"This year's trials will be in honor of Iza, who sees what's hidden and who grants glory to the worthy and silences the weak." His eyes seem to float over the contestants, not quite making contact, showing no reaction upon reaching me.

"Each realm has chosen contestants, units to represent them. Courage, cunning, sacrifice—these shall be weighed, not in gold nor titles, but in blood, bone, and resolve."

Another cheer goes up, the crowd clamoring for the entertainment to begin. The sound repeats outside the arena, giving the impression of an echo. At the mention of blood and bones, I have the sudden urge to carry Ara out of here. What was I thinking? I should have kept her out of it.

"Tread carefully as you cross into Iza's sacred grounds, where no other can shield, and no lie can guide—for secrets, once uncovered, cannot be buried again."

Ara shifts next to me, muttering something under her breath, too low to catch it over the roar of the masses around us.

My father's eyes come to me, and when his words follow, I'm not surprised.

"Perhaps some of you hope the trials might restore what was so willingly cast aside, but you'll soon realize this is not for the faint of will, and only the worthy walk out unchanged."

He already made it plenty clear that I'm the disappointment in the family, that I let him down. I hold his gaze, not giving him the satisfaction of showing any emotions. If that's all he got, I'm not worried. What worries me more is my brother's smug grin once his eyes fall on Ara.

I clasp her hand, squeezing it, reassuring myself that she is right next to me. She smiles up at me, and I can't help but mirror it. My brother's face has darkened with fury when I look back at him, and I have the sudden urge to rub it in by leaning down and kissing her.

But I don't, because there are more eyes on us than just his. And I certainly don't want to do anything that would upset Ara.

I'm sure the two oldest Blackstones are in attendance too, since there are competitions held for infantry as well. They also seem the kind of tight-knit family who would show up solely to support each other.

"This year, we honor not only the flight games, but the turning of the age they herald. Upon the final eve, when the trials are done, and the goddess satisfied, my son—Prince Frederick—shall be crowned king to the throne of Belarra."

He pauses longer this time since the crowd expresses its adoration for my brother.

"While another cast aside this legacy, he has stood in the light — steadfast, loyal, and unshaken, so to him the crown shall pass." He motions my brother forward, who is once more all smiles and charm.

"And now. Let the veils fall and the truth rise. May your steps be silent, your eyes sharp, and your hearts unshaken." He pauses.

"Let the trials begin."

The roar of the crowd is deafening this time, but breaks off into hushed awe when a golden flare of light draws everyone's gaze up to the ledge at the top of the arena, displaying the gods. A few gasps sound when one statue starts to move. Iza.

She steps out of the image as if she has had enough of lounging around with other gods and instead takes a few steps forward. The ledge places her well above everyone in the arena, even the king.

Golden light surrounds her, and where her image was beautiful to behold, her presence now is so brilliant, so terrifyingly striking, it's obvious she is no mortal. Her eyes trail over us standing in front of her, beneath her, and she smiles.

"I've waited so long for this," she breathes, and still her voice thunders through the stands, echoing off the building around her. "So many beautiful secrets," she purrs, and I don't like the way her eyes rest on Ara for a moment. "We will have so much fun together." She claps her hands. "Let the games begin."

# THIRTY-NINE

## ARA

I guess I have to take back the words I said to Lorcan, because in front of my blinking eyes stands a goddess. The hood of the cloak, normally shadowing her face, is thrown back, gleaming red curls spilling out over the soft leather and cloth of hunting clothes. Brown and green replace the previous white of the statue's garments, and a quiver and bow rest on her back.

Glowing as if there is more than just the sun illuminating her, she smiles down at us. But her smile isn't reassuring or soft. It's sharp-edged and cutting, her eyes assessing like a hunter gauging its prey.

At the clap of her hands, the sky above us swirls, dark clouds move in and build up, stacking, twisting, growing. I wonder if she asked her brother Tempos, the god of weather and winds, for help in this.

The clouds gather above the arena until a giant diamond-shaped cloud blots out the sun, plunging the city into shadows. The structure is restless, moving, lightning illuminating it in flashes. Harsh winds whip at it, some parts swirling.

Everyone stares at it.

"What is that?" Zaza breathes, and Tate shuffles closer, his presence reassuring and protective next to me.

"Welcome to your first trial." Iza's voice vibrates around us. "You'll prove your abilities in the cloud maze today." It's a statement, a challenge with no room for doubt.

"Not one to waste time," Joel mutters, and I have to agree, the goddess caught all of us by surprise. No one mentioned that today would be the actual start of the trials.

"Every team starts at one of the golden lights. Trust is the key. Whoever reaches the center first is the winner and takes away a clue for the last competition. The teams that lose a member or fail to reach the center in time are out." She pauses, an expectant silence dropping over the arena.

"How do you know the time is up? Oh, you'll know." She cackles. "Have fun." And with a boom and a flash of light, she vanishes from sight, her statue once more unmoving, resting at the place she was before, unchanged. Or is she? I didn't study her closely enough to truly say.

Unsurprisingly, the men from Kystis are the first to leave on their writhing mounts, getting smaller and smaller, and soon seeming no bigger than a fly against the mass of clouds.

"Now, doesn't that look like fun?" Calix murmurs, his eyes on the maze that's waiting for us.

"Do you think it will be just a maze?" Mariel asks.

"No," Calix and I answer simultaneously. "Her ominous 'have fun' at the end..." I shake my head. "This promises to be much more than just a maze if you ask me."

"Trust is the key," Mariel mutters. "Couldn't she have been clearer than just that?"

"We're no more than game pieces for her. Risking our lives is her entertainment." Tate's eyes are on the dark, boiling mass above us.

Our birds land, and while everyone heads to their bonding partner, Tate catches my hand, keeping me in place just a moment
longer.

"No unnecessary risks, Ara, please. And I'm not saying this
because of the trials." And when I catch the plea in his eyes, I rest my
hand on his cheek.

"I promise," I say. He covers my hand with his, leaning into it for
just a second before letting go. We both walk over to our birds, ready
to tackle the first trial.

I don't know what I expect, but not the sinister, murky darkness
enveloping us as soon as we enter the labyrinth. It reminds me
strangely of the mists, which puts me on edge. Will something be
lurking beneath the cloud cover?

Tate's command is simple. "Stay close." But it turns out it's not
that easy to implement. Crosswinds threaten to scatter our flight
before we even enter, turning our orderly structure into chaos within
seconds.

Every bird fights to stay on course, but the Rukhs, the smallest
and lightest of our group, have to fight the hardest against the winds.

At least the surrounding walls are built from clouds, so there is
nothing to collide with ... or so I thought.

Only seconds later, a high-pitched screech has me whipping
around. Tempest, Mariel's Rukh, careens into one of the walls. And
going by her sound and Mariel's expression, it must hurt.

*"Tempest says not to touch the walls. It feels like being struck by
lightning,"* Solaris informs me.

*"Well then, we'll do our best."*

On Tate's command, we change formation, taking the three Rukh
in our midst, so the Strix, as well as Solaris and Daeva, shield the
smaller birds.

*"Is it only my imagination, or are the walls closing in?"* I ask
Solaris, and he curses but confirms my observation, relaying it to Tate
via Daeva.

It gets worse the deeper we delve into the maze. As it turns out, the paths are not just getting smaller, but are also changing and moving, as if the clouds were living things, trying to trap us.

Soon, the tunnels get too small to keep up our clustered formation, and we have to spread out, flying in a stretched-out V, too narrow to harbor anyone in our midst.

With every turn that gets us closer to the center, something else comes on top of what we are already dealing with.

"Scatter." Daeva passes down Tate's command. Our birds react before they even relay the message to us, and not a second too early.

A giant cat—no, a Sphinx—pounces for the spot where Calix and Aella had been only moments earlier. The creature throws her head back and laughs, but the voice spilling out is the goddess's.

"Avoid the black mist," she purrs, but the warning comes too late, since it materializes right in front of me. Solaris flies through it, and for a second, I think we are fine. But then his wings falter.

"*Solaris,*" I call out to him, but his presence is muddled, sleepy.

"*Solaris,*" I try again.

"*I'm so...*" He doesn't even finish his sentence before his wings still, and we nosedive.

"*Solaris.*" I try to reach him again, panic slowly taking over my stomach. We head for the wall below us. The sting has to wake him up, right?

Only we pass through it without a problem. It just swallows us up.

We're surrounded by a dull grayish white, with no signs of up or down, no sign of where we come from or where we need to go. Solaris spirals, and I cling to the harness, trying to stay awake and upright.

I might not see much, but we are falling ... quickly.

## TATE

I GLIMPSED THE LAST GLOW OF SOLARIS'S LIGHT BEFORE THE clouds beneath swallowed it.

The white shifts and erases any lingering signs, once more a cozy cushion, looking like a feather-soft resting place, but it's not.

We dive after them, but the cloud doesn't let us pass. Daeva gives a furious scream of pain and rage. We try two more times, but no matter what we do, we can't follow.

Images of broken bodies, shattered on the ground, crowd my mind, paralyze me. I want to turn around and go back to find them. But the passage has shifted again, and if she continues to fall through the clouds, there is no way I'll reach her before she lands on the unforgiving ground far, far below.

*"You have to trust that she will get out of this, that she will find a way,"* Daeva tells me. *"We need to move on."* And she is right, the clouds are closing in on us, nevertheless, I can't just leave.

*"I'm sorry."* Daeva makes the decision and heads farther into the maze, leaving the spot I saw them last.

*I failed her.*

*I lost her.*

The maze doesn't even give me time to let the shock settle before the voices start. Some loud, some whispering, some begging, some demanding, cursing, but all of them familiar.

Ara's plea for help has me whipping around, only for her voice to come from the other direction a second later. There is Louis, Leo, my uncle, all of them crying out for help or cursing me a second later, accusation mixing with desperation. What it means that I hear Ara's voice next to theirs is something I can't dwell on, or I will lose my mind.

*"Trust her to get out of it,"* Daeva repeats. *"She is capable, she is strong, she is smart and ruthless if need be."*

She's right, and I try to hold on to that. The rest of the flight looks as unsettled as I feel. Eyes are darting around, faces anguished, and Mariel Tethys is openly crying.

Only training and our birds keep us in formation, keep us going, when all we want is to dive for the voices of our ghosts and make them stop.

It goes on forever, the shadows of our past dragging up every missed opportunity, every failed chance, every regret until my insides feel raw. We are close to our breaking point when they stop. The silence is deafening and quickly filled by inner voices, continuing the slaughter. One agonizing thought louder than any other.

*I failed her.*

Ara's voice pops into my head again. This time her tone is mocking, telling me to change course or die. No pleading, no accusations. When nothing else follows, I call out to her.

"Wait, what?" She sounds startled.

"Ara? Is that you?" I ask again.

"Tate? You can hear me?" she breathes, and my throat is suddenly too tight.

"Are you dead?" I press on, dreading the answer.

She snorts. "I'm not dead. Dammit, this goddess has one weird sense of humor. But I love to hear your voice."

I smile at that.

"Let's get to the important stuff," she continues. "I will guide you, and you follow my directions, no exceptions."

My brow furrows. "And if we don't?"

"You'll die." Her voice sounds rough. "Iza used more fluff, but I'm pretty sure that was her core message. I'm also sure she intentionally separated me." When I don't answer right away, she adds, "Just trust me. Okay?"

"How will you navigate us if you aren't even here?" I ask, skepticism strong in my voice. What if this is another trap, another trick of the goddess?

"I can sense magic. The token, object ... whatever is waiting in the middle of this monstrosity, is magical, and all of you are gifted. I can sense that. Okay?" She pauses. "And yes, you were right." I nearly hear her eye roll in her voice. And it's that little detail that sways me.

"So we'll follow your directions blindly, or die?"

She sighs. "I know you hate the thought of relying on someone else, but can you do it for me? Please?"

I curse under my breath. But I also remember what the goddess said.

*Trust is the key.*

Just bloody why does she have to choose something that goes against my nature? The thought of handing over control makes me itchy. I huff out a breath.

"Okay," I grumble.

Ara laughs. "I promise I'll take good care of you," she purrs.

"You're enjoying this, aren't you?" I accuse, but that sobers her quickly.

"No, I'm terrified," she admits quietly. "Terrified of the fact that one mistake could kill you all." She's silent for a moment. "Can you tell me whenever you come to a branch off or a crossroad? And I'll warn you if anything else comes up."

"You can do this," I murmur. "You'll get us there safely."

"I sure hope so." She sighs. "And I'll do my damn best to get back to you."

"I sure hope so." I mirror her words. And gods, do I pray she does.

# FORTY

## ARA

I observe my flight path through the maze by following their gifts, then I turn to Solaris. We are both standing on a surprisingly solid cloud that stopped our fall. It's in the center of an open space, the wall of clouds around us, riddled by countless openings leading back into the labyrinth of corridors. The atmosphere is bleak, like on those rainy days that make you question whether the sun even exists.

The sickening crunch at our landing alerted me that something wasn't right, and I'm still trying to adapt to the sight in front of me.

*"Don't look at me like that. I know I'm not pretty right now, but it takes time, okay?"*

*"You look terrifying, but you're still beautiful to me,"* I tell him. And I mean it. Had he been anything but a Phoenix, had he not shielded me with his body, we would not be standing here. My right arm, the one I braced myself with, hangs uselessly at my side, my ribs

sting with every breath, and my entire body whimpers while I shuffle over to him.

But we're alive.

Even though Solaris doesn't look like it at the moment. He is mainly blackened bones. A few sparks run along them now and then, and some of the bones glow like he is still smoldering. He had gone up in flames shortly after our crash and came out like this.

Seriously, he looks like something that belongs in the realm of death, rather than the living.

*"You're staring again."*

*"Just admiring your resilience,"* I tell him, and he makes a sound close to a snort. There is almost no tissue on him yet, and only clumps of black feathers remain. *"Are you sure you can fly yet?"* I ask and pull myself onto his back, wincing when my bad arm gets jostled in the process. *"Can I help in any way?"*

*"Just a bit more. I'm concentrating on restoring my wings first. Give me half an hour and we'll be fine."*

Maybe this is the moment to tell him about the signatures coming in our direction—ten of them.

*"Umm, how about five minutes?"* I ask and show him what I mean. Solaris curses.

*"Then I do need your help. I don't have enough magic for that kind of healing in such a short time."*

*"Tell me what to do."* Solaris describes how to transfer magic to him without harming either of us, while I keep an eye on the contestants coming closer and closer.

The first attempt makes me hiss in pain when I try to channel too much of my gift at once. It feels like my nerve endings got fried.

I try again, but I'm getting anxious about the incoming group, causing my gift to become erratic and unstable.

*"Steady. You need to hold it steady,"* Solaris groans. This time, it sounds like he's in pain.

*"Shit. Sorry."* I break it off and take a few deep breaths, but

calming down when you know you only have minutes to get this right is easier said than done.

"Breathe. Relax. You can do this." I motivate myself, trying to envision Tate's calming presence next to me. And thank whoever-the-fuck-listens, it works.

My gift settles, and I let it seep into my bird in a soft, slow trickle. After a moment, the feathers on his wings lengthen, thicken, and start to cover more of them. But not nearly enough to support us.

I don't have to look up to know when our competitors come into view. The shouts and cheering when they see us are obvious enough.

I don't acknowledge them, just increase the flow from me to Solaris, concentrating on holding it steady. Dizziness accompanies the dwindling gift, but I ignore it. If we don't get airborne soon, I'm not sure we ever will again, or at least not me.

Only when there is movement in my periphery do I look up, and my breath stalls. One of the lindwyrms snakes its way over to us. A broad, cruel smile mars its rider's face. I push even more of my gift to Solaris, my vision blackening at the edges, but I'm strapped in ... mostly. I couldn't do it on the side with my injured arm, but one secured leg and one good arm should keep me up here.

"Okay, we are at the next branch off," Tate's voice announces, and I give him directions, struggling to keep my gift flowing and my voice uneventful.

"Nearly there," Solaris promises. He shuffles to the opposite edge of the cloud we sit on, keeping an eye on the wyrm, who starts to pick up speed, his wriggling motions getting more streamlined and quicker.

I push all I have left of my fire gift at Solaris, my world going dark for a blink or two, and then there is a giant jolt.

For a second, I think we're too late, that the beast rammed us. But it's Solaris launching himself off the edge with everything he's got. His wings flare wide, and my stomach somersaults when we drop more than I'm used to. Then his wings come down, and we gain height, slower than usual, but steady.

A hissing snarl causes Solaris to throw himself to the side, and I nearly lose my seat. I grasp for something, anything to hold on to, while the wyrm misses us, but barely.

Solaris rights himself, and I find my hand closed around one of his ribs.

*"Quite handy that you have handholds now,"* I tease.

*"Sure, make fun of me while I'm flying for our lives,"* he grumbles.

*"Don't be so prickly. I meant what I said. You are still beautiful to me."*

The wyrm strikes for us again, and his companions circle, trying to cut us off. Solaris spirals to evade him, and that is the moment Tate needs directions again.

I concentrate on the dots of my friends twirling around in my mind in relation to my position.

"Left, no wait ... right. Yes, it's right," I tell him, gritting my teeth when my hand starts to slip from the smooth bone.

"What is going on?" The concern in his voice is audible.

*"Into the maze,"* I tell Solaris, but he is already diving for it.

"Ara." My name is a warning growl that on any other occasion would spark heat.

"Um, nothing," I tell him because what use is there in worrying him when he can't do anything to help?

Solaris gives everything he has, but since he is not yet back to his full self, the wyrm slowly gains ground, every strike at us coming too close.

"Spit it out, Ara," Tate commands.

"I might be occupied with escaping a wyrm." *Or ten,* I add in my mind, but it seems I did not separate that properly.

"Get out of there now," Tate bellows. There is terror in his voice now.

"Kind of working on that," I reply dryly. *"Dive into the clouds,"* I instruct Solaris as I throw my magic gift around both of us, hoping we'll be able to pass through.

My gift is the fallback in case we encounter lightning or whatever caused Mariel's pain.

We head for the cloud, and I squeeze my eyes shut, holding on as tight as I can, in case we bounce off. But nothing comes.

"Ara?" It's a plea.

I open my eyes tentatively, and white surrounds us once more.

"Still here to annoy you some more." I laugh, then release a deep breath. "Damn, that was scary," I admit.

"Yes, it was," Tate answers with a sigh. "Please come back to me, Ara."

I promise to do my best and continue guiding my flight while Solaris and I use the cover and shortcut of the clouds to get back to them.

## TATE

I stare at a field of lightning bolts barring the way in front of us. They seem to come from everywhere, crossing the corridor like a giant spiderweb, flashing in and out too fast to pass them.

Jared's and my gaze collide. Well, shit. It's written all over his face, making words unnecessary, not that everyone isn't thinking the same.

There is a crackling hiss with every violet strike, but no thunder, giving the image an eerie quality.

I motion everyone closer. At least there is no wind, making circling easier.

"Any ideas?" I shout so everyone can hear me.

Mariel raises her hand, and I stir closer.

"It's a pattern." She gestures back to the sizzling light. "They always strike exactly the same location." I look again, and she's right. "So if we weave through them, we should be able to get to the other side," she continues.

"I gladly let you try first," Boko comments, drawing glares from Cassius and Ilario.

"By replicating the pattern, we can try without harm," Jared offers and points in the other direction, letting a mirror image of the lightning appear.

"I'll go first," Zaza offers. "Rukhs have the advantage here."

And that's what we do.

After Zaza scouts out a way, we repeat it three times each to memorize it, but our time is slowly running out. The darkening of the clouds around us and the slow shrinking of the maze are clear indicators of that.

"I'll go first," Zaza repeats her earlier offer while we circle in front of the original challenge.

"No, I'll go," Jared jumps in, but Zaza waves him off. "That would be incredibly stupid. Zephyr takes up much more room."

*"Sunshine, where are you?"* I ask, and I'm relieved when she answers immediately.

*"I'm close. I should be there soon."*

"Zaza, you'll go first," I order, ignoring my best friend's death glare. "Cassius and Tethys follow, after that the Strixes and Daeva, and I will be last."

"I hate you right now," Jared grumbles, and I totally understand, but I'm hoping for Ara to get here. She could shield the bigger birds from the lightning. So I just ignore him and watch Zaza with bated breath, maneuvering her way through the rays.

Mariel is next, and she starts strong, but then slows down.

"She'll hate me for this," Ilario says and fixes his gaze on her. Mariel immediately picks up speed again. "She was drifting into fear," he explains, and with fear comes doubt. I nod my agreement.

"Okay, do the same for everyone else," I instruct. "And you can blame it on me if it helps," I add as an afterthought, making him grin.

I monitor the corridor we came from, but Ara is still not in sight when it's Daeva's and my turn.

I refrain from contacting her, since I can't be distracted, or I'll risk burning Daeva and me to a crisp. The walls have closed in considerably by now, and I question the wisdom of my earlier decision to let the smaller birds go first. It will be a tight fit.

*"I've got this,"* Daeva promises, and I have to trust her in this since there won't be a way back once we start.

*"Then let's go, beautiful. I'll let you take the lead here."*

*"You should do that far more often,"* she comments and shoots off into the flickering obstacle course of light.

The space seems to shrink with every passing moment, and I crouch low over Daeva's neck, making myself as small as possible, keeping my weight centered so I don't risk throwing her off balance.

I hold my breath more than once while she maneuvers her big body through spaces that should have been impossible to fit through. Despite that, the closer we get to the end, the closer the strikes come.

My hair stands on end from the surrounding static, rising as if it has a life of its own. We will not make it.

*"I've got you."* Ara's soothing voice calms me, and I relay it to Daeva.

*"Go!"* I yell while I put our lives into the hands of the woman I love, trusting her to keep us safe.

Lightning sizzles around us, cascading over our bodies, the violet sparks on Daeva's black feathers like a thunderstorm in a night sky. And then we rip free, finding eight horrified gazes on us. We circle around, my eyes already searching the space we just left.

And there she is, like the goddess of death coming to claim the souls of the slain. She sits upright and proud, not cowering from the sizzling light around her. Solaris is the embodiment of a man's nightmare beneath her, Ara's hair flowing around her like she is under water.

They don't even bother to evade any of the strikes. The sparks dance over her skin and the bare bones of Solaris's body like tiny fireflies paying homage to the queen of another world and her loyal mount.

"Now that is a dramatic comeback," Jared comments, breaking the hushed silence, but I can't take my eyes off her.

*"Good to have you back,"* I tell her.

*"I could say the same thing,"* she replies. Now that she is closer, I see the strain on her face, her motionless arm, and the blood and bruises.

*"What happened?"*

*"We crashed."* That is her simple answer. *"But we survived."* She is free of the strikes now and joins us. *"Let's get to that center so we can go back."*

The maze is nearly pitch black by the time we reach the epicenter. Daeva and I take the lead, Ara right behind us, and the others follow, while we speed through a passage barely wide enough to accommodate a single bird.

The moment we reach the middle, we are back over Avina, the ominous cloud black and threatening above us. We land in formation, audible gasps rippling around us when they catch sight of Solaris.

I'm by their side before Ara can slide down on her own. I hold on a bit longer, a bit tighter than I need to when I set her back on the ground. At the same time, my healing magic seeps into her, repairing the worst of the damage. And she leans into me with a sigh before straightening again.

"Okay?" I ask before letting go.

"Much better." She smiles at me. "Thank you."

Only seconds later, there is a thunderclap above us, and when our eyes come back down from the cloud, they land on a pile of bodies in the center of the arena.

Arms, legs, claws, wings, and hair. Beasts and humans tangled together, motionless, lifeless. The first fly lands on an unseeing, unblinking eye.

Twelve flights, that's how many made it. The rest ... didn't survive.

Gasps break the horrified silence. Ara sidles up to me, squeezing my hand. This could have been us. We arrived not long ago, and the maze was already dark.

I swallow.

"How could she ... why did she do this?" Ara whispers, and maybe the goddess hears her. There is a flash of light, and a booming voice answers.

"The loser of a hunt always ends up dead. Remember that." There is another boom, and the bodies vanish.

Ara looks sick.

"What is it?"

"She said these are her trophies now."

# FORTY-ONE

## ARA

After the horror of the trials, all of us are exhausted and quiet, so we head off to our rooms, not in the mood for conversation. But I don't want to be alone either, so I follow Tate and, when no one is looking, slip into his room instead of mine.

He pulls me into his arms as soon as the lock clicks behind us and simply holds me. Wordlessly, he guides me into the bathing chamber and helps me out of my dirty and bloody armor, his fingers tracing and erasing the marks still left on my skin until only soot and dried blood mar it. I help him with the buckles on his armor with the same reverence, appreciating that both of us are still alive. He checks the temperature of the water before pulling me into the shower with him.

"May I?" he asks, holding up the soap, and I nod.

Slowly, deliberately, he starts soaping up my body. The slippery feel of his hands sliding over me makes my skin tingle while the piney, cool scent that is him envelops me. I inhale, savoring it.

"I might have to steal your soap," I say, making him grin.

"Hmm, I like the thought of my scent on you," he hums while he rinses me off, his hands chasing off the bubbles, his movement appreciative but not overly sexual. He enjoys taking care of me and maybe even needs it to reassure himself I'm still in one piece.

He soaks my hair next, his fingers fanning through the matted strands.

"You don't have to, I can—" I start.

"But I want to," he murmurs, pressing a kiss to my shoulder. "Let me take care of you. Let me savor your being here with me."

I smile at him over my shoulder. "Savor away then."

He laughs softly while his hands spread soap over my hair and then start massaging my scalp. It feels freaking amazing.

I moan.

His hands stop for a second.

"My plan was to clean you up and hold you while you rest, but if you keep up those sounds, that intention goes down the drain with the soap," he warns.

I laugh wickedly, and he lets his head fall to my shoulder in mock exasperation. "Now I've done it, haven't I?" he murmurs against my skin before pulling my hair aside and kissing his way up to my ear.

He gets back to my hair, and sure enough, I let him know how much I like it, audibly.

As soon as he is done, I snatch up the soap before he can reach for it and turn to him, arching one eyebrow in challenge. With a small smile on his lips, he holds still while I relish the feeling of his soap-slicked skin and hard muscles under my fingers. I let my hands roam over the ridges of his abdomen, the wide expanse of his chest, and his strong shoulders, only to run them down his arms. I step closer, my arms coming around him, soaping up his back while I press my body against his.

He reaches for me then, but I shake my head with a playful smile, and he humors me.

I tease him, taunt him, tug on his control with every sweep of my hands, with every press of my lips, until by the time I wash his hair, both of us are panting. With wet, slick skin heated by more than warm water, we step out of the shower. Our eyes lock again and again while we dry off, and I'm wrapping a towel around my hair when he sweeps me up into his arms.

"You're taking too long," he growls, and I giggle while he carries me over to his bed.

"I'm just making sure your bed isn't getting wet."

"And who the fuck cares?" He throws me onto his bed, and I bounce, before looking up with mock indignation.

"I'm not sleeping in a wet bed."

"Oh, that is another matter then." He grins at me. "Let me make sure we didn't miss a spot." He crawls onto the bed, kissing his way up my body, making me squeal whenever he finds a spot I'm ticklish and moan when he finds my weaknesses. And he finds them all.

Soon, I'm writhing under him, tugging him up, desperate to have his lips on mine and his cock buried inside me.

The laughter made room for a quiet intensity, and his mouth catches my sigh when I welcome him into my body. Our movements are filled with appreciation, worship, and giving. We share long, slow kisses while we get lost in each other, both of us basking in the glory of being alive, of being together.

It's much later, when I'm curled into him, his fingers tracing lazy circles on my skin, that I tell him about everything that happened today—of our crash, the goddess, and how she gave me the ability to talk to him. Unfortunately, that ended as soon as the trial did.

Or maybe it's for the better since there is no way I could keep my secrets with him in my head.

"What is it?" Tate asks, as always, too perceptive, but I smile it away and distract him instead.

Tonight, I'm all about enjoying what I have instead of mourning what I'll lose. Who knows if we even survive these trials? Iza killed nearly half of the participants in the first round, and it had been close for Solaris and me as well.

The following morning comes much too soon, and I scurry to my room for clean clothes before anyone else wakes. Or so I thought.

At breakfast, Calix watches me with a knowing grin while I shovel food into my mouth.

"What?" I ask as soon as I have swallowed.

"Nothing, just glad you're feeling better, is all," he says, and Mariel nods enthusiastically.

"Yes, I feel much better, actually." I smile. He gives me a knowing smirk, and I narrow my eyes at him.

I don't have to wait long to hear what that was about. We are on our way to the arena for training. Calix is walking next to me and grins again.

"What?" I ask.

"Look at you, all relaxed and glowing." He bumps my shoulder. "And since I not only saw you sneak out of his room but also saw our centurion press a kiss to your temple when he thought no one was looking, I don't even have to ask who is responsible for it." Calix grins at me. "Guess he doesn't hate you, hmm?"

I swat his arm, my cheeks heating, but nothing can wipe the smile off my face today.

We talked for a long time yesterday, and Tate now knows everything about the last months and what happened since our fight at the palace—well, almost everything. I still have to tell him about my bargain with Tynan, my grandmother's plan, and my promise to his brother.

I opened my mouth a thousand times to say something, but somehow I know that a confession a la "Oh, and I spy for the enemy now" wouldn't have gone over well. And it's not like I can tell him much, anyway. And Frederick ... honestly, I like to pretend he doesn't exist.

It's wrong to keep this from him, but I can't regret it. Not if it's the price for mornings like today. I sigh.

"That good, eh?" Calix asks, winking. I slap his arm, but laugh with him. Gods, I need more moments like this, like last night.

The arena is empty when we arrive, and nothing reminds us of yesterday's massacre, not even a discoloration of the sand.

We go through our usual drill and sparring, and maybe my perception is skewed, but I could swear Tate is going easier on us today. It's a sunny day, and even here in Avina, the coming summer slowly shows. Tate lost his shirt during training, and keeping my eyes off him is damn near impossible.

Now that the others have left, it's only us, and I don't have to pretend anymore. He is setting up targets for me to practice my gift. Biting my lip, I watch his muscles ripple with the movement. His golden skin is already turning a darker shade from training out in the sun in Telos, and the sunlight playing over it makes my fingers itch with the desire to do the same.

He clears his throat, and my eyes fly up, only to find him watching me with a smug grin on his gorgeous face.

"Focus, Ara, and I don't mean on my body."

"Hmm, I was only in thoughts," I reply airily and strip out of my shirt, which leaves me naked from the waist up, apart from my wrap. His eyes turn molten.

"And what thoughts were those?" he asks, his voice a little rougher. I bite my lip to keep from smiling.

"Eh ... more memories, really." I wink at him.

"Put your shirt back on," Tate says calmly, but a warning vibrates through his words.

"And why would I do that? There is no one here but you and me, and you have already seen it all." I shrug, stepping closer, then turn my back on him.

"How am I supposed to concentrate like that?" he mutters, and I grin.

"You started it."

"You've probably seen me train without a shirt a hundred times by now."

"And it's a testament to my swordsmanship that I didn't hack off my foot while I did," I reply dryly, making him laugh.

By the time we're done, my skin is slick with sweat and my breath labored, but I'm grinning triumphantly.

"We're getting there," Tate says, and I stick my tongue out at him.

"That was damn near perfect, and you know it."

He scoffs, but the corner of his mouth twitches.

"Hah, I saw that." I point a finger at him. "Now admit it." I step closer, cupping my ear. "I'm waiting."

"For what?" He takes a step toward me, and I'm overly aware of the heat radiating off his skin, or maybe it's his gift that blazes like a sun next to me. "Are you waiting for me to tell you how good you did, or how perfect you are?" he rumbles. I swear it goes straight to my core even though he isn't touching me ... yet. Goose bumps spread over my skin, and he smirks.

What can I say? Playing with fire is kind of my thing.

I step closer and look up at him through my lashes.

"Yes, please," I breathe. "Tell me what a good girl I am." I bite my lip and watch with satisfaction as his eyes darken with desire. We stand there, frozen, neither of us breathing. The pull between us is too strong to step away.

"Are you done here?" a voice calls, jolting us.

Right, we are still standing in the middle of an arena that is open to the public and used by more people than just our flight. I take the first breath in what feels like hours and force myself to take a step back.

"Yes, we are done *here*," Tate calls back, his eyes still on me, conveying that he is far from done with me.

"We are supposed to meet the rest," I remind him. "And then we have to attend this celebration." I give him an apologetic shrug and grin when he curses under his breath.

# FORTY-TWO

## ARA

The following days are full of training and boring functions, as everyone who thinks highly of themselves is eager to host something in our name. Never mind that two full flights of Belarra's riders died in the last competition, not to mention countless others as well.

I stand between the others in someone's fancy home just outside Avina, and it seems like he has invited all the remaining competitors and everyone who matters in Avina's society. I'm pleasantly surprised when I spot my brother across the room.

"I'll go say hello to Dar," I whisper to Tate, who has stayed glued to my side since we arrived. A glance and a nod, and I'm moving through the room. Tate is incredibly tense tonight, but then he never seems to enjoy any of the parties we're at, and his glare is more effective than a fence in holding off people.

"Hey, stranger." I slide next to my brother and grin up at him. He gives me a small smile, but seems tense as well. What is it with them? Do they know something I don't? My gaze sweeps over the crowd, and Tate's smile when our eyes meet makes me feel instantly better despite my brother's unusually cool greeting.

"Did I do something to piss you off?" I ask, turning back to him.

"No, of course not," he replies gruffly and pulls me into a hug, holding on for a long moment.

"Dar, are you alright?" I study his face more closely now. He looks as calm and collected as always, but there is tension next to his eyes, and they are shadowed. His hair doesn't look as perfect as usual either.

"Yeah, just a lot with the trials and everything." He waves away my concern.

"But you'd tell me if I could do something for you, right?"

He gives me a smile, but it looks strained and his eyes are missing their warmth.

"Is Elena alright?" I prod again.

"Would you stop harassing me? Everything is fine. Elena is visiting her parents."

"Ah, you miss her," I conclude. "You're so sweet." I laugh when I pat his cheek, and he swats my hand away, scowling.

"General, just the man I wanted to talk to." An older man interrupts us, and I leave my brother to his dealings.

"Just who we were looking for." Morgan steps up next to me with a stunning red-haired woman at his side. "Ara, this is my sister. Marina, this is Tamara Blackstone."

"I've heard so much about you." Her voice has me openly gaping. It's the quiet lapping of waves, promising a thundering strength beneath. It's sultry, mesmerizing, and alluring, like a cool breeze on a hot summer day. And it spreads magic with every word, hooking everyone within earshot. A crowd surrounds us in seconds. She sighs, causing everyone to lean in, then signs something to her brother.

"That is why she avoids speaking when people are around," he explains, and Marina rolls her eyes. "Most people lack the self-control to resist a siren. It has a polarizing effect. People hate or obsess about her."

"Shit, I'm sorry," I say, making her giggle. The expressions, especially of the surrounding men, turn feral. She rolls her eyes again and signals something to Morgan.

"She is delighted to meet you and would love to meet up somewhere quieter. But we'll go now before it turns unpleasant." A warning glare accompanies his last words to anyone still fixated on his sister, completely out of character for his usual light and charming personality. He reminds me so much of my brothers that I can't help but like him even more.

On my way back to Tate and the others, I pass a group from Kystis. The wyrms draped around their necks declare them part of the games. One of them lets his eyes run over me, only to say something that makes all of them laugh.

Unease snakes up my back and gets even worse when I recognize the lindwyrm around his neck as the one who chased Solaris and me. At least it's the same color. Other than that, all the beasts look the same to me, just like their riders.

They are tall, pale men with long pale or sometimes reddish hair, their faces half obscured by beards that are carried long and often braided.

I dismiss them and keep walking, but a voice with a hissing lisp makes me stop.

"You cheated, witch," the man snarls. That word again. The same as the man in the alley called me—witch.

I turn around and eye the one I noticed before. He is glaring at me now. I shake my head.

"Go tell someone who cares," I say and walk away.

A few steps later, I nearly run into Tate, who is coming the other way.

"Where are you going?" I ask.

"I was coming to you," he says, his eyes running over me. "What did they say to you?"

I shake my head, smiling at him. "Nothing important. What do you think? How long do we have to stay until we can leave?"

"Too fucking long," he growls, and I laugh while we make our way back to our friends.

TATE

Large gatherings always make me wary. That Ara looks like a dream, and I'm not the only one noticing, isn't helping. I'm not sure if she is oblivious or if she enjoys driving me crazy.

Either way, it's working.

I grind my teeth while a blond fool, old enough to be her father, holds on to her hand far too long. When he steps even closer, I clear my throat. His eyes flit to me, and he drops her hand, taking his leave shortly after.

The next one is a persistent little bugger, and unfortunately, he seems to know Ara. He holds on to her hand as if he has a right to it and ignores my subtle warning. When his hand lands on her shoulder, I've had enough.

I'm next to him in a heartbeat, removing his hand while keeping it in a painful grip. I increase the pressure while giving him a smile that lets him know I mean business. Sweat pops up on his brow, and Ara nearly chokes on a laugh.

"Tate Kyronos, Pascal Devont, heir of the Devont family." Ara makes introductions since I don't make any efforts. So this little shit thinks that because he has money, he can disregard Ara's personal space. Not on my watch.

I lean in so only he can hear my next words.

"There are things you don't get to touch, no matter how much money you have," I whisper. "Unless you want to lose your hand or your life. Do you understand?" I pin him with a glare.

The man nods frantically and hurries off as soon as I release him.

"You are in a rare mood today." Ara slips her arm through mine. "Let's get some fresh air before Avina's high society is missing a few of its members." She grins. I look down at her arm circling mine. Seems like we stop pretending for tonight, not that I'm complaining.

"So you don't like parties?" she asks once we step out into the night air.

"It depends," I answer.

"On what?"

"The party."

"I have seen you now a few times in surroundings like this." She makes a sweeping gesture. "And you did not look like you enjoyed yourself."

I wonder why, when someone always seems to think they have a right to what's mine, and I can't challenge them openly for it.

And then it's hard to keep track of everything when so many people are around. Even though I had been within sight, it had taken me some shoving and precious minutes to get to Ara when those shits from Kystis talked to her. I grip the stone railing so hard my knuckles turn white.

"Hey, relax." Ara trails a finger over the back of my hand, tracing the marking. At her touch, the tension seeps out of me, replaced by awareness. Her gaze is fixed on the back of my hand, on the featherlight touch that sears my skin. "We don't have to go back in there right away," she murmurs, and my heart stumbles.

"What," I say, then clear my throat. "What do you want to do instead?"

She gestures to the dark garden beyond the balcony. "How about a walk?"

Hasn't she realized yet that I would follow her to the depths of the mists without a second thought?

I nod.

The night air is heavy with the scent of jasmine and roses. The laid-out gardens are serene and dark, the sound of people blissfully muted and fading against the crunch of gravel beneath our feet.

A quiet giggle to our right tells me we are not the only ones with the idea of a night stroll, and I gently steer Ara in the other direction.

My body hums with her walking next to me, and I pull her into my side as soon as we are out of the light. Her quiet sigh and the way she leans into me settle me.

"I'm not good with crowds," I confess. "Ever since..." Even mentioning the attack is hard, like something constricts my throat.

"The attack?" Ara inquires. "The one where you lost Jared's brother, right?"

My eyes snap to her.

"Jared told me," she says softly, "I'm sorry that happened to you. I'm even more sorry you had to deal with it on your own and the shit people made up about you. Don't look so stunned." She smiles up at me.

"I thought..." I swallow against the tightness in my throat. "What you said before I left..."

"You thought I believed it?" Her eyes widen, her hands reaching for my face. "No, baby, gods no. I would never..." She shakes her head. "I know you did everything you could."

"It wasn't enough," I mutter, and the words taste bitter.

But she shakes her head at me and pulls me down, sealing my lips with hers, replacing the bitterness with something sweet. The kiss is soft, reassuring, soothing. I pull her closer. What would I give to stay in this moment with her?

She pulls back with a soft sigh, then turns and snuggles into me, her back to my front, my arms circling her waist, her hands resting on mine. She leans her head back against my shoulder and takes in the stars above us, then contentedly hums in her throat.

"Whenever I look up at the stars, my problems shrink until they are insignificant. What are the thoughts and worries of one person compared to all of this? To everything that came before me and will follow?"

I tighten my hold on her. "Nothing about you is insignificant. Not to me."

She turns her head and kisses my jaw. "Tell me about it."

I tense.

"I can't," I whisper, and when she stiffens, I prepare myself for the accusation, for the doubt, for everything that typically follows, but it never comes.

"They made you promise?" she hisses with anger on her face, but it's not directed at me; it's on my behalf. And if I didn't love this woman so much already, I would fall for her right here and now, while she looks up at me, her eyes blazing, her jaw set, ready to go to war for me.

# FORTY-THREE

## ARA

I'm agitated while pacing the keep's kitchen. Lyla and Lorcan watch me from the table—one of them amused, the other concerned. The rest are out scouting for a raid, and I don't know how they can sit here so relaxed knowing that.

"They will be fine," Lyla soothes. "Or is that not the only thing on your mind?"

She's right. Ever since I found out last night that Tate is bound by a promise too, I've been unable to stop thinking and worrying about it. Not being able to talk about what happened is eating him alive. I can see it. He had guilt written all over his face as soon as I mentioned the attack, and I can't help him if I don't know what happened.

I left while Tate was showering after training, and I know he'll be pissed about it when I get back, but this is important. I look at two of the people I consider friends by now, and no one knows more about magic than Lorcan.

"Is there a way to hide a promise?" I ask him. "And is there a way to break one without killing the person involved?"

Lorcan cocks an eyebrow. "Planning to blackmail someone into submission?"

I roll my eyes at him. "Is it?"

"They say the divine can break a promise, but I haven't seen it. And yes. Some gifts can mold them, bend them, and if the person already has markings, you could hide the promise between them."

And suddenly it all makes sense. Tate's obsession with the trials, his despair when we failed at first. What did Janus call it? A favor from the goddess? Tate needs to win, to free himself from this promise. Determination spreads through me. I will get him this favor, whatever it takes.

"Does it have to be a specific god? Or can any of them do it?" I ask.

"What?"

I scowl at him. "Come on, you have hundreds of years of experience. Surely, you can guess what I'm asking. Which god can break a promise?"

"I don't know," he snarls, his temper rising at my rude tone. "Even if you think I'm old enough to have been walking the earth next to them, I'm not."

"You're not very helpful," I grumble.

"Talking about helpful, do you know why your brother is looking for a dragon?" Lorcan asks, and I furrow my brow.

"Darren?"

"Yes, the general," he confirms impatiently, as if I don't have more than one brother.

I shrug. "Are you hired for anything else but fighting?"

"Tracking." Lorcan leans back in his chair. "Is he looking for someone?"

"I don't think Tate talked to him about the attacks, so... Your guess is as good as mine." I shrug again. We are quiet for a while.

"Someone called me a witch last night," I tell them, and Lorcan's gaze turns watchful.

"Someone from Kystis?" he asks, and I nod.

"It's an old word for someone controlling magic. They still use it in Kystis to refer to someone with your gift."

I frown. "How would he know about that?" I ask.

"That's what I'm worried about." Lorcan nods. "It means someone either suspects or knows what you are. Be careful. Don't use your gift around others if you can help it."

"Why do they hate us so much?" I whisper.

"Do you want to hear a story? A true one?" he asks, and when I nod, Lyla rises.

"I'll make some tea and get out the biscuits," she singsongs, her grin wide. "I love to listen to Lorcan's stories," she explains for my sake.

"She badgered me into telling her one every night when she got here," Lorcan grumbles. I laugh because I can picture it perfectly. "You would think in the last hundred years she would have grown tired of it."

"A hundred years?" I splutter, my eyes flying to Lyla.

"She's held up well, hasn't she?" Lorcan says, then laughs when Lyla shoves his shoulder, while setting down mugs.

"All Tynan's fault," Lyla says at my questioning look, and I'd bet that's another story worth hearing.

Lorcan settles in, getting comfortable, while Lyla bustles around us and sets down a plate filled with cookies and a pot full of steaming tea. He starts only once Lyla sits, shaking his head at her eager smile. And as soon as he starts, I understand her fascination. He always has a pleasant voice—deep, rumbly, and calm—but as the story begins, it becomes almost hypnotic, captivating.

"Now, this was about 400 years ago, when a newly crowned king coveted the princess from the neighboring realm. Not only was she beautiful, but her magic gift was one of the strongest ever recorded." He smiles wistfully. "She was strong and not just in magic, but also in will, and she saw no benefit in giving up the right to her throne to reign second to a husband in another kingdom."

"Understandable," I agree, and he gives me a scolding look, so I shut up.

"Well, the king didn't want to accept it. The more she denied him, the more determined he was to make her his." He takes a sip of his tea. "And then he made the mistake of stealing her from her home and bringing her back to his palace. While he was sure he could woo her, she was enraged beyond belief. She wrought devastation on his castle and his kingdom. But that wasn't enough." He looks into the distance as if he remembers it. "She wanted to humiliate him for his audacity to force her hand, so she took his throne and made it hers."

"The ease with which she overpowered him, the most powerful man of Belarra, sparked fear in rulers of neighboring kingdoms, fearing for their power. Everyone was afraid to face her. And her end came quietly in the dark of night." He clears his throat. "Long story short, their helplessness in the face of her gift frightened them, so they outlawed it."

His voice turns more distant. "It spiraled from there and ended in what you know today. Were they right to fear her power? Maybe." He pauses. "If all of you who gathered under Tynan's protection were to rise and decide to take the throne, you could." His eyes rest on me. "Well, taking the throne is still the plan, only peacefully."

I ignore his comment and the twist in my chest. "So, essentially, they hunt us because one of us had a well-deserved tantrum," I ask.

The dragon's mouth quirks. "Yeah, essentially."

"Talk about actions having consequences," I mutter.

We are quiet for a while, and Lyla covers Lorcan's hand with hers, squeezing it.

"Thank you for the story." She smiles.

"What realm was the princess from?"

"It doesn't exist anymore. She was one of your ancestors. Well, technically, her brother was," Lorcan says.

So one of my ancestors had to marry the king of Belarra, which resulted in her laying waste to the kingdom. A shiver works its way up my spine. This is too close for comfort.

A commotion in the entry hall makes Lyla jump up. "They're back." She rushes out of the room. Lorcan and I sit there in silence, both of us caught up in our thoughts.

But it isn't long until Lyla comes back, with a wide smile on her face.

"We have someone who will be glad to see you," she beams, and my brow furrows, but then Tynan steps through the door, and after him follows...

"Alessia!" I run to the girl who is no longer a slave. I wrote to Tynan, but I never thought... "Wait, you went to get her?" At Tynan's nod, I whirl around to Lyla. "Why didn't you tell me?"

She shrugs. "I didn't want you to be disappointed if it didn't work."

"Thank you." I throw my arms around Tynan, who looks perplexed at the gesture.

Lyla giggles behind me. "I told you I'll keep her. Finally, someone who the lot of you doesn't intimidate."

I help Lyla get Alessia settled in one of the guest rooms, and when I come back down, I'm already later than expected, so I decline Lorcan's offer to train my gift and head back to Avina instead.

# FORTY-FOUR

## TATE

I'M IRRITATED WHEN I RETURN TO AN EMPTY ROOM, BUT I conclude that she must have slipped out and is with the others. I love the time I get with her, but it pisses me off that we have to sneak around. Why can't she just break the betrothal?

In the last few days she's slept more nights in my bed than in her own, but every time I try to talk to her about it, she either distracts me or changes the topic.

I get dressed, but when I knock on Ara's door, she isn't there, and she isn't down with the others either. Through Daeva, I learned she took Solaris for a flight, and they headed east. What the fuck? If she wanted to visit her family, why didn't she just tell me?

Relief and irritation war inside my chest when she comes into my room in the late afternoon.

"Where were you?" I snap.

"Were you worried?"

"Of course, I was worried. Don't evade the question."

She saunters over to me, straddling me with a seductive smile on her lips, her hand coming up to caress my cheek. "I was perfectly safe, I promise."

"That doesn't answer my question."

"Then don't ask questions." She leans in, placing kisses along my jaw. "We have two options: we can fight about it or use our time for something much better. I know which option I'll pick. What do you say?"

Damn that woman and her secrets.

"I will get to the bottom of this," I say, but my hands run down her sides and I pull her closer.

She hums in approval. "Right choice," she murmurs before her mouth devours mine. The kiss is hungry, and a husky laugh leaves her lips when I twist so she ends up on the bed underneath me.

"You drive me fucking insane, sunshine," I growl, and she laughs again.

"Insanity looks good on you, though," she teases.

I bite her neck just where it smoothes out into her shoulder, frustration and possessive need coursing through me. She consumes me.

"Marking me as yours?" she teases, laughter in her voice.

"I would stamp it across your brow if I could," I growl, and she laughs again.

"I'll be yours for as long as you'll have me," she whispers, her voice soft now, while she traces my face. And her eyes are full of unspoken words. I just wish she would spit them out.

"Then plan on forever," I murmur.

Our next kiss is softer, savoring, appreciating.

I want answers, but she's right. We have so little time alone, wasting it on a fight seems a shame. So I trace her every curve and dip again and again even though I've already committed them to memory by now.

I love the way her sighs turn to breathy moans, the soft hums of approval I can draw from her lips, and I drink up her sounds, keeping them.

Our clothes disappear piece by leisurely discarded piece, while I worship every part of her on my way to her pulsing core. The sounds she makes, the way she responds to my fingers, my lips, my tongue, is addictive, and I watch tension gather in every line of her body, mesmerized, until she shatters with my name on her lips, her body going from taut and writhing in pleasure to languid and boneless. Motionless apart from her heaving chest.

I kiss my way up her body, and when her eyes flutter open, I push into her. I groan at the sensation, her moan mingling with mine. No matter how often I have her, this first moment of invasion and surrender gets me every time.

"I love the way you fill me," Ara whispers, as if she read my mind. Her inner muscles squeeze me, and I groan again, her quiet laughter a delicious vibration running through both of us.

"Like this?" I push deeper and savor the way pleasure clouds her eyes.

"Yes," she moans.

"And this?" I pull out and slam into her, burying myself even deeper than before.

"Gods, yes."

"The gods have nothing to do with it," I tease.

"Oh, but they made you just for me."

"Or you for me."

"Who cares as long as we end up right here, right now?" she pants, meeting every one of my thrusts.

Our fingers intertwine, skin slickens, and as her body arches off the bed like an offering worthy of a god, my mouth finds her breast. Mine. She is all mine.

Watching her surrender and demand at once, to see her fire and fight tempered by pleasure, is the best kind of reward. It doesn't take long until she tightens around me, her muscles quivering. Ara bites my shoulder to muffle her scream while she ripples, squeezes me, and almost takes me over the edge with her. But I'm not done with her yet.

I pick up her pliant form and carry her over to the desk, settling once more between her legs while she wraps her arms around my shoulders, burying her face in my neck.

"Insatiable," she mumbles against my skin before kissing my neck.

"You were the one telling me to make good use of the time, and I don't know how long it'll be until we have time alone again."

"True, and that was not a complaint." She kisses up my neck before she finds my lips, our pace slower, more savoring this time. When she goes over the edge again, pleasure consumes me, and I hold her close while I let go.

We don't get much sleep that night, but my only regret is having to wake her in the early morning hours when she fell asleep in my arms not long ago. She grumbles at me and pulls the pillow over her head when I pepper her face with kisses.

I chuckle at her adorable attempts, but pry the pillow out of her fingers and away from her face.

"We have to get up, sunshine," I tell her.

"Just tell them you broke me last night," she mumbles, and I laugh.

"Are you sure that's what you want me to tell them?"

"If it means I can spend the day in bed snuggled up to you, yes, then I'm sure." She sounds more awake now, and I love the picture she paints. One day, we'll have that.

"Come on, we have to get moving." I scoop her up in my arms and carry her over into the shower.

Showering together makes us slightly late, and we hurry through breakfast, but neither of us minds.

Jared's eyes wander from me to Ara and back before he grins.

He leans into Ara and whispers something, and I raise my eyebrow in question when Ara laughs.

"He thanks me for your good mood," she murmurs, relaying his message. I shake my head and grin. Cheeky bastard.

Someone clears his throat behind me, and when I turn and find a messenger bearing my family's colors, my stomach drops.

"Your Highness, the queen requests your presence."

# FORTY-FIVE

## ARA

THE KING IS DEAD. WHILE TATE HAD STILL BEEN GONE, THE news had made the rounds, and I dread what that means for me, for us.

*Frederick can't just change the promise,* I remind myself, but still, there is a tension in the air, a foreboding I can't quite ignore. Frederick is king now, or will be after the ceremony tomorrow. I suppress a shudder when I think back to his words at the ball.

*You don't tell a king no.*

Jared and I took the time to answer all the questions raised by the messenger's appearance. At least Joel and the girls had already known, but the rest of Tate's flight had been stunned by the news. Understandably so.

Tate comes back late at night, but I'm waiting in his room for him. I wouldn't have been able to sleep anyway. He looks tense, troubled, and defeated when he steps through the door. But the tired smile he sends me makes me breathe easier, and I'm by his side in an instant.

"Are you alright?" I whisper, helping him out of a formal coat I never saw on him. I'm even more relieved when he lets me help him. The memory of how he had pushed me away the last time he had been hurting had had my stomach in cramps for the past hours.

"I guess I am... Yeah..." He swallows, then shakes his head.

"No, I'm not," he corrects himself. "I should be. My father's and my relationship was ... strained is not even close. No matter what I did, it was never good enough. I always disappointed him." He lets out a long breath, then chuckles humourlessly. "Damn, the bastard is dead, and I should rejoice, but..." He shrugs. "When I talked to Fred weeks ago, he said Father made him feel inferior by comparing him to me." He pauses. "Why couldn't he have said any of that to me? Anything. Literally. Any halfhearted, 'you didn't do too bad, son' would have been great." He shakes his head.

"He will never know the reason for my decisions. Fuck." He grips his hair. "I was his biggest disappointment. The last time I saw him, we barely spoke ten words. I'll never be able to explain." He laughs again, mockingly.

"Not that it would have made a difference. But... Maybe I should go and shout at his sarcophagus." He shakes his head and exhales through his nose.

"So in short, I'm a fucking mess at a time when I should be concentrating. There are people after me. After you. The trials. My brother plans only the gods know what. And here I am, falling apart because my father didn't ... pat my back?" He shakes his head. "Fuck, that's pathetic."

I step up to him, grabbing his face with both hands.

"Now, you listen to me." I look into his eyes. "You're an amazing man. You're perfect the way you are. And if your father couldn't see that, that's on him. He's the one who missed out." I place a soft kiss on his lips. "If he is the reason you are always so hard on yourself, then rotting in a crypt somewhere is too good for him. I'm sorry you're hurting, and I wish you'd had the chance to make things right with him." I search his eyes to make sure he understands me. "Not for him. I don't give a rat's ass about him. But for you. And it's alright to still mourn his death. He was your father. And I guess on some level, you can't help but love him, even if he was an asshole."

That makes him release a breath that almost sounds like a laugh.

"Just because he was a cold-hearted bastard doesn't mean you have to be cold too. I see you. And I wouldn't change a thing. Not even your annoying habit of showing up when I'm in trouble and saving my ass whether or not I want you to."

His lips quirk.

"Now let me spoil, pamper, and distract you. And tomorrow, we will tackle all the other problems. Okay?"

"Pamper?" He arches an eyebrow at me.

"Yeah." I grin at him. "Something tells me that for a pampered prince, you got little of that."

He chuckles, and my world lights up again.

"And what would you know about being pampered, my warrior princess?" he teases.

"A lot." I grin at him. "Because even if I fought it sometimes, I grew up pretty pampered. You might have noticed I have a way to wrap everyone around my finger and get exactly what I want."

"Do tell." He chuckles again and wraps his arms around me.

I grin up at him, and he places a kiss on my brow.

"You are pretty amazing, and I'm a lucky guy."

"Yes, you are."

"And so very humble," he deadpans, then grins.

"Who wants to be perfect?" I ask. "That would be incredibly boring. Don't you think?"

I'm content to see the light back in his eyes.

"You know you're going to be stuck with me, right?" he asks me softly. I turn to him, rising to meet his lips, while something in my chest twists.

"And there's no place I'd rather be," I tell him between kisses, giving him the only truth I can, while I try to convince myself that I can enjoy the stolen moments as long as they last and that they are better than nothing.

# FORTY-SIX

## ARA

Despite the king's death and Frederick's rushed coronation, the games go on as if nothing has happened, and maybe no one has a choice. I can't see Iza paying regard to the affairs of a human, even a king.

We are once more gathered within the arena's curved walls. Only today, Frederick is occupying the king's throne, his mother stoic and regal next to him.

Fewer flights occupy the sand, and with Avina, we are the only contenders left from Belarra. Harea and Ilyn have only two groups left, too, but Kystis and Muntos fared better, with three flights remaining each. Their heavier animals were probably an advantage in the maze.

The sky is blue above us, not a cloud in sight, and I can't help but hope it will stay that way. A gleaming letter waiting on the table this morning summoned us. It's been ten days since the last round, and I hope whatever the goddess has for us today will be kinder. Solaris has just reached his old glory, and I don't know if I can stand another week of complaining.

*"I have to listen to you pine for him all day, too,"* Solaris counters, and I snort.

*"The only one who has it even worse than me is Daeva,"* he teases. *"Tell me more."*

He snorts. *"Just look at him."*

And even if I want to, I keep facing the front. I don't want to hand Frederick any excuses to use his newly won power.

A shower of light announces the goddess, who this time sits on the ledge, dangling her legs over the edge.

"Today is about... No, let's not make it that easy." She leans back on her hands. Her eyes sweep over us. "Every unit has to rely on its members..." I don't like the way her eyes rest on me. "I'll pick some-one"—her eyes jump to Tate—"no, let's make that two in every flight to compete for their team."

I'm not surprised when only seconds later I'm bathed in golden light, and Tate doesn't fare any better. Of course, she would pick us.

Two people from each flight are illuminated. Iza makes a shooing motion, and everyone else leaves the arena. Our flight gives us worried glances, but I put on a reassuring smile and hope failing just gets them kicked out, not killed.

The space around us transforms. Sand-colored walls rise around us, and I hastily step in Tate's direction when one wall approaches me. They grow higher and higher until the sky is just a small band above us, and Tate and I are alone in a room without any of the other contestants in sight.

Iza speaks again.

> "I'm the door you dread to choose,
> through me, friends and hearts to lose.
> Yet whisper once what hides in shade,
> and I will vanish, challenge paid.

. . .

Hold your tongue, keep truth confined,
then test your strength and sharpened mind.
For every hour you don't speak,
the path grows dark, the end more bleak."

WE STAND IN A SMALL ROOM, THE SAND-COLORED WALLS around us are smooth and bare. Without a crevice in sight —unscalable.

There is only one exit, and when we step toward it, a wall of flame surges up, barring it.

*Okay, maybe this isn't so bad.*

I reach for the flames, but when my hand makes contact, I jump back and look at my stinging fingers. It burned me.

"The flames of truth," Tate says, eyeing the silvery-blue fire dancing in front of us. He's right. The flickering wall barring our way looks just like it's described in the stories. I guess we *are* playing with the gods here.

"Something you dread and hides in the shade..." Tate murmurs.

"Causing you to lose friends or love, and it vanishes when whispered," I complete the clues.

We look at each other. "Secrets."

"Who would have guessed from the goddess of the hunt and secrets?" I comment dryly, trying hard to keep the dread from showing. My stomach just dropped to the ground and buried itself so deep in the sand that I have no chance of retrieving it.

There is no way this can end well, not with the secrets I'm keeping and what Tate means to me. *Are you fucking happy now?* I direct the thoughts toward Iza, and I think I hear faint laughter.

Hissing comes from behind us, and we both whirl around, only to find a snake writhing on the ground. She rises, showing us her blue underside. Suddenly, I remember pain in my leg and a blue-bellied snake flying through the air. The rest of the memories follow in a rush —how my magic gift fought and eliminated it, how it drained my gift, painful walks and sweaty nights, falling into the river, Calix fishing me out...

"I remember," I whisper. "One of those beasts bit me during Picking, and it drained my gift."

"A blue-belly bit you during Picking?" Tate asks, pulling me behind him.

"Yes, and I survived it." I step in front of him. "You are the one with healing powers here, so better I get hurt than you."

"Mists, no. That's not how it works."

The snake shimmers, and suddenly, there are two.

"So we kill the snakes and get out of here? Maybe we should hurry." The snakes shimmer and multiply again, leaving us with four of the beasts.

"Wait, there was something about whispering what hides and the challenge being paid, wasn't there?" Tate says, while I only have eyes for the hissing, writhing creatures in front of us.

"So we blurt out secrets and can walk out?" I ask. *Maybe I'd rather fight those snakes.*

*"Don't be ridiculous, just talk to him."* Solaris chimes in.

*"I'll lose him."*

*"You'll have to tell him at some point."* I know Solaris is right, and I will tell him ... eventually.

Tate takes my hand and squeezes.

"We'll get through this," he whispers, but he doesn't know what he's talking about. There is no way he'll look at me the same way if this goes as we suspect.

"I love you." I blurt out the words I was too scared to voice until now. The hissing stops. "I need you to know that, to remember that, okay?" I whisper, and Tate's heated gaze sets my skin ablaze. His eyes linger on my mouth before returning to mine with a look of pure agony.

"You have the worst fucking timing ever," he grumbles. "Couldn't you have told me that while we were alone and preferably somewhere with a bed?" He gives me a wicked grin. "Or a desk?" Heat thunders through me at that reminder. He looks around. "And not at the beginning of a competition that ensures that I have you next to me for who knows how long without being able to touch or kiss you?"

And gods do I hope he still wants to once we reach the end.

The room is once more empty and silent around us, and the doorway is open, with no flame in sight.

"How about taking turns?" Tate asks, and I nod weakly while grasping his hand tighter, holding on to him.

The next room seems empty at first, but as soon as we step into it, flames shoot up in front of the other exit, and there is a rumble above us. When we look up, a grate with spikes starts to descend.

"Lovely," I comment.

"I joined the skyriders solely for this trial," Tate says, and it stops.

"To break the promise," I whisper, and he nods. "Is it bad?"

He nods again.

"And you can't tell me anything about it?"

He sighs. "I had to leave." And I know there is more to his statement. He is trying to tell me something.

Still holding hands, we walk through the door and down a corridor, only to end up in a room just like the ones before. Familiar flames surge up as soon as we enter. And water pours in from the sides.

"Something bad would have happened if you had stayed," I say, and the spark of excitement in his eyes tells me I'm right. Maybe I can't promise him forever, but I won't give up on him either. I'll give him back his freedom, even if it's the last thing I do.

Every room gives us less time before something threatens our lives, but it stops, and the flames clear our path as soon as one of us reveals a secret. And as we work our way through the maze of rooms, each question brings me closer to the truth behind his promise, and soon I am sure it has something to do with the succession to the throne.

It's fine in the beginning. There are small secrets to share, things we don't have a problem confiding. But soon, only the heavier ones are left, and both of us have secrets we can't even share because promises bind us.

Dread stacks up in my gut like lead weights.

Once again, we stand before the flames. It's my turn, and I rack my brain looking for anything I could declare a secret while ignoring the ones pressing in on my mind. But I come up empty. Neither of us moves, neither of us speaks, while we look around trying to spot the danger.

There is a buzz like a bowstring being released, and Tate throws himself over me, a puff of air leaving his lungs when we land. He throws up a shield around us before he lets me sit up. I look around, but there is no arrow in sight. Tate winces.

"Could you?" he asks, turning his back to me, and there it is, lodged in his left shoulder. Despite the armor he's wearing. My breath catches. About a hand span to the right, and it could have hit his heart.

More arrows fly, and voices start around us, cursing, begging, pleading, but neither of us pays attention since Tate's shield holds, and we have more important things to take care of. I help unbuckle his armor, and with a sympathetic wince from me and a muffled groan from him, I pull the arrow free, using my foot as leverage against his back.

Blood gushes from the wound, and I press my hands to it while Tate heals himself.

"Done," he says, and only now do I dare to remove my hands from his bloody skin. Only a pinkish patch of skin remains. I slip my arms around him from behind, my head resting against his back, while I simply hold him for a moment. When I slacken my hold, he lifts one of my hands to his mouth, kissing my bloody palm, then turns around in my hold, facing me.

"I hate when you get hurt," I murmur.

"I'm terrified of losing you," he whispers, and he's not the only one. I swallow and wipe at my face when a single tear escapes. I can't lose him.

The arrows have stopped, but I'm not sure if it's because of Tate's admission or because we waited them out.

Tate rolls his shoulder, and I help him back into the armor with care, paying attention to every latch I close. I make sure it sits and protects him properly, even if divine arrows seem to go through it.

He has a smudge of blood on his cheek, probably from my hands, and since I wiped at my face, I can only imagine how ghastly I look—with my hands, my face, and the front of my armor stained in his blood.

The next room instantly fills with smoke. No, not smoke, mist. And suddenly, I have a terrible feeling about this.

*"Just tell him,"* Solaris urges, but I shake my head. I can't tell him. If I tell him, I'll lose him.

A burn starts on my skin, where the mist touches me. I suck in a breath and step back, closer to Tate, but otherwise stay silent. Tate throws up a shield around us, keeping the mist at bay, while I search for another secret.

"I honestly can't think of anything," he mutters. "Nothing I would get over my lips at least." And I know he's talking about his promise.

"Me neither," I murmur, but his eyes flit to me, alert, like he knows I'm lying. My stomach cramps.

The mist gets thicker, tendrils snaking along Tate's shield, reaching for us. A clicking sound starts, reminding me of the beasts hiding in the mists. Shit.

There is a voice, and by the way Tate's eyes search the mist, he hears it too.

Then I can make out the words, and I freeze.

"Hey, little warrior," Lorcan purrs. *No. Please, no.* But despite my plea, Lorcan steps out of the mist, his eyes fixed on me.

Next to me, Tate is now as rigid as I am. I grip his hand, afraid he will step away from me.

"Do you want to take up where we left off the last time?" Lorcan asks. Those are the same words he spoke weeks ago, but this illusion steps up to me and reaches for me in a way that makes it seem all ... all wrong. And I realize in this instant that if I don't talk, I'll lose Tate for sure.

# FORTY-SEVEN

## TATE

The moment the mist solidifies, Ara becomes as tense as the stone wall surrounding us. I step closer, but she doesn't react.

What is she hiding that she lies about having more secrets? What is so bad that she would rather risk our lives than reveal it?

There are voices, and then the dragon steps out of the white fog around us. Trepidation settles in my chest, and my mind flashes back to the way he cornered her that night in Platoria. Her grip on my hand is so tight her knuckles turn white.

The dragon reaches for her, and jealousy rushes through me, hot and vicious. The implication that she let him touch her... Is that why she tried to push me away, even after I cleared up the misunderstanding? Is that why she said I couldn't fix it? Had she already moved on?

I take a step back, but that jerks her out of her stupor. She whirls around, releasing my hand and grabs my face, holding on like her life depends on it.

"It's not like that. I haven't been with him, I swear." *Truth.* "I... I got the information he owed me." *Truth.* "I barely know him." *Lie.*

Information always comes at a price. My heart sinks when I remember the promise on her skin.

"What did you give him?"

She pales. "Nothing important." *Lie.*

I ask her more questions to understand why she is lying to me, but it gets worse and worse. She lies at every fucking turn. And every single one of her lies hits like a thrown knife, splitting me open. She doesn't trust me.

"You're hiding things from me." It's a statement, not a question. But she answers anyway, shaking her head in denial.

"No." *Lie.*

"You still don't trust me." When she opens her mouth to answer, I hold up my hand. "Stop fucking lying to me," I snap.

"I'm not."

I laugh, but it's hollow and dead. "Oh, how I wish that were true." I shake my head at her. "I'm a truth-teller."

The illusions and the flames disappear. I turn and head to the exit. When I look over my shoulder, Ara is still standing in the exact spot I left her, her eyes huge, her face pale.

"I hope your secrets are worth what you're willing to pay."

I step into a circular room with twelve doors, and in the middle of it is a stone block with a shining golden ball resting on it.

We are the first to arrive, but I feel defeated.

## ARA

Tate walks away from me, and my chest feels frozen to the point where it's hard to breathe. Everything inside me aches, calls out for him to turn around, to come back, to look at me, to hold me. But he doesn't.

Truth-telling.

My mind stumbles over everything I said. I was so desperate to hold on to him that I barely remember what I said. But I know I lied … a lot. I flinch.

Isn't that what I always do—hide, lie, and keep secrets?

I look down at my hands, flexing them, as if being cared for and loved is something physical I could hold on to. My knuckles turn white, and still it slips through my fingers, leaving my chest empty.

I don't know how to make it right. The harder I try, the worse it gets.

But I have to try.

"I'm bound by promises, too," I call after Tate, and he stops but doesn't turn around.

"I'm used to your fucking secrets, Ara." He pauses. "But not to you lying to me."

"But—"

"I can't do this right now," he rasps, the sound so defeated my throat closes up. My body grows numb while he keeps walking away from me.

His hand reaches out and closes around the golden globe, securing us the win. Yet defeat is all that registers with me.

The ground shifts, nearly sending me to my knees. My body is heavy, and all I want is to bury myself in the sand, hide, shut out the world, but we are bathed in greyish sunlight and free of the walls, hundreds of eyes trained on us. Our flight waits off to the side, their faces lighting up the moment they see us.

The sand beneath my feet feels like mud as I make my way over to them. Every step is dragging me down while I keep my head high and my spine ramrod straight.

"You did it!" Calix throws his arm around my shoulder, pulling me next to him. I nod numbly. Behind me, Jared congratulates Tate.

I force air through the tightness in my throat and stare straight ahead, unblinking, until the world becomes a whirl of colors. But my cheeks stay dry.

I knew I couldn't keep him and still ... I had hoped for a little more time.

And he doesn't even know about Tynan or his brother yet.

I allow myself to lean into Calix. His gaze rests on me, questioning, but I ignore it.

"Are you hurt?" he whispers, and I shake my head, lying yet again.

No matter what I do, my thoughts come back to the man standing a few steps away. Four steps to my left and one step back, to be exact —that's how pathetically aware I am of his presence.

I have no idea how long it takes, but finally, a rumble starts up and the walls sink into the ground, revealing too many dead contestants.

*I hope your secrets are worth what you're willing to pay.*

Tate's words circle through my mind, and I'm afraid to consider the cost.

Of the ten flights entering this round, two have been reduced to eight members, and only three remain complete.

The powerful twang of a bowstring makes me flinch. The dull impact of something heavy hitting the ground draws my eyes to the two heaps of bodies where the competing flights, with the fewest members, stood before. All of them felled by an arrow through the heart. My stomach heaves.

Iza places her bow next to herself, still dangling her feet like she is unconcerned, that she just killed sixteen warriors at a whim. Outraged shrieks and roars sound above us as the slain riders' mounts turn on the goddess. But she only smiles, and with a wave of her hands, the sound and the creatures are gone.

"Another addition to my eternal hunting grounds." She smiles.

My shock switches over to anger. If Tate and I had failed, she would have murdered my flight, my friends. Was that the cost Tate had been speaking of?

"Why did you do that?" My accusing words carry in the shocked silence, and all eyes whip to me. There are groans around me, but my whole flight steps closer.

The goddess's eyes rest on me as if she can't believe I dare to question her.

"I had no use for them." She shrugs. "Humans are incredibly boring to hunt."

She would have killed my friends because they weren't fun to hunt?

"So you kill them? That's wrong," I tell her. Calix's arm around my shoulder tightens in warning, but I step out of his grip, my skin heating.

Iza laughs, a cruel, haunting sound.

"You dare to lecture me on wrong and right?" There is a clear warning in her tone.

"Clearly, someone has to." I glare at her. "Being a god doesn't give you the right to do whatever you want," I challenge, and there is a collective intake of breath, which leaves the air in the arena too thin, too tense to breathe.

"Lucky for you, I decided to see the games through to the end." There is no way to miss the threat in her posture and voice this time. "I would have thought you one of my most loyal worshippers. You value your secrets, do you not?" Her smile is calculating and cold. She disappears in a flare of light and a thunderclap so loud my ears ring.

"You think angering the goddess who oversees the games was a smart move?" Mariel hisses.

"But calling her out like that was pretty badass," Calix throws in.

"Let's hope we'll survive it," Zaza adds glumly from behind us.

There I go again, making things worse. The initial high mood after our win has morphed into something darker, and I don't even dare to look in Tate's direction.

"Are you okay?" Joel sidles up to me while we leave the arena and head back to the house.

I give him an overbright smile. "I'm splendid."

He shakes his head at me. "My offer still stands. My ear and my shoulder are all yours."

I give him a tired smile. "Thanks." And even though I crave physical comfort, it's not his arms or shoulders I want.

## TATE

Jared and Calix do their best to brighten the mood, and soon, laughter and joking hum in the air around us while we head back. And why shouldn't they celebrate? Only one trial is left, and with the token, we have a clear head start. Our odds stand better than ever.

Ara and I are like the silent eyes of a storm between them, the tension growing, and the trust between us unraveling. The fragile net frayed by the words that stay unspoken.

My eyes wander over her. How can it be that she has no problem calling out a goddess, but can't bring herself to tell me what is going on in that pretty head of hers?

Her eyes are downcast, her answers monosyllabic, while she looks like the weight of the world drags her down. I can't take it any longer.

I grab her arm and hold her back, waving her friends on, until we are at the end of the group.

"No matter what you would have told me, I would never have given up your secrets," I whisper. "Do you still not trust me even that much?"

"It's not about trust," she huffs out. She opens her mouth again, but closes it, saying nothing, and marches off, following the others.

"It is," I call after her, the words a challenge. She whirls around and comes back.

"No." She shoves against my chest. "It isn't." She shoves again, then huffs out a breath and continues much softer, "I will only say the wrong things..." She pauses. "And you'll walk away again."

"You don't trust—"

"This is not about trust!" she yells. "I just don't have the right words to make you want to stay."

"I don't need the right words, just what is going on inside you," I demand, and step up, erasing the space between us.

"You want to know what's going on inside me?" She hits her chest with a broken laugh. "The ground is crumbling beneath my feet while I'm trying to outrun it. And saying too much causes holes that make me stumble. But if I fall, it will not just hurt. It will shatter my life into jagged shards ready to carve up everyone I care about." Tears run down her face, and she looks down as if she is trying to hide from me. But I tip her chin up, bringing her eyes back to me.

"It feels like the fates hate me," she whispers. "Like I can't get anything right, no matter how hard I try... And then this past week..." She closes her eyes for a moment before looking at me again, and the pain, the despair in her eyes, shreds me. "Having you back, keeping us a secret, knowing—"

The need to comfort her, to take her pain away, is overwhelming, and her sentence breaks off in a surprised gasp when my fingers glide along her jaw until I frame her face. Her brow furrows, her eyes jumping between mine, and I close the distance, sealing her lips with mine.

They taste salty from her tears, and for a heartbeat, she tries to pull away, but my hands keep her in place. Her surrender is like a sigh, like something settling in both of us.

Her arms come around my neck, and I pull her closer, trying to erase the distance caused by the trial. She angles her head, letting me in, while her urgency, her desperation, color a kiss that suddenly seems to have a predefined timeline.

Can't she feel I want her, no matter what the fates have to say about that? I slide a hand into her hair, and I tilt her head back, holding on while I get lost in her.

Whistling and clapping register dimly, but I only pull back once we come up for air.

"Fuck the fates," I tell her while kissing the tears off her face. "And I can't walk away, I've tried." A stray tear runs down her cheek, and I catch it with my thumb. "I love you, Ara, and nothing you say or do will ever change that." Her beautiful eyes fill with hope, and I get lost in them. "Trust me to stay—you own me anyway, body, heart, and soul."

"Finally!" Jared shouts, shattering the moment, and I flip him off without looking. Laughter swells up, and Ara's lips curve into a small smile. I tuck her into my side before turning to our friends.

"Whew," Zaza comments. "Now I'm hot and bothered."

"Oh, I can help with that," my best friend purrs and laughs when Zaza slaps him. "You want me to show you?" He wiggles his eyebrows at her, and she huffs out a laugh.

"Watch it, Venti. There would be a lot of sounds but no laughter when I'd take you up on your offer and crawl into your bed tonight."

I chuckle when my best friend swallows, scrambling for a comeback.

"That's what I thought," Zaza says, winking, while Jared looks slightly dazed.

"Better watch out." Tanner slaps Jared's back. "You just heard it. The girls of our flight don't take prisoners ... they take slaves. Isn't that right, Kyronos?" They all erupt in laughter at my rude gesture.

There is a lot of teasing and laughter while we amble through the streets, but I don't mind. Not with Ara by my side.

Miller offers to be Ara's slave too, making her laugh while I narrow my eyes at him.

"You don't even want to joke about that," Jared advises. "Those two are more possessive of each other than a dragon of its treasure."

And he may have a point there. I kiss Ara's temple, marveling at the fact that I can do so while out in the open.

We are close to the house when Ara tenses.

"What is it?" I ask, but before she has the chance to answer, three figures step in our way. My eyes take them in, gauging the situation, while I pull Ara behind me.

"There are more," Ara whispers, her hands settling on my sides.

People flood the street, dressed in dark clothes, their faces partially hidden behind cloths despite the balmy temperatures. Even without precognition, it's obvious they are up to no good.

"Jared and Cassius stick to Ara like flies to honey. Tanner, Boko, Zaza, you take the back. Ilario, Tethys, Miller, you're with me. Don't let them push us back. If they can maneuver us into the crossing back there, they can surround us."

"They are above us, too!" Ara shouts, and a quick look up confirms it.

*"Don't worry about them,"* Daeva tells me. *"Solaris and I are already on it."* By the blank gazes of the other flight members, they are calling their birds as well. So we don't have to worry about anyone coming at us from above, but the alley we are in is too narrow for our birds to get us or be much help down here. No one doubts that this isn't a coincidence.

I should've seen it coming. I varied our training schedule, so the official contests were the only times they had a chance to plan an ambush. My eyes find Ara's, reassuring myself that she's here, and we'll be fine.

A horrified scream ends in a sickening thud, telling me our birds are working their magic already. The sound catapults our enemy into action. Steel meets steel and reverberates from the surrounding walls, soon joined by curses and grunts.

We act as a unit, standing side by side. While Zaza's team guards our back, we take on everyone coming from the front. Ara, Jared, and Cassius stay between our lines, jumping in wherever a hand is needed, keeping an eye out for additional danger, and warning us when necessary. Keeping Ara safe is a need so deeply ingrained in my bones that I wouldn't be able to shake it even if I wanted to, especially with everything that has happened in the past months.

Our lines are steady, eliminating the enemy strategically, mercilessly. But there are only ten of us, and a lot more of them. They didn't underestimate us this time. If anything, the opposite. The narrow street is the only thing saving us from being overrun.

Slash follows slash, magic sparks, shouts, and curses bounce off the walls, but we hold our ground.

Another attacker collapses to his knees in front of me, burying the body already occupying the floor, and I chance a look behind me, assuring myself that the other side is holding up, and Ara is fine.

Fallen bodies and enemies turned to stone by Cassius's gift slowly create walls on both sides, making it easier to defend the space we carved out for us, but closing us in at the same time. I don't know how long the fight has already lasted, but when Ara screams my name, my heart nearly stops.

# FORTY-EIGHT

## ARA

"Ara, watch out." I whirl around at Joel's warning, only to witness him going down, revealing the menacing grin of an ice wielder behind him. It just takes one blink to take in what happened, but it chills me to the bone. Joel's skin is eerily bluish-white. He took a hit that was meant for me.

The guilt is instant and staggering, and only surpassed by my rage at the man who is responsible.

With a scream, I throw my fire at him and watch in satisfaction as he goes up in flames, his horrified shrieks multiplying when others catch fire too, increasing the surrounding chaos.

I'm next to Joel in two steps and pull him behind two of his stone creations and out of the line of fire. Today is the first time I have seen his magic in action, and it's chilling and fascinating at once to see men turn to stone.

Falling to my knees next to him, I try to assess the extent of the damage. His skin is too cold and cracked in places, and I flinch when there is a crackling sound while I search for a pulse. His heartbeat is slow and sluggish. Maybe it's just the hypothermia? I sit against one of the stone figures and pull his torso up until his back is leaning against my chest.

"Why did you do that?" I mutter, throwing his helmet aside, but of course, he doesn't answer. Slowly, I let my body heat, concentrating on not bursting into flames.

"Don't you dare die on me, Joel Cassius. I can't tell Ben you died trying to protect me." A sob catches in my throat. I swallow it down, but can't do anything against the tears running down my face. Joel is the only close friend my twin has. Losing him... No, I will not let that happen. Not because of me.

"He'll understand." The words are whispered so softly that I first think I imagined it, but Joel's eyes are open, watching me.

"There you are." I give him a watery smile. His skin is still ghostly pale, but a little less blue. It's working. "I've got you," I tell him. "We'll warm you up in no time. You'll see."

He smiles at me, his eyes trailing my face as if trying to memorize it.

"Tell Ben and my parents I love them ... and Mariel, I'm sorry. I..."

"Don't you dare say shit like that. You'll be as good as new in no time. All you need is to get your body temperature back up, and lucky for you, I'm a walking furnace."

"You always were hot." He gives me a lopsided grin.

"See, you're already back to joking." The weight of a boulder rolls off my shoulders. "If that is not a good sign. I don't know what is." I grin. I'm immensely relieved. I check his pulse again, and his heart rate is already coming up.

It takes a while before I realize the blood.

As I warm him up, the cracks I observed earlier start bleeding. They're superficial, but I would still feel better if someone could heal him. My gaze wanders to the other line of defense, instantly finding

Tate. He's battling two men at once, and I watch him cut them down one after the other. As soon as the second man goes down, his eyes sweep the space between us, and his movements become harsher, agitated, until our eyes meet. A mix of concern and relief washes over his face.

Another black-clothed figure rushes him, drawing his attention away, and my breath catches when his opponent's sword misses him with no room to spare. I realize I'm holding my breath when black dots start dancing before my eyes. I exhale slowly, but only relax once Tate gains the upper hand.

"Tate will fix you up in no time," I murmur to Joel.

I don't get a response, and when I look down, his eyes are closed. I shake him and call his name, but his eyes only open after I pinch him.

"There you are. You scared me," I tell him, trying to laugh it off, but something isn't right. I feel it. He looks too pale, and his eyes are already drooping again.

"Don't you dare give up on me now, Joel Cassius," I threaten.

"But you were never mine to keep." His voice is barely a whisper, and I lean closer, my cheek resting against his. "...when to give up."

"No, please, Joel, not like this." But he doesn't respond.

"Tate!" I scream his name in a plea for help. Tate's head snaps to me, nearly getting impaled because of my distraction. I suck in a breath.

While it's getting quieter behind me, there are still too many coming at Tate's side. He doubles his efforts while Joel slips through my fingers.

My twin's best friend, my friend, my childhood love... I'm begging now while I recount all the fun the three of us had back home as if memories could keep him here.

Tate kills his opponent, but is delayed by yet another man stepping up to him, and I know in my bones that he will be too late.

"Hold on, please hold on a little longer."

"Honor ... the dead." Joel breaks off, his breath too fast, just like his erratic heartbeat.

"...by living." I finish his sentence, choking on the last word.

"Love ... be happy," he says, and his eyes flutter closed. I tighten my hold on him.

"I'll do my best," I promise while all I want to do is rant and scream at him for stepping in front of me in the first place. But I clamp my mouth shut, my body wracked by silent sobs, while his heartbeat becomes weaker and weaker and finally stops. His markings go up in smoke. And a shriek full of pain spreads over the city. I look up, and Asta, Joel's Rukh, falters, losing height, as if she took a physical hit when their bond ripped. She cries out again, and her pain singes my bones.

*I caused that.*

Her wings falter again and again, and she seems disoriented and dazed. She drifts off, and I lose sight of her.

I have no idea how much time passes. It could be seconds, minutes, or hours. Tate suddenly crouches down next to me. He touches Joel's body, and I can read in his eyes what I already know ... too late. He's gone.

I squeeze my eyes shut as if that could somehow turn back time. Maybe all of this is a bad dream.

A soft tug on Joel's body makes my eyes fly open. I glare at Tate and tighten my hold when he tries to pull Joel off me.

"You have to let go, baby," he murmurs soothingly. But I can't. I don't know how. How do you let go of someone who gave everything for you?

I shake my head. "Do something, please, Tate. Do something." My plea is a broken whisper. "He can't be gone."

"Gods, how I wish I could." His voice is raw, and the way he looks at me is even worse. There are too many emotions when I don't want to feel anything.

"Do something," I scream and try to tug Joel closer. My head collides with the marble statue behind me. The bright flash of pain dulls into a throb, and I welcome it. It's so much better than the pain in my chest.

Then Tate is there. He gently pries Joel from my numb arms and pulls me up into his chest even though I fight him.

Anger fills my veins—at Tate for taking so long, at Joel for stepping in front of me, for not holding on like I told him to. At myself for not calling Tate over earlier. And above all, for not telling Joel the truth. If he had known, if I had trusted him ... but I didn't, and it cost his life.

My palms sting and tingle from hitting Tate's armored chest repeatedly. My movements slow down and finally stop, my hands coming to rest on his chest, and my brow follows. He wraps both arms around my shaking form, holding on while grief and guilt threaten to shatter me.

Self-loathing and anger swirl and writhe, building up to a tidal wave, battering my control, wearing it down until it splinters.

I throw my magic gift around all the familiar signatures around me, just in time before raw, vicious heat rolls out from me, like a detonation. Causing every attacker to tumble to the ground, writhing in pain, screaming in agony. Those who were closest to me don't move at all.

"He stepped in front of me," I choke out. "The attack should have hit me." And I would have survived. But Joel didn't know that, because I didn't tell him. Tate simply holds me, not trying to offer words that wouldn't change a thing.

Not trusting Joel killed him, and I'll have to live with that. The rest of our flight forms a circle around us, and Mariel falls to her knees when her eyes land on Joel's now unmarked skin.

"What happened?" she chokes out, her accusing gaze finding me right away, as if she knows.

"He stepped in front of me," I whisper, my voice unrecognizable even to my own ears. I step out of Tate's arms because it would be too easy to stay, to hide from the truth.

I doomed us all. Our flight is no longer complete, and I have seen how Iza deals with that earlier. Bodies hitting the sand, studded with arrows, unmoving, flash through my mind.

Mariel reaches out, and her marked hand lands on Joel's pale cheek, and for less than a blink, I see a flicker, or a twitch, too quickly gone to say for sure. And I remember my promise ... anything.

"Mariel," I whisper. "Call him back." When she doesn't react, I repeat my request, stronger this time. "Mariel, call him back." There are uneasy glances around me, and Mariel stares at me with a horrified expression.

"Call him back," I demand. "Now."

# CHAPTER
# FORTY-NINE
## TATE

ARA CHANGES BEFORE MY EYES. HARD, ICY DETERMINATION settles over her like full-body armor. She is lost in thought and doesn't even notice the stunned and wary looks the others give her.

Mariel does as she asks and binds Joel's soul back into his body, but it costs her. She trembles and can't even look at Joel, who now walks next to her.

Her gift erased the signs of the attack, and as long as you ignore his too pale complexion, missing markings, and heartbeat, and that he isn't breathing, he looks just like before. Unless you look into his eyes, they are filled with a quiet intensity, with a burning ire he never displayed while living. Either he is pissed someone killed him, or he's pissed at Mariel for calling him back and binding him to her. It's hard to tell.

At first, I thought it was Ara's grief talking, that she was trying to erase his death with this parody of life under Mariel's control, but then I understood her reasoning, and it's brilliant—cold, but brilliant.

Bodies, soot, blood, and destruction mark the alley we leave behind—a battlefield. However, no one stops us, and the fact that the fight alerted no guards in the first place suggests that someone powerful is behind this.

We are quiet when we arrive at the house, its emptiness somehow more noticeable now. All eyes are on me, while Ara heads for the stairs without looking back.

"I'll talk to her. Keep him here for now," I tell Mariel, and she nods, but she is nearly as pale as Joel, and her bottom lip trembles. Calix throws his arm around her and starts murmuring soothingly, and I would not be surprised if he uses his gift to support her. She is clearly teetering on the edge.

"No one goes out. Strategy meeting in an hour," I command, before following Ara.

She is sitting on her bed, with her knees tucked under her chin, her eyes dry but unfocused, staring at the wall. I close the door behind me.

"You were right." Ara whispers, "I should have trusted you." She swallows. "And if I had trusted him, he would still be alive." She looks up at me with trembling lips. "How do I go on? How did you do it?" She sounds lost, and I sit down next to her, pulling her into my arms.

"I know." I swallow, my voice rough and barely above a whisper myself. "You'll learn to live with it, even if it doesn't feel like it now. And I'll always have your back ... fight by your side."

"Frederick pressured me into a promise." There are tears in her eyes when she finally looks up at me.

"What kind of promise?" My voice is hoarse.

"To marry him as soon as I graduate."

"You won't," I tell her. "He's not getting you," I murmur and bury my face in her hair, breathing her in.

She tells me about her grandma's plan, her family's reasoning, and her conversation with my brother. I have a feeling there is more, especially since she said nothing about the dragon. But today is not the day to push.

"Fred and I aren't close, as you noticed, but his hate didn't start until after the attack or even after I left." I pull her closer. "I shouldn't have left the way I did. I'm so sorry you got roped into all of this."

"Hey, that can't have been easy for you either." She nuzzles my neck. "Cut yourself some slack."

"Look at you, defending me again." I catch her face in my hands, running my thumbs over her cheek, and lean my brow against hers. "Don't worry, we'll figure it out. We have time. We'll get you out of it." I promise. And I mean it. No matter the costs, I'll help her choose her own future.

The hour is filled with quiet comfort, promises and whispers, and passes much too quickly.

I offer that she can stay up here, that I will fill her in later, but just as I knew she would, she gets up. The tentative smile she puts on her face is a testament to her strength.

She takes my hand, and her grasp gets tighter the closer we get to the room. The low rumble of voices indicates everyone is already gathered. Her eyes find Joel right away, and she flinches. For anyone not familiar with him, he may appear the same, but he isn't. His pallor and his eyes are the most noticeable changes, but his mimic is off, too.

"I don't know why we are planning. We are already disqualified and as good as dead," Boko mutters.

"That's not true," I retort. "What Ara realized, even if most of you still don't, is that the rules only state we have to stay complete as a flight. Not that all flight members need to be alive." My eyes come to Mariel. "So even if this is not a comfortable situation, as long as you keep him with us, we are still in and safe from any repercussions a disqualification might have."

Mariel grinds her teeth but nods. She's suffering. Her hands clench, and her eyes close for a moment. Maybe I'll have to set Calix on her to keep her emotionally stable.

"That is something I wanted to discuss with all of you. No promise that the attempt wouldn't get us killed, but if you want to try to get out, now would be the moment."

There are a few snorts around the room.

"We all knew from the start we could die," Zaza states. "So, no, I'd say we fight."

"Even if I made our lives harder by pissing off the goddess?" Ara whispers, and her eyes wander to Joel again. And getting one of us killed? It's in her eyes, even if she doesn't say it.

"He says it wasn't your fault." Mariel's voice is scratchy, watery. "And he says he would do it again in a heartbeat." A sob escapes her, and she hides her face in her hands. "I'm sorry."

"I, for my part, think it's great that you said what everyone thought," Jared addresses Ara. "It takes bravery to stand for your beliefs, no matter what. So don't worry about it." His eyes meet mine. "Let's do this. Let's make a stand." And I know we both think of Louis.

"Let's do this" is echoed around the room, and we plan until late into the night. Ara is only half present, and if I had to guess, I'd say she is planning something else.

We clean out the hall that was used for eating and deposit all the stuff into the entrance hall, creating temporary fortifications. This leaves us with one big room we can use for practice.

"I also paired us up for the nights," I tell them. "We'll charm all the entrances, but going by the trouble someone went through to cut us down, I think pairing up is the safer option. So, Zaza and Mariel, Joel and Calix..." I continue reading off names until only Ara's and mine are left.

"That was very smooth." Jared chuckles, and Zaza turns to him with a quizzical look until her eyes fly from me to Ara and back, and she grins.

"Are you alright—" I ask Calix.

"With sharing the room with the dead guy? Yeah, I'm fine unless he smells, then I'll throw him out." He winks at Joel, who doesn't react. "Hmm, his humor didn't improve with death." He shrugs.

"Calix." Mariel wields his name like a whip, and he flinches.

"Damn, Blue, you nearly slashed me in two with my own name." They go on and on, and even if his comments seemed insensitive at first, he gives her exactly what she needs—a distraction. The color returns to her cheeks, and she looks more alive the longer their bickering lasts.

I pull a frowning Ara into my arms. "Did you really think now that they know, I would let you sleep anywhere else?" I murmur.

"Couldn't you have warned me?" She grumbles, and I smile into her hair.

"And give you the chance to say no? I don't think so." A small smile forms on her lips, and I take it. I'll take everything she is willing to give.

# FIFTY

## ARA

IT'S BEEN TWO DAYS SINCE THE ATTACK, AND WE ARE ONCE MORE at the palace for another fancy celebration. I'm absolutely positive that if I have to attend another one within the next year, I'll scream. That Tate is fidgety doesn't help either. Okay, fidgety might not be the right word, since only his eyes are moving, constantly checking for threats, but his gift is restless too, and it freaks me out. He and Jared flank me, and I'm not even sure they would let me go to the bathroom by myself.

"Could you please relax?" I whisper. "You're giving me palpitations."

Jared gives me a funny look. "What are you talking about? We hardly shifted our weight in the last twenty minutes." He peers past me at Tate. "Is he even breathing?"

"Ha, ha, not funny," I whisper back. Too aware of the undead, non-breathing Joel in my back to appreciate the joke.

Mariel and I spent a good part of this morning painting markings on his right arm. And placing him at my back, flanked by Mariel and Calix, is mainly so no one can get too good a look at him.

My stomach roils, and I have the urge to put distance between us, which isn't fair since all of this is my fault. My stomach lurches again, probably because I have hardly eaten anything in the past few days.

"I'll grab something to eat," I declare and don't wait for an answer before making my way across the room. Tate was the one constantly pushing food on me the last few days, so I don't think he will object, especially since I'm never leaving their view.

I step up to the elaborate buffet and pick a cookie and an apple. Dar stands close, talking to Deliah, but I don't linger. For once, I'm glad he is preoccupied. We've kept Joel's condition a secret so far, and I don't plan to change that anytime soon. It will be hard enough to tell them about his death without adding time spent as an undead into the equation.

Nausea runs through me, and for a moment, I'm worried I'll decorate the floor with the few bites of the cookie I've eaten so far. Telling Ben about Joel is something I don't look forward to. I press a hand to my mouth, waiting for my stomach to settle again.

"Are you not feeling well?" Deliah whispers next to me, and I flinch. When did she become so good at sneaking up on people?

"Oh, it's fine," I say. "Maybe something didn't agree with me." *Or it's the thought of telling my twin I got his best friend killed.*

"I can keep a secret," she says, and my eyebrows jump up, but Deliah is busy taking in my dress.

My brow furrows. Does she know something?

"Tell you what?" I ask, feigning ignorance.

"It's Alec's, right?" Now she has completely lost me. I narrow my eyes at her.

"What are you talking about, Deliah?"

"The child."

I look around, but there is no child in sight. When her eyes run over my flat abdomen, the coin drops, and I bark out a laugh.

"I'm not pregnant." I shake my head at her. "Sheesh, Deliah."

"Are you sure?"

I roll my eyes at her. "I think I would know if I were pregnant."

Strangely enough, the thought of carrying Tate's baby doesn't scare me nearly enough. But gods, that would be the last thing I'd need right now.

Deliah doesn't look convinced, but I only shake my head at her. I will not argue about something like that in a place like this. Otherwise, tomorrow's rumors will have me carrying triplets for sure.

I turn my back on her and make my way over to my blissfully ignorant, imaginative baby daddy and snort at the thought of telling him that. But for a second, I wonder if he would be happy or horrified about such news. Then I shake my head at myself. What's wrong with me? I'm no closer to solving my Frederick-shaped problem. I still have to find the courage to tell him the rest of my secrets, and we might not survive the last trial. And I'm considering starting a family with him?

Aware of the many eyes around us, I still can't help but brush past him, seeking contact. His hand finds mine for just a heartbeat.

"You look pale," he comments. "Are you alright?"

"Killing your brother's best friend might do that to a girl," I joke, before adding, "I'm fine," to reassure him.

I glance at him, only to find his focus already on me.

Dammit, I want to kiss him. His lips twitch as if he knows what I'm thinking. Well, I am staring at his mouth.

He steps closer until he stands partly behind me. "If you keep looking at me like that, I will find a quiet corner to have my way with you," he rasps right next to my ear.

I look up at him. "Promises, promises." And my core tightens when his growl fills the air between us.

"You'd better stay right where you are for a moment," he says. "Otherwise, everyone will know what you do to me."

Not looking at him, I sneak my hand behind my back and run it over his crotch, making him hiss. And he wasn't lying.

"So ready for me," I purr.

"Are you?" he asks.

"Soaked." And gods do I want him to take my mind off all the problems crowding my head, to remind me that we are still alive and what we're fighting for.

"Fuck." The word is a stretched sound of agony. "Let me give you a tour of the palace." He grabs my hand and is about to pull me to the next door when a servant stops right in front of me.

"The king requests your presence, Lady Blackstone."

I nod, resigned. Only a few more days of this, a few more days, and we'll be back in Telos ... or dead. I send Tate a grimace and follow the man in front of me.

## TATE

Frederick's gaze rests on me with a smile, while Ara is on her way over to him, and tension seeps into every fiber of my being. I hate this. I hate her being this close to him, and I have no qualms whatsoever about tuning into their conversation.

"Only five more days," Frederick says.

"I'm aware when the last competition is, thank you," Ara mutters, looking bored. My lips twitch. Mists, I love her defiant, stubborn ass. And I love the annoyed frown on my brother's face.

"You'll probably be glad to know that should you win, I'll graduate you and your friends early." At his words, her eyes fly up to his, and my gut sinks. So much for having time.

"You wouldn't dare," she snarls.

Frederick's smile is slow and smug, his eyes wandering from her to me.

"How about a kiss?" he asks, and she recoils. Then, everything happens too fast to intercept. Understanding and disgust flash over her face, and I'm moving.

I wasn't around when Frederick's gifts woke, but going by Ara's reaction, I have a pretty good guess, since it runs strong in our family —influencing. If she resists, he'll learn her secret, but I can't see her—

Ara's hand connects with my brother's cheek with a crack that has everyone whirling around. The room freezes into shocked silence, while I move faster.

"Fuck you, Your Majesty, fuck you and your sick games." Ara hisses, and then she moves toward the balcony doors.

*"Tell everyone to get out of here,"* I instruct Daeva.

Ara is already outside and reaching for Solaris when I catch up with her.

"Ara, wait." She stills at my request, and her body deflates with a sigh before she turns. I'm right in front of her, and she has to see the questions in my eyes, but instead of answering, she pulls my head down and kisses me with a desperation that makes my stomach clench. This feels too much like goodbye.

"He tried to compel you." My voice is strained, clipped.

"And I screwed up. I'm sorry," she whispers. Her eyes trace my face.

"Be careful." I tuck a strand of hair behind her ear and then help her up onto Solaris's back. My hand rests on her leg while she sorts out her dress. I don't want to let go, but to save her, I have to. So I step back.

"I'll come back, I promise."

There are heavy footsteps, and Ara's eyes dart behind me. Solaris launches into the air before I have the chance to do more than shake my head. Not that it would have made a difference.

*"Where are you?"* I ask Daeva.

*"About one minute out."* A heavy hand lands on my shoulder.

*"Circle above the palace,"* I tell her, and then face the guards behind me.

"Come along, Your Highness," the man requests, and I recognize him as Corin's second in command. I don't protest or correct him about my title but follow while he leads me into my father's study. *It's Fred's study now.*

I step in and nearly snort when all five guards follow and surround me in a semicircle. Do they think they have a chance of holding me here? I'm only here to salvage whatever is possible. But at least if they go after me, that means they are not going after the others.

*"Update,"* I request from Daeva, while we wait.

*"Ara left to the northeast. No one followed so far. Solaris requested that we not follow either. No one stopped the rest of your flight. They are confused, but back at the house. I ordered them to lock down."*

*"You are the best."*

*"I know."* She preens, and I smile.

The door opens, and Frederick walks in, his left cheek still red from Ara's hand, and my grin widens, but the high deflates when I notice the man behind him.

Four years have turned his once salt-and-pepper hair completely white, and the lines on his face a little deeper, but his eyes are still alert, his back straight. My father's truth-teller. He taught me everything I know about my truth-telling gift and how to interrogate people.

He acknowledges me with a nearly imperceptible tip of his chin.

"You knew," my brother accuses me right away.

"Be more specific than that, Your Highness," I drawl. "I know a lot of things, but not everything."

"Do your job," he spits at my former mentor. "Or do I have to remind you of your loyalties?"

"Your Majesty, I have served your family since I made my promise of loyalty fifteen years back, and I do not intend to break it." He looks at me with those last words.

I'm fucked.

I had hoped... I don't know for what, since he is bound by a promise.

He turns to me. "Ready when you are, Your Highness," he addresses me, and my brother bristles.

"He was stripped of his title. Don't address him like that."

"Of course, Your Majesty." He bows to my brother before turning back to me. "Let's start, shall we?"

I nod at him, and he steps next to me, both of us facing my brother now, who sits behind my father's—his desk.

"How did you meet Ara Blackstone?" my brother asks.

"I met her when we were children on the palace grounds," I answer.

"True." Comes the confirmation next to me.

"No, I meant, how did you meet her the second time?"

"I saw her four times in total when we were children, and—" My brother cuts me off with a wave of his hand.

"True."

My brother's jaw works. "No, by Otero's patience, how did you meet her now that she is a grown woman?"

"She was assigned to my division."

"True."

My brother continues to pester me with questions, but it seems my father didn't concentrate on interrogation. He grows increasingly frustrated, and I get a twisted satisfaction out of answering his questions as unsatisfactorily as possible.

Finally, we get to the part I dreaded from the start, confirming my suspicion about his gift.

"Do you know what she is?"

"Yes, she is reckless, smart, funny—"

"True."

"Stop testing my patience. Did you know she is cursed?"

I frown at him. "I've healed her multiple times," I say, and a smug smile starts on his face.

"True."

His eyes jump to the truth-teller. "What?"

"It's true, Your Majesty."

"But that is ... impossible," my brother sputters, and for a moment, I think it's over, but unfortunately, I'm wrong. "Did *you* know Ara Blackstone is cursed?"

"No." I don't blink, and I don't hesitate. And even if he were to torture me, my answer would be the same.

"Truth," the truth-teller declares, but I hear the lie in his voice. Which raises two questions: why did he lie for me, and how did he survive it?

My brother's shoulders slump, and with a wave of his hand, he dismisses all of us. The guards accompany me to the gates, thwarting the chance to speak one-on-one to my old mentor.

# FIFTY-ONE

## TATE

Four days have gone by since Ara disappeared. Four days without a word, with no sign that she is still alive. My brother's men searched our house eight times during that period. This, combined with the fact that they ordered me to come in after their last search an hour ago, brings me relief.

He doesn't have her.

But the relief is short-lived. Frederick has no problem laying out his plans in disgusting detail.

"You can't be serious," I growl, shaking with rage, while my brother looks calm and pleased about the execution he's planned for the woman he wanted to marry only days ago.

"It's the law," he states calmly as if he couldn't change that if he wanted to.

"You don't have proof," I snap.

"I don't need it," my brother retorts.

He doesn't, and that turns my stomach.

"She won't come." I hold on to this hope. She has to know it's a trap.

"Oh, but I have the perfect bait." My brother grins at me. "I already spread the word. It's your life or hers. What do you think she's going to do?"

I feel sick. I know what she'll do. Mists, I hope I'm wrong. I hope she never hears about this.

My brother watches me intently. "I will have guards circle your house and accompany you to the arena tomorrow. If you try to warn her, I'll kill every one of your friends. Do you understand?"

I nod, grinding my teeth. "And if she doesn't show?"

"You'd better hope she does. Iza hasn't proven to be very merciful so far, either, has she?" He grins mockingly. "I won't start my reign by pardoning a dangerous individual, who already attacked—"

"She slapped you." I shake my head at him with a sneer. "If you think that was an attack, you are even softer than I remember."

"It would give the wrong impression," he insists.

"What, and now her connections aren't important anymore?"

"Her family will understand." He grins. "General Blackstone has already distanced himself from his sister."

I mask my shock. Why would a brother who was ready to kill me for not letting him see her just ... abandon her?

But this plays perfectly into my brother's hands. He wanted to see me suffer, and now he gets that without binding himself to a woman he doesn't even want.

I turn and leave the room before I kill him because the gods know, I'm tempted. It would land me on the throne, and I would do it in a heartbeat to protect her, but it would also put me under their control, and I know they want her dead as badly as my brother does, maybe even more so.

The way back to the house barely registers through the haze of rage and icy numbness. My teeth clench so hard that the muscles in my jaw are cramping.

The house is more of a fortress now. Not physical, but magical fortifications make it impossible to enter without our permission. We set up rotating guarding duties and sent all the servants away after they stocked the storage rooms and kitchen. Thankfully, Calix turns out to be an excellent cook.

Where is she? I heeded her wish and didn't attempt to find her so far. Now, I have to.

Everyone is gathered in the big room, and eyes drop along with shoulders as soon as they spot me.

"I guess that means bad news from the king," Jared says and steps up to me. "Stop worrying. We are good at what we do ... and so is Ara," he continues more softly, throwing his arm over my shoulders.

He's right, and she would tell me the same thing, along with a kiss and something like, *Pests are hard to kill, remember?* But I have to see her, warn her.

"Then go," Jared urges next to me.

"Since when have you become a mind reader?" I raise my eyebrow at him.

"Since your eyes become all soft and gooey when you think of your woman," he replies and snickers at my frown.

But he is right, I have to at least try.

It's dark by the time I meet Daeva on the roof of our house. The clicking of her talons on the slate shingles sounds like shattering tableware in the quiet night.

"Shhh," I hiss, but there are no hurried steps, no sign that my brother's guards heard anything. Maybe he thought a warning would be enough to deter me.

Tonight is my last chance to talk to her. To convince her to stay away. I would rather lose the games, my chance at revenge, and my life than lose her. I've made plans to get everyone else out. Now I only have to convince her.

Half an hour later, I stare in shock at the white river of mist lazily swirling below me. Moonlight highlights the pristine surface, where once lay a sunny valley filled with life and color.

Fortress Blackstone and the village next to the mountain base are gone. If not for the river continuing to Avina, I would question whether it ever was here to start with.

*"Did we... I don't know, mix up the location?"* I ask Daeva, but she negates that as I knew she would.

"What did you do?" I mutter the words, the wind stealing them from my lips, carrying them off to the sea of white beneath me.

*"She told you not to come looking for her,"* Daeva chastises. *"I guess she made sure you couldn't find her."*

*"We could go down—"*

*"Only if your stubborn ass learned to fly. Otherwise, you'll have no choice but to accompany me back to Avina,"* my bird informs me. *"She had to trust you to stay. Now you'll have to trust her to come back."*

*"I do trust her to come back. That's the problem here."*

Sleep doesn't come easily, and the following morning comes much too soon after I've spent nearly all night pacing my room.

I strap on my armor with quiet determination, fastening every strap with precision and donning every blade I have. I meet my gaze in the mirror and promise myself that whatever else happens today, she will not die.

# FIFTY-TWO

TATE

WE ARE LED TO THE ARENA LIKE CATTLE. FIFTY OF MY brother's men surround and herd us through small alleys. They go through significant efforts to avoid the crowds congesting the streets, chanting in anticipation of the games. Our birds follow, but they have no way to reach us in the small space.

The arena is crowded like never before. Many carry torches, their chanted words muddled by too many voices and our guards' relentless requests to hurry. We are hustled along with no chance to observe what is going on around us.

We step into the arena and are immediately ushered down into its intestines, full of corridors and rooms. The air is cool, smelling of stone dust, and the faint echo of sweat and fear.

A dull pounding rises in volume, and the corridor slowly lightens from black to gray the closer we get to the fighting ground. A glaring white square awaits us at the end of the tunnel, and when we step onto the sand, the sunlight momentarily blinds us.

The mass around us is stomping, cheering, and the ground vibrates with the sound. The other two teams are already here. Whispers start, and the cheering dies down once they realize we are missing our Phoenix rider. Ara's name ricochets off the walls, and I pray she can't hear it.

Kystis's flight is openly gloating, while the one from Muntos looks confused. No sign from Ara so far, which gives me hope.

My brother sits perched on his throne, his eyes sweeping our group repeatedly. My mother is absent today. Maybe she doesn't agree with the spectacle Frederick plans to make out of her best friend's daughter.

Frederick rises and steps forward—watching, waiting. The crowd hushes, but he stalls, still waiting for Ara. Finally, he nods to the guards lining the arena's perimeter, and they file out.

The gates close with a finality that echoes through the space around us.

Ara isn't here. A relieved breath leaves me while Jared stiffens next to me. And when I shoot him a questioning look, he sports a broad grin.

Frederick steps up to the balustrade of the royal terrace.

"Welcome to the finale of the flight games. We have three teams left fighting for the title of victor of the current flight games. But..." His eyes come to us. "Since one flight has only nine members..." One gate opens, drawing everyone's attention. I whip around, but it stays empty, the black mouth gaping, waiting. A tense silence hangs over the arena, making it hard to breathe.

"Well, good that at least some of us can count, isn't it?" A collective gasp follows the drawled words. And there she is, sitting cross-legged in the center of the arena, sending a dagger tumbling up in the air before catching it again as if she doesn't have a care in the world.

Jared and Calix are the first to chuckle, and it spreads like wildfire.

Her eyes are fixed on me with a wide grin on her face.

Mists, that woman is something. I shake my head at her, too relieved to see her unharmed to even attempt fighting my smile.

She rises, dusting herself off, and mockingly bows to my brother.

"I didn't want to interrupt your speech. Go on, Your Majesty." She gestures for him to go ahead before sauntering over to me. She stops right in front of me.

"Hi," she breathes. "I give you two seconds to object," she says before deliberately stepping into my personal space. Her hands land on my chest, slowly sliding up to my neck. "I'm done hiding," she whispers before our lips meet. The kiss is slow, sweet—a declaration.

"No matter what happens today, I choose you. I'll always choose you, and if it ends today, I only regret that we didn't have more time."

"If you get yourself killed saving me, I won't forgive you," I warn.

"I know." She kisses me. "But that's a worry for another life." Her fingers trace my jaw, her eyes are serious. "And I will find you again."

"Guards, seize her!" my brother shouts. I clasp her hand, and our flight surrounds us, all of us drawing our swords. Only Zaza, Joel, and Tanner have arrows notched and ready to fly instead.

If they want her, they'll have to fight us. Their advance slows down.

A flare of light. "No one interrupts my games. Call your dogs back, king." The goddess's voice booms, while her eyes lazily run over our clustered formation. "I still have a bone to pick with her." Her smile is cold.

"Three rounds of fights, and the last man—or woman—standing is the winner," she announces. "Every flight will face one of my creatures. If more than one team is victorious, I'll pick a champion from each to battle the other. The order is: Kystis, Muntos, Belarra." Her gaze swings to my brother. "No one touches my competitors before I've had my games," she growls. "Once done, you can do with her whatever you wish." She pauses, a slow smile curling her lips. "If there is anything left."

Guards lead us into a room under the arena. It's small and bare, apart from one table with two chairs. It has no windows since we are underground. The air is stale and cool, stone dust tickling my nose.

As soon as the door closes, everyone clusters around Ara and me.

"Where were you?" Calix asks.

"That was a damn epic entrance." Jared laughs. "I'm glad you asked me for help." The last comment earns him narrowed eyes from me while I wrap my arms around Ara's waist from behind. She leans into me.

"I think neither our king nor Iza is a fan of you," Tanner cautions.

"Whatever is coming won't be easy," Zaza predicts.

"Guys, slow down." Ara laughs. "I was with friends," she answers Calix's question first.

"You shouldn't have come," I murmur, and she turns in my arms.

"Tell me, how could I have lived with myself if I hadn't shown up today? We all know how Iza has disqualified most flights so far." She huffs out a breath and settles her hands on my shoulders. "Yes, I remember the part about you going out of your mind when I'm in danger. But you have to trust me, too," she whispers. "Trust me to hold my own."

I know she's right. "But what if—"

She lifts on her tiptoes, placing a kiss on my lips, silencing me.

"Whatever happens, happens. All I'm asking for is your trust. And I'm way too stubborn to die," she jokes, resting her hand on my cheek. I trap it with mine, holding it there just a little longer.

"I trust you to hold your own," I tell her.

"Okay then," she breathes. "Now I have a little confession to make."

"Are you sure?"

She nods and turns back to our friends. She tells them about her curse, that it's another name for a gift that controls magic as an element. That she is still learning to handle it, and that my brother found out when he tried to compel her to kiss him at the palace.

"So basically, his plans for me changed from marriage to execution."

There is stunned silence, interrupted only by the faraway roar of a beast.

"So cursed people don't suck out their fellow humans and destroy villages? Damn, you ruin all my favorite childhood stories," Calix complains, earning him a jab from Mariel and a relieved laugh from Ara.

"I don't." She winks at him. "I'm too busy sacrificing myself for my friends." Earning more laughter. "So we are okay?" Her eyes wander over our friends.

"You came back for us, knowing there is an execution waiting for you. Well, and pretty boy, of course." Jared dodges my punch, laughing. "Shit yes, we are okay."

The sentiment is echoed all around.

"One last thing," Ara says. "If I say go, you'll leave, all of you."

And we're back to arguing.

## ARA

THE BEAST THAT GREETS US ONCE WE ARE BACK IN THE ARENA looks like an unfortunate mix between a wyrm, a medusa, and a sphinx. A long, scaly green body ends in a woman's head, crowned by wriggling snakes of the same green. Two black feathered wings, four furry paws, and a tail with a tip that would make any scorpion proud complete the ensemble.

It whirls around with a hiss as soon as we enter. And it seems she has been snacking on whoever was unfortunate enough to die in one of the previous fights. Her teeth are too sharp, too pointy to belong to a human, and what at first looks like smudged lipstick turns out to be blood, which she licks off leisurely.

"Oh shit, it's an Ophisyx," Mariel breathes next to me. "Their gazes turn living—"

Miller has the bad luck to meet its gaze first and turns to stone, cutting off Mariel's explanation.

"Close your eyes," Tate shouts, and we all obey, switching to our birds' view, who are circling above.

It's disorienting, and curses are flying all over the place, while we adjust to navigating without getting bitten, stung, or sliced up.

Remains of temple ruins sit throughout the arena, the rubble making the ground more treacherous, especially if limited to a bird's view from above.

"She is truly not making it easy for us," Mariel mutters.

"*Spread out.*" This time, Tate's command comes via our birds, easily reaching everyone without alerting the Ophisyx.

"What else do you know about this, whatever-it-is-called?" I ask Mariel while we creep along the walls until we surround the beast.

Tate is on my right, Calix on my left, with Mariel and Joel next to him. Joel is the only one not impaired by the creature's gaze, as it only affects the living. With his connection to Asta severed, he wouldn't have a bird to rely on anyway.

"Its sting paralyzes, while the victim stays fully conscious."

"Lovely," I mutter, nearly stumbling over a shattered pillar, since a crumbling wall hid it from Solaris's view. Our birds have to stay in motion and can't hover unless they catch a favorable air current.

I curse audibly since I stubbed my toe, but freeze when the Ophisyx's head swings around to me.

"Hey, pretty girl," Calix calls out, drawing its attention before hiding behind a wall.

"Really? Now you're flirting with monsters, too?" Mariel grumbles.

"What? Calling it ugly seemed unfair." Calix shrugs. "Who knows what her beauty standards are?"

"Maybe I'll keep you around, human," the creature whispers,

showing off good hearing and a split tongue, while slinking in our direction.

I groan. "He can't help but sweet-talk every female around."

"Holy mists. You three are worse than Jared," Tate grumbles, making me chuckle and Jared protest. "Could you shut up already?"

A volley of hailstones draws the creature's attention to the other side of the arena, and she turns.

*"Just because she is the most obvious doesn't mean she is the only threat in here,"* Solaris relays Tate's warning. *"So, keep your eyes open, and let's collect everything we know about Ophisyx."*

Our collective knowledge is rather sobering. Ophisyx are Iza's preferred hunting companions. Next to turning living things into stone with their gaze and paralyzing victims with their poison, no matter if a sting or a bite of their "hair," their aura triggers nightmare-like hallucinations if they come too close, and their teeth and claws are sharp enough to shred us to ribbons.

Safe to say, not a creature I want to get to know more intimately. Oh, and then there is the teeny detail that the scales are too thick to be penetrated by a blade or arrows, leaving only the throat, where the scales run out into skin.

We have to get close to her to kill her. Awesome.

"It'll have to be me," I state the obvious.

"No," Tate cuts me off before I even finish my thought.

"I'll do it," he offers. Jared says nothing but shakes his head, and I'm reminded of the nightmares he mentioned.

"Tate," I say, but he clenches his jaw.

"Let's make it a group effort," Jared suggests. "With all of us going in, she'll have it harder to concentrate on one target."

Tate nods, my next breath coming easier.

On Tate's command, we move in, doubling and tripling in numbers as Jared uses his gift. His illusion mirrors our movements.

Zaza and I throw flames at the Ophisyx, while Tanner batters her with ice. Mariel is using Joel to get closer to her, hoping the aura won't affect him either.

We are nearly close enough to strike when everything happens at once.

Jared's illusions drop, and Joel freezes when the creature pounces, landing too close to Mariel and Jared. Tate rushes in to pull Jared back, only for whatever hits him to make him stagger.

The gasp of the crowd registers as a missed beat of my heart. I rush forward, focused on getting to Tate before the creature does. But Daeva is faster. She swoops down, gripping Jared and Tate with her talons, and dives out of the Ophisyx path. The creature's sting misses her only barely, and then the beast unfurls its wings as if it wants to go after Daeva.

But I step into her line of sight. Taking Calix's cue from earlier, I address her to draw her attention.

"You have very thick hair ... and so wriggly."

"Aren't you scared, human?" She stalks toward me. "No nightmares terrorizing you?"

"Oh, plenty," I tell her. "But I'm not good at giving in."

"I can still shred you, paralyze you, eat you."

I wrinkle my nose. "No, thanks. I'm not a fan of that either. And I've heard I'm more of an acquired taste."

In my periphery, the others advance again while I do my best to keep the Ophisyx's attention on me. And I'm relieved to see Jared and Tate back on their feet. While my friends close in, ice and fire bounce off the creature without doing damage. And I realize there's only one way to end this, only one way to get all of them out of here alive.

# FIFTY-THREE

## TATE

THE CLOSER WE GET TO THE CREATURE, THE STRONGER HER influence tugs on my sanity, swamping and crowding me with memories until it becomes harder and harder to hold on to reality. But I fight my demons, keep them at bay, because one person in here is more important than anything else.

And she is currently walking back and forth in front of the Ophisyx, distracting her to give us a chance to end it. And for her, I'd do anything.

Ara has her eyes closed, just like the rest of us. But her posture betrays her seconds before she moves.

"Don't do it," I whisper under my breath. "Stick to the plan, sunshine. Stick to the fucking plan." But of course she doesn't.

She runs forward, throwing out her hands, releasing her magic at the creature, in the same moment as the paw hits her, throwing her through the air, where she bounces back from the wall of the arena, staying down while the beast goes wild between us, barring my way.

*"Daeva, I need you to get me."*

*"On it,"* she says and dives, but she has to break off her advance when the Ophisyx lunges for her. And since Daeva heads the other way, I can't see Ara either.

I snap, the terror that had been paralyzing me before boils out of me. Wind hisses, whipping up the surrounding sand, ripping at hair and clothes. My friends stagger back, and the beast cowers, trying to protect its face with its paws. As the gusts become stronger, my gift permeates the air just like the metallic, stinging scent of magic. Raw power spills over, ready to flay the skin of the creature that stands between me and her, one tiny slice of sand at a time.

And then I feel it.

Ara taps into my power, and I open up even more for her.

Finally, she rises, tall and proud, and advances on the Ophisyx.

My gift dances around her, caressing her skin, playing in her hair, worshipping her, while it batters everything around us. Her face turns toward me, and she opens her eyes to meet my gaze, holding it while she strides through the arena. Her gift is nothing visible, but there's a tension, a looming danger surrounding her, so vivid the air nearly crackles with it.

She is magnificent, powerful, unyielding. A queen in her own right.

"I'm sorry," she mouths.

I shake my head. But I know she'll do it anyway. An "I love you" dances over her lips, before her gaze whips to the creature in front of her.

Her hands come out, and she releases her gift in one brutal strike of raw magic. Showcasing that she is undoubtedly more than merely gifted, proving that she is cursed.

Her gift hits the Ophisyx, running through it, arching out, affecting everything that Iza created within the arena. Her creature and the ruins crumble, churning up a massive cloud of dust that shrouds us, obscuring our surroundings in a pale, sandy beige, hiding us from view.

The dust settles slowly, revealing shapes and moving figures, and there's silence, eerie, shocked silence. And no way to deny what Ara is.

"You scared me, sunshine," I tell her when she stops next to me.

"I know," she says.

"This will have consequences." I turn to her and pull her closer.

"I know," she answers. "But I'm done hiding."

"I know," I tell her and claim her lips because who knows, it might be the last time I get to do it.

The goddess claps above us, breaking our kiss and the silence.

"Impressive," she says. "I underestimated you. But then, it's not over yet."

She claps again, and a gate opens. In walks a warrior from Kystis.

My body goes rigid. And Ara takes my hand, linking her fingers with mine.

"I can do it," she murmurs.

"I know you can. That doesn't mean I have to like it."

She grins up at me. "True."

Our fingers are still linked, and once more, I open my gift for her.

"Take it. Take all of it." And as if my gift reacts to my words alone, it seeps into her, while I pull her into my arms and kiss her one last time. We're one, the connection of our gifts as intimate as if our bodies were joined as well. I get lost in her taste, the feeling of her lips moving against mine, her tongue teasing me, her teeth nipping. The way she fits into my arms and how she melts into me when I pull her closer—I stow away all of it.

"Kill him," I breathe against her lips. "And don't keep me waiting."

She nods.

"We've gone through so much already," she murmurs in my ear. "We can do this."

She is right because there is no other fucking option than her coming out of this alive. There simply isn't.

WE LEAN AGAINST THE STONES OF THE ARENA, AN INVISIBLE wall separating us from the fighters. The arena is vibrating with the energy and anticipation of the coming fight. And the crowd salivates with a morbid fascination for blood.

The energy is so heightened that the structure is on the verge of bursting with it. And I don't feel any different. Only the energy running through my blood is dark enough to swallow everything around me.

They start, and my breath catches in my throat. Her opponent fights anything but fair, using his ice magic, weight, and strength to drive her back. He tries to dominate her. But my girl is quick, cunning, and ruthless. She looks deadly beautiful, her movements fluid.

Ara counters his ice with her fire. The magic collides, and sparks of hot and cold sizzle between them.

There is no hesitation, no doubt in her strikes, and when her opponent moves arrogantly, carelessly, she uses the chance and draws first blood by opening a wound on his thigh. He curses and pulls back before she severs tendons.

Red paints the previously immaculate sand, and a vicious smile blooms on my face.

*That's it, baby. Just like that.*

A triumphant call from Solaris, circling above the arena, and his bursting into flames draws every eye. Ara laughs, and that's the moment hesitation enters her opponent's movements. He underestimated her.

"She is fucking beautiful to watch," Jared murmurs next to me. "I would say your training sessions paid off. She has improved immensely. Or maybe that is because you keep her satisfied and relaxed."

He laughs at my glare. "What? The fluidity has to come from somewhere."

The longer the fight lasts, the less secure Ara's opponent seems. Time is on her side. The man becomes increasingly vicious, using brutal force in both his magical and physical strikes. He knows he's losing and, in an act of desperation, drives her back with his onslaught, forcing her to shield herself with her magic gift.

Both of them are now covered with shallow cuts, and I flinch every time she receives a new one.

She retreats step by step until her back collides with the curving wall behind her. A volley of sharp ice splinters reaches her just when her shield falters, and she cries out in pain, erupting in flames a second later, melting the ice. The tiny wounds paint her skin red.

"Only superficial," Jared murmurs next to me. "You will have her fixed up in no time. Don't worry, she can do this."

But there is confusion on her face, and I don't like the way she takes a tentative step toward her opponent. He brings up his sword, and she meets it, but barely.

She shakes her head before driving him back, slash for violent slash, to the center of the arena.

Repetitively, she blinks, shakes her head, and clenches her jaw as if she tries to clear her head. Then she falters, lowering her blade. I can't breathe.

Why isn't she fighting?

Her eyes are fixed on the man in front of her, who is talking and slowly advancing on her. But she still doesn't move.

"Come on, baby, show him what you're made of," I whisper under my breath. Her shoulders are bowed, and she looks pained. What the fuck is he saying to her?

"Come on, sunshine." My words are a plea. Nevertheless, the only movement on Ara's side is the rise and fall of her chest.

Her opponent takes another step, one hand reaching for her face, and a snarl works its way up my throat. He slowly raises his sword.

"Move!" I shout even though I know she won't be able to hear me. My stomach turns. This can't be happening.

I rush forward, my hands pressing against the barrier between us. It burns, but I pound against it anyway.

# FIFTY-FOUR

## ARA

I blink, but he is still there. But is he? Or is he just an illusion?

Is this another sick game of the goddess?

I hesitate while the man I love raises his sword.

"Now it comes down to us," Tate whispers, and it's his voice. "I'm sorry, Ara, but I've worked so long for this. You understand, don't you?" He takes a step toward me. "I'll make it quick. You'll be a good girl and stay just like this, won't you?"

I swallow. He takes another step toward me and reaches for me.

And I strike.

His eyes widen in shock, and Tate's face disappears. The man from Kystis sinks to his knees, my dagger embedded in the cutout under his arm.

"This means war," he whispers as his sword drops to the ground next to him.

"Well, let your death be the first then." I leave the dagger. A message. A promise. "Your illusion had a massive fault, by the way. Tate would never expect me to give up. And he would never sacrifice me for his goals."

The crowd erupts in cheers, chanting two words that reverberate around me: Phoenix rider. The words rise, joining my bird circling above, matching the pounding of my heart, and drowning out my enemy's curses.

I grin while I turn to find the eyes I need to see most.

There he is, unharmed.

I exhale, tension seeping from my body. My hands come up in victory while his gaze sweeps over me like I'm beautiful and not covered in blood, sweat, and wounds. Strands of my hair are stuck to my face and neck, and a coat of sand and dust seals it all. I shake my head at him, still grinning, and try to catch my breath.

Rage takes over his features just when Solaris cries out, *"Behind you!"*

I whirl around, grabbing my sword with both hands, and with a scream of rage on my lips, using the force of my turn, my honed blade bites into his unprotected neck, decapitating him.

His sword clatters once more from his hands before his body and head hit the ground separately, the hollow thumps too loud in the shocked silence around me.

The roar of the spectators is deafening.

The barrier falls, and Tate is next to me in seconds, lifting me with a whoop that splits my face into a grin. The rest of our flight is not far behind.

"You were fucking amazing, Gray!"

"I bow to you, my queen," Jared shouts, sweeping into a deep bow, and snickers when Tate scowls. "She chooses her own king, of course."

"I'm so proud of you, girl."

The voices of my friends blur together like the surrounding colors when Tate twirls me around, his grinning face looking up at me, the only thing that is crystal clear.

We fucking did it. We won the games. We survived.

A thunderclap startles me out of our celebration.

Right, there is a goddess and a king left to deal with. I look at the body lying behind my friends, coloring the sand a dark crimson, and my eyes snag on a small mark still visible in the crook of his arm, now prominent since the rest of the markings have vanished.

Three interwoven triangles.

It reminds me of something, but I can't place it. Tate lets me slide down his body until my feet hit the ground again, but he never lets go, and I'm content with leaning into him.

A flash of light has me turn around in his arms. The goddess stands before us, and the power radiating from her is staggering. Her beauty is blinding, but her smile is anything but warm.

"Congratulations on your win. The trials have been enlightening." She pauses, studying me. "Maybe Maita was right." She flicks something my way, and I catch it out of reflex.

A golden coin burns my palm when I grasp it, its glow slowly subsiding. It bears a laurel surrounding runes on one side, and when I flip it over, I gasp.

Not because of Iza's image on the other side, but because her likeness is now burned into my palm, like a brand. I look up in question.

"Choose your side wisely and your wish carefully. Remember, magic always has its price." With those words and another boom shaking the arena, she is gone.

I slip the coin into Tate's hand and close his fingers around it, fulfilling part of my promise to myself. He protests, but I stop him by placing a kiss on his jaw. Now I only have to make sure he gets out of here alive.

"I want you to have it. I already have everything I could ever want and took care of everything I needed to."

"Why did you falter?" Tate whispers against my hair, his arms tightening.

"He suddenly looked and sounded like you."

"Now I'm a little disturbed that you killed him that easily," Tate jokes, and I huff out a laugh before kissing him like it might be the last time.

"The bastard made a mistake," I tell him when I come up for air. "Your doppelgänger chose the win over me and expected me to give up without a fight."

His arms tighten around me. "Then he didn't know either of us."

"Hence the dagger in his chest." I look up at him. "You've seen me at my worst, know my darkest secrets, and still didn't run for the hills—that has to count for something, right?"

"You trust me," he whispers, awed.

"With my life, my heart, my soul, and all of my secrets." I grin at him. "Guess that means I'm yours now."

Tate tightens his hold on me just when a fanfare blares. His body tenses.

Maybe he only now remembers what I've already been waiting for. I turn in his arms when the main gate is thrown open. Guards swarm in and surround the arena. Frederick and his entourage follow, Dar included.

I try to catch my brother's gaze, but he stares stubbornly ahead, his face unreadable. I sigh.

Standing taller, I squeeze Tate's hand before stepping out of his arms.

I can't pull him into this. I can't pull any of them into this. So I step away from my friends to face the king. And he is not one to hesitate.

"Tamara Summer Blackstone, I declare you guilty of using forbidden magic, of deception, and treason." The king's voice booms through the arena, amplified by the gifted by his side. "Your execution will be public. The date will be set shortly."

Everyone seems to hold their breath while I swallow the rising dread and give him my best infuriating smile. Slowly, I walk toward him.

*"Get everyone ready, handsome,"* I tell Solaris, and he grumbles his displeasure about my plan, but I know he will do as I ask, because we have been over this a hundred times within the last days.

Frederick takes a step back, clearly not sure what my reaction means. His gift strengthens, but never reaches for me, perhaps because it didn't work last time. Good thing he doesn't know I spent all of mine during the fight.

"Seize her," he commands, but no one moves; too fresh is the image of me bringing down Iza's beast.

"Don't you dare come even one step closer," he threatens, but I laugh.

"What could you possibly threaten me with? Even slaughtering everyone in here wouldn't make a difference." I shrug and study my nails. "But how about you send for a priestess?" I ask, too quiet for anyone else but him to hear, raising my eyebrows. "You were so adamant about marrying me, and a throne seems what I'm missing, don't you think?" I smirk at him, and he clenches his jaw.

"I'd never marry you, never. You're a—"

I tsk at him. "But you promised, so..."

"Tamara Summer Blackstone, I release you from your promise to marry me." Frederick hisses, and my grin widens.

"But then I would be stupid to agree, wouldn't I?" I shake my head at him. "And I'm not." I shrug. "So I guess you have to postpone the execution." He pales. "Unless you want to make another deal."

Someone steps up behind me. I whirl around, raising a dagger, but it clatters to the ground even before I see the person's face. I recognize his gift. Cool shackles close around my wrists, draining my remaining magic, while I look up into familiar eyes.

"I knew it would be you," I say, and he flinches, then I give my friends the command they never wanted to hear. "Go." And while my brother drags me out of the arena, my eyes are on Tate. Two rows of guards separate us, closing in on my flight. I softly shake my head.

Denial, horror, grief, anger, betrayal flash through his eyes before

I'm too far away to tell anymore. This is not what we agreed on, but if I were to flee with them now, the king would hunt us down.

Without me, they have a chance. It's a simple choice to make.

And for the second time today, I tell Tate that I'm sorry and hope he'll forgive me.

Our birds swoop down, picking up their riders, and Solaris grabs Joel. My eyes come back to Frederick. I expect him to gloat about seeing me in chains, but his expression is thoughtful. It's another person who looks gleeful, and that's when it clicks. Suddenly, I realize why the mark on the man from Kystis seemed so familiar.

I'm ushered out of the arena to the waiting carriage, with my hands constrained behind my back. And as soon as the people outside catch sight of me, unrest starts in the crowds surrounding us.

Angry voices demand my release. "Phoenix rider" is a chant that spans the entire square. There's fire everywhere. Torches decorated with stylized silhouettes of rising Phoenixes are held high.

People are pushing and shoving to see me, to touch me. The faces of the king's men are growing more irritated by the second. I grin.

I'm thrust into the carriage, the door slams closed, and the curtains are quickly drawn, blocking me from sight, but they can't block the noise that follows us to the palace.

# FIFTY-FIVE

## TATE

I'm still reeling from the day's events when I slip into the palace unnoticed. It's easier than one might think when you've spent all your life playing, hiding, and exploring in and around it. That Daeva can set me down in the dead of night, and that the guest wing is not the most heavily guarded part, helps too.

The note Ara left and Solaris helped me understand her reasoning, but I'm still angry with her for sacrificing herself.

My first stop is my old mentor. He worked around his promise, and I need to know how he did it.

The old man's face breaks into a grin as soon as he sees me.

"I was wondering when you would show up," he says, while he leads me to a seating arrangement close to the fireplace. Despite the balmy temperatures, he has a fire going, and a relieved sigh slips from his lips once he has settled down. From the way he moves, I know it's his back that is bothering him.

Wordlessly, I reach out a hand, and his eyes crinkle when he places his in mine. His face smoothes a bit, and he sits straighter as soon as my healing gift flows into him. He pats my hand before releasing it.

"Thank you. You were always a good boy. Just a bit too serious. But that is hardly surprising."

I shrug.

"But you are here about the lie," he continues.

"Yes." I lean forward. "How did you get around your promise?"

He smiles. "I didn't. When I was sworn in fifteen years ago, the king had me promise to always speak the truth unless a lie would serve him better. But I didn't only swear fealty to him, but also to his successor, and at that time that was—"

"Me," I whisper.

"And Frederick never swore me in anew." He shrugs. "I tried to give you a hint. But you didn't need my help for the most part anyway." He grins.

"So, if I asked you to lie for someone else?"

"No," he shakes his head. "It's not that easy. The connection has to be deeper than just your word."

I leave half an hour later, my thoughts swirling with possibilities and plans, while I make my way through dark corridors.

My knock is loud in the surrounding silence.

Confusion and weariness war on Darren Blackstone's face when he finds me in front of his door. I lift one eyebrow in question, and he steps back, letting me in.

The silence between us stretches.

He clears his throat. "I'd have thought I'd have your fist in my face by now."

I chuckle and hand him the note I brought.

"What is this?"

I shrug. "Open it."

His eyebrows jump up before he follows, and then the man I thought could take anything without flinching disintegrates in front of my eyes. Guilt, shame, and relief flash over his face while the note drops to the ground, and he staggers to his desk, bracing on it.

I snatch up the note.

*They are safe, and you are forgiven.*

A small bird is drawn on the paper below. A sparrow.

I give him the time to fall apart, and what I see tells me Ara was right about him.

"If not for her, it wouldn't have been my fist but my blade that met you," I tell him, and he gives me a grim nod.

"And I would have deserved it." His voice is rough in the confession. "How?"

"Ara figured it out. The first thing that struck her as odd was that your daughter wasn't there to meet us when we visited Blackstone. Then Ian told her they were here with you, while you said they were with her parents. The fact that she is amazing at reading people who hide their feelings probably plays a role as well." I give him a crooked smile, and he answers with a broken laugh. "And when Lorcan told her you were looking for a dragon." I shrug. "Your wife and daughter are well and in hiding, and I'd advise you to leave Avina tonight."

"And leave her? After everything she did for me?" He scoffs. "Not fucking likely."

"I kind of hoped you would say that." And for the first time, we understand each other.

"She told you to walk away, didn't she?" he asks.

I nod. "But she'll learn what I already told your brother."

"And what is that?"

"That I'm hers, and she's mine. And not even death could keep me away."

"I think you'll grow on me." Darren Blackstone gives me a crooked smile.

"Let's see if you still think that after hearing the rest of my plan."

# ARA

THE DOOR TO MY CELL CLOSES WITH A METALLIC CLANG. THE sound of the lock sliding into place is loud in the silence and emptiness surrounding me. I get as comfortable on the wooden excuse of a bed as I can. Waiting.

The clacking of boots on rough stone grows faint and fades away. Darkness and silence claim once more the small cell that, apart from the wood I lie on, just holds stone and metal. It's cold so deep beneath the palace, and the dried blood and sweat on my skin make matters worse.

They were careful to remove everything flammable from my cell. I look at the suppressors circling my wrist and chuckle softly. Lorcan was right. They have forgotten everything.

I don't have to wait long before the rhythmic clicking of approaching footsteps pierces the silence again, the sound too high, too sharp to belong to the boots of a prison guard, the steps too hurried. No, they belong to a woman in heels, and ever since I saw her face at the arena, I knew she would be coming.

The sound grows louder, soon joined by the rustle of skirts. She stops right in front of my cell, but I don't acknowledge her, staring at the ceiling instead.

"You poor thing, they didn't even give you a blanket. I will talk to Fred," Deliah coos, and I snort.

"You can drop the act, Deliah. You should have suppressed your glee at the arena if you planned to continue your charade."

She chuckles. "It was just too damn satisfying."

"What have I ever done to you?"

"You stole my man, my crown. And you think I would just let you get away with that?"

I sit up facing her. "You and Frederick?" I ask and she laughs. But there's no warmth, no joy in that sound.

"He was mine," she says. "And then you came along, with your family ties, your beauty, your charm, your Phoenix," she spits out. "You stole my man, my crown, and then I had to play your friend for weeks." I'm stunned by the venom in her voice. "You ruined everything."

She starts pacing in front of the metal bars, fidgeting with her pendant again, the one that has the same form as the marking I saw on my opponent's skin—three overlapping triangles—disguised as mountains.

"You are from Kystis," I say, and she whirls around to face me. "Were you planning to marry Frederick and then kill him off and rule by yourself?"

"No," she snarls. "I will reign by his side. I'll fix the mess you made and show them they won't need Alec."

My heart stutters. "What do you mean they won't need Alec?" But she only sneers at me. I get up and advance on her, slamming my hands against the bars, rattling them, and Deliah jerks back. It's then that the light of the lamp she brought glints off something secured at her waist. My eyes widen.

"Where did you get this?" I ask, my eyes glued to the blade my father once gave me.

"Since you didn't even part from it when going to a ball, I thought it would be a safe way to identify you. Imagine my surprise when I received the message that you were dead, only for you to enter the ballroom surrounded by your friends a few days later." Her laugh sounds shrill. "Three times. I tried to kill you three times. So, of course, I celebrated when they arrested you."

"And you think you'll get away with all of this?"

She snorts. "You should pray for my success, or your precious prince will be my cousin's puppet as soon as he sits on the throne." My eyes widen as more puzzle pieces fall into place, but Deliah misunderstands my surprise. "I saw how you look at each other. I even told Frederick, but he didn't want to listen. He was obsessed with the thought of marrying you." She sneers at me, her gaze wandering over me before she turns. "Anyway, I just wanted to make sure you are still here. Wouldn't want you to miss your own execution."

I stare after her and shake my head. So Frederick didn't share our little secret with her. Since our promise would backfire on him if he causes my death, I'm not too worried about an execution, but the news Deliah spilled is another story.

I stay where I am, holding on to the bars and listening to her fading steps until there is only silence. I straighten. Seems like I'll have to adjust my plans. Not all of them, of course, since some are already being implemented.

I walk back to the wooden plank and lie down with a grim smile on my face. Maybe the king forgot who raised me, but I haven't, and what should I say... I was always more of a daddy's girl.

The warmth of familiar magic and the crinkle of paper let my eyes snap open. And there, light on the dark ground, close to the metal bars of the cell door, lies a piece of paper. I get up and crouch down to pick it up. It flutters with my movements like a moth lost in the dark. The magic softly trails over my cheek before it's gone.

I open it, and a smile warms my chest while my thumb caresses the words and the blackened, broken crown drawn beneath it.

*I take care of what's mine.*

# EPILOGUE

Close to Kystis's border
(the day before the final fight)

THE LITTLE GIRL HUDDLES CLOSER TO HER MOTHER, SEEKING her warmth. She is exhausted, tired, and cold, and even if she would never admit it, frightened. The men are rough and mean, speaking a hissing language she has never heard before, and if her daddy were here, he would have killed them already for the way they treated her and Mom.

Suddenly, there is so much wind. The tent around them shakes. There are screams, and the ground vibrates, as if it were trembling alongside her.

"Mom." She shakes her mother, who is wide awake as soon as she notices the strange noises around them. Only moments later, the flap to their tent is thrown open, revealing a strange man with glowing orange eyes and slitted pupils. Golden scales retreat from his skin, while she watches, fascinated by it.

"Lady Blackstone," he addresses Mom, and the girl feels safer right away. He knows how to speak properly and uses the right language as well.

"Did my daddy send you?" the girl asks, stepping forward while her mother pulls her back.

"No, princess, your aunt did," the man rumbles.

"Are you Sparrow's friend?" she asks, and when he smiles and nods at that, she tugs her mother forward.

"Sparrow, huh? That fits." He chuckles. "What do you say about getting out of here and meeting a siren?" His face scrunches up at the word siren as if he smelled something bad, and the girl giggles.

"So you like sirens, huh?" he asks, and the girl nods. "How about dragons?" And when she nods again, he grins. He leads them out of the tent, and as soon as they are out in the open, he turns into a massive beast.

"Get on," he rumbles. His voice is now the sound of mountains shifting. But the girl is not afraid. If he is Sparrow's friend, he is her friend as well. She pulls her mother with her, and the dragon welcomes them onto his back. He flares his wings, and Mom makes a choked sound, but the girl giggles when the dragon launches off the ground and soars off for the faraway coastline.

Telos ( Night of Ara's victory)

True to his name, there isn't a sound when the black shadow slips through the door of a villa close to the academy grounds.

The atrium is big and much more elaborate than you would expect for a deputy commander's pay. But then, Silence knows of his other sources of income. The guard stationed inside the house opens his mouth, but his eyes widen when no sound comes out, and before he can recover from his shock, he lies motionless on the floor. Not even the thump of his falling body disturbs the night's peace.

That is the benefit of being sound-gifted in this kind of profession.

The stairs and the wooden floor on the upper level of the house, where the bedrooms are located, are smooth, with a faint scent of lemon and beeswax.

Again, too lavish, too expensive for his status in this society. A man he would have had to deal with sooner or later anyway.

It's an easy job, and one Silence would do a hundred times for what he gains for it. Ara settled Sloan not just in the mists, but right in Tynan's very keep. Nothing and no one will get to her now.

For Sloan, he would do anything, so her cousin's request was as good as done as soon as she contacted him.

Foley snores softly, oblivious to the fact that he is already dead. That's how it always is, but somehow that doesn't do tonight. Silence shakes him awake, and his dagger and his words slide home at the same time.

"Tamara Summer Blackstone sends her regards." The soft rasp of his voice right next to Deputy Commander Foley's ear is the only sound in the room, while he dies in silence. Understanding and horror on his face, and Telos's new ruler of the underworld by his side.

Thank you for picking up *Trials of Embers and Trust* and joining me, Ara and Tate on this journey. If you enjoyed this story so far and would like to read more, sign up for my newsletter to receive exclusive bonus scenes as well as information about upcoming releases and more. Your email address will never be shared, and you can unsubscribe at any time.

And while this journey isn't finished and there is much more to come, I would be forever grateful if you take the time to leave my book an honest review and share your thoughts so others may discover this story.

Thank you so much,

K.J. Altair

# Acknowledgments

I can't believe I finished another book—and that you're now holding it in your hands!

When I sit down to write, I only have a vague idea where the story is going, but Tate and Ara are good at taking over the reins and making the story their own... and I love it when that happens. Even if it means I have to throw out perfectly good scenes because they no longer fit. ;)

Until a rough, messy draft becomes a book, there are a few moments when you doubt it'll ever happen, and a lot more people are involved in getting it there than just me. Their role might sometimes be more, other times less obvious, but important nonetheless.

Let me start by thanking my family, who made writing this book possible.

First of all, my wonderful husband—thank you for taking over the chores and the kids so I could sit down and write. Thank you for enduring my complaints when something wasn't working, and for listening to my nonsensical ramblings about people and places that don't exist. You were always ready to brainstorm with me, even though I gave you only the bare minimum to work with.

To my sweet girls, a big thank you for being so understanding whenever my head was stuck in another world. And I'm incredibly proud of you for creating your own stories. You are the best!

To my amazing beta readers: Tyesha Nauslar, Aleighsha Parke, and Chantelle Kerr—thank you. Your feedback was invaluable and encouraging, and it helped make this book so much better.

A heartfelt thanks also goes to my editor, Jenny Sims of Editing4Indies. You gave the story its final polish and helped me catch all the little things, so the story can shine now.

To all my awesome book girlies on TikTok and Instagram—thank you for your excitement and support. You are incredible! Your sweet and mind-blowing feedback about *Feathers of Ash and Hope* kept me going and motivated me more than you'll ever know.

Most of you are also part of my amazing ARC reader team, and I'm beyond grateful to share my books with you. Hearing that you enjoy them is the best reward I could ask for. Thank you for reading early and taking the time to let others know about Ara and Tate. It truly means the world to me.

And last, but absolutely not least, thank you, dear reader.

Thank you for reading this book, for letting my characters live in your head and heart, and for coming on this journey with me. I had an absolute blast writing *Trials of Embers and Trust*, and I hope you enjoyed it just as much.


Love,
K.J. Altair

# About the Author

K.J. Altair is the author of the Flameborn series, a fantasy romance filled with sizzling tension, banter, high stakes, and a dash of spice. Ever since she learned to read, books have been her constant companions and—apart from her husband and kids—she loves nothing more than getting lost in another world.

When she's not writing, she can be found devouring novels (mainly fantasy and romance), indulging in dark chocolate, or traveling and enjoying the magic of the real world.

Follow her on: Booktok, Bookstagram, or Goodreads, and join her newsletter to stay up to date on new releases and more.

tiktok.com/@kjaltair

goodreads.com/kjaltair

amazon.com/author/kjaltair

instagram.com/kjaltair

threads.net/@kjaltair

www.ingramcontent.com/pod-product-compliance
Lightning Source LLC
Chambersburg PA
CBHW021402310726

48971CB00005B/1165